Two Mysteries

OTHER MYSTERIES BY JOAN LOWERY NIXON
AVAILABLE FROM DELL LAUREL-LEAF BOOKS

JOAN LOWERY NIXON

• Two Mysteries •

The Other Side of Dark

The Name of the Game
Was Murder

Published by
Dell Laurel-Leaf
an imprint of
Random House Children's Books
a division of Random House, Inc.
New York

This edition contains the complete and unabridged texts of the orginal editions.
This omnibus was originally published in separate volumes under the titles:
The Other Side of Dark copyright © 1986 by Joan Lowery Nixon
The Name of the Game Was Murder copyright © 1993 by Joan Lowery Nixon

Visit us on the Web! www.randomhouse.com/teens

Educators and librarians, for a variety of teaching tools, visit us at
www.randomhouse.com/teachers

ISBN: 0-553-49453-8

Printed in the United States of America

First Dell Laurel-Leaf Edition May 2005

10 9 8 7 6 5 4 3 2 1

OPM

Contents

The Other Side of Dark

The Name of the Game Was Murder

The Other Side of Dark

For Susan Cohen
with love

Chapter One

The dream is too long. It slithers and slips and gurgles deeply into midnight pools in which I see my own face looking back. It pounds with a scream that crashes into earth-torn caverns and is drowned; it surges with the babble of voices that splash against my ears; it whispers over words I can't understand.

I have cried out in my dream. I have called, and ages ago someone answered.

"Mom? Mama?"

My voice violently shakes the dream. I open my eyes, as with a trembling roar the dream rushes from my mind and my memory.

I'm in bed, but this is not my room. Across the room is a statue of a nurse. Her pencil is held in midair above her chart; her mouth is open enough that I can see some bubbles of saliva on her tongue; her eyes are stretched and glazed.

"Where's my mother?"

The statue comes to life. "Oh!" she says. "Oh, my, you're awake!" Fluttering like a moth between too many lights, she pats at my bed, jabs at the controls that rest on the nightstand, and trots to the door. "I'll be right back, Stacy," she says. She takes a step toward me with palms up as though she wanted to hold me where I am and repeats, "I will. I'll be back in a minute," then scrambles through the door.

"Where's my mother?" I call to the empty room. I try to sit up, but I can't. It makes me dizzy. My mouth is dry, and there's a spot on my left hip that is sore. What is happening to me? The blanket and sheet have slipped to one side, so I pull them up to my chest.

I gasp as my hands feel breasts that are rounded and firm. My shaking fingers slide past my waist, exploring, as the horror grows. I lift my head to look down, down at toes that lump the blanket near the foot of the bed, and the horror explodes in a scream. I am Stacy McAdams. I'm only thirteen years old, and I'm in the wrong body!

My room explodes with people, and they buzz like white-capped bees, reaching for my wrist, wrapping something around my left arm, and squeezing it until something beeps. And all the time I'm shouting, "Go away! I want my mother!"

A man with a trim blond beard sorts himself out from the confusion. He leans over me, studying me from under shaggy eyebrows, one hand gently stroking my forehead. "Stacy," he says, in a voice that pours like dark molasses, "I'm Dr. Peterson. I don't want to sedate you. I want to talk with you. Will you please stop shouting?"

I'm trembling so hard it feels as if the bed were shaking, and my voice is a raspy whimper. "Where's my mother? I need my mother. I'm afraid."

"Of course you are," he says, "but you don't need to be afraid. Everything will be all right." His hand keeps soothing my forehead, sopping up the fear until the trembling is gone and the bed is still.

The nurses have disappeared, except for a short, round one standing by the door. For some reason I notice that her blue eyes are surrounded by crinkly laugh lines, so I don't mind if she stays.

Dr. Peterson sits on the edge of my bed. My right hand disappears into his. "Now then," he says, "the members of your family are being contacted. They'll be here as soon as they can make it."

"My mother—"

But he hasn't finished. "You're in Houston's Braesforest Medical Center, under my care. You were brought here after hospital treatment for a gunshot wound."

I groan and screw up my face, trying to think, trying to remember.

"Relax," he says. "It doesn't matter now if you recall what happened. That can come later. The fact is that you've come out of what can best be called a semicomatose state, a type of coma."

"Dr. Peterson, listen to me!" I clutch both his hands, and my voice grates like a rusty gate. "There's something wrong. My body. It's not right. It's—"

"You were thirteen when you were brought here, Stacy. We've tried to keep you in a good state of health —as good as your condition would allow—so your body has grown and matured naturally."

"But I *am* thirteen!"

He shakes his head. "No, Stacy. You're seventeen."

"When my mother comes, she'll tell you that you're wrong!" I don't want to listen to what he has to say. I try to tell him to go away; but I can't talk and cry at the same time, and the tears get in my way.

He reaches to the table by my bed and hands me a fistful of tissues. They're soft, but they're heavy. My hands are heavy, my eyes are heavy, and the bed is a warm cocoon, shutting away the things I don't want to hear and see. Deliberately I slide into sleep.

This time I wake slowly, scrunching up my eyes, stretching and twisting and arching the way I love to do. "You wake up just the way Pansy does," my mother always says, as she shoos our lop-eared cat off the foot of my bed and tousles my hair. "Stacy, our other little cat."

"Stacy? You're awake?"

I open my eyes quickly at the sound of my father's voice. "Oh, Daddy, you're here! You're here! I need you!"

He quickly wraps me in a long hug. His chest, under his smooth white cotton shirt, smells cozy and warm, but my cheek grows wet from his tears. I hold him away, puzzled. "Daddy? I've never seen you cry."

There are hollows under his cheekbones, and his brown eyes seem strangely faded. His hair is thin on top. He's my father, but he isn't my father—at least not the way he was yesterday.

"Daddy, the doctor told me I've been here four years, that I'm not thirteen, I'm seventeen. It's not true, is it?" But as I study my father's face I know it has to be true, and I gasp, "How did it happen to me?"

"Nobody completely understands it. Not really.

You were shot, and the bullet did something to you that caused a kind of coma; but you didn't need life support. You were breathing on your own, and your vital signs were good. It's just that you were in a world of your own, and you couldn't or wouldn't leave it. The people here were able to help you sit in a chair and walk and even feed yourself if someone was with you. You have a physical therapist who has worked with you on exercises every day."

"I don't remember any of this."

He pats my hand. "I know, sweetheart. Mentally you weren't responding."

"Then why did I wake up?"

He shakes his head. "No one knows exactly. They can just guess. You fell and cut your hip. Then last week you developed an infection in the cut, and the doctors treated it with antibiotics and even some minor surgery. They think that maybe it was the reaction to the anesthetic that brought you out of the coma. I'm doing a bad job of telling you about it, I guess. Dr. Peterson can do a better job of explaining it to you than I can." My father wipes his cheeks with the back of one hand, then spots the box of tissues, wads one, and rubs it over his eyes.

The door opens, and a familiar face peers through. Donna's the original. I'm the carbon. "That beautiful dark hair, those tilted green eyes," Dad would say, and wink at Mom. "We've certainly got lovely daughters, Jeanne."

Donna shyly whispers, "Stacy?"

"Donna!" I hold out my arms to my sister, laughing

as she hurries through the door. She clumsily bumps against the end of the bed as she rushes to hug me.

"I like your hair that way," I mumble against her ear. "But don't ever scold me again about munching Twinkies. You're getting fat, big sister!"

She sits back and beams at me. Her tucked-in smile reminds me of so many times when she has been where I couldn't follow: her first dance; the red-haired basketball player she thought she was in love with when she was sixteen; the dorm friends she wrote about when she started college.

"I'm pregnant," she says. "In just two months you're going to be an aunt."

My mouth is open, and I know I'm making owl eyes, but I don't know what to say.

"Last year," she says, "Dennis and I were married." She glances at Dad from the corners of her eyes. "I had to promise that I'd get my degree, and I will—in May of next year. See, Dad, I'm keeping the promise."

"But I wasn't there!" I wail. "I was going to be your maid of honor. You always told me I could be."

She holds the palm of my hand up against her cheek. She's still smiling, but I see a terrible sorrow in her eyes. "Stacy, love, things were—well, so different. Dennis and I didn't have a big wedding. Just a few people and the priest."

"But you always said when you were married, you'd have a train six feet long! And loads of bridesmaids, all in blue, and wear the pearls that Grandma left to Mom."

Dad clears his throat as though he were about to say something, but Donna interrupts. "It doesn't matter," she says. She shakes her head, lays my hand gently on the blanket as though it were made of fine china, and awkwardly gets to her feet, one hand pressing the small of her back. "I can't wait till you meet Dennis. Dennis Kroskey. Hey, you'll have to get used to my new name!" She walks to the door, turning to say, "He's patiently biding time out in the hall because I wanted to see you first."

Dennis enters the room, and Donna props open the door. He's tall, with skin tanned the color of his reddish brown hair, and he has a summer smell of lots of soap and showers. I'll bet he plays tennis.

"I've met you before," he says, "when you were—sleeping."

"You came to see me?"

"Lots of times, with Donna. She introduced us, and she talked to you about our wedding, just in case you could hear her. Your family talked to you about everything that went on."

"Maybe that was part of my dream." There were so many voices, and they came and went for so long a time. I can't remember what they said. I don't want to remember. He's smiling, too, so I hurry to add, "Donna told me about the baby. I'm glad you're going to have a baby."

"So are we." He hugs Donna in such a special way that I ache right in the middle of my chest. I wasn't there when she fell in love and when she got married and when she first found out she was going to have a baby. I have to get used to all this at once, and it makes me feel lonely and shut out, no matter what they tell me.

I take a long breath, trying to keep things going right. "I'll baby-sit for you whenever you want. I guess I should say I'll baby-sit if Mom gives me a chance. She'll be so crazy about that baby the rest of us might not get to hold it until it's old enough to go to school."

No one laughs. No one answers. There's a funny kind of chill, like when you open the freezer door on a hot day and the icy air spills over your feet. "When's Mom coming?" My words plop into the cold. "Where is Mom?"

Dr. Peterson is suddenly there, head forward, his shaggy eyebrows leading the way like the prow of a ship. "Donna and Dennis," he says, "we'll keep your visit short. Why don't you come back to see Stacy tomorrow?"

Donna quickly kisses me, Dennis pats my feet, and they disappear before I can protest. The door swings shut, and the room is silent.

Dr. Peterson lifts my wrist in strong fingers and looks at his watch.

I try to tug my arm away from him. "You interrupted," I tell him. "I was asking a question, and I want an answer!"

"Take this," he orders. He hands me a pill and a glass of water from the table.

"Not now."

"Yes, now."

As I obey, quickly gulping the pill, he nods at my father, and Dad leans forward, holding my hand again. His skin is clammy and hot, and he has to clear his throat a couple of times before he can talk.

"Honey," he says, "all along we've had faith in you.

We knew you wouldn't give up. Remember even when you were just a little girl and you'd be so independent and set on getting your own way? You've always had a lot of courage, Stacy, and—"

"Daddy, tell me now. Where's Mom?"

He is hurting, and I can't help him. I don't even want to help him. My toes and fingers are warm and relaxed, and a numb feeling is seeping through me. It's like the drowsy waking-sleeping in the early morning after the alarm has been turned off. But I'm awake, and I hear what he's saying.

"The day you were shot—" His words are jagged pebbles on a dry, dusty road, and his voice trips as he stumbles through them. "Your mother was shot too. But Jeanne—oh, Stacy, Jeanne was killed."

"No," I answer, because I don't believe these strange words that are as hollow as shouts inside a tunnel, ringing and echoing and sliding away. My father is gray and crumpled, and he's crying. I try to pat his hand with fingers that are too heavy to lift. Something is wrong. Maybe it's still part of the dream, and I'll wake up and tell Mom about this crazy dream while we're making breakfast, and she'll give me a little swat on my backside and say, "For goodness' sake, stop talking and eat, or you're going to be late for school."

"Tell me everything that happened," I murmur, wanting the dream to be complete. "No one has told me."

It takes a few minutes for my father to answer. His voice seems farther away, but I clearly hear every word. "Donna said you were going to the backyard to sunbathe," he begins.

I remember. I was wearing my new red shorts, and I had Pansy with me. There wasn't any smog, and it was a golden day, and I wanted a head start on my tan.

"We don't know what happened next," he says. "Donna went to the grocery store down at the boulevard to get a couple of things. She came home and found that the front door was unlocked. Your mother was lying in the den. Donna said she screamed at Jeanne to get up, but she didn't move. Donna telephoned for an ambulance, and then she remembered you. She ran outside and found you lying on the grass near the back porch steps."

I hear the words, but I don't feel them. I am in a tunnel, but I can still hear what Dad says. Except that his words get mixed up with the other sounds and voices that are in my head.

There's a weird noise, like a yelp. It's coming from inside our house.

But a hand begins stroking my forehead. A deep voice says, "Go to sleep now, Stacy. Relax and sleep." I want to open my eyes, but I can't.

I run toward our back porch, and the screen door bangs open. Somebody runs out. He stares at me.

"Is she asleep?" Dad asks, and the voice murmurs, "Not yet."

This guy on the porch stares at me. I can't see his face, but I know he's staring. I feel it, the way words and ideas I need to know seem to sift through my skin and pour into my mind. He's scared. I know that too.

"Daddy, did they catch him?"

"Don't worry about that now," he says.

"But did they? I have to know!"

"No," he says. "They couldn't find out who it was. There were no witnesses."

It's harder and harder to speak. There's a humming in my head, and it moves Dad farther and farther away. I whisper, wondering if my whisper is real or only in my head. "I'm a witness. I saw him, Daddy."

"Hush, Stacy," Daddy says. "Don't try to talk now. Go to sleep."

The sounds in my mind melt together and dissolve the words. I am so tired. I don't ever remember having a dream in which I felt tired. I wonder what my mother will tell me about this dream.

Chapter Two

When morning comes, gray light poking around the edges of the venetian blinds, I wake and know this has not been a dream. As though a tape recorder were inside my brain, part of last night's conversation comes through loud and clear.

A picture appears. I am standing in our backyard. I'm listening, wondering what it was I heard. "Mom?" I call as I walk toward the porch steps. "Are you all right?"

But the door suddenly slams open, hitting the siding on the house with a clatter, and someone races out. He pauses on the second step as we stare at each other. But I can't see his face!

"Show me your face," I say aloud. "You're someone I know. I remember that much!"

The face is blank. But there's something in his hand. It's a gun. He points it at me. I can't move. I can't make a sound. I want to cry out, "Mom!"

Mom.

Some part of my mind has clutched and hidden what Dad told me about Mom; but now his words spill out, and I have to face them. I roll onto my stomach and cry, the pillow stuffed against my mouth. I cry until no more tears will come, and dry, hiccuping shudders shake my body. The soggy pillow smells sour, so I push it to the floor. I'll never see my mother again.

The door snaps open, and a tall, angular nurse, who matches the crispness of her uniform, strides to my bed. "Well, hi," she says. "I'm Alice." I can tell that she's taking in the pillow on the floor and my swollen eyes, but she doesn't react until all the temperature-pulse business has been accomplished. She checks under the bandage on my hip, makes a note on her chart, puts it down, and for the first time looks at me as though I were a person. "How about a shower before breakfast?" she asks. "It will help you feel a lot better."

"Yesterday I got kind of dizzy when I tried to sit up."

"That was yesterday, and that was the medication."

"Have I got out of bed to take showers before?"

She smiles. "Every day, and I'm usually the one who's given them to you."

My face is hot. I'm embarrassed that I blushed, but she doesn't seem to notice. The shower does make me feel better on the outside. I hold my face up to the water, feeling its sting on my forehead and scalp.

But nothing has helped on the inside. Maybe I can't be helped, because a hollow has been carved in there, and inside that hollow there are no feelings at all.

Alice, making sure I'm steady on my feet, leaves me to towel-dry my hair. She hums under her breath as she makes my bed.

There's a small mirror over the sink in my bathroom. I drop the towel and study myself in the mirror. It's the weirdest sensation. I feel that I'm looking at Donna the way Donna looked when I was thirteen. The person in that mirror is different from the one I was used to seeing. The face is thinner with shadows under the cheekbones. I remember when my best friend, Jan, and I would stick our faces toward the mirror and suck in our cheeks and say, "This is what we'll look like when we grow up and are beautiful!"

I wonder how the eyes in the mirror can droop with so much pain when I feel absolutely empty inside.

Alice brings me a short gown sprigged with blue violets. "The nurses thought you'd like something pretty," she says, adding, "Norma picked it out."

I don't know what to say. I think I mumble, "Thank you."

She glances at me from the corners of her eyes. The shyness doesn't match her efficient look. "We're all so glad that you recovered. We really care about our patients, especially the young ones. Especially you, Stacy. You've got most of your life ahead of you, and we—" She stops, and the briskness takes over. "Your sister's going to bring some of her clothes for you."

"Don't I have any clothes here? What did I wear?"

"During the day we put you into cotton knit jumpsuits, which you could wear when the therapist helped you ride the exercise bike and use the other equipment." She reaches into the small closet, pulls out a shapeless gray thing, and holds it up, its arms and legs dangling. It looks like an ad showing what happens when you use the wrong brand of soap.

All I can say is "Yeech!"

She laughs and tucks me between the stiff sheets, cranks my bed until I'm sitting upright, and hands me a hairbrush so that I can brush my hair.

Breakfast is brought in, and while I'm munching through the eggs' curly brown edges, a girl appears in the open doorway.

She looks at me as though she were afraid of me, and for a moment I don't know who she is.

"Stacy," she says, still in the doorway, "I'm Jan. Can I come in?"

"Jan?" I know I'm sitting there with my mouth open, but it's hard to believe that this tall auburn-haired girl in the pink, tailored shirt and tight jeans and makeup that looks like a cosmetic ad is my friend Jan Briley.

Her knees seem a little stiff—or maybe it's the jeans. She shoves a small package toward me, backs off, and perches on the edge of the armchair across from the bed. "It's not much," she says. "Just some lipstick and eye shadow and mascara and stuff I thought you'd need."

"Thanks." This isn't Jan. It can't be Jan. I shiver and push the breakfast tray away.

"You look—you look good, Stacy. How do you feel?"

"Okay."

"You'll feel lots better when your makeup's on and you've done something with your hair. Do you have hot rollers?" She looks embarrassed. Her fingers are white from gripping the arms of the chair. "Of course you wouldn't have them here. I should have brought mine, I guess."

"It's okay." I look at her hair closely. "You never used to wear your hair like that. You used to wad it up in those big brown barrettes to keep it out of your eyes when we played baseball. Do you still play on the team?"

"Team? Oh, no." She gives a funny little laugh and says, "There's a mirror in the package. Why not get it out?"

"What for?"

"So you can put on your makeup."

"Mom lets me—let me wear lipstick, but I don't know what to do with the eye stuff."

"Oh. I didn't think about that. I just take makeup for granted, like brushing my teeth or wearing shoes."

"How long have you worn real makeup?"

"Well gosh, Stacy, for ages. After all, I'm seventeen." She pauses. "And so are you."

I shake my head. "I've got to get used to that. I still feel like I'm thirteen. I feel like everything took place yesterday."

"I'm sorry about what happened—all of it. When they took you to the hospital and thought you might die, I wanted to die too. I couldn't bear to lose you. And then last night your father called me, and I couldn't believe it. I just sat right down on the floor and cried and cried, I was so glad you were going to be all right again." Jan leans forward, forearms resting on her knees. "Do you want to talk about it?"

I can't help it, but I feel as though she were one of Donna's friends, not mine. It's hard to answer. "I haven't remembered all of it yet."

"Oh," she says, and looks relieved. I don't know

what I expected. Sympathy? Maybe even curiosity. This Jan doesn't want to know what I could tell her.

I have no idea what to say to her. I guess, from the way she starts squirming as though the chair had lumps in it, that she feels the same way. This is my best friend, Jan, to whom I told even my secret thoughts, and now I'm blank.

But I make a desperate stab. "What are things like at school?"

Jan sits upright, looking thankful, as though she'd just passed a math test she hadn't studied for. "Oh, same old grind. Suzie—you remember Suzie Lindly—anyhow, poor Suzie got married last week to a guy who is really out of it. I mean totally out. Only everybody knows she had to."

"Why did she have to?"

Jan blinks a couple of times, her mouth open. "Honestly, Stacy. You know. Because she's pregnant."

"Oh." I feel myself blushing again, and I'm mad at myself for being so dumb, for being a little kid.

Jan takes a deep breath and picks up speed, like a train making up time after almost getting derailed. "And Bick is quarterback and is the big thing in the sports section of the newspaper each weekend and has a ton of colleges wanting him next year."

"Bick—that skinny guy in ninth grade?"

Jan rolls her eyes. "He's no longer skinny, needless to say, and he's a senior and really something to look at. I dated him a couple of times." She smiles, and I can see that she's waiting for me to be impressed.

But I giggle. "I'm sorry, Jan. All I can see in my mind is gawky, skinny Bick who likes to make those awful loud burps while we're eating lunch. Remember, he sent you a note in study hall one day and got yelled at by Mr. Hadley, and you said you'd rather drop dead than have anything to do with Bick?"

There's a long pause. Finally her voice comes out as tight as a stretched rubber band. "I'd forgotten. That was such a long time ago."

We stare at each other for a few moments until I stammer, "I guess it was." Desperately I blurt out, "Well, tell me about yourself."

"Sure. B.J. talked me into joining the camera club. You remember B.J., don't you?"

"The quiet girl with the blond braids."

Jan laughs. "No more braids, and B.J. really blossomed. We're all jealous. Anyhow, I went into photography in a big way and got some black-and-whites and one color shot accepted for the yearbook last year. So I'm on the staff this year, and B.J. and I are saving our money for a camera trip in Yellowstone Park in July. B.J. says—"

"Sounds like B.J.'s a good friend."

"My best. She's so much fun, and—" Jan stops. "Of course, you've always been my best friend, too, Stacy, and when you get back to school—"

We just look at each other. I don't feel jealous because this Jan is another person in another world. This isn't my comfortable, forever-and-ever best friend, Jan. Besides, the hollow place is still inside me. I can't feel anything at all.

Jan jumps to her feet. "I've got to leave pretty soon. Let me get some makeup on you first."

I'm still clutching the package. "You don't have to."

"I want to. Really. You can use the little hand mirror to watch."

She has taken the package out of my hands and tears it open, so I don't object. I just let her smear on creams and oils and all sorts of stuff, obeying directions as she tells me to close my eyes, open my eyes, and hold my mouth just right so she can add the lipstick. She gives me instructions as she goes, but it's hard for me to pay attention. I keep thinking about the Friday nights when she'd stay over at my house or I would at hers, and we'd put on our pajamas and sit on the bed eating cookies and cheese puffs and all sorts of junk while we watched TV and rolled each other's hair. I wish she'd go away.

Finally she steps back, stares at me and gasps, "Stacy, you're really beautiful! Look in the mirror. Look at yourself."

Dr. Peterson comes into the room, stands at the foot of the bed, and studies me so appreciatively that I don't have to look into the mirror.

"Seventeen, going on twenty-six," he says. He's not talking to me. It's to someone else who's sitting here, someone I don't even know.

I introduce him to Jan, who beams at him like a beauty contestant meeting the judge, grabs for her handbag, and says, "I know you're busy, and I'll get out of your way."

"Stick around if you like," he says.

But Jan squeezes my hand and rolls her eyes upward in a way I remember, meaning, "Isn't he gorgeous?" and backs through the door, saying to me, "I'll see you tomorrow."

I can't help giggling, but it surprises me by sounding like a sob.

"Don't cry," Dr. Peterson says. "One thing I learned when I was married is that crying does ugly, smeary things to a woman's mascara."

"I don't know anything about mascara."

"Well, you've got plenty of it on."

For the first time I look into the little mirror and feel even more alienated than before from the body I'm in.

"Want to wash your face? I can wait."

"Yes." I start to climb out of bed, then change my mind. I kind of like the way that girl in the mirror looks. Maybe I can save it for just a little while. Maybe I could get used to looking like that. "Never mind," I murmur. I tuck the blanket around my hips and sneak another look in the mirror.

He sits on the side of the bed. "Do you want to talk to me?"

"About what?"

"About what you remember."

I know I'm scowling, screwing up the muscles in my face until they hurt, trying, trying, trying so hard to think. "I don't remember enough."

"Don't work at it so hard. It will all come back to you."

"What if it doesn't?"

"I think it will. You said you saw him—the guy who shot you."

"I didn't think that you heard me."

He doesn't answer, just shifts his weight, making the bed wobble, and waits for me to go on.

I hug my knees against my chest. "I can't see his face, but I know his name. It's somewhere in my head!"

"Take it easy. One thing at a time."

"If I could just remember, I could tell the police. I could identify him. What if he gets away?"

"It's been four years already since the crime took place. A little more time won't matter. Why don't you talk to me about the way you feel? You've had to make a lot of mental adjustments in the past few hours."

"I don't want to talk about anything."

"I'd like to talk about your mother."

"No!" I sound so angry I'm surprised, because I don't feel angry. I don't feel anything. I'm a robot with nothing inside but gears that make me move and talk. I try to soften my voice and add, "I can't. Not yet anyway."

"Okay," Dr. Peterson says. "I'll be here when you want me."

My breath comes out in a long shudder. "I want to go home."

He smiles. He has a nice smile. It melts across his face, matching the deep syrup of his voice. "Pretty soon," he says. "We just have to make sure you're over the infection and the anesthetic and all that stuff."

In spite of the way I feel, I can't help reacting. "Doctors don't say things like 'all that stuff.' "

"Oh? What do doctors say?"

"You know. All sorts of professional things that nobody can understand."

He stands up, pats my hand, and moves toward the

door. "Okay. There must be a medical book around here someplace. I'll look through it and find something that sounds good."

The door plops shut behind him, and the room settles into stillness. I remember in Grandma's house how she'd go through the living room and dining room every evening, pulling down the window shades against the dusk, one by one shutting out the night, shielding the house, enclosing it in a white-fringed safety. My mind is doing the same thing. I know that thoughts should be racing through my mind, tumbling over each other. I should be rolling in memories, wading through pain to all the new things I've seen and heard. But bit by bit my mind is shutting itself in, shielding itself from everything but one thought: *Who was the person I saw on our back stairs?*

It's his turn to die.

Chapter Three

A reporter comes to my room.

But Donna arrived first with a suitcase filled with blouses and jeans and underwear and a pair of brown sandals, so I'm sitting in a chair, dressed in jeans that are too loose and short and a T-shirt that's definitely too snug and sandals that actually fit.

"I had to guess on sizes," Donna said as she tugged at the belt that keeps the jeans from falling around my hips. "I didn't realize that you'd grown so tall and that you're so slender. I guess I keep thinking of you the way you were when you were thirteen."

"That makes two of us," I answered. I wish Donna hadn't helped me get dressed. I felt the same way I did last year—no, the year I was twelve—and took swimming lessons and all the girls had to change clothes together in the dressing room. Some of them were starting to grow breasts, and I'd sneak little looks while I was trying to keep my own chest covered, feeling miserable, hoping no one was looking at me.

I know, Donna's my sister. But in a way she isn't my sister. She's a grown woman, with a baby growing inside her, and it makes her so different I really don't know her at all.

There's a quick knock at the door, and it opens before either Donna or I can answer. A woman steps in and takes in Donna and me and everything around us with a glance that sweeps the room like a vacuum cleaner.

Seemingly satisfied, she looks directly at me. "Hi!" she says, and her grin is broad and full of teeth. She's skinny, with frizzy blond hair that sticks out in every direction. Loose strands straggle over her eyes and fly away from her forehead. Straps for her handbag and camera case are tangled on her left shoulder.

For a moment Donna and I just stare at her, so she quickly adds, "Didn't they tell you I was coming? I'm Brandi Mayer, a reporter from the *Houston Evening News.*" She peers at me. "You're Stacy McAdams?"

I watch a strand of hair flop across her glasses. They're huge and round and too big for her. She pushes her glasses up on her nose but doesn't seem to notice the hair in her eyes. "Yes. I'm Stacy," I answer.

Donna steps slightly in front of me, taking charge. "I'm Stacy's sister, Donna Kroskey. Maybe I'd better call the clinic's supervisor. No one here told us a reporter was coming. I really don't know if you should be here or not."

Brandi pushes up her glasses again and perches on the edge of my bed, since I'm in the only chair. "Communication foul-ups," she says. "Happens all the time. Drives me absolutely batty." She pulls a tiny tape recorder out of her handbag. The strand of hair drifts back over her forehead. "You mind if I tape this?" she asks.

"Tape what?"

Brandi says, "If you don't know, I'd better fill you in. I'm doing a story for the *News* about Stacy. My editor is real soft on human-interest stuff, and he thinks that what happened to Stacy, coming out of a coma and all that, ought to make a good feature story."

"But how did he know about Stacy?" Donna asks.

"Easy," Brandi says. "Medical news is a regular beat. We check the hospitals and clinics all the time, and we have people who call us about things they think might make stories." She smiles at me. "Okay. Now that you know what I'm doing here, do you want to talk?"

Donna answers. "Not yet. I'm going to call the supervisor's office and make sure this is all right. But first, we're going to ask Stacy if she wants this interview."

I shrug. "I don't care." A puff of hair drifts over Brandi's glasses again. She probably doesn't know what a mess her hair is. It looks as if she were caught in the rain and then in the wind. So I say, "Look, before you ask me any questions, do you want to comb your hair? You can use my bathroom mirror."

"Stacy," Donna mumbles. She looks embarrassed.

Brandi just gets up, goes into the bathroom, and comes right back. "Looks the way it's supposed to look," she says. "I worked hard to get it like this."

"I can't get mine to do that," Donna says. "I think it's the wrong length."

"You're kidding," I tell them. "You mean it's supposed to look messy?"

"Stacy! You're being rude."

But Brandi grins. "It's the latest thing, kid. But you wouldn't know that. You're still into what was going on four years ago. That's great! Real reader-interest stuff. How do you feel about the new cars and new movies and—"

"Wait!" Donna says, so while Donna telephones we sit and stare at each other. Brandi impatiently fiddles with her tape recorder.

Donna hangs up the receiver and says, "The woman in the supervisor's office says it's all right, but maybe I should try to get in touch with Dad and see what he thinks."

"Could I just take a couple of pictures and get some basic answers from Stacy while you're doing that?" Brandi looks at her watch. "I've got another appointment in less than an hour, and it's over near the Loop."

"It's all right with me," I tell them, so while Donna makes the call Brandi quickly aims her camera at me and snaps a few pictures. Then she tucks away the camera, turns on her tape recorder, wiggles into a shoulders-back alertness, and says, "Stacy McAdams—and that's spelled M-C and not M-A-C. Right?"

"Dad's not in his office right now," Donna says. She comes to stand beside me and rests a hand on my shoulder.

"If I ask anything you object to, just stop me," Brandi says. And without waiting for Donna to answer, she asks me, "What did it feel like, Stacy, coming back to the real world after four years asleep?"

The question throws me. "I—I don't exactly know yet. There's a lot to get used to."

"New songs, new fashions, new television shows," Brandi says. "Sleeping Beauty, coming back to the world. Hmmm. That's good."

"No. That's wrong. Sleeping Beauty slept for a hundred years, and everyone else slept with her. Everything would be the same when she woke up."

"Details, details. Doesn't matter," Brandi says. "What did you remember when you woke up?"

I close my eyes for a moment, thinking, trying so hard to think. I can see our screen door flying open. I can see the guy with the gun running out and pausing as he sees me standing there. And I can see him raise the gun, pointing it at me. But I can't see his face!

"She's getting tired." Donna breaks in.

"No. I'm trying to see his face, and I can't!"

"Whose face?" Brandi asks.

"The guy who shot Mom. He ran out our back door. The screen door slammed open. I was standing there. We looked at each other, and he raised the gun. He shot me. I know him. I know his name. I think that's why he shot me."

Brandi leans toward me eagerly. "You're an eyewitness! You saw your mother's murderer!"

"Yes."

"So tell me about him."

"I can't remember his face."

"But you said that you know him."

"I do!"

"Do you remember his name?"

I scrunch up my face. Trying to remember hurts. It aches. "It's in my head. It's like I can touch it. But it won't come close enough."

Brandi's eyes sparkle. "Think hard. Maybe all of a sudden it will all come back to you."

Donna interrupts. "I don't think we should even talk about it. Maybe it would be traumatic for Stacy to remember. We ought to leave it up to Dr. Peterson. Stacy is all that's important. The rest isn't."

I speak up. "It's important to me to know who that guy is. He killed my mother!"

Donna's arms are around me. "Shush, shush. It's okay, Stacy. Don't get upset."

"I hate him, Donna!"

"And you want to see him get what he deserves!" Brandi's eyes are bright.

"Yes!" The hollow inside me begins to fill, churning upward with boiling bubbles of anger, until there is nothing inside me but a burning red hatred for the man I saw, the killer, the murderer, the person who took my mother away from me.

Donna's cheek is against mine. She's holding me tightly. "Stop!" she says to Brandi. "Please stop and get out of here. This isn't good for Stacy."

"Listen to her. She wants to remember."

"Go away!" Donna stands and takes a step toward Brandi.

"Okay," Brandi says. She climbs off the bed and smiles at Donna as though they were best friends. "I'm going. I'm gone." She fishes a business card from her pocket and hands it to me. "Thanks for the interview, Stacy. If you remember anything else about this guy who shot you, please give me a call. Okay?"

I just nod and stuff the card into the pocket of my jeans.

Donna follows Brandi into the hall, and in a couple of minutes she comes back with Alice.

"Got a little excited, did we?" Alice asks. Before I can answer, she wraps a cuff around my left arm and takes my blood pressure. She beams at Donna and at me. "Very good. Nice and normal. No harm done."

"I still don't think they should—"

"The supervisor has a new secretary. She didn't know—"

"Patients should have privacy, and—"

"I agree. I agree. Unfortunately they don't let nurses make the rules, although—"

I get to my feet, and the walls of the room lean a little to the left and then to the right. So I rest my head against the wall to steady it.

"Oh, Stacy," Donna says, and her arms are around me. I can feel the warm bulge of her belly against mine.

"Donna," I murmur against her hair, "I want to go home. Take me home."

"As soon as the doctor says so."

"Where is he?"

Alice gently pulls me away from Donna, leads me to the bed, and pats me into place. "Mrs. Montez is your physical therapist, Stacy. She'll be in soon. She wants to talk to you. Just be patient, honey. You'll be home in no time." Task accomplished, Alice rustles from the room.

I close my eyelids. The anger glows against them. "I wish I could see his face."

Donna leans over to kiss my forehead. She gives a little grunt as she bends, and I'm very much aware of the baby who is making her body so thick in the middle that it's hard for her to lean over the bed.

"I'm going to let you rest now," Donna says. "I have to get to class. I'll see you later."

Her face is close to mine, and I can see the tiny beads of perspiration that lie on her upper lip like a glistening mustache. "Donna," I say, grabbing her right hand and holding it tightly, "do you remember a couple of years ago when Mom was pregnant?"

"That was more than a couple of years ago, Stacy. You were only ten."

I groan. "Ten—whenever. Oh, Donna, I was so excited about Mom's baby, and I'd rest my hand on her stomach and feel it kick. And when she lost it, it hurt so much it nearly killed me."

There are tears on Donna's cheeks. "I know. It hurt all of us."

I struggle to sit up and wrap my arms around her. "I didn't mean to make you cry. I'm so mixed up. I mean, I think about Mom having a baby, but not you. And now that you're grown-up and pregnant I can't get used to it. It's like you should be Mom and not Donna, and it makes me feel strange and faraway and—oh, Donna, I don't even know how to tell you what's in my head."

But Donna soothes me, patting my back and nuzzling her cheek against mine. "It's okay, Stacy. It's okay. Calm down. Everything's not going to happen at once. It's going to take awhile for you to get things straight. Don't punish yourself by trying to rush it. Just relax. Just take each day as it comes."

We hold each other without talking. The room is warm. The window spills sunlight onto the beige tile floor, and the voices in the hall hum in the background like contented bees. Donna is the big sister, the comforting one, yet the hurt we share is the same, and it flows between us. I can feel how much Donna misses Mom too. I begin to realize that there'd be questions she'd want to ask Mom, little scary sparks that Mom could pat out with a smile and a few words. There'd be the baby clothes to buy together, the excitement to share about the first grandchild.

As I close my eyes I see our screen door fly open. Someone runs out and pauses on the steps. He stares at me. He raises the gun and points it at me. But where is his face? For Donna, for me, I must see his face!

Donna leans back, holding my shoulders. "Are you all right now, Stacy?"

I nod. The storm blew away some of the clutter in my mind, and I found my sister. "Thanks, Donna."

"Whenever you need me, I'll be here," she says.

I pat her stomach and smile and answer, "Whenever *you* need *me*. I'll be here too."

Alice opens the door in a hurry, nimbly stepping back, saying, "Stacy, this is Mrs. Montez."

The physical therapist bursts past her into my room, leaning forward a little, breaking a path with her chin and the end of her nose. She's short and solid with clipped gray hair, and she's packed into a rose velour jogging suit. She checks the chart at the end of my bed, grins at it and then at me.

"All that good, regular exercise has paid off," she says. "Aren't we proud of ourselves!"

"I don't remember exercising," I tell her. "And I'm sorry, but I don't even remember you."

Her left hand chops at the air, as though she were cutting off something unnecessary. "Doesn't matter if you remember or not," she says. "What matter's is that I kept you in good physical shape. Once you're over the temporary effects of your operation, you'll find yourself in fine condition, thanks to my care and skill."

Behind Mrs. Montez's back Alice winks at me.

"You may think this all sounds immodest," Mrs. Montez says, half turning to include Alice, who blinks and looks embarrassed, "but the body is like a machine that must stay fine-tuned in order to operate correctly. And keeping you in condition was my job." She beams again, looking so pleased with herself she reminds me of the Cheshire cat in *Alice in Wonderland.*

"So," she says, bouncing a little on her toes, "if Dr. Peterson allows it, tomorrow morning I'll put you through your paces. Then, after you return to your home, you can keep up the good work. Do you have a swimming pool?"

"No."

"Exercise cycle?"

"I don't think so."

"Rowing machine? Oh, never mind. Of course, you don't have any of the things you'll need. No one ever does. Well, I'll just trot off and see what we can do about it."

Without another word she charges from the room. Alice smiles sheepishly and whispers to me, "She's really awfully good. One of the best."

A white-coated orderly with shaggy yellow hair comes in with a lunch tray. His gap-toothed grin is friendly as he arranges the tray on the table by my bed and swings it around in front of me.

"Thanks, Monty," Alice says.

"No problem," Monty says, and dashes off before Alice can hoist me up and plump up my pillows.

There's nothing special on the tray, but I'm hungry. I don't pay much attention to what I'm eating. I'm tired, and after I've finished my lunch, I push the table away, lie back, and go to sleep.

The dreams don't make sense as they lap one into another, trailing through the afternoon. I wake to long shadows in a room lit with late orange sunlight.

The light touches Donna in her chair, brushing brightness into her hair and on her cheek. Her head is bent as she reads a newspaper, and a little worry wrinkle flickers on her forehead.

I stretch lazily, arching my back, and Donna looks up.

"You're purring," she said. "I remember how Mom said you were like a little cat the way you stretched. You always used to purr."

"I must have slept a long time."

Donna sighs and hands me the newspaper. "I wish I hadn't let that reporter interview you."

I wiggle up, sitting cross-legged, the newspaper on my lap. There, on the front page, are two photographs of me—one my class picture when I was thirteen and in the seventh grade and the other the picture Brandi took this morning. Two girls, so very different, yet they're both me. One I recognize, but the other is someone I don't even know. I keep staring at the photos until Donna says, in the same tone of voice she'd use if she'd found a roach in the bathtub, "She even used that 'Sleeping Beauty' stuff." ⌐

For the first time I read the headline over the pictures and story: SLEEPING BEAUTY AWAKES TO NEW WORLD. "Does she write what I said about her messy hair?" I ask Donna.

Donna groans. "Read it."

So I do. Brandi's story is not too bad, just a little dramatic, and she did put in the part about her hair, only she didn't use the word *messy*. She made everything seem more exciting than it was, especially the part about how I was the only one who could identify my mother's murderer.

I throw the newspaper on the bed and complain to Donna, "She didn't write things the way they happened. She makes it sound like any minute now I'm going to remember who I saw. But I can't! I want to, and I'm trying, but I still can't!"

"It's my fault that story was written," Donna says. "I should have sent her away."

"Don't blame yourself. It's not your fault." I sneak another look at the girls in the photographs. "I wonder where she got my seventh-grade picture."

"Not from Dad or from me," Donna says. "She might have got it from your school or from one of your friends."

"Maybe Jan." I study the picture the reporter took. Am I really as grown-up as I look in that second picture? Donna sighs and mumbles something else about making a mistake, so I quickly say, "It doesn't matter. It's just a dumb story. I bet nobody will even read it."

"Of course, they'll read it!" Donna says. "And what worries me is what if—"

I wait a moment, watching worry pucker her forehead and turn down the corners of her lips. When she doesn't finish what she was saying I ask, "What if what?"

"Nothing," Donna says.

"You were going to say something. Don't just stop like that. I want to know what's bothering you."

Donna tries to smile. "Stacy, my thoughts were just wandering around. I don't even remember what I had in mind."

"But—"

She stands up and hugs me. "I've got to get home and put something together for dinner. Dennis made dinner the last three nights, and I promised I'd take my turn tonight. He comes home starving to death, and I need to stop by the grocery store and get lettuce because we're out . . ."

Donna is talking nonstop, not letting me get in another word. I remember that technique of hers, and I have to smile. Okay. She doesn't have to tell me now what she has in mind. She'll come out with it sooner or later.

"Dad will be here to see you tonight," she says as she reaches the door. "And I'll be back tomorrow morning. Bye, Stacy." The door closes before I have a chance to answer.

I turn on the bedside lamp, take another quick look at the photographs, and go to the bathroom mirror. As I comb my hair I study my face. This is me, Stacy McAdams, and I have to start getting used to it. This is how

other people see me. This is how people who read the
newspaper will see me. This is how—

I suck in a deep breath and hang onto the edge of
the basin as what Donna meant suddenly socks me.
Brandi wrote that I could identify the murderer. What
if the killer reads that? What will he do?

"Somebody help me!" I whisper to the girl in the
mirror. "I've got to be able to see his face!"

Chapter Four

The bones in my legs are like Jell-O, and chills shiver up and down my spine. Somehow I make it back to the chair and drop into it, trying to think, wondering what I can do.

A voice makes me jump. "That Sleeping Beauty stuff was cornball."

"Dr. Peterson! I didn't hear you come in."

"Obviously. What makes you so jumpy? Did you think I was another reporter?"

"No. I just had a lot on my mind. I—" I look right into his eyes. "I was scared. I *am* scared."

He sits on the bed and rests his elbows on his legs, leaning toward me. "I didn't know that reporter had been allowed to visit you," he says. "We have someone new on the front desk, and she didn't understand the situation. I'm sorry it happened. No one else from the media will be allowed to see you while you're here."

"It's not your fault."

"Your sister chewed us all out." He smiles.

"What if the guy who murdered my mother reads that story? It says I'm an eyewitness."

He nods. "He may not read it. That was four years

ago. He may be thousands of miles away from here. He might even be in jail somewhere. Or dead."

"What if he isn't?"

He shrugs and looks as though he wished he had an answer. "Don't worry about him," he manages to say.

Don't worry? Oh, sure. I grip the arms of the chair. But the telephone rings. Someone at the front desk tells Dr. Peterson that two detectives from the Houston Police Department have arrived, that they want to talk to me.

Dr. Peterson opens the door wide and leans against the wall, arms folded, waiting for the detectives to join us.

"You don't have to stay," I tell him.

"I don't have anything important to do," he answers. "A head transplant, but that can wait."

"I don't need a baby-sitter."

"Doctors never baby-sit. Their fees are too high."

"I'm not going to laugh at your jokes. It will only encourage you."

Two tall men block the door for a moment. Smoothly one steps aside, then follows the other into my room. They look the way I'd imagine detectives should look. Their business suits are taut across their broad shoulders, and they're both big men. They have brown hair, and one has a mustache. It's their eyes, I think, that label them as detectives. It doesn't matter that the mustached one has brown eyes and the other has blue. I know they really see me, every detail of me, and they're trying to probe below the surface, poking at the doors to my mind.

Markowitz and Johns, they tell me and shake hands

with Dr. Peterson. Markowitz has the mustache. I'll try to remember that.

A voice comes from the doorway, and Dad appears. "What is this? Stacy, are you all right?"

Dr. Peterson fills Dad in, and everyone goes through the introduction thing again.

Dad shakes his head. "I don't think Stacy is up to this yet." But his words come out in a question, and he's looking at Dr. Peterson, not at me.

"Stacy can handle it," Dr. Peterson says.

"Hey, look at me, Daddy. I'm dressed and out of bed. I'm feeling a lot better. Honest!" I stand up and give Dad a hug.

He hugs me tightly, awkwardly. The shock I feel takes away the comfort I used to feel in my father's hugs. My head once fitted snugly against his chest, and now I find myself looking over his shoulder. We stand back and stare at each other.

"You might want to sit down, Stacy," Detective Johns says to me. "We won't be long. Just a few questions." He shoves his hands in his pockets, then takes them out again. He doesn't seem to know what to do with his hands. I bet he's trying to stop smoking.

"It's about that newspaper article, isn't it?" Dad asks as I move away from him and sit in the only chair. Everyone else is standing, and it makes me feel kind of strange.

"Yes," Detective Markowitz says. "Stacy, according to the interview you gave the reporter for the *Evening News,* you saw a person run out of your house, the person who shot you."

I nod. "But—"

"It's been four years," Detective Markowitz adds. "How good is your memory? If we show you some books of mug shots, do you think you might be able to recognize him?"

The sound that comes out of my mouth is a kind of desperate wail, and it shocks me as much as it does everyone else in the room. "I can see it happening in my mind," I tell them. "It's almost like a movie, running over and over. He comes out of the back door and stands there, staring at me. And I know him. I know that I do. But I can't see his face!"

The detectives glance at each other quickly, then back at me. Johns rubs at an invisible spot on his chin. "Maybe it would help if you tried to describe exactly what you saw at the time," Markowitz says.

And Detective Johns adds, "Like what he was wearing. Jeans? A T-shirt? Maybe a white one?"

"Yes, jeans," I say quickly. "But not a T-shirt. It was kind of a plaid shirt—red, I think. Yes, red, but faded, and the sleeves were rolled up."

Markowitz is writing. "Very good. What else?"

"What else? Uh—he has a gun in his right hand." There's a long pause as I try hard to remember. "Help me!" I beg. "I have to know who he is. He killed my mother, and I hate him!"

Dr. Peterson gives me a quick look. I'm startled myself at the bitterness I can taste in my words.

"Take it easy, Stacy," Detective Johns drawls. "Just try to relax. We'll ask some questions, and see if you can come up with the answers."

He uses the telephone on the table next to my bed. The receiver almost disappears inside his hand. While he makes his call Markowitz asks me to go over the physical description I have given and try to add to it. He asks a lot of questions: Did I hear a shot? How close was I standing to the back door? Had I heard a car on the street before it all happened? And how old was the guy I saw?

"A few years older than I was," I tell him.

"Someone you knew at school?"

"No. Older. He goes—went—to high school."

"How old was he?"

I squeeze my eyes shut so tightly that they burn. "I should know!"

"He lives in your neighborhood? Your mother knew him, too?"

"Maybe. Oh, no. I don't think so. I don't know."

I try so hard, but I still can't see the murderer's face.

Finally Markowitz pauses. "I think that's it for now," he says.

"Wait. Let me ask you something," I say. "Why was this guy in our house? Why did he kill Mom?"

"It's listed as robbery," Markowitz answers. He looks at Dad, and Dad nods.

"He took my wife's wallet out of her handbag," Dad says. His voice rises as though he still couldn't believe what he's telling me. "And it was only ten or twelve dollars. She asked me that morning if I'd stop by the bank on the way home from work."

"Ten dollars? And he killed her?"

"One of the policemen who came after it had happened said he guessed the killer was someone looking for money to buy drugs, and he probably thought the house was empty. Maybe he panicked."

"Why did it have to be Mom?" I cry out. "Mom was gentle and loving and funny and kind. And she trusted everybody!"

Even when I was a very little girl, I wanted to be like Mom. But I wasn't like her at all. I'd get mad and shout and stamp, and Dad would march me off to my room to "think things over" and cool down. Thinking things over never seemed to help much.

Dad sighs. "Honey, we just don't know what was in the—murderer's mind. There's no way of knowing."

"We'll know when we arrest him!"

They look at me, and Markowitz says, "To make a solid case, the DA needs two kinds of evidence: an eyewitness to place someone at the scene of the crime and physical evidence that the person was there."

"I'm the eyewitness! I'm going to remember! I am! And you must have something from the house!" I think about some of the detective movies I've seen. "What about fingerprints? Could you look for fingerprints?"

Dad reaches down and takes my right hand. His forehead is wrinkled with worry. "Calm down, Stacy. Don't get overexcited." He looks at Dr. Peterson as though he were begging for help, but Dr. Peterson just gives a barely noticeable shake of his head.

"Granted, fingerprints can last for years," Markowitz tells me, "but chances are any fingerprints were cleaned up long ago."

I impatiently tug my hand away from Dad's. "But what about when the police investigated after Mom was murdered? Wouldn't they have taken fingerprints then?"

Markowitz nods. "We'll pull the file and see what they've got. There may be a chance they got some prints. Maybe even some clear ones. Obviously, if they had them, they didn't get a make on them; but maybe our boy's been in trouble since then, and we'll be able to match them. There may be some other physical evidence that may help. With luck they'll have the bullet that killed your mother. We won't know till we check it out."

"What good will the bullet do without the gun?"

"It might be worth something. It might not. It's our job to find out."

"Will you tell me? The minute you know?"

"These things take time," Johns says. He turns to Markowitz and mumbles, "Got a cigarette?"

The look Markowitz gives his partner is enough of an answer.

"Okay, okay, forget it," Johns says. He turns to me. "We'll try a computer search. May just luck out."

"Computer?"

Dr. Peterson smiles. "You've got a lot to catch up on, Stacy. Everyone does everything by computer now."

"What will happen to the murderer after you arrest him?"

"He'll go through all the legal processes," Johns says.

"Will he get the death penalty?"

Dad looks startled, but Johns takes the question as though he'd heard it over and over again. "Depends on the jury," he says. "In Texas the death penalty can be given if robbery, sexual assault, or kidnapping are associated with the murder. With this one we've got a robbery charge."

Markowitz tucks his notebook into his inside coat pocket. I get a glimpse of a gun in a shoulder holster. I remember another gun, and I shiver.

"I'm afraid we're tiring you," Markowitz says. As though they could read each other's mind, he and Detective Johns turn toward the door at the same time.

I climb out of my chair and walk a few steps with them. "I'm not tired. I won't get tired. I'll do anything I can to help you."

Markowitz hands me his card. "You can reach me through this number at any time. If you need us, don't hesitate to call." They stride from the room.

Dad follows them. So does Dr. Peterson. Because they've left the door open, I can hear the deep rumble of their voices, but only a word or two, so I stand just inside the door, where they can't see me.

"Well, yes, there is a possibility," Johns says. "But it's a slim one."

Dad is demanding. "But he could be a danger to Stacy."

There's a pause, and Markowitz answers, "Yes. It's a long shot, depending on where this guy is and whether he saw that newspaper article and how his mind works, but I suppose we could say there's a possibility that Stacy could be in danger."

"Then shouldn't we get protection for her?" Dad asks.

"If you don't mind, I'd like to butt in." Dr. Peterson

doesn't wait to find out if he can or can't and just goes on talking. "It's important that Stacy lead as normal a life as possible so that she can get all the pieces together."

"But I think—"

I don't hear the rest of what Dad says as they move farther away. I lean against the wall, waiting for Dad to come back to my room. I'm tired. I'm angry. And I'm scared because I don't know what will happen next. The guy without a face who murdered my mother. And Stacy McAdams. Who's going to find the other first?

Chapter Five

When Dad comes back to my room, he tries to hide his worries under a broad smile, but his eyes give him away. He hugs me again and mumbles against my hair, "Oh, Stacy, you can't know how wonderful it is having you back. You just can't know!"

It's warm inside Dad's hug. It's safe. "I don't want to stay in this clinic," I murmur. "I'm feeling all right now. Really. I want to go home with you."

He backs off and smiles at me. "Dr. Peterson says most likely you can come home the day after tomorrow. Only—"

When he doesn't finish his sentence, I ask, "Only what?"

For a moment he's silent. Then he says, "Only you'll be home alone, and I think someone should be with you."

I open my mouth to say, "But Mom will be there," and I have to remind myself that she won't. It's still so hard to believe. Dad is watching me, so I manage to stammer, "School. I have to go to school, Daddy."

Dad takes my hand and leads me to the bed, sitting beside me. "There are a lot of things to work out, Stacy.

And school is one of them. You were just finishing the seventh grade when all this happened to you. But your classmates are now in the eleventh grade. You aren't prepared for eleventh-grade courses, and naturally you won't want to go back to seventh grade. So maybe tutors? Home study? I don't know yet. It hadn't occurred to me to find out what to do."

"I don't want to go to school at home by myself."

Dad rubs a hand over his forehead and sighs. "No, no. Of course not. You'd be lonely."

"Maybe they'd let me take exams for the courses I was taking in seventh grade and make up eighth grade in summer school. That way I'd be in high school in the fall. I'll work real hard, Daddy, and not stay on the phone too long or watch too much television, and Mom will—"

The word enters us like an ache, and we just sit there, staring at each other.

"I—I'm sorry, Dad. I keep forgetting."

He puts an arm around me. "Honey, I still do. So many times I come home in the evening and for an instant actually expect Jeanne to call out to me."

"It hurts so much."

"Yes, it does."

"Will it ever stop hurting?"

"I don't know. We'll never stop remembering, but I don't know if the hurt will always be part of the remembering. I wish I could give you an answer that would help."

"If we had wishes, I'd wish none of this had happened. I'd wish we could go back. Have a second chance."

"Life doesn't give second chances, Stacy."

"Then I don't like life very much."

Dad's arm is strong, and he tightens his grip a little on my shoulder. "At some time or another everyone gets hit by problems that seem almost impossible to handle. You can give up without a fight, or you can climb over those problems and move on, because there are lots of good things ahead for you to discover."

"You make it sound too easy, Dad. Maybe you could do it, but I don't know yet if I can."

"You can." He makes a strange sound that startles me. I don't know if it's a laugh or a sob, so I twist to look at him. I can see the tautness of the muscles that are throbbing in his cheeks and chin. "Stacy, when Jeanne died, I wanted to run away, to hide, to do anything in order to escape all the pain."

"But you didn't."

"I did."

"I don't understand. You're here, Daddy."

"And I'll continue to be here with you, honey." I listen to footsteps pass my door and to someone laughing down the hallway. It seems a long time before Dad continues. "I drank a lot. Too much. It didn't help me escape anything. It just made it all worse. It was a stupid thing to do."

"Don't say you're stupid, Daddy! It wasn't your fault. It was the murderer's fault."

"You can't blame him for everything, Stacy. I'm certainly not going to blame him for something I chose to do."

"Well, I blame him. I hate him!"

"Hate isn't the answer. Think about your mother and what a forgiving person she was."

"I can't forgive him! I don't want to!"

He shakes his head sadly. I don't know why he can't understand how I feel.

"What we've been talking about is all part of growing up, of maturing," he says.

"Those are just words grown-ups like to use. Teachers say them. 'I expect you to be mature.' *Mature* doesn't mean anything."

"Yes, it does. It means a responsible way of looking at things, a more thoughtful way of making decisions."

"So if I grow up, then I'll automatically be mature."

"Stacy, I don't know how to explain it. It's something you'll feel inside. You'll find it out for yourself." He sighs. "Maybe your mother would have known how to explain these things to you."

I don't know what to say to him to make him feel better. I take his right hand and hold it tightly. "I love you, Daddy."

He gives his head a little shake, as though he were trying to toss away a lot of painful memories, and says, "I love you too."

The door slams open so suddenly that I gasp. Monty, the shaggy-haired orderly, bursts into the room, carrying my dinner tray. He must have startled Dad, too, because Dad jumps to his feet, standing between me and the orderly. "What are you doing?" Dad snaps.

"Well, hey, I got to deliver her dinner tray." Since Dad doesn't move, he says, "Here. You want it? You can give it to her. No problem."

Dad takes the tray, and as the orderly turns to

leave, Dad adds, "From now on, knock, and come in carefully."

"Hey, they know we're coming. We don't have to knock on doors around here."

Dad's voice is firm. "I said, from now on I want you to knock on this door before coming in. Understand?"

"Sure, sure," Monty says, and disappears.

Dad puts the tray on the bedside table. There's a deep pucker between his eyebrows, and he looks terribly tired. "I don't like that kid's attitude," he mutters.

"Daddy, he's okay. He's just always in a hurry. Maybe it's part of his job to get the trays around fast."

He looks at his watch. "I'd better grab a bite to eat pretty soon. It's almost time to get to the office."

"You have to go to your office? But it's so late."

"Uh, extra work," he says. The wrinkle between his eyebrows deepens as he looks at me. "Are you sure you'll be all right, Stacy?"

"Are you afraid something is going to happen to me?"

"No! Oh, no! I just meant, do you need anything? Can I do anything for you while I'm here?"

His glance slides away from mine. He's not telling me the truth.

"Better hurry, so you won't miss dinner," I answer. He holds me tightly in a big hug, then leaves, pausing at the door to give me one last, searching look and an attempt at a smile.

I'm staring at the dented metal top that covers the plate on my tray, wondering if I really want to take it off and find out what's under it, when a nurse with hair so red she looks like a lit candle pokes her head in the door. "Turn on Channel Two!" she says. "Quick!"

I move toward the television set that is mounted on the ceiling, but she bounces across the room and grabs a remote-control device that was lying behind a large box of tissues. She quickly presses buttons until she gets the right channel.

A man and a woman are tasting spaghetti and rolling their eyes with delight.

"It's going to be after this commercial," she tells me.

"What is?"

"You!"

I sit on the edge of the bed, wondering what she means. "There weren't any television reporters here."

"Oh, they were here. They just didn't get in to see you. The office put you under tight security."

"Security!"

"Oh, didn't they tell you that? There's a real cute off-duty policeman stationed in the hall to keep out the reporters and photographers. Norma's been walking by him so often she's wearing a path in the tiles."

"But what—"

She holds up a hand to hush me. "Listen. Here it is."

The newscaster is saying, "Stacy McAdams, Houston's sensational Sleeping Beauty, two days ago awakened from a four-year-long comatose state to announce that she is a potential eyewitness to a murder. However, she is just as inaccessible to reporters as the original Sleeping Beauty was to the rest of the world."

As he speaks the front door of the clinic is shown on

the screen. So that's where I am. It's a white one-story building that seems to ramble over a large area, and there are lots of pine trees shading it. There are people standing on the steps of the building and, on the grass, some of them carrying cameras. A policeman is facing them, his back to the closed doors.

On the screen appear the same two photographs that were in the newspaper.

"—called a model student by her teachers," the newscaster continues.

"Oh, no!" I groan. "That's not true. I wasn't a model student. I hated algebra. Anyhow, what he said makes me sound like a creep."

"You can't hear what he says if you don't keep quiet," the nurse answers, but a picture comes up of a group of protesters at the city hall, and the newscaster is off on another story.

The photographs of the two girls stay in my mind. Especially the one taken by the newspaper reporter. "Do I really look like that?" I whisper to myself.

The nurse hears me. "Sure you do! You're just as pretty as Sleeping Beauty was too! Remember the Walt Disney one, with her dark hair and big eyes?"

"That was Snow White."

She shrugs and laughs. "Doesn't matter. You're a really good-looking girl. You're going to have lots of dates and lots of fun."

She scurries out of the room. It's just as well, because I'm suddenly too surprised to talk to her. Dates? I don't know how to date. I don't even know what to say to a guy. Oh, sure, there were cute guys in my school, but Jan and I and my other friends didn't talk to them much, except when we worked up enough courage to say things like "You were real good in the game yesterday." And when they weren't around, we giggled a lot about them and talked about what we'd do if a guy wanted to kiss us. Suzie told us she'd been French-kissed, and she described what it was like and a lot more, but Jody kept yelling, "Yuck, yuck, yuck! That's gross!" so Suzie said we were babies and she wasn't going to tell us any more. We didn't care. We'd all read the same book Suzie had.

Jan and I asked our mothers when we could date, and they both said not until we were in high school. Jan and I made a real fuss about it. I guess now that was pretty silly, since none of the guys had asked us for dates.

Jan. Jan would know how to date, but I can't ask her what to do. She'd think I was really dumb. She's not the Jan I used to know, and I feel shy with her. Maybe I can ask Donna what to do.

I flop on the bed, nearly overturning my still-covered dinner tray.

From where I'm lying on the bed I can see the bottom edge of the door. It's open just a crack, just enough so that someone must be holding it open, just enough for someone to be watching me.

Quickly I scramble off the bed and manage to stammer, "Who—who's there?"

The door opens wide, and Monty blinks and grins. "Hey, it's just me."

"What do you want?"

"Your tray," he says. "I'm collecting them."

"You just brought it."

He shrugs. "Go ahead and finish," he says. He comes into the room, shoving the door so that it shuts behind him, and sprawls in the armchair. "Saw you on TV," he adds.

"You're not supposed to be in here."

"Gotta take a break once in a while. They really work us hard around here."

I grab the tray and shove it at him. "Here. Take it."

"You didn't eat anything. Aren't you hungry?"

"No."

He still doesn't move to take the tray. "You're a celebrity. You know that?"

"Go away."

Slowly Monty bends and curls as though it were taking a lot of effort to pull his body together and out of the chair. When he gets to his feet, he says, "You're not very friendly. I just thought it would be kind of interesting to ask you about what happened."

"I don't mean to be unfriendly. I just don't want to talk about it."

"You're scared. Right? But you don't have to be scared of me." He moves a step closer. "You can tell me. What did the guy look like? Do you know his name?"

I can't answer. I try to back up, but the bed is behind me. Only the tray is between us.

Monty's voice lowers. "It's sort of like a movie, you being the only one who can identify the guy who shot you and your mom. If it was a movie, you know the guy would come hunting for you, and it would probably be Jack Nicholson or somebody, and you'd try to hide out and—"

I drop the tray, and he hops backward, grabbing his left foot.

"Whadja do that for?"

"Get out of here!" I yell at him, and I jab at the call button.

A petite nurse with cropped black hair comes in as Monty is picking up the dishes and trying to wipe up the globs of food that decorate the floor.

"What's the matter?" she asks.

"She did it, not me!" Monty complains.

"I told him to get out! He kept trying to ask me questions!"

Monty stands, holding the messy tray. He grins at the nurse. "She's a celebrity. I just wanted to talk to her for a few minutes."

"Get back to your job," she says sternly. "You could get fired for deliberately annoying a patient."

She glares until he leaves the room. Then she smiles at me. "Don't mind Monty. He's not the brightest person around this hospital, but he's harmless."

"He wouldn't leave when I told him to. He frightened me. He asked too many questions."

"He was just curious," she answers. "Naturally the staff has been talking a lot about you, and he probably wanted to brag about getting some inside information. I'll tell the head nurse to chew him out, and he'll leave you alone. Want another dinner tray?"

"No, thanks. I'm not very hungry."

"Okay now?"

"I guess."

She leaves, and I sit on the edge of the bed, thinking about what happened. I guess I overreacted and got scared of Monty because I'm scared of so many things now. I don't want to be on television! I don't want a policeman guarding me in the hall! I don't want to be afraid anymore! I wish I were still thirteen!

I don't have time to think about Monty or policemen or anything else the next morning when the day snaps into place with doors banging open, blinds clattering up, breakfast, a shower, and Alice changing the dressing on my hip.

"Looks lovely," Alice says. "It's healing nicely. Dr. Peterson will be pleased."

"*I'm* pleased," I tell her.

Alice laughs. "That's taken for granted." She hands me a clean pair of jeans and a slightly faded T-shirt with a strange face on it. "This was my daughter's," Alice says. "I thought you'd like it."

"Is that your daughter's picture?"

Alice giggles. "No, honey. That's Glory Beans."

"Who's Glory Beans?"

"Why, she's—" Alice stops and stares at me with wide eyes. "Oh, my, I didn't think. You wouldn't know, would you? She's a very famous punk star. All the kids are crazy about her."

"Punk?"

"Whew!" Alice shakes her head. "I guess the best thing to do is bring you a four-year stack of newsmagazines, so you can catch up."

Mrs. Montez hops into the room as I pull the shirt over my head. "Fifteen minutes," she says. "I wrote your appointment on the schedule. Meet me in the physical therapy room on time!"

"Where is the—" But she's already galloping down the hall.

Alice gathers her tray of things and heads for the door. "Just turn left and go straight down to the main desk, then turn left again. It's at the far end of that wing. You can't miss it."

I go into the bathroom and brush my hair. It needs a trim. I could probably use a haircut, a new style. What are the new styles? Maybe there's a choice. Jan's hair looked good, not like that reporter's. I study my face. I'm getting a little more used to it now. It's not too bad. I wish my nose weren't so long and my eyes were bigger, but on the whole I kind of like this face. It's so much like the face I was used to seeing on Donna.

Quickly I get the lipstick from the drawer of my bedside table and run back to the bathroom with it. I smooth it on with my little finger. There. Maybe later I'll try some of the eye stuff. Not now. I remember Mrs. Montez's order to be on time.

As I enter the hallway I hear some voices to my right, down at what must be the nurses' station, but the hall to my left is empty. What happened to the policeman who was here? The hall is long, but at the end I can see a desk, or counter or something, and a lot of potted plants. That must be the main desk. Feeling like a six-year-old who's allowed to cross the street for the first time, I start down the hallway, following the directions Alice gave me.

Suddenly someone swoops up from behind me and grips my upper right arm. As I stiffen, digging in my heels and trying to pull away, a voice says, "What's with you? I'm just trying to help you escape the mob."

The voice belongs to Monty. He smiles at me, and I try not to stare at the wide gap between his front teeth.

I tug my arm out of his grasp. "What mob?"

"Down at the main desk."

As I take a skeptical look in that direction, he says, "Well, it's not exactly a mob, but a couple of reporters there are asking a lot of questions about you."

"I don't see anybody."

"They're by the main door. The cop is with them. If you go past them, they'll see you."

"I have to go by the main desk to get to the physical therapy room."

"Not if you use my shortcut. That's what I've been trying to tell you."

It makes sense. I don't want to have to talk to any reporters right now. So I shrug. Okay. Which way do we go?

He takes my arm again and pulls me down the hall to a swinging door, where he jerks me through. We're in a corridor that's narrower than the main hallway. I try to pull away. "You're hurting my arm. Don't squeeze it! And don't go so fast!"

"C'mon. You don't want to be late."

I nearly stumble, trying to keep up with him. The corridor turns, and I begin to realize that we're going in the wrong direction. We're heading toward what must be a back door to this building because in the upper half of the door is one of those crinkly-looking opaque glass windows, and I can see light shining through the window.

I grab his arm with my other hand, tugging and yelling, "Stop!"

When we're almost at the back door, he does stop, so suddenly it throws me off-balance. I bang into the wall, and the only reason I remain upright is that he's still hanging onto my arm. His eyes dart to each side as he nervously looks at the row of closed doors. "Don't make so much noise," he says.

"Let go of me!" I try to kick his leg, but he jumps aside.

His face is close to mine. I can smell the salty sweat on his forehead. "Hey, hold on. You'll get me in trouble if you don't shut up."

As I open my mouth wide to scream he claps a hand over it and in a low voice says, "Listen to me, will you? I'll get twenty bucks from one of the reporters if I bring you to the back door. The guy just wants to ask you a couple of questions and get a picture of you. That's all. You don't have to say much if you don't want. Okay? I mean I can really use the twenty bucks."

He takes his hand away from my mouth, and I spit and rub the back of my left hand over my lips, trying to wipe away the taste of his fingers.

"Well?" he asks.

"I don't think a reporter would do that."

"Look, who asks questions? Twenty bucks is twenty bucks." He smiles, as though he were trying to put me at ease; but his eyes narrow, and for an instant he looks away. I think he's lying.

Suddenly the knob of the back door rattles, and I look up to see a shadow through the glass. The door is locked, so the person on the other side gives up and presses against the glass, trying to see through it. The glass distorts his face into a monstrous blob with squashed nose and two dark spots for eyes. Can he see me? Those dark spots shift and seem to be staring in my direction. The doorknob rattles again.

Chapter Six

I yell at the top of my lungs, and now my kick connects with one of Monty's shins. He shouts an obscenity and grabs his leg. Two doors fly open, and people crowd into the corridor, squeezing behind and around each other, squishing Monty against the wall, where he squirms and struggles like a beetle on its back.

Maybe I don't make much sense, but I shout at everyone about what happened. The policeman arrives and dashes through the back door, but he comes back to say that whoever was at the door has got away. He grips the back of Monty's neck and marches him off.

Someone has an arm around my shoulders and is trying to calm me down. People are demanding, "What did she say? What happened?" But a loud, firm voice shatters the confusion.

"Now!" Mrs. Montez says, clapping her hands into the silence. "We are already well off schedule, and I will have no more of this silly chitchat in the corridor. We will all get back to work. Stacy, you come with me."

I follow her through a room that connects with one of the major hallways. Rubbing my arm where the orderly had held it, I ask, "If the man outside the door was a reporter, he would have stayed, wouldn't he? He wouldn't have run."

"Don't think about it," Mrs. Montez says without breaking her rapid pace. "That is the policeman's job. Your job is to pay close attention to what I will show and tell you."

We march into a room that is like a small health club with all sorts of exercise equipment, some of which I recognize, some of which I've never seen before.

"Did I use any of this?" I ask her.

"Of course," she answers. "How does your hip feel?"

"Alice says it looks good."

"I didn't ask how it looks to Alice. I asked how it feels to you."

"It's okay."

"Very good, Stacy. Then hop on the bicycle."

There is no question but that she should be obeyed. I can't imagine anyone ever questioning her authority. I begin to pedal, and she sets a timer. She acts like the queen of the world, but she's really not so bad. I can tell that she's made a shell to hide in so that people can't see that she really cares. But I look at the warmth in her eyes, and I know she does care. I pedal a little faster and glance at her and smile.

And I do pay close attention to what Mrs. Montez tells me. She's arranged for the loan of an exercise bicycle and insists that I also walk at least a mile or two a day. Believe me, I'm going to keep doing the exercises and stay in good shape because I've got a lot to do. First on my list: As soon as I can see the face of the guy with the gun and they catch him, I'm going to make sure he's convicted of murder.

The policeman comes by to report. Whoever was at the back door of the clinic was probably an inexperienced reporter who chickened out when the fuss began. Lots of apologies that I was upset, and please don't worry. No real problem, except for the orderly, who was in big trouble with the clinic manager.

I nod and make all the right answers, but something at the back of my mind keeps nagging uncomfortably that the orderly's answers were too easy. I don't believe it was a reporter. Why would a reporter use such sneaky tactics to meet me? But who else would it be?

Dad arrives to check me out soon after I get back to my room. Dr. Peterson joins us, and Alice comes in to help me pack. I am starting to get a little shaky, thinking about what it will be like to be back in our own house without Mom there too, when the phone rings. It's Detective Markowitz.

"They told me you were checking out. Will you be able to come downtown this morning to look through some mug shots?"

"Do you think that will help me remember?"

"It's worth a try."

"Then, I'll be there."

"Ask your father," he tells me, so I do.

Dad takes the receiver and talks to Markowitz. Then he turns to me. "Are you up to all this, Stacy? It's going to be an emotional strain."

I stand as tall as I can. "I can do it. I have to do it. I hate him."

"Hate isn't the answer, Stacy. It won't solve anything."

"It will send the murderer to prison. That's all I care about."

"There are other things to care about," Dad says, but then Norma and one of the other nurses crowd into the room to say good-bye and interrupt him. I hear Dad tell Markowitz he'll take me home first, then bring me to the downtown station. I gather up the rest of my things, wad them into a small suitcase Dad has brought, and say good-bye to the nurses and to Dr. Peterson.

"Take it easy, Stacy," Dr. Peterson says, and suddenly wraps me in an awkward hug.

I wish he hadn't. When he releases me, I stare at the floor and hope nobody notices my cheeks are hot. "He hugged me. Really!" I'll tell Jan, who thought he was gorgeous. But I suddenly remember that the Jan I want to tell doesn't exist anymore.

I just stumble close to Dad and hang onto his arm as Dr. Peterson smiles and says, "I'll see you in two weeks, Stacy. Just change the gauze pad on the incision each day, and call me if you have any problems."

We're met outside the front door of the clinic by a couple of reporters and cameramen. For a moment I can only stare at them.

"Not now," Dad says. He makes a shooing motion with the arm I'm not clinging to. "Stacy has nothing to say to you now."

We make a dash for the car.

Dad and I don't talk much on the way home. I can tell that he's trying hard to think of just the right things to say, and I am, too, so our wary words back off and circle each other. We make sense, but that's all you can say for our conversation.

I enter the front door of our house and walk past the living room back to the den. For a few moments I stand with one hand braced against the top of Dad's reclining chair. Everything looks the same. I wish it had changed. I wish someone had painted the walls blue, or bought a new chair, or put flowered pillows on the sofa —anything to make it different. It's just the way it was when Mom was here. Only Mom isn't here now, and she won't be back.

I glance around the room. "Where's Pansy?"

"Oh," Dad says, "I guess I forgot to tell you. Pansy just, well, disappeared last year. She was getting old. She—" He gulps, looking miserable, and quickly adds, "The Coopers have a cat that's going to have kittens soon. Maybe you'd like one of her kittens. We could ask. People usually want to get rid of—"

"Who are the Coopers?"

"They live next door, in the Hadleys' house. The Hadleys moved to Dallas a little over a year ago. You'll like the Coopers. They're a nice family. Three little girls."

I move to the window, studying the backyard, which is deep in the ragged color of spring. The grass needs mowing, and the althea bush is spewing limbs of lavender blossoms with abandon. The pink and white geraniums have overgrown their bed, and the confederate jasmine vine on the back fence waves loose tendrils in the breeze as though it were deranged.

In the large oak rests the funny little shack of boards, with its open door and oddly shaped windows,

that Donna and I so carefully hammered together—
with a little help from Dad. It had been my sanctuary,
my quiet place, so many times in the past. I suddenly
want to climb the oak and curl up in the tree house
now. "It's been so long since I've been in the tree
house," I murmur to myself.

But Dad is standing next to me and hears. "Don't
climb up there, Stacy. It isn't safe now. One of the
supporting limbs broke off in a storm, and the whole
thing could come crashing down. I should have taken it
apart long ago, but I just don't seem to have enough
time."

I take his hand. "I'm sorry, Dad."

"It's not your fault, honey!" He suddenly brightens.
"I've been talking to Donna and Dennis, and well, how
would you like it if we set a date for all of us to drive
down to Padre Island for a weekend? We know how
much you always loved Padre Island. Remember? We
used to go every year. I think it will be nice to have a
family outing, don't you?"

The last thing I want to do is go to Padre Island. It
holds too many memories, but Dad is looking so uncomfortable, so hopeful, that I smile and say, "Sure."

A worry wrinkle flickers on and off across his forehead as he asks me over and over again if I'm sure I'll be
all right.

"I'm fine. Honest, I'm okay," I tell him. "Let's go
see those mug books. The sooner the better."

It doesn't take long to get to Riesner Street, and on
the way I gawk out the car window like a tourist. Downtown Houston is a collection of sharp-edged, shining

new buildings which stretch high over their old, ornate brick neighbors like a collection of slender giants and chunky munchkins. Much of what I see is new to me, but the police station squats in a very old part of town and looks as though it had been there forever. Dad parks in the lot in front of the station. I climb from the car and stand there, staring at the building. All sorts of people are bustling in and out of the front doors.

"Would you rather go home?" Dad asks, and I realize that I'm visibly trembling.

I just shake my head and, clutching Dad's hand, blindly follow him into the building and across the lobby with its olive green asphalt-tile floors. There is a sudden crush of bodies as we enter the central room. Someone pushes against me. The shoulder of his plaid shirt is damp and sour with sweat as it rubs against my cheek. A woman who is bulging in her faded cotton dress follows the man, swinging sharp elbows and talking all the while in rapid Spanish. She treads on my toes.

"Ouch!" I mutter, and stare after her, but she's unaware of anything but her own problem. Beyond her two men are talking. A man in a business suit has his back to me, and a tall, light-haired guy, who is probably close to my age, faces me. For a second our eyes meet, but a fat character in khakis, puffing, muttering, and pushing between us, follows his protruding stomach through the crowd. An elderly woman and man come through one of the doors, clinging to each other, looking terrified. Are all these people here because they're in some kind of trouble?

"This way," Dad says. He leads me into the elevator and up to the second floor. Just down the hall is the homicide room and Detective Markowitz's office.

Markowitz tugs a handkerchief from his pocket and wipes the sweat from his face. "Air conditioner went out yesterday. Hot weather, even for Houston. Feels like midsummer already." He gives me one of those searching looks and asks, "Ready to get to work, Stacy?"

"I'm ready."

Markowitz seats me at a table at one side of the room and places five huge scrapbooks in front of me. Dad sits at the table next to me. "Take your time," Markowitz says. "Look at each face carefully. I'll be working here in the room most of the time. If you think you recognize the face in one of those photos, just call me."

"Okay," I tell him, and open the first scrapbook.

At first I'm hopeful, but by the time I've gone through the third book I'm discouraged. When I finish the fifth, I slam it shut with a groan.

Markowitz comes to the table. "No luck?"

"His picture's not in those books."

"Maybe it's there, but you can't remember him."

Dad stands up, the legs of his chair screeching against the floor. "I think this is enough for now. Stacy needs to get some rest."

"I'm not tired," I insist, but Markowitz looks at Dad and nods.

"She might need a little more time," he says. "Let's put it on the shelf for a few days."

"I'm going to remember," I tell them.

"I'm counting on it," Markowitz says. "But I'd like

to wait and have you remember the face naturally, instead of forcing your memory."

"How do you mean, *forcing* it?"

He looks at Dad again, then back at me. "Well, for one thing, I've given some thought to trying hypnosis."

"That's a great idea!" I grab Dad's arm. "Can you do it?"

"We've got some people in the department who are trained to hypnotize, and there are a number of M.D.s who can do it. But there's a big problem, and that is, it doesn't always hold up in court."

"But if I could remember—"

He shakes his head. "I'd like to catch this guy and see that he's put away so carefully there won't be any technicalities for a sharp lawyer to use like a key to get him out. Understand?"

I nod.

"So I'll get in touch with you next week," he says, and walks with us to the elevator.

We're in the same squeeze of bodies as we leave the building. I'm glad to get out of that place.

It's good to be home again. Dad was right. I am tired.

"Are you sure you don't mind staying alone?" Dad asks.

"Of course, I don't." I lie, so he leaves to go back to the bank where he works. The aching loneliness of the house soon creeps around me, clinging, crawling, trying to seep through my skin to the hollow inside of me. I push myself out of the deep armchair and hurry to the backyard.

As I walk to the center of our backyard I take a deep breath of the mingled sour-warm geraniums, honeyed jasmine, and spring-sharp air, remembering, remembering, and turn to face our house.

The screen door flies open, and someone races through. He pauses, stares at me—his pale eyes frightened and glittering—and raises the gun.

"No!" I shout, backing away in terror. He evaporates, and the memory turns as blank as unexposed film.

"I saw his eyes," I whisper, furious at myself for giving in to the fear that erased the face I was almost able to see.

I know I should walk that mile Mrs. Montez insisted on, but I'm reluctant to leave the house. Finally I find a book to read and settle back into the armchair, deliberately forcing myself to concentrate on the book. Slowly I manage to relax and curl into a cocoon of sound spun by the hum of the air conditioner.

The sudden jangle of the telephone smashes the silence of the late afternoon. I drop the book and jump from the chair, staring at the phone, wishing it would stop.

On the third ring I answer and sigh with relief and gratefully flop back into the chair as I hear Jan's voice. "Stacy! Your dad said you'd be home. I'm so glad!"

"I'm glad too," I answer, and wonder what to say next.

It doesn't matter because Jan says, "You're going to a party!" She doesn't give me time to answer but probably has guessed what my answer would have been because in one long breath she adds, "You've got to go, so don't say no. The party's being given in your honor.

Besides, it's important for you to meet some of the kids."

"Jan, I'm not ready to go to a party."

"You are too. You just don't know it."

"But everyone's different. I mean, they're like you. They've grown four years older, and—"

"Hey, Stacy, cut it out. We're friends. Remember? I wouldn't make you go to this party if I didn't think it was right for you, and it is. It's going to be Friday night at Tony's house. You know Tony. And he's got this great house that is super for parties, and everyone is going to be there. Not just the kids you remember. All sorts of people will be there. There always are at Tony's parties. I mean, most of them are really neat, but some—oh, well, I'll brief you on those, and they won't bother you anyway. All in all, it will be a great party."

"Jan, listen to me. I can't go. I haven't got anything to wear."

Jan sighs so elaborately I have to laugh. That dramatic sigh hasn't changed. "Everyone is wearing jeans. You have jeans. I know you have. You're going."

"I don't have a date."

"You don't need a date. It's not a date party. B.J. and I will pick you up at eight Friday night." She giggles. "That brings me to the best news of all."

"Jan, listen to me! That party's just the day after tomorrow. I'm not ready!"

"Hmmm," Jan murmurs. "That's partly true. I'm going to come over early and fix your makeup. We'll be there at seven, so don't argue anymore."

"You haven't given me much chance to argue."

"There. You see? It's all settled. And I've been talking long enough because you've got to come over to my house right away."

"Why?"

She giggles again. "Wait and see!"

"Jan?" But she's no longer on the phone.

The party's a dumb idea. I don't want to go. Who are these people now who used to be in the seventh grade with me? What are they like? Will they think I'm just a stupid kid?

I walk into the bathroom and study my face in the mirror. No, I'm not a stupid kid. "Who knows?" I say to the green-eyed girl who is staring back at me. "The party might be a lot of fun."

I grab my house keys and make sure the door is locked. It doesn't take long to walk to Jan's house, which is just a couple of blocks from ours; but the air is humid and sticky, and my shirt begins to cling to my back. My finger is still on the doorbell when the door flies open and Jan says, "Stacy, guess what?"

She takes a long look at me and rolls her eyes. "Thank goodness we have time!"

"Time for what?"

"You'll never believe this. No one will believe it. Jeff Clinton is coming over!" Jan grabs my arm and pulls me inside and down the hallway.

"Come on, Jan. Make sense," I manage to say. "Who's Jeff Clinton?"

"He's a guy at school," Jan says, "and we're talking real hunk. He comes to some of the parties, but he doesn't date. He told Bick once that there's a girlfriend in Michigan, where he came from, and they're sort of going steady, which makes this whole thing absolutely amazing. B.J. will die when she finds out!"

"Finds out what?"

Jan glides into the den with one of her elaborate sighs. "Pay attention, Stacy. I'm telling you. Jeff Clinton called me and said he'd be going to the party, and he'd like to meet you, and one thing led to another, and I said how about today, and he's coming over in a few minutes, so let's get some makeup on you."

"Jan! You fixed up a date for me?"

"It's not really a date. We'll just get acquainted and talk and drink some cola. And you and Jeff can get acquainted."

"Wait a minute!" I back away from her. "Why did he want to meet me?"

Jan's eyes open wider. "I don't know. Maybe he saw your picture in the paper and thought you were cute."

"That's not a good reason."

"Honestly, Stacy! That's as good a reason as any." She studies me, her head tilted to one side. "What's the matter? You look so—I don't know—suspicious. And that's silly. There will be lots of guys who will want to get to know you."

"But I want to know why."

Her mouth makes a large pink O. "I get it. It has to do with the guy you saw on your back porch, the one who—"

I interrupt. "Jan, I still can't see his face!"

"He wouldn't be Jeff. I told you, Jeff just moved here from Michigan last year. And anyway, you can't go around being suspicious of everybody."

I lean against the wall and sigh. "You're right. I guess I sound like some kind of nerd. It's just that—" Jan is looking at me with so much concern that I change the subject. "When he's here—Jeff, I mean—what am I supposed to do? I don't know what to say to him."

"Oh, you will." She tugs at my arm, dragging me into the bathroom. "Aren't you using the makeup kit I gave you?"

I shrug. "Sometimes."

"You're supposed to use it, Stacy! Look at you. Naked faces are not *in!*"

"In what?" I ask, trying to be funny, but Jan doesn't appreciate my humor. She's too busy doing things to my face.

The doorbell rings, and she hisses, "Here's the lipstick. Quick!"

"You answer the door," I tell her. "I'll put it on."

"Not much," she says as she runs from the room. "Just enough to count."

I stare at my reflection in the mirror, startled again by the girl who looks back. I like what Jan did. There's a kind of peach color over my eyelids, with a brown eyeliner. It makes my eyes look bigger. I fumble for the lipstick and put on just a little, following Jan's directions.

Taking a deep breath, I give one last glance at the mirror and head for the den, where I can hear Jan chattering.

As I enter the room a tall sandy-haired guy pulls himself up from Jan's father's reclining chair and faces me. His pale blue eyes crinkle at the edges as he smiles at me.

I can't help smiling back.

He's wearing snug jeans and sneakers without socks and a white T-shirt and a light kind of unbuttoned jacket with the sleeves pushed up to his elbows. It looks strange. It's probably another new style. He must work out a lot. I wonder if he's on the football team. His shoulders are broad, and even the jacket doesn't hide the muscles in his arms.

Jan introduces us and says, "Sit down, Stacy. I'll get something for us to drink."

Suddenly I'm shy. I clasp my hands together and stare at them, wishing I knew what to talk about to a guy.

"Have you thought yet about going back to school?" Jeff asks. "Will they let you make up some of the classes in summer school?"

I'm so thankful that he didn't ask me about Mom or the murderer that I stumble all over myself answering his question. "Dad and I were talking about that. I don't know what they'll want me to do. I do know one thing. I can't go back to junior high school. I'd be so much older than everyone else." I stop for breath. "What I'd like to do is study the things I've missed. I could study hard and make up some of the work. If they'll just let me."

Jeff smiles. "It's hard to study alone. Maybe some of the kids could help tutor you and get you ready for exams. If you could pass exams, they might give you credit for the courses."

"That's a great idea."

"I'll volunteer to be a tutor. I'm pretty good in math."

"Really? You'll help me learn the math I've

missed?" Maybe it's excitement. Maybe it's the way he's leaning forward just a bit, looking at me as though I were the most interesting person he's ever seen. I feel myself blushing.

Jan comes into the room, balancing a tray with three glasses of cola and a plate of chocolate marshmallow cookies. She remembered. They're my favorite.

Jan looks at my red face, and one eyebrow rises and falls.

But Jeff starts talking about how much he likes math and how he once tried building a computer, and it gives me a chance to calm down. Afternoon sunlight tilts through the window next to him, highlighting his face. I study it, liking it. For some reason Jeff seems much older to me. I can't explain it. Maybe it's something I see in his eyes. He seems more knowledgeable, more aware than kids his age should be. Strangely I have the feeling that I've seen him before. It can't be, but there's something familiar, something I should remember. I don't know what it could be.

The conversation has shifted to the party. I don't know most of the people Jan is rattling on about, and Jeff begins to look kind of bored.

He stands up and smiles at me. "I'd better go, Stacy. If you'll check into the books you'll need for algebra and geometry and get an okay from one of the counselors, we'll start on the tutoring anytime you say. I can come over to your house every afternoon and work with you."

Both of Jan's eyebrows go up this time, but I don't think Jeff notices. He's looking at me. Jan dashes into the kitchen, so I walk to the front door with Jeff. "I appreciate it, Jeff. I really do."

He smiles again. "See you at the party," he says, and walks to his car. It's a plain vanilla gray sedan and looks like the cars I remember, so it's probably four or five years old.

"Stacy!" Jan hisses, and I realize I'm still standing in the open doorway, watching Jeff, so I close the door and hurry back to the den.

"He likes you!" Jan shouts. "It's obvious instant infatuation! B.J. will go out of her mind!"

"He just offered to tutor me in math," I tell her.

"Math is as good an excuse for seeing somebody as any other excuse," Jan says. She's so pleased with herself that she practically purrs.

The clock in her den chimes five times. I automatically count along with it. "I'd better go home," I tell her. "Say hi to your parents for me."

"Mom will be disappointed that she missed you. She didn't know you'd be here. She keeps asking me how soon you'll be able to come over for dinner."

"As soon as possible. Your mom is a great cook."

Jan opens the front door and calls to me when I reach the sidewalk, "I'll see you tomorrow! This is going to be some party!"

When I get home, I poke through the refrigerator. I never really learned to cook. Oh, well, I can make grilled cheese sandwiches for dinner.

Donna and Dennis come over, and Donna says next time I have to go back to the police station she'll go with me since Dad doesn't think he can take any more time off his daytime job, and Donna has only one class and can skip it.

That's when I find out that Dad has been holding down two jobs, so he can pay all my medical bills. I hate the guy who murdered Mom even more.

I wish so hard I could see his face. How do I explain to Dad or to Detective Markowitz about my weird feeling that if I don't discover the identity of the murderer pretty soon, I may run out of time?

Chapter Seven

Early-morning mists from the Gulf slither inland, mingling with the pollution from the northeast factories and refineries, giving us a day that's gray and grimy with smog.

Donna arrives, waddling smugly. She puts a covered bowl into the refrigerator. "The baby kicked all night," she complains, but she looks delighted. She studies the green cotton shirt and jeans I'm wearing. "We're going to Foley's this morning. You have to get some clothes that fit you, Stacy."

"When do you want to go?"

"As soon as the store opens."

Later, all the way to Foley's Memorial store, she chats about the kinds of clothes I'll need: jeans and shirts. I feel comfortable with those. But she gets me a couple of dresses, and they're weird.

"I wouldn't buy you a 'weird' dress." Donna is firm. "You just don't know anything about the styles for your age yet. Trust me."

"You're being bossy," I tell her as she pulls out Dad's charge card. "You're trying to act like Mom, but Mom wasn't bossy."

"I'm trying to help you." Donna looks at me the way she used to when I'd yell at her that it wasn't fair she always beat me at Monopoly.

I take a deep breath. "I'm sorry. I didn't mean it." I really don't care about the dresses. What to wear is just one more stupid thing to have to get used to, and right now it seems unimportant.

Donna buys some bras, panties, and a slip. She decides that I've got everything I'll need for a while, so she drives me home.

I dump my packages on the sofa in the living room.

"I'll hang them up for you," she says.

"I can do that myself."

"Better do it now, so the dresses won't get wrinkled. I promised Dennis I'd call him before I started home."

As she heads toward the kitchen phone I scoop up my packages, take them to my room, and drop them on the bed.

A persistent pat-pat on the window greets me. It's a loose branch of a scraggly, climbing Queen Elizabeth rose. I open the window, soaking in the pungent-sweet smells of the garden, the sounds of a dog barking down the street, and the laughter of the children in the yard next door. The Cooper children. They don't see me, so I watch them play.

The two younger girls are playing tag. The older girl—Donna said she was twelve—leans against the solid trunk of their old elm tree, laughing at her sisters, yelling encouragement to the little one, who's trying so hard to catch her sister. They're look-alikes, with round, freckled faces and light brown hair.

For an instant I ache to join them. The twelve-year-old—she looks almost thirteen—would be close to my age. She might like to be friends and—

But I'm no longer thirteen. I turn and see myself in the full-length mirror that hangs on the door. I'm seventeen, in a world I don't want, that I'm not ready for. I bang my fists against the wall. *You, with the gun—whoever you are, I hate you. I hate you!*

"Stacy."

I hurry back to the front hallway to join Donna, who's fishing in her handbag for her car keys. She has to go, and I have to let her. I fight the fear I know will come with the lonely house.

"Are you sure you'll be all right by yourself?" she asks as she studies my face.

I take her by the shoulders and laugh, trying to sound braver than I feel. "I'm a big girl now. Remember?"

She smiles and hugs me. As she presses against me the baby moves, so I feel it too. I want to keep holding her, so that I can feel the baby again, sharing it with her. But Donna steps back and says, "If you need me, just call. Oh—there's a chicken pasta salad in the refrigerator."

"Thanks for everything, Donna. Thanks for shopping for me."

"If you decide you really don't like the dresses—"

"They're great," I say. "Go on. You've got things to do." The longer she stays, the harder it will be to let her leave.

"The blue one is especially—"

"I love it! Get going!"

I throw open the front door and shriek at the face that's staring bug-eyed into mine.

"Oh, dear!" the woman on our front porch says. She brushes back the brown bangs that hang over her eyes and pushes her oversize glasses up on her nose. "I didn't mean to startle you! I saw you come home a few minutes ago, and I was just going to ring the bell."

Donna steps up beside me and holds out a hand. "Mrs. Cooper, you must come in and meet Stacy." She turns to me. "Remember, Stacy? I told you that Mrs. Cooper and her family live next door."

We say all the right things to each other as Donna moves us into the living room.

"I can't stay," Mrs. Cooper says. "I just wanted to greet Stacy and tell her the entire neighborhood is glad she's back and feeling good again."

"Thank you," I say.

"Oh, I know we weren't here before; but we're so fond of your family, and that includes you too."

"Thanks."

"And I am planning to send over a casserole or something. It's just that I've been so busy with the little girls, and you do understand, I know. It's just PTA and the church society and dental appointments and one blessed thing after another. You certainly are a pretty girl."

"Thank you."

"So much like Donna."

"Yes. Thanks."

She hardly pauses for breath. "I was wondering if you'd baby-sit my girls this evening. One of my husband's clients invited us out to dinner—at the last minute, wouldn't you know?—and we'd need you for just a short time. Could you make it seven o'clock? We promise to be home by ten, so you won't get too tired."

Donna holds up a hand. "But Stacy is—"

I interrupt her. I don't want to tell Donna that I'm still feeling jittery about being alone in the house. I'd just as soon Donna didn't know. "I'll be glad to babysit," I tell Mrs. Cooper. "I don't have anything I have to do tonight. Sure. I'll be there."

"Maybe we should ask Dad," Donna says.

Mrs. Cooper manages to look both puzzled and horribly disappointed at the same time. "But it's just right next door," she says. "And the girls are all well behaved."

"Dad will be at work anyway," I tell Donna, and I smile reassuringly at Mrs. Cooper. "See you at seven."

Mission accomplished, she's off and away, and Donna leaves after one more reassuring hug.

I start puttering around in the kitchen, reading cookbooks as though they were messages from a secret power and I were a decoder with the CIA. Why didn't I ever learn to cook anything besides fudge? I peek inside the bowl of chicken pasta salad that Donna made. What's a pasta salad? It sounds terrible.

To my surprise I find a recipe for a casserole that seems to match up with the carrots and onions and ground beef I pull out of the refrigerator. That's such a good start I tackle the putting-together part with real enthusiasm. After it's been in the oven awhile, it starts to bubble and actually smells good. I'm really proud of myself.

I carry the little TV set to the kitchen and listen

while I'm setting the table. It's the local news, and the newscasters talk about a rapid transit system and things I don't know anything about. Then I hear my name and look up to see that scene outside the clinic. Did I really feel as scared as I look? Yes. I guess so. But they're off now on a story about a convenience store shooting. A couple of times I glance at the telephone. I wish it would ring. I wish it would be Jeff. But the telephone is silent.

Dad comes home, kisses me, and says, "I think I'll just settle down with the newspaper for a few minutes before dinner's ready."

I make a lettuce salad, but according to the timer, we have fifteen minutes to wait for the casserole. So I join Dad in the den. He's asleep in his chair, the newspaper spilling from his lap. Carefully I pick up the classified section. It gives me an idea.

As I turn the pages they rustle. Dad's eyelids flicker, then open. He smiles at me. "Guess I had a little nap." He sits up, stretches, then notices what I've been reading. Before he can say a word, I speak up.

"I want to get a job."

"Stacy, we talked about your catching up on your schoolwork."

"I can do both. I'll study hard, Dad. I know how much work I've got to make up. But there's no reason I can't get a job too. I want to help."

"It will be too much for you. We won't discuss it."

"We have to discuss it!"

He sighs. "Stacy, I'm afraid you got your stubbornness from my side of the family, but maybe that's good because I can be as stubborn as you can." Dad smiles, and I know he's trying to ease things between us as he says, "I remember once when we met head-on about whether or not you were old enough at twelve to go on a date, and your mother said the two of us were like that pair of rams in the Disney movie, banging their heads to the tune of the 'Anvil Chorus.' "

"You won that argument," I say.

"I'm going to win this one too."

"I just want to help. You work at the bank in the daytime and do bookkeeping at night, and it's too much."

"We won't discuss it."

"You already said that. You make me so mad, Daddy! All I want to do is talk to you!"

He sits up and leans toward me. The lamplight in the room casts shadows that deepen the hollows under his eyes. "Honey, I want to talk to you too," he says. "I want to talk to you about your mother."

My shoulders are stiff, and there's a tight place at the back of my neck that begins to throb. "There's nothing to talk about."

"Yes, there is. I'm worried about you because you haven't mourned her."

"Yes, I have."

"I think you're holding your feelings in, afraid to let go and face what happened. That's not good, Stacy."

I can't tell him about my feelings. How can I explain about the burning fingers of hatred that claw at my mind?

The oven timer buzzes, so I scramble to my feet. "Dinner's ready!"

He studies me for a moment, then says, "Okay,

Stacy. Just remember, when you're ready to talk, I'm ready to listen."

There isn't anything I want to say now. There's too much to think about to wonder about my feelings. That will come later.

Dad praises me over and over for the wonderful casserole. I think it tastes a little flat, but he has second helpings, so I suppose he really likes it. I tell him I'm going to baby-sit the Cooper kids. He starts to frown but changes it to a smile and says it's all right. Maybe he's got a limit of one argument going at a time. Maybe he thinks he'll have his say about the big things and let the little things go by. Who knows what parents think?

After the dishes are finished and Dad has left, I make sure I've got Detective Markowitz's card in my pocket. I leave the lights on in the den, lock the house carefully, and cross the lawn to the Cooper house.

Mrs. Cooper opens the door. She reminds me of one of those dust devils that whirl across the open lands in Texas as she darts and swoops into the den, introducing me to Keri, Meri, Teri, and Mr. Cooper. She points out the emergency numbers in the kitchen and the phone number where they can be reached. Then she disappears for a moment into a closet, emerges with a handbag, bobs over her daughters with a good night kiss, and is out the door, carrying her balding and bemused husband with her.

The girls stare at me.

"Help me get your names straight," I tell them, knowing that it had to be their mother who had named them.

"Think of it as alphabetical," the oldest one says. "*K* before *M* and *M* before *T*. I'm Keri. I'm twelve."

Teri, who looks as though she were about six, pipes up. "Mom said you're the Sleeping Beauty. Are you the real Sleeping Beauty?"

"No," I say. "That's just a make-believe story." I glance around the room. It doesn't look a thing like it did when the Hadleys lived here. Everything is flowered chintz with red poppies and ruffles. A big bouquet of matching artificial flowers is on an end table, and dozens of photographs of the girls are on the wall over the sofa. The wall has been paneled in a light birch wood. How can this house look so different when our house looks so much the same?

On the floor, nearly covering a round scatter rug, are Barbie dolls, dresses, houses, cars—the whole works. I wonder where Daddy put my Barbie dolls. Maybe they're packed away.

"You've got a lot of clothes for your dolls," I tell the girls. "Do you care if I look at them?"

"Wanna play?" Meri asks.

I shrug. "Why not?"

We sit near the edges of the rug, and in a few minutes I'm putting a red net ball gown on one of the dolls, and Keri's doll is driving over to visit mine.

"Three movie stars are going to be at the dance," Keri's doll says.

"Who cares about movie stars?" my doll says. "Have you heard? The duke of York is going to be there."

"And I'm going to sing with the band," Meri's doll says. "I'm a famous singer."

"You sing like a frog," Keri says, and we all giggle.

The game goes on until Teri steps in the middle of the rug and stamps her foot. "Nobody listens to me! I tried to tell you what I saw upstairs!"

"You were upstairs?" I'm startled and worried, because I didn't realize she had left the game.

"I told you I was going to the bathroom!"

"I'm sorry, Teri. Sit down. Our dolls are going to the beach. Do you want the purple bathing suit for your doll?"

"No! If you're not going to listen to me, then I won't tell you."

I put out my arms to her and pull her down on my lap. "Hey, I'm sorry. I'll listen. What do you want to tell us?"

"About somebody who's in your yard. I looked out the window upstairs, and I saw somebody trying to look in your windows."

We all jump up. Meri screeches, and I shush her. "We don't want him to hear us. We'll have to be quiet."

But we race upstairs, ahead of Teri, who's now filled with her own importance. She joins us in the dark room and leads the way to the wide bedroom window that overlooks our house and yard.

"Look," she whispers.

I lean over the heads of the three girls, straining to differentiate between the shapes and shadows. One shape moves, and I see it step back from the side of our house, where it has apparently been trying to see into my bedroom window. In an instant it has slid through the darkness and disappeared around the back of the house.

Keri clutches my arm, and I feel her tremble as she whispers, "He's in your backyard! Stacy, what if he gets inside your house?"

Chapter Eight

I step back from the window, pulling the children with me, and try to sound calm. "We'll call the police. They'll take care of it."

"I want my daddy!" Meri is so terrified that Teri puckers up and begins to wail. That sets Meri off, and it takes me a few minutes to quiet them down, so that I can make the telephone call to Detective Markowitz.

The woman who answers my call tells me that Detective Markowitz is not there, but she'll get in touch with him, so I explain why I'm calling. She says that she'll send a squad car out to investigate, then try to reach Markowitz.

The Cooper children and I huddle together in the living room, where we can press our noses against the picture window and watch for the police car to arrive. Maybe one of us should stay at the upstairs window and watch for the shadow to appear again, but we're all too frightened. We want to stick together.

"Let's call Mama," Teri says. Her lower lip wobbles, and I hug her tightly.

"In a few minutes," I tell her. "It will be safer if the

police check things out before your mother and daddy get home."

"They said they'd be home by ten," Keri answers, "and it's almost ten."

"You were supposed to put us to bed at our bedtime," Meri accuses. "Mama's going to be mad at you."

"So you want to go to bed right now?" I ask her. She shakes her head vigorously.

"I want Mama," Teri whimpers.

Maybe I expected sirens and screeching tires, something like what I've seen in police movies. But a police car comes quietly down the street and parks in front of the Cooper house. Two policemen climb out. One stays in the yard, studying our house next door, and one comes to the Cooper front door.

I nearly trip over Teri, who dashes under my feet as I run to open the door, but I manage to hang on to her and tell the officer what happened.

Teri keeps interrupting, shouting, "I saw him first!"

"Just stay put and keep the door locked," the officer says. "We'll look around."

He shuts the door firmly. We rush to the large window again and see him and his partner walk toward our house, flashlights sweeping a crisscross pattern of light ahead of them. In a few seconds they are out of sight.

"Let's go upstairs and watch out the bedroom window," Keri says.

She tries to squeeze past me, but I grab her arm. "No! We're safer here. The policeman told us just to stay put. Remember?"

There's a little brass clock on the mantel, and it chimes ten times. It's not just the Coopers who are due home at ten. Dad told me that he usually gets home a little after ten o'clock too. I don't want them to come now. Not with whoever it was prowling around our house! What if someone gets hurt?

The telephone's ring is so shrill that we all jump, and Meri screams.

"It's just the phone," I say, but they cling to me and shove against me as I hurry to answer it. We're like a pack of puppies, bumping and pushing against each other.

Just after the third ring I manage to grab the receiver before Keri can snatch it.

"What's up?" Markowitz asks me. "Where are you?"

I fill him in, and he says he'll be right over. "Tell the officers to stay until I get there," he adds.

The sound of his voice is like a pat on the back, an arm around my shoulders. "Everything's going to be all right," I tell the girls. "Let's go back to the window."

As we reach the front window and settle against the glass, one of the officers appears, cutting across the lawn. He comes to the front porch and rings the bell just as the Coopers' car pulls into the driveway.

"Oh-oh," Keri says.

Oh-oh is right. As I open the door Mrs. Cooper flies across the lawn, screeching, "What happened to my children?"

"It's all right, ma'am," the officer says, and at the same time Teri shouts her story at the top of her lungs. Meri rushes into her mother's arms, crying loudly, and Keri yells that there's a prowler outside and everybody should get in the house and lock the door.

The perpetually puzzled Mr. Cooper appears, and Dad, who has also just come home, and the other officer join the scene.

"Let's all be quiet," Dad says in a loud, firm voice as he checks out everyone in the group, "so we can find out what's going on."

Apparently Mrs. Cooper has been counting noses, too, and is satisfied with the tally, so she's ready to listen. Miraculously she is able to quiet her children by firmly saying "Hush." I wonder if there's an unspoken "or else" behind it.

One of the officers explains about my call. "But we couldn't find anyone in your yard," he adds to my father. "The windows all seemed to be locked, and both the front and back doors were secured."

The other officer speaks up. "Could be your daughter is a little nervous. Can't blame her. And people sometimes think they see things in the dark, things that aren't really there. You know, shadows and tree branches moving in the wind, stuff like that."

"But we all saw him," Keri says.

"I saw him first," Teri shouts.

"It was a 'him'?" Mrs. Cooper asks Teri. "A boy? A man?"

Teri thinks for a moment. "Maybe it was a monster."

There's a pause, during which the adults all look at each other. Then the first police officer says, "There's no one there now," in the tone of voice that implies he doubts there ever was. He turns to Mrs. Cooper. "We checked your yard out, too, ma'am, just to be sure."

"Thank you," she says, takes a deep breath, and

immediately begins to order her children inside, ask if they've brushed their teeth, why they aren't in their pajamas, and have they completely forgotten the rule about picking up their toys before they go to bed?

I just quietly shut the door and leave with Dad and the policemen. Mrs. Cooper didn't remember to pay me, but it doesn't matter. I wasn't a very good baby-sitter, and I'm not going to baby-sit again—not until the murderer is found and he's in prison. I don't know what happened tonight, if anything, but if I'm in any danger, I don't want to involve anyone else.

Markowitz arrives and talks to the policemen. They leave, and he checks out the yard himself with a high-powered flashlight. He bends and stoops and examines the ground under each of the windows as Dad and I follow along behind him. "If we'd had some rain, we might have been able to get a footprint," Markowitz finally says, snapping off his light and tucking one end of it into the pocket of his jacket. He thinks for a moment, then looks carefully at me.

"Stacy, I think it was a false alarm."

"We saw someone."

"Male or female?"

"I don't know. I couldn't tell."

"Why?"

"It was too dark. It was just a shadow."

He shakes his head and says, "That's what I mean. It is dark tonight, too dark to know what you saw. I'm inclined to think it was too much imagination."

Dad puts an arm around my shoulders and lets out a sigh. "I thought so, but I'm glad to hear you say it. Would you like a cup of coffee, Mr. Markowitz?"

"No, thanks," Markowitz says. "This was a long day. I'm beat." He walks with us to the front door. "Want me to check inside?"

"Do you think you should?" Dad asks.

"Nope. Your house was locked up tight. We would have found signs of forced entry if anyone had tried to get inside." Markowitz smiles at me. "Take care, Stacy. I'll be in touch with you soon."

Dad seems satisfied, and so does Markowitz, but I'm not. "What if—" I begin, then don't know how to say what I'm thinking without getting Dad all upset.

But Markowitz knows, and he answers. "Nothing's going to happen to you, Stacy. We'll watch out for you. You're our star witness."

Is that all he cares about? That I might be able to testify against whoever killed my mother? Maybe that's all that would matter to me, too, if my job were trying to catch criminals. He's smiling, but I don't trust his smile because I don't believe everything is as simple as he makes it out to be. I know that I saw someone prowling around our house tonight, and nothing Markowitz or the other officers have said is going to make me change my mind.

I don't sleep well. In spite of the air conditioning, the air is sticky and clammy, and the sheets are a tangle around my legs. I doze and wake, alert to every little pop and creak of the house. Somewhere nearby the sharp trill of a mockingbird shatters the dark, and my eyes fly open. What is it? What?

Every time I close my eyes I see the screen door open, the hand raise the gun, the face—I can't see the face! I know I'm trying too hard, but I've got to be able to see it.

At breakfast the next morning I tell Dad I'm going to make an appointment to talk to the counselor at Glen Creek High School, and I tell him about the party tonight.

Dad looks uncomfortable. "When Donna was your age, your mother took care of those things," he says. "I can't remember all the questions I'm supposed to ask." He thinks for a moment, then brightens. "Who will you be going to the party with?"

"Jan and B.J."

"I know Jan, but who's this guy B.J.?"

"Dad, B.J. is a girl. You met her—a long time ago. And it's not the kind of party where you have to come with a date."

"Will this party be supervised?"

"I don't know."

"Well, do you know where it will be?"

"Tony Maconda's house."

"Do you know him?"

"Sure. I've known him since kindergarten. His family used to live just a couple of blocks from us, and then his father got to be vice-president or something in the oil company he worked for, and they moved to one of those big houses near the bayou."

There's something else I should remember about Tony, something nagging my mind, but for now I can't think of it. I do remember that he got caught shoplifting once, and there was one day when he bragged he had marijuana in his locker, only that time he didn't get caught. I used to think Tony was a creep. But then, I thought Bick was, too, and Jan says he's wonderful. People change a lot in four years.

I tell Dad, "Tony's short and plump and—" I lean back in my chair. "Oh, Dad, I don't know what he looks like now!"

"Okay, Stacy. I know who you mean. I've met Tony's parents. They seem like reasonable people."

He stares at the table, and I know he's trying to think up the other questions he's supposed to ask, but I'm tired of this. I hadn't wanted to go to the party, but now it's become a challenge. There's no reason why Dad shouldn't let me go with Jan.

"At seventeen I should be old enough to make up my own mind about going to a party!"

"It's just that you're not quite used to the world as it is now," he says. "There's a problem with drugs and—"

"Daddy!" I interrupt. "Kids were taking drugs when I was thirteen! And you don't have to worry about me. I'm not dumb enough to take drugs."

He reaches across the table and takes my hands. "Stacy, I wasn't intimating that you'd take drugs. I was —oh, honey, I want to protect you, and I don't know how to do it."

I squeeze his fingers and smile at him. "Daddy, you're doing a good job of protecting me. Just don't overdo it. I've got to be allowed to grow up."

He nods and tries to smile back. "Well, you'll be with Jan. She's a good girl. And I know where you'll be. What time are you leaving for the party?"

"Jan's going to be here at seven to help me get ready."

He looks puzzled. "Do you need something special to wear?"

"No, Dad. It's informal. I'll wear my jeans. Jan's going to help me with my makeup."

"I feel so lost," he says. "I wish your mother were here."

I fight back the hot pressure behind my eyes, answering, "I wish she were here too," and adding quickly, "but you're doing a great job, Dad. And Jan will be glad to see you."

He carries his coffee cup and empty cereal bowl to the sink. "Not tonight, I'm afraid. I almost forgot to tell you. I'll get a hamburger for dinner because we've got to go over some reports that came in from one of the branches. It's going to mean that I'll be there later than usual, maybe until eleven or even midnight."

"I may get home before you do," I tell him.

He bends down to kiss my forehead. "Have a good time at the party, Stacy."

"Thanks," I answer, wishing I didn't have to go.

In the afternoon a delivery truck comes with an exercise bicycle.

The moment the deliveryman leaves the telephone rings. "Is everything all right, Stacy?" It's Mrs. Cooper's voice.

"Yes. Everything's fine."

"Well, you know how it is in a neighborhood—everyone checking on everyone else, and I saw a delivery truck, so I thought—" She interrupts herself to tell me about some friends who had a delivery truck parked in their driveway, and none of their neighbors thought a thing about it, except it really wasn't a delivery truck, and most of their furniture was stolen.

"This one was a real delivery truck, and it brought my exercise bicycle," I tell her.

"I guess I'm just being too careful," she says. "But one thing and another, like that excitement last night and that same car that seems to be cruising this street, although my husband says I'm just looking for trouble, and—"

"What car?" I have to interrupt.

"I don't know," she says. "Just a car. Next time I see it I'm going to write down the license number."

"How often have you seen the car?"

"Oh, three or four times."

"What kind of car is it?"

"Goodness, I have no idea."

"What color is it?"

"Plain. You know."

"Brown? Blue?"

"Yes. Something like that. Nothing special."

There's no point in asking her any more questions. Besides, the car she saw is probably no more a threat than the delivery truck that brought my bicycle.

"One more thing." Mrs. Cooper continues by telling me she's sorry she forgot to tell me about the girls' bedtime, and she's sorry we all got so excited. She forgot to tell me that Teri has an overactive imagination, and she apologizes for forgetting to pay me for babysitting. If I come over tonight or tomorrow, she'll have the money for me. By the time we end our conversation I feel like gasping for breath.

I climb on the bicycle and follow all of Mrs.

Montez's instructions, working up a real sweat. Next comes a steamy, hot shower. I feel good, really good.

As I turn off the shower I hear the telephone ringing. Wrapping the towel around myself, I run to answer it. How long has it been ringing? Whoever is calling must know that I'm home. Maybe it's Donna or Dad.

"Hi," I gasp into the receiver.

A whispering voice hisses, "What do you remember, Stacy?"

"Who are you?" The whisper is weird, but I'm too shocked to be frightened.

"It's been a long time," the voice says. "Why don't you just forget? It would be safer for you to forget."

I hear my own voice as though I'd stepped outside my body and were looking and listening to someone else. I expect to be afraid, but I'm not. It's as though I were made of glass, with a red, churning anger bubbling up inside me. Words drop like chunks of molten glass as I ask, "Are you the one who killed my mother?"

The whisperer doesn't answer for a while, so I ask again, "Are you?"

The voice over the telephone is softer now. "I heard that you don't remember my face."

"But I will," I say.

"Then I'll have to do something about it."

"Not if I find you first."

There's a pause, then a chuckle. It sounds almost as though he were talking to himself. This guy is weird. I can't make out the first few words, but I hear him say, ". . . have a friend."

I interrupt. "What are you talking about? What friend?"

"You haven't got a chance, Stacy," he whispers.

There's a click as the line goes dead. Slowly I put down the receiver. I didn't know that hate could be this strong. He has torn up my life. He's destroyed four years that belonged to me. And most horrible of all, he's taken my mother away from us. I shiver as I realize I actually hate him enough to kill him.

Chapter Nine

The late-afternoon sun is rapidly being swallowed by dusky shadows, so I hurry through the room, fumbling with trembling fingers, turning on a couple of lamps. The light helps. And the movement brings everything back to normal. I think about the person who made that telephone call. Why did he laugh and talk to himself? He might have been high on something, some weird character who was playing games. Our telephone number's in the phone book, easy for anyone to find, and there are a lot of crazy people who might think a call like that was funny. No. I'm sure he wasn't the murderer. The murderer wouldn't call me. Of course, he wouldn't.

The doorbell rings. Hesitating long enough to take a deep breath, I open the door. Jan stands there beaming at me.

"Here we are, right on time and ready to make you gorgeous!" Jan announces. She steps into the entry hall, B.J. behind her. Jan looks super, but I stare at B.J. and wish I could go to the party with a paper bag over my head. Nobody should razzle-dazzle her good looks like

B.J. It's unfair to the rest of us who have to live in the same world.

My expression must show what I'm thinking, because the corners of B.J.'s mouth turn up, and she gleams at me. "Stacy, you have great possibilities. With a little makeup and a new hairdo we'll work wonders."

"You should have seen her in the clinic after I did her makeup," Jan says quickly. She holds up an overnight case. "I've got everything here! Even hot rollers and scissors."

"And we'll choose something for you to wear," B.J. adds. "Oh, isn't this fun!"

I take a step backward, bumping into the wall. "Wait a minute. You said to wear jeans. I'm wearing jeans."

They both examine me slowly from head to toe. "They're *new* jeans," B.J. says. "Besides, they're a little baggy. You haven't shrunk them yet, have you?"

"Well, no. I mean, why should I shrink them? They'd be too tight."

"We've got time to shrink them. Take them off."

Jan giggles. "Stacy, you aren't going to wear that flowered cotton shirt?"

"I like this shirt."

Jan puts down her case and opens it. Triumphantly she pulls out a bright red T-shirt with short sleeves and a V-neck. "I brought you a present," she says, handing it to me. "With your dark hair you'll look super in red."

I try to step back again, but there's nowhere to go. "Look," I say, "why can't I just go like I am?"

B.J. tucks her chin down and stares at me with determination. "Because you have something to live up to, Stacy. You're the Sleeping Beauty, coming back to the world, and you have to make an impact on it."

"Don't call me that," I plead.

Jan grabs my hand and pulls me toward my bedroom. "We don't have much time. Let's stop all this talk and get to work!"

They've got a goal, and I'm it. I can't fight the two of them, so I give up and follow orders, getting into a robe as B.J. marches to the laundry room with my jeans and Jan lays out an array of bottles and jars and cans on the bathroom ledge.

She shampoos my hair and plops me into a chair that B.J. has brought from the kitchen. I'm facing away from the mirror over the sink, but that's all right because I'm nervous about what I'll finally see. I just hope Jan knows what she's doing.

Chunks of my hair fall into my lap, and I squeeze my eyes shut. I may need that paper bag after all.

She squirts a handful of some kind of foam into her hands and rubs it all through my hair. Then come the hot rollers.

"So far, so good," Jan says with satisfaction, and B.J. nods approval.

"Now for her face," B.J. says, and reaches for a bottle.

They seem to take turns patting and smoothing things over my skin. Finally I say, "Isn't that enough? This seems like an awful lot of trouble."

"Keep quiet," B.J. says. She picks up a blue pencil. "If you talk, we might make a mistake."

"But—"

"You're going to be our masterpiece," Jan says, and

she giggles with excitement. "Wait till you see yourself, Stacy!"

I can wait. Believe me, I can wait.

"Wait till everybody sees you. Wait till Jeff Clinton sees you!"

"I heard the big exciting news about you and Jeff," B.J. says. From the expression on her face I guess the excitement must have passed her by.

"It's no big deal about Jeff," I tell them. "He just offered to help me learn math. That's all."

"Stop talking," Jan says. "I'm getting to your mouth."

They make enthusiastic comments to each other, which I try to ignore. Finally they step back and grin at me. "Don't look yet," Jan says.

She takes out the rollers, pulls me from the chair, and leads me out of the bathroom back into the bedroom. "Put on your T-shirt before I comb your hair, so your hair won't get all messed up."

"But where are my jeans?"

"Here they are." B.J. comes into the room, holding them out before her. "They're still a little bit warm, but they're dry now."

It takes the three of us to get me into the jeans. I have to lie on the bed and wiggle and grunt and hold my breath until the zipper is up. "I told you they wouldn't fit me!" I complain.

But Jan says, "Of course they fit you. They look just right now. Pretty soon you'll learn how to put them on by yourself. You have to wiggle in just the right way to make it easy."

"You'll get the hang of it," B.J. says, and she helps

me sit up. Stiffly I swing my legs over the edge of the bed. My knees can actually bend. "Good," she says. "Now, don't move until we finish your hair."

As Jan brushes my hair I sneak a quick glance at the clock by my bed. "It's already eight o'clock. We're going to be late."

"Of course we are. Nobody's ever on time," Jan says. "If we get there at eight, they'd think we were nerds."

B.J. sighs. "Stacy, you've got so much to learn!"

Jan steps back. "What do you think?"

B.J. studies my hair, then pokes gently in one spot with the end of the comb. "Perfect," she says, and reaches for the hair spray.

I squeeze my eyes shut as the spray hits my hair, but Jan cries, "Don't ever do that, Stacy! It does terrible things to eye shadow!"

B.J. takes one of my hands, Jan the other. "Come look at yourself," B.J. says. "The Sleeping Beauty emerges."

"Don't call me that!"

But Jan interrupts. "Not the Sleeping Beauty. *My Fair Lady*. That's it. Stacy is like Eliza Doolittle."

"No, I'm *me!*"

By this time I'm in the bathroom. They push me in front of the large mirror over the basin and stand on either side of me. "Well, look!" Jan says.

My hair is shaped so that the front strands barely reach my shoulders, and it's full and wavy and soft. A few tendrils escape over my cheeks and forehead. I reach up automatically to push them back, but Jan grabs my hand. "It's supposed to be that way," she says.

The shadows under my eyes are gone. They're under my cheekbones now, highlighting them. My eyes seem brighter, my lips softer. Jan was right about the red T-shirt. Red is my color. In the T-shirt and jeans I'm snug and straight and so rounded in all the right places that I blush and hunch my shoulders forward a little. B.J. still shines in her own orbit, but now I have nothing to complain about. I won't need that paper bag after all.

I laugh. "Is that really me?"

"Stand up straight," Jan says, and pokes me between my shoulder blades hard enough to make me jerk my shoulders back.

"But I—" My voice drops to a whisper. "I'm so—I mean, on top I—" My face grows even warmer.

"You look just the way you're supposed to," Jan says. She studies me in the mirror. "Don't you like what we've done?"

I have to admit it. "I do. I really do!" I give Jan a quick hug and turn to B.J., but she steps back quickly.

"Don't do that," she says. "Only grandmothers hug."

The telephone rings. Forgetful of everything except the girl in the mirror, the new Stacy, I run to answer.

It's the same voice I heard earlier. The same whisper. "Where are you, Stacy?" it says. "The party's started. We're waiting for you."

This time I slam down the receiver. I'm not going to talk to this jerk. I'm not going to give him the satisfaction of knowing that he's really getting to me. I'm scared at the sound of that horrible whisper. It isn't funny!

I turn around to see B.J. and Jan watching me.

"Is something wrong, Stacy?" Jan asks.

"Somebody I know has a warped sense of humor," I answer. "He thinks he's being funny by trying to scare me."

"What did he say?" Jan asks.

I shrug. "Nothing much. Just whispering about will I be at the party. Real dumb stuff. Second-grade humor."

B.J. and Jan look at each other. "Mort?" Jan asks. "He thinks he's so humorous, and he isn't at all. Remember when he pretended to throw up in Mrs. Watkins's wastepaper basket in front of the whole class?"

"Disgusting," B.J. says, "but I don't think he was invited to this party. At least I hope not."

"Buddy likes to play practical jokes."

"I doubt if it's Buddy."

"It wasn't nice to do to Stacy," Jan says, "and when we find out who it was, we'll totally ignore him."

Each name pops a face into my mind, but I see seventh-grade boys full of mischief, loud belches, and side glances with snickers. Some of them were okay, I guess, but a few were spoiled mean. That was the time of the big oil boom, in which some families in Houston bought bigger houses and guard dogs and handguns and let their fat wallets spill out all over their kids, who grabbed for what they could get and more.

B.J. picks up her handbag. "Let's go," she says.

Their conversation has made me feel better, even though I don't know who they were talking about, so I grab my handbag and follow them to B.J.'s car, making sure a light in the den is left on and the front door is locked.

"You'll have to learn to drive, Stacy," B.J. says. "You can't get around Houston without a car."

"There's a bus to school, isn't there?"

Jan and B.J. give me one of those wide-eyed looks. "We're talking about *after* school, weekends, doing things," B.J. says.

Oh, no. I said the wrong thing again. Embarrassed, I slump against the car seat.

"Sit up, Stacy!" Jan exclaims. "There are a couple of other things you've got to get used to!"

We giggle all the way to the party.

The one-story Maconda house sprawls across an oversize tree-shaded lot that backs onto Buffalo Bayou. Tony opens the ornately carved front door and ushers us into a huge entry hall. Part of my mind takes in the marble and gold and mirrored glass, so that I remember it later, but for the moment I concentrate on Tony. The chubby little boy I knew in seventh grade has changed into someone who is tall with broad shoulders and is very good-looking. He grins at me so appreciatively that I blush.

"Hello, Sleeping Beauty," he says. "You were worth waiting for."

He steps toward me, but B.J. takes his arm, tosses her handbag on a nearby chair, and leads us toward the den. "Come on," she tells him. "We've got to let everybody else meet Stacy."

I follow her into a large wood-paneled den. "Stacy's here," she announces loudly. People crowd around me. Even a woman dressed in a maid's uniform peeks out from the door to the kitchen. I'm overwhelmed by the faces, the voices, the curious stares, the giggles, the questions.

"What was it like, being asleep for so long?"

"How does it feel to be a Sleeping Beauty?"

"Did you have amnesia, Stacy?"

"Do you remember being shot?"

I feel as if I were in a nightmare. The faces are all familiar, yet they're all different. Everyone has changed. I try to match these faces to the faces I remember, and it makes my head hurt.

Suddenly it's more than I can stand. "I don't want to talk about it!"

Jeff has elbowed his way through the group, and he takes my hand. "She means she *can't* talk," he says.

"What do you mean, can't talk?" a girl named Debbie asks. "You make it sound mysterious."

"C'mon, Debbie," Jeff says. "You've seen police shows on TV. You know that nobody's allowed to talk about a case until it goes to trial."

"Oh." Debbie shrugs and looks at me as though I'd suddenly gained a new importance.

A small dark-haired girl in a maid's uniform, who's carrying a bowl of snack mix, pauses for just an instant to stare at me. I hate being a curiosity! I just want to be myself!

I glance around the room. So many faces. Some of them are drifting into groups; some of them are still staring at me. One of the people in this house must be the one who called me, trying to frighten me. How can I look past all those smiles to find out who it was?

"Do you know many of the people here?" Jeff asks.

"No," I answer.

But a stocky guy steps forward. He has brown hair and hazel eyes so light they gleam yellow. He's wearing a linen jacket with the sleeves shoved up. It's almost a twin to Jeff's jacket. For just an instant he glances at Jeff, and I imagine that I feel Jeff's fingers tense. I glance at Jeff, too, but he's standing easily, smile in place.

The stocky guy is staring at me. "Don't you remember me, Stacy?" he asks, and grins.

"No." I shake my head.

He laughs. "Four years make a difference. I'm Jarrod Tucker."

I didn't know Jarrod Tucker well. He was a few years ahead of me in school. He lived down the street from Jan, so I saw him around his house once in a while. Mostly we ignored each other. Jan didn't like him. She said Jarrod was spoiled rotten and bragged that he always got his own way about everything. He's probably changed too. Look at Bick. Four years ago Jan and I thought Bick was sickening, yet across the room she's hanging on his shoulder and looking into his eyes as though he were the most fascinating thing in her life.

"I remember. You lived down the street from Jan."

"Still do," he says.

"But you're a lot older. I mean, this party—you're not—"

He laughs again at my embarrassment. "You're trying to ask why I'm at the party since I'm older than everyone here? Look around. Not everyone. Some of the people who were in high school with me are here too."

"I'm sorry. I didn't mean—"

"Tony and I are good friends," Jarrod adds. "You might say I'm a fixture at most of his parties."

Tony calls out, "Who changed the radio station? All we're getting is commercials." He heads toward the built-in equipment across the room. Jarrod follows him.

A freckle-faced girl edges toward me. "What was it like being out of your head all that time? I mean, did you dream or what?" She looks as spacey as her question.

"No more questions," Jeff says. He murmurs to me, "Let's get you away from the inquisition," and leads me toward a small library. "You need a chance to sit down and relax."

I look around the room. "I like this."

"So do I, and we're lucky. No one else has discovered it yet, so we get a chance to talk."

I sit on the wide sofa that's in front of a wall of bookshelves, and he sits next to me, twisting so that he faces me. I get the peculiar feeling that he's trying to memorize my face.

"Your friends are glad to see you again," he says.

"Are they? I feel like something on exhibit."

"No. It's not like that. Your story is new and different, and they're excited about it."

"But I don't want to be different. I want to go back to school and just be me."

"It will all settle down soon. You'll probably get more questions, but just hang on." He smiles.

"I ought to go home. I feel like I used to when I was a little kid looking on at my big sister's party. I don't belong here."

"It's hard to grow up all of a sudden."

"How do you know that?"

"I can put myself in your shoes. I can imagine."

"Nobody else has tried to do that," I tell him.

"Maybe they just haven't told you."

I shrug. "I don't think so. You're—you're different." I'm furious at myself as I feel my cheeks becoming hot and red. "I'm sorry. I mean— Darn! I sound like a kid. I say all the wrong things."

He laughs as he stands and holds out his hands to me. "You'll learn in a hurry. Come on. Let's get back to the party."

I'm reluctant to join the others. Jeff pulls me to my feet, but I hesitate. Maybe I'm trying to stall. I find myself saying, "I know most of the people in there, but I don't know you. Tell me about yourself."

"There isn't much to tell."

"When did you move to Houston?"

"Around a year ago."

"Where did you live before that?"

"Michigan. Come on, I'm hungry. Aren't you? Somebody said there was going to be pizza."

"Did I know you before, Jeff?"

"I thought you didn't like a lot of questions."

"It's just that I get the feeling that we've met somewhere."

"Where could we have met, Stacy?"

"I don't know."

He heads for the den, pulling me with him. "Maybe I'm just the man of your dreams. Let's check on that pizza."

But as we reach the crowd in the den Jeff and I are

separated, and I see him near the kitchen, talking to B.J.

Jarrod pulls me off to one side and pushes a Styrofoam cup at me. "You've got to be thirsty by this time. Here's something to drink."

I can smell it. Making a face, I hand it back to him. "No way. That's got liquor in it."

He leans close to murmur in my left ear. It tickles. "Come on, Stacy. You're not a kid anymore. This will help you loosen up. You want to have some fun, don't you?"

"Forget it."

"Okay. One soft drink coming up." He squirms a pathway into the kitchen and is soon back with another Styrofoam cup. "Lemon-lime okay?"

Carefully, suspiciously, I smell it, then take a sip. It's all right. "Thanks," I tell him.

I start to move toward the kitchen, but Jarrod says, "The pizzas aren't ready yet. Talk to me." He takes my arm and leads me to a small garden room with floor-to-ceiling glass windows overlooking the backyard and patio with a lighted pool. At the far end of the room a couple has snuggled together in a wicker swing. He's nuzzling her neck. I turn my back on them quickly, blushing again.

Jarrod grins at me. "You really are a Sleeping Beauty, aren't you?"

"Don't call me that!" Angry at him and at myself, I take a long swallow of the soft drink.

"Okay," he says. "You're a beauty anyway." He puts an arm around my shoulders. I stiffen.

"What's the matter?" he asks.

"Nothing," I answer. I'm very much aware of his arm and of the warmth of his hand that is kneading my shoulder. What am I supposed to do? No guy has ever put an arm around me.

"I wonder where Jeff is."

I didn't mean to say it aloud. Jarrod tilts his head to look into my eyes. "You didn't come with Jeff," he says.

"No. I just wondered. I—"

He moves a little closer, and his breath blows warm against my right ear. "It's a pretty night. Want to go outside for a little while?"

The swing creaks, and the girl on the swing giggles. I'd like to get out of this room, so I quickly answer, "Okay. By the pool?" The underwater lights add a glow to the yard that is almost as bright as the lights in this room.

"Better yet," Jarrod says. "Out in front. I've got a new car. I'd like to show it to you."

"Well—"

"Don't you want to see it?" He sounds hurt. "I'm real proud of it. Wire wheels and all sorts of gadgets— even a makeup mirror on the passenger side that lights up. You'll like it. Come on, Stacy." He puts on a little-boy grin. "If you knew me better, you'd know I always get my own way."

I suppose if I had a new car, I'd want to show it off too. "Okay," I say. "I'd really like to see your car."

I look for a place to put down my cup, but Jarrod says, "Drink up first."

I take another long swallow. "That's enough."

"Hey, I got that 'specially for you. Chugalug it."

It's a small cup, and there's not much left. Obediently I take another drink, emptying the cup.

Jarrod takes it from me, grins, and puts it on a nearby table. Holding my hand, he leads me past the couple on the swing, who don't seem to notice us. We go back through the den and the entry hall to the front door. No one seems to notice us. Jarrod quickly opens the door, and as soon as we step through he shuts it behind us.

The night air is still warm, and the light from a large, low-hung moon blurs the dark sky. The sharp, pungent fragrance of early ligustrum blooms is making me dizzy. I find that I have trouble focusing my eyes.

"I feel kind of funny," I tell Jarrod. "I'd better sit down." And I plop onto the top porch step. The bricks are rough and hard.

Jarrod sits next to me. "Get up, Stacy. It's just a few more steps to the street."

"I don't know what's the matter. I'm kind of dizzy. Maybe I'm coming down with a virus. I'd better find Jan."

"Don't bother Jan. You'll be all right. Come on. I'll help you walk."

I try to stand up, but I can't make it. "Let go, Jarrod."

But he doesn't. "Shhh," he says. "Just relax. Just lean against me. Close your eyes, and some of the dizziness will go away."

Maybe he's right. I close my eyes and do feel a little better. As I relax, my head rests against the warm hollow of Jarrod's neck. We sit there quietly for a few minutes. Then he begins stroking my arm with the tips of his fingers, and my skin tingles.

"Feel a little better now?" he murmurs.

"I guess so. I don't know what happened to me."

"You just had a little too much to drink. I didn't know it would hit you this hard, but it won't hurt you."

"What are you talking about? I didn't have anything to drink." It's hard to think. It's hard to figure out what he means.

"Just a little vodka, Stacy. I knew you couldn't taste the vodka."

"Jarrod, you weren't supposed to—" I say, but he interrupts.

"Let's go to the car now," he says.

"No. I think I should go home."

His voice is smooth. "Okay, Stacy. I'll drive you home."

He helps me up. My legs wobble as though the bones weren't connected while we make our way down the three or four brick steps.

As we reach the walkway Tony's front door slams open. Someone leaps down the steps, grabs Jarrod by his collar, and flings him aside. I stagger backward onto the grass and see Jarrod jump up to the top porch step.

"Leave her alone!" Jeff yells.

I stare up at the porch and into Jarrod's eyes.

The screen door bangs against the wall, and I can clearly see the guy who has run from our house. He's scared. I can feel his fear as he stares back at me. His eyes are glittering with terror. They're so light and pale they're almost yellow. I can see his face. He has a gun in his hand. He raises it and points it at me.

"Jarrod!" I scream. "It was you! You killed my mother!"

Chapter Ten

Yelling, screaming with rage, I stagger through a red haze toward Jarrod and directly into Jeff's path as he leaps toward the porch. Jeff and I fall, legs and arms flailing wildly. Jarrod jumps over us and runs to a car that is parked on the drive, facing the street. Jeff stumbles to his feet and races after Jarrod. He slams against the trunk of the car as Jarrod takes off with a screech of tires.

People explode from the house, shouting questions, and I can't stand it. I collapse on the grass, my hands over my head.

"What happened?"

"What's the matter with Stacy?"

"Jarrod? Really? It was Jarrod? I can't believe it!"

"Somebody ought to call the police!"

"Tell them—tell them Jarrod keeps a gun in his car."

"How do you know that?"

"We were on a date. He opened the glove compartment, and I saw—oh, what difference does it make. Someone should tell the police. I don't want anyone to get hurt!"

"Is Stacy all right?"

"Did Jarrod hurt her?"

"Why does Jarrod keep a gun in his car?"

"C'mon. A lot of people do. Tony does."

"Hey, keep me out of this! Anyhow, that's my dad's gun."

"Look, everybody, what should we do about Stacy?"

The questions become a roar, and the words don't make sense. Where is Jeff? Where is Jan?

A hand firmly clasps mine and pulls me to a sitting position. "Open your eyes," Jeff says. "Jan is getting you some coffee."

Jan arrives with a mug of coffee and helps me drink it.

"I hate coffee," I mumble into the cup.

"It doesn't matter," Jeff says. "It will help you wake up."

I can open my eyes now. He's watching me carefully.

"Okay, everybody," Jeff says to the row of white faces with huge, lemurlike eyes. "You can go inside now. I'm going to take Stacy home."

"I'll go too," Jan says.

"You don't need to," Jeff tells her. "She'll be all right."

"But what if Jarrod—"

"The last place he'll come tonight is to Stacy's house."

"Shouldn't we call the police?"

"It's taken care of," he tells them. He turns to me.

"Stacy, is there a particular detective you should talk to?"

"Yes. Detective Markowitz."

"Let's take you home. You can talk to him there. It will give you a chance to calm down."

Jan gives me a questioning look, so I tell her, "I think Jeff is right."

As I watch them leave I mumble to Jeff, "I didn't know what Jarrod was going to do. He wanted me to see his new car." I feel as though I have to explain. "I didn't know about the vodka."

"It's okay, Stacy. You don't have to tell me about it."

"I'm glad you came when you did. Thanks."

"Drink some more coffee."

The coffee has cooled down a little, so I take a big drink. "You came right away."

"I was looking for you. Feeling a little better?"

"Why were you looking for me?"

As I wait for his answer I sip at the coffee. I can think more clearly now, which is unfortunate because I'm getting more and more embarrassed. To make everything worse, I look up at Jeff and hiccup. His face twitches as he tries unsuccessfully to suppress a laugh.

"Home is a good place for you right now," he says. He puts the empty coffee mug on the edge of Tony's front porch. "Come with me, Stacy. My car is across the street."

My legs are working now, but I hold his hand tightly while we walk to the car. In a few minutes, as we pull away from the curb, the nearby streetlight flashes across his face, and again I get the strange feeling that I've met Jeff before.

"You're different," I tell him.

"You said that before."

"I can't explain it. It's like you're not exactly what you seem to be."

He turns to look at me. "You'll find out that many people aren't exactly what they seem to be, Stacy."

"What does that mean?"

"Questions, questions," he says. There's a long pause until he surprises me by asking, "How well did you know Jarrod Tucker?"

"I just saw him around the neighborhood. I knew who he was."

"Did you see him with other people?"

"I don't know. Maybe. I didn't pay any attention. Why?"

"Just asking," he says, but for an instant he gives a strange smile.

"My turn." I sit up straighter. "Do you know Jarrod Tucker?"

He turns and looks at me. "I've seen him around."

"You didn't answer my question."

"Sure I did. Pay attention."

"How come you get to ask all the questions? When I ask you questions, you don't answer or you change the subject."

"Changing the subject right now is a good idea. What do you want to talk about? The party?"

"I don't even want to think about the party." A large hiccup shudders through me, and I clap my hands over my mouth.

The muscles at the corners of his mouth twitch again. He's laughing at me! I open my mouth to tell him that he's rude, but all that comes out is another hiccup. I feel so stupid that I hunch back against the seat and don't try to talk. He doesn't talk to me either. There's such a muddle of feelings stirring inside me. I don't understand them. I sneak a couple of glances at Jeff from the corners of my eyes. I like him. I like to be near him. But there is something about him I don't understand. It's like a secret he doesn't want me to discover.

In a short time we park in the driveway to my house. Jeff leads me up to the front steps, takes the key from my purse, and opens the door. I look at him and gulp. Now what do I do? Will he just say good night? What if he kisses me? I'm terrified that he might, but at the same time I desperately hope that he will.

A rectangle of light suddenly spills from the open front door of the Cooper house, and Mrs. Cooper steps out.

"Is that you, Stacy?"

"Yes, Mrs. Cooper," I call back.

"Your father said you'd be at a party. When I heard a car, I thought I'd check."

"I came home early," I tell her.

"Are you all right?"

"Just tired." I remember my manners. "This is a friend of mine—Jeff Clinton. Jeff, our neighbor, Mrs. Cooper."

They nod at each other, but Mrs. Cooper doesn't go inside. She stands there, watching, as Jeff hands me the key and a scrap of paper.

"My phone number's written on that," he says. "You might want it sometime."

"Thanks," I answer. I wish Mrs. Cooper wouldn't stare at us. "Would you like to come inside?"

From the corners of his eyes he glances at Mrs. Cooper and smiles. "What would your watchdog say about that?"

"I don't care. I—I wish you'd look through the house to make sure no one's there. I'd feel a lot safer."

"No one's there, but if you'll feel better about it, I'll check it out."

I start toward the door with him, but he says, "Stay here. Your watchdog will protect you."

I lean against the rough brick and smile at Mrs. Cooper. "He's checking the house for me," I tell her.

She nods. "Good idea." She still doesn't go inside.

I feel as though I should be making conversation, so I stammer something about what a warm night it is, and she quickly agrees. I'm relieved when Jeff appears in the doorway.

"Everything's okay," he says. "Call Detective Markowitz as soon as you're in the house."

"How did you know his name?"

"You told me."

"I did? Oh. I did. You have a good memory."

"Yes," Jeff says. "I do." Even with Mrs. Cooper watching he leans down and kisses my forehead. "You'll be okay now," he tells me.

As he starts down the walk toward his car I shut the door and lock it, then lean against it, thinking about what a nice guy Jeff is. But why is he such a mysterious person in some ways? He doesn't want to talk about himself. Why? And what did he mean about people not always being what they seem to be?

A thought breaks through the fuzzy fog that has settled on my brain. I realize that Jeff didn't ask me my address. He didn't ask where I lived. But he came here as though he had been here before.

I hear the whispery voice on the phone, the voice that mumbled, "Yes, I have a friend."

What if Jeff is Jarrod's friend?

Detective Markowitz calls me before I can call him. "I got the word on your identification," he says. "They told me that someone at your party phoned it in."

"Yes. I think it was Jeff. A lot of what happened is kind of mixed up in my mind."

There's a pause, and his voice is deeper, quieter. "How about the identification, Stacy? Could that be mixed up too?"

"No. I'm sure. I'm very sure." Then I tell him everything that happened.

"I've got his record in front of me," he says. "Minor stuff. A couple of charges on possession of drugs, but because of his age he was given probation."

"But he's a murderer!"

"That's what we'll have to prove."

"He is! I told you! He is!"

"Take it easy, Stacy. I believe you."

"What are you going to do now? Are you going to try to find Jarrod?"

"There are a number of things to do," he answers.

"I'm working on them. I'll get back to you tomorrow. You okay?"

"Yes. I'm okay."

"Don't worry about anything. It's up to us for now."

I remember that Jeff said my house would be the last place Jarrod would come to, but I can't help asking Markowitz, "What if Jarrod comes here?"

"He won't," he answers. "Go to bed. Get some sleep."

"Are you sure?"

"Stacy," he says, and I can tell he's trying to be patient and is probably tired and wishes he could be home in bed. "As I told you, I'll get back to you tomorrow."

When I put down the receiver, the house seems awfully quiet, as if it's listening along with me. I shake my head. No. I can't frighten myself like this. I'll read a book. I'll watch something on television. I know what I'll do. I'll take a shower.

A shower is a perfect idea. The water is hot and strong. I take a deep breath, then tilt my face up under the shower head, so that the steamy water beats against my forehead. When I can't hold my breath any longer, I twist and duck, letting the force of the water massage my neck and shoulders. It's warm in here and comfortable, and I wish I could stay here for an hour. But finally I turn off the water and stretch for a towel that's on the nearest rack.

The silence in the steam-filled room makes me nervous. I'd forgotten that with the noise of the shower and the bathroom door closed, I wouldn't be able to hear anything else in the house.

But what would there be to hear?

In the distance the telephone rings.

I fumble with my pajamas and robe, scrambling into them, accidentally turning a sleeve of my robe wrong side out in my haste. I jab at the inside-out sleeve, nearly ripping it as I manage to get it in place so I can pull on the robe.

My hand is on the knob of the bathroom door when I realize that the phone rang only once. That's funny.

Open the door. Don't move. Wait. Listen.

Someone must have known it was a wrong number. Right? Or decided not to call after all. Sure. That's it.

But just to be positive, I cautiously walk through the bedroom hallway. The lights are on in the den, just as I left them. I take another step, and a floorboard makes a snapping sound.

There's a creaking sound in the den, a shadow against the wall, and a voice asks, "Stacy?"

"Daddy?" My voice wobbles. "Is that you?"

He appears at the other end of the hallway. "I thought you heard me come in."

"I didn't. I was in the shower."

"Did I startle you, honey? I didn't mean to."

I run to him and hug him. "It's okay. I didn't expect you to get home so early."

"The reports they sent us were incomplete, so there was no chance to do the work tonight." He turns back to the den, where I see part of an apple on a plate next to his chair. "I was having a snack. There are more apples in the refrigerator. Want to join me?"

"No, thanks." I perch on the end of the sofa. "I thought I heard the telephone."

"You probably did. One of those calls where it dawns on someone that he has the wrong number, but he doesn't say anything and doesn't hang up until he finally figures it out."

"I saw him tonight, Daddy."

"Saw who?"

"The guy who killed Mom. He was at the party. I recognized him."

Dad gives a choking gasp, stumbles toward me, and grabs my shoulders. "What happened? What did you do? Does Detective Markowitz know?"

I hug my father tightly. It makes it easier to tell him about Jarrod and Jeff.

When I finish, Dad drops onto the sofa, next to me. "This Jeff shouldn't have left you alone. He should have stayed with you until I came home."

I'd thought the same thing but found myself defending Jeff. "He said I'd be all right. He did check out the house. Besides, Detective Markowitz told me the same thing."

"Who is Jeff?" Dad asks. "Have I ever met him?"

"Daddy! He just took me home. That's all. He said good night while Mrs. Cooper watched us, and he left."

"Mrs. Cooper?" Dad suddenly looks guilty.

"Did you ask Mrs. Cooper to keep an eye on me?"

"Well, not exactly. The conversation came around to you, and Mrs. Cooper is one of these concerned people, and—" He stops and sighs. "Stacy, I'm doing my best."

"So is Mrs. Cooper!"

Dad laughs, and I have to laugh too. In a way it's funny. "I have to admit, I was kind of glad to see her," I tell him. "I wasn't sure how I was supposed to say good night to Jeff."

"With a firm handshake," Dad says.

"Daddy!"

It's good to hear Dad laugh. It's good to laugh together. But the telephone rings again. Dad reaches for it.

"Hello," he says, and pauses. "Hello? Hello?" He puts down the receiver. "Probably the same idiot."

But I know these aren't just wrong number calls. And I can see in Dad's eyes that what he said was designed to put me at ease. He doesn't believe these are wrong numbers either.

"Are you cold, Stacy? You're shivering."

"I guess I'm just tired," I tell him. "I'd better get to bed."

As soon as the dark seeps through my eyelids I can see Jarrod's face. "I'm not going to let you ruin my life," I whisper to those yellow eyes, "because I'm going to ruin yours!"

Chapter Eleven

Saturday. Long after Dad has left for work, I stretch from strange, troubled dreams into wakefulness. Saturday mornings used to be filled with waking to sunbright windows and the buttery-sweet fragrance of Mom's pancakes. I almost expect to hear the purr of the lawn mower, which would become a roar as Dad guided it under my bedroom window. Tousle-headed, I'd press my face against the window, squishing my nose, and yell, "You're making too much noise!" Dad—who would follow the game, even though he couldn't hear me over the noise of the mower—would shout back, "Get up! Get up! You've slept away half the morning."

No lawn mower, no pancakes. I make some toast to go with my glass of orange juice. At least there's one Saturday routine I can continue. Today, after breakfast, I'll clean the house.

As I walk into the kitchen the doorbell rings. I freeze, trying to breathe. It rings again. I force myself to shove the fear aside and go to the door. Through the peephole I see a woman standing on the porch. She's well dressed in a denim skirt and pink knit cotton blouse, but her youthful haircut doesn't match the web of tiny wrinkles that stand out under the makeup around her eyes. Beyond her a large black Cadillac is parked at the curb.

I open the door and say, "Hi."

She blinks a couple of times, then raises her chin imperiously. "May I please come in and talk to you?" she asks.

"Why? Who are you?"

"I do apologize. I assumed you would remember." Her stare becomes even cooler. "You're probably having a great deal of trouble remembering people from four years ago—even your neighbors. I am one of your former neighbors."

I still must look blank because she quickly adds, "My name is Eloise Tucker. I'm Jarrod Tucker's mother. I think we need to talk."

I step out onto the porch, shutting the front door behind me. "Could we talk out here?"

"It's warm outside." Her tone is peevish. "You don't have to be afraid of me. I simply want to talk, to clarify a few things."

The porch isn't large enough to have a porch swing on it, so I gesture toward the steps. "I'm sorry, Mrs. Tucker, but—"

She sighs with annoyance and settles on the top step, wrapping her skirt around her legs. I sit on the same step, only as far away from her as possible. She's wearing a perfume that reminds me of dead roses.

She stares at her hands for a moment, then says, "It's about the terrible, unbelievable situation you've created. About your ridiculous statement that Jarrod was the person you saw in your house."

"But he was."

"No, dear," she says, "you're wrong because during that day it all happened, that particular day, Jarrod was visiting my sister in San Antonio."

"He wasn't."

"My sister and a close friend of hers are going to testify that he was."

"They'll be lying!"

"It will be your word against theirs. It won't do you much good to insist on your version.

"As we all see it," she says, "when this tragic incident happened four years ago, it was a terrible shock to you. This morning my husband spoke with a noted psychiatrist who feels that it is entirely possible you may have—well, shall we say, some mental and emotional problems that are confusing you?"

I lean over, resting my elbows on my legs, clasping my hands in front of me. "Mrs. Tucker, are you trying to talk me into changing my mind, or are you threatening me?"

I suppose I expect her to get angry, but instead, she calmly says, "To quote our minister, who said he would be glad to be one of Jarrod's character witnesses, Jarrod is a willful boy, but he wouldn't shoot anyone."

"He did! He shot my mother. He shot me."

"You saw the gun. Is that right?"

"Yes."

"You had your eyes on it."

"I—I guess so."

"Perhaps you were watching the gun so carefully

that you didn't really take a good look at the face of the man who was holding it."

"But I did!"

"That will be hard to prove."

Now *I* feel like crying, but my tears would come from frustration, from rage. "Mrs. Tucker, no matter what you say, I *know* who was on that back porch. I *know* who shot me. And I *am* going to testify! Where is Jarrod?"

Her tone is sarcastic. "That is what my husband and I have been asked repeatedly by the police, thanks to you. Unfortunately we don't know." She clenches her fingers so tightly the knuckles look like shiny white knobs, and her voice lowers and softens as she adds, "He didn't come home last night."

I lean back against the railing around the edge of the porch and see, from the corners of my eyes, Mrs. Cooper busily sweeping her front porch. I pretend not to notice Mrs. Cooper.

A gray sedan pulls up in front of the house and parks behind the Cadillac. The driver's door opens, and Jeff climbs out, calling "Hi, Stacy!"

"Jeff!" I jump to my feet.

Mrs. Tucker quickly gets up, leans close to me, and murmurs, "Think about what I said."

Jeff's long legs have brought him to the foot of the porch steps. He looks at Mrs. Tucker. For an instant I think I see a spark of recognition in his eyes before he puts on a smile and a bland look and politely says, "Hi."

"This is—" I begin, but Mrs. Tucker, ignoring Jeff, hurries down the walk, jumps into her car, and drives away.

"You know her?"

"Yeah," Jeff says. "I've seen her around. Jarrod Tucker's mother. Right?"

His smile is open and charming, and I want to believe him. I open the front door and hold it wide. "Would you like to come in?"

"Hello, Stacy!" Mrs. Cooper calls.

I wave back. So does Jeff.

"I'm going to come over in just a few minutes," she says. "I made a tamale pie. All you have to do tonight is just stick it in the oven."

"Thanks, Mrs. Cooper," I call back.

"Shut the door," Jeff says. "We can sit here on the steps."

I settle on the same step, not quite as far away as I had sat from Mrs. Tucker. I wish I had the courage to scoot over close enough so that our bodies would be almost touching. There are all sorts of strange feelings inside me, some of which I like and some which kind of scare me because I don't understand them.

"What did she want?"

"Who?"

"Mrs. Tucker."

"She tried to convince me I had the wrong person. She tried to talk me out of testifying. She even told me that her sister and a friend would testify that Jarrod was with them in San Antonio." I look at Jeff. "Could they do that?"

"Sure. Witnesses can say anything they want."

"But they'd be lying!"

"Some people do lie."

"What if the jury believes them and not me?"

"That can happen."

"Then Jarrod could go free?"

"Yeah. I guess so." Jeff cocks his head as he looks at me. "Instead of asking me all these questions, you ought to ask your Detective Markowitz, who's working this case."

"You're right." I have to smile. "I don't know why I just took it for granted that you'd know."

I pause, and he fills in. "Because I'm obviously wise and highly intelligent and probably know all the answers to everything."

"You're laughing at me."

"No, Stacy. I just tried to cover what you didn't want to say."

"How do you know what I was going to say?"

"Because I have a little brother who's twelve—no, thirteen last month—and he thinks because I'm older than he is I know everything—or ought to know."

I wiggle the toes of my sneakers and watch them intently. I feel so stupid, but in a way I'm glad for what he said. "You told me that you understand. I guess you do."

The telephone rings. I don't care. I like sitting here with Jeff, and I don't want to answer it.

"Get your phone," Jeff tells me.

"It's probably not important."

He jumps up and pulls me to my feet. "On the other hand, it could be. Are you going to answer it, or do you want me to?"

He follows me into the house. I run the last few steps and catch the telephone on the sixth or seventh ring.

"Hello!" I shout. I take a deep breath and try to calm down. "Hello," I repeat, trying to be quiet and dignified.

It's Detective Markowitz. "We picked him up," he says.

"Jarrod? You did? Really? But his mother was just here. Did she know?"

"We're trying to reach his parents. No real urgency, though, since Tucker's an adult."

"What did Jarrod tell you?"

"Nothing," he answers. "I didn't expect him to."

"His mother said her sister and friend would testify that Jarrod was in San Antonio that day. But I know she's lying."

"Oath or not, a lot of people lie, trying to save their own skin or someone else's."

"But I saw him! I'm a witness!"

"I think I told you, Stacy. Placing someone on the scene of the crime is just half of it. We need physical evidence to prove he was there."

"And you don't have any?"

"We may. They did come up with some fingerprints which they couldn't make at the time. We have the casing, which was found in the room, and the slug taken from— Well, at least now that we know what we're going on, there's a slim chance that we might tie Tucker into the scene. To be perfectly honest with you, though, these factors may work out, they may not. That's all I can tell you."

"You also told me about a computer search. What about that?"

"Zilch."

I'm confused and feeling more frustrated by the minute. "What can we do?"

"Come down for a lineup," he answers. "That's as good a place as any to start. It might help us hold Tucker a little longer."

"You mean he might get out?"

"Depends on the judge and what we can come up with to convince him the guy shouldn't be allowed bail."

"I'm going to come to the station right now," I tell him.

"Is anybody there with you?"

"What do you mean?"

"I mean, someone who could drive you?"

"Oh. Yes. A—friend is here. But I'll call my sister and ask her."

As I hang up the receiver Jeff says, "I'll go with you."

"Thanks, Jeff. But I'd better tell Donna where I'm going." I dial her number and give her the latest news.

"I don't know Jeff," she says. "I think your family should be with you. I'll drive you."

"But, Donna—" I don't know how to tell her, with Jeff standing beside me, that I wish she'd butt out for now, that I'd like to be with Jeff.

"I'll be right over," she says firmly, and hangs up.

I turn to Jeff. "She wants to come with me."

"Sure," he says, and smiles. "She's your sister."

He stays until Donna arrives. She smiles and chats, but at the same time she gives him a sharp once-over. Apparently she's satisfied that Jeff is a nice guy because

I can see her relax. She presses a hand to the small of her back and says, "Stacy, we'd better be going."

"I'll be glad to take you there," Jeff says. "It's a good half-hour drive."

I'm hoping she'll agree, but Donna smiles and says, "Thanks anyway, Jeff, but this is going to be a difficult situation. I think it had better be just family."

"Sure," Jeff says. He walks to his car and watches us climb into Donna's. I wish I could turn around and see him drive away.

"He's nice," Donna says.

"I think so too."

I want her to say more about him, but she talks instead about the party and Jarrod Tucker and all the things Dad told her until we reach the police station on Riesner.

As we leave the parking lot Detective Markowitz suddenly comes out from the police building and trots down the steps to meet us. He leads us through a side door. Remembering how busy the lobby was the last time I was here, I'm grateful to miss the crowds.

We enter the homicide room, and he bends to look into my face. "Ready for the lineup?" he asks.

"I'm ready."

He nods, picks up a telephone, punches a couple of buttons, and tells someone to set things up. He puts down the receiver and turns to me. "A few other people will be in the viewing room with us. One of them will be Tucker's attorney. He won't talk to you, but he has the right to be there to make sure everything is done legally, that no one leads you to make a decision. Understand?"

"He has an attorney already?"

"We reached Tucker's father right after we talked to you. The attorney was here within twenty minutes."

I'm glad that Donna is hanging on to me. I don't pay attention to the route we're taking. I can't see anything except Jarrod's face, which has glued itself to my mind.

We're led into a small room. Chairs are facing a glass wall, and beyond the wall is a stage with a height chart made of horizontal lines painted on the yellowed wall behind the stage. Detective Johns is in the room, as are some other men. Donna and I speak to Johns, but no one introduces us to the others. I wonder which one is Jarrod's attorney.

Markowitz tells us to be seated and relax. "The men you'll see out there won't be able to look in at you. This is a one-way glass," he says. "So don't be afraid."

"I'm not afraid."

A door opens at the left. A policeman comes in and picks up a microphone. Then a line of seven men come into the room and file across the stage. Each one is wearing a number on his chest. They all look something alike. "Turn right. Turn left. Face forward," the policeman drawls, as though he'd given these commands so often he could say them in his sleep.

I study the men facing me. I spot Jarrod immediately. His jacket is wrinkled and smudged. He needs a shave. The men with him must have been carefully picked. One of them looks about Jarrod's age, one a little younger. All of them have dark or brown hair. Two of the men are staring at their feet. One has his chin tucked down, throwing his face into shadow.

"Tell them to look this way. Tell them to look at the window," I say to Markowitz. "There's something I want you to see."

Markowitz picks up a receiver and relays my command to the policeman, who barks it out.

The men look upward, to the window that separates us. I look into the pale yellow eyes of the guy who tried to get me away from the party last night. Was it an attempt to get rid of me? If I had gone, would he have succeeded this time in killing me?

What if I identify Jarrod, and he is released on bond? Will he try again? "You won't have a chance," I whisper, as though he could hear me.

Donna is startled. She quickly turns and stares at me. I hear one of the men shuffle his feet. Another coughs.

"Jarrod Tucker is second from the right, and I want you to look at his eyes," I tell Markowitz. "Four years ago those awful yellow cat eyes stared into mine just before Jarrod shot me. I'll never forget his eyes! Never!"

The men in the room look at me sharply, and Donna nervously squeezes my hand. I realize that my hatred for Jarrod has made the room come into focus. I can smell sour body sweat and stale cigarettes, and my tongue curls at the edges with a taste like bitter lemon.

"You're positive?" Markowitz asks. He sounds pleased.

"Merely a formality," one of the men says. "She saw him at the party last night."

I twist toward them. "I'll identify him from photographs," I say eagerly. "Give me his photograph from four years ago, along with others, and I'll pick him out. I promise!"

"Stacy." Detective Markowitz's voice is low as he firmly squeezes my shoulder. It's a signal to be quiet. It doesn't matter. None of them answered me or acted as though they had heard me.

Detective Markowitz speaks to the policeman in the lineup room. In turn, the policeman tells the men to turn around. They file out as they came in, and the door closes behind them.

I stay in my chair, staring into the room. I can still see Jarrod Tucker's yellow eyes.

"That's all for now, Stacy," Detective Markowitz says. "Thanks for coming. We'll be in touch with you."

I stand and look up at him. "How about the gun? Was it in Jarrod's car?"

"We found a gun in the glove compartment."

"And?"

"It wasn't the murder weapon. Different size caliber."

"Oh. I hoped so hard that—" I take a long breath. "Okay. What happens next?"

"Someone in the district attorney's department will want to talk to you, and Tucker will be arraigned."

"Does that mean the trial?"

"No. That means the district attorney will bring a brief summation of the charge against Tucker before a judge, he'll plead not guilty, and his attorney will ask for a trial."

"Then what happens?"

"Among other things, the judge sets the amount of

bail for Tucker or decides if he should be allowed out on bail."

I hear Donna gasp. "You mean he might be set free until his trial?"

"That's a possibility," Markowitz says. "In court we'll present a strong plea that he not be allowed bail, and for now, we can hold him for twenty-four hours without a formal charge."

Donna says, "But even if he's released on bail, surely he won't try to hurt Stacy. He'd have to be insane."

For a moment there's nothing but silence. I know we're all thinking the same thing: *Who says that he's not?*

"Will you let me know what happens to Jarrod?" I ask Markowitz.

"You'll know. You're our witness."

As he talks he moves toward the door. Donna and I follow him out of the room and down the hallway.

Without warning an intense light nearly blinds me, and someone says, "There she is!"

"Don't worry," Markowitz tells us. "It's just a TV crew. They seem to be the only ones who wanted to follow up on the story. The others on the police beat are covering a convenience store shooting on the north side."

Donna is nervous. "What do they want? Can't we get them to go away?"

"I'll chase them off if you say so," he answers, "but Stacy might agree to talk to them for a few minutes. They'll just ask her a couple of questions. They've got word by now on the result of the lineup, and it won't take long. If they ask anything they shouldn't, I'll step in."

"Sure," I say. "It's okay."

A woman with short dark hair is working her way toward me. She's holding up a microphone. The bright light snaps off, so I can see the cameraman with the light and the camera on his shoulder. He's right behind her.

I take a step toward the reporter, ducking around a guy who is being steered through the hallway by a police officer. The guy's face is all scrunched up, as though he were trying not to cry. I don't think he's any older than I am.

Suddenly there's space, and just as suddenly I find myself face-to-face with Jarrod Tucker. He's wedged between two sturdy officers, his hands cuffed in front of him.

His eyes turn to narrow slits as he recognizes me.

Detective Markowitz snaps, "Get him out of here!"

Donna tugs at me, the reporter shouts at the cameraman, and I throw up my hands against his instant blast of bright light. Jarrod is jerked past me, the officers with him ordering people to get out of the way, but he manages to twist toward me. Through all the confusion I hear only a snarl of words: "My friend!"

Just as quickly I cry at him, "You're crazy!"

For just an instant, before he's pulled away from me, Jarrod's lips part in a wide grin, and his eyes gleam.

"Donna!" I shriek, but Donna seems to be trying to head off the reporter. Frantically I look for Markowitz, but he has followed Jarrod and the officers down the hall. Nobody's reacting to what Jarrod said to me. Didn't they hear him? Am I the only one?

What did Jarrod mean? That's the second time he's mumbled something about a friend. If Jarrod can't get to me, will one of his friends try?

Markowitz appears at my side. He takes my arm and leads me into a nearby room. "You're shaking," he says. "Sit down." He nudges me toward an ugly chrome and plastic chair.

"I want Donna."

"I'll get her."

I'm alone and more frightened than ever. When Markowitz appears with Donna, I jump up and run to her. I hug her as closely as I can, hanging on as though she were an anchor that would keep me from being swept downstream.

"Don't be afraid," Donna says as she strokes my hair. "Stacy, honey, he's locked up. He can't hurt you."

"He said something about a *friend.* I think he was threatening me. I think he meant his friends would take care of me!"

"He spoke to you?" Markowitz scowls. "I didn't hear him."

"When they took him past me. That's all he said. Just the words *my friend.*"

"Are you sure?"

"I'm positive! Don't you believe me?"

Donna speaks first. "There was a lot of noise, a lot of confusion, and you were afraid. Maybe you just thought—"

"The words *my friend*—if that's what you heard— could mean anything, Stacy."

I interrupt them. "I didn't imagine it. I heard Jarrod. I think I know what it means."

Donna wraps her arms around me and says to Markowitz, "There was so much noise, and we were all distracted. It makes sense that Stacy heard him and we couldn't."

"Okay, okay," Markowitz says. He leans against the desk. "I've seen guys like Jarrod Tucker over and over again. They're all brave talk on the outside, cowards on the inside. Threats? Sure, he'd try to scare Stacy out of testifying against him."

"Maybe she shouldn't testify." Donna's chin wobbles, and I know she's close to tears.

I push away from Donna, take a deep breath, and say, "Look, I'm scared. He scared me a lot. But I *am* going to testify against him. Nothing Jarrod can do will scare me out of that!"

Markowitz nods. "We won't let him get to you, Stacy."

"It isn't fair," Donna says, and she suddenly sits on the hard, ugly chair. There are brown smudges under her eyes, and her face looks thin and pale.

"Donna! Are you all right?"

"I'm just tired," she says. "I'm tired of all this. We were a happy family leading normal, average lives. What went wrong? Why should all this happen to us?"

"I'm sorry," Markowitz mumbles, and his eyes do look sorry.

It's not an answer, but for the moment it seems to satisfy Donna. "May I please have a glass of water?" she asks. She sits up a little straighter and rests her hands on her abdomen. Her fingers make a little patting motion, as though she were reassuring the baby.

"Right away," Markowitz says, moving toward the door. But he pauses. "And when you're ready to leave, we'll get you out the back door and away from here. No problem."

"Thank you," Donna says.

But my mind is on Jarrod and the words he whispered at me. He meant to frighten me, and he succeeded. What did he mean? I know what I'm up against with Jarrod. But who is his friend?

Chapter Twelve

On the way back to our house I tell Donna my idea. "I'm going to find out who Jarrod's friends are. As soon as we get home I'm going to call Tony. Jarrod goes to Tony's parties. I bet he'll know."

"It might help," Donna says. Her smile can't cut the worry in her eyes.

But I don't have a chance to call Tony. As Donna parks the car in front of the house, a gray sedan pulls up behind us. Jeff jumps out, lopes over, and opens Donna's door for her.

He walks with us into the house, asking, "Did everything go all right?"

"Yes." For some reason I don't want to talk to him about it.

"Want some iced tea?" I ask him. We follow Donna into the kitchen.

She pulls a large covered pitcher of iced tea out of the refrigerator and hands it to me. Then she pries the lid off a casserole dish and asks, "Why didn't you eat the chicken pasta salad?"

"Because I don't know what it is."

She looks at me oddly. "Oh, Stacy," she says, "I guess none of us did until a couple of years ago."

There's a knock at the back door, and I hear a young voice calling, "Stacy!"

Donna opens the door, and the three Cooper kids tumble inside, each one trying to beat the others in coming out with what they want to say.

"Slow down," I tell them. "Let Teri go first."

Teri quickly shouts, as though the rules might be changed at any minute, "Can we play in your tree house?"

"Oh, no!" Donna says before I can answer. "It's falling apart, girls. It's really dangerous. Dad is going to take it down because it's a hazard."

"I'm glad you asked," I tell them. "You were smart to ask."

"We asked you because when we asked our mother, she said we couldn't," Meri answers.

Keri speaks up. "Can you come over and play, Stacy? We can play dolls again."

I gulp with embarrassment, frantically trying to think of the right thing to say, but Jeff smiles at them and answers for me.

"Not until she baby-sits you again. She'll see you later."

They're out the door like a pack of puppies. I hear them shout their way to their own backyard.

Jeff puts the tips of his fingers against my cheeks. They're cool against my hot skin. "When I was a kid, one of our baby-sitters used to play cars with me by the hour," he says. "I thought she was neat."

"Thanks," I murmur.

"Why don't you stay for dinner, Jeff?" Donna asks. "Dennis will be here soon, and Dad gets home early on Saturday."

"I'd like that," Jeff says. "Mind if I use your phone?"

Donna waves toward the kitchen telephone. Jeff dials and says, "Hi. I'll be here for a while. Okay. Sure." He hangs up.

"In a way I hope the baby is a girl," Donna says. "Girls talk to their mothers."

Jeff laughs. "I'll set the table," he says.

In a moment he and Donna are laughing together, but the telephone call makes me remember. I can't call Tony and ask about Jarrod's friends while Jeff is here. Would Jeff know that much about Jarrod? I can't explain it. I don't want to ask him.

Dad's home on Sunday, and Jan comes over. For some reason Jeff doesn't show up and doesn't call. The maid at Tony's house says the family is at their beach house for the weekend. She'll tell Tony to call me when he gets back, but they might not return until late Sunday night. I keep thinking of Jarrod and wondering why Markowitz doesn't let me know if Jarrod is still in jail or is out on bail. Finally he telephones to say they have a temporary order that will keep Jarrod in jail without bond. A hearing has been set for Tuesday afternoon. There's a lot of talk about the case on the evening news, but all the discussion about possible evidence seems to be rumor. I try all the channels, and no one has any real facts.

Monday morning comes, and Markowitz calls again.

"Regina Latham, one of the assistant district attorneys, is going to work on the Tucker case. She wants to talk to you."

"When?"

"This morning."

"I'll have to call Donna to see if she can take me downtown."

"No need to bother your sister. Just let her know where you'll be. I'll send a car for you. Can you be ready in about twenty minutes?"

"I guess so."

"Okay. I'll meet you there."

"Wait! Don't hang up!"

"What's the matter?".

"I—I don't know what's going to happen. What will she do?"

"Don't worry about that. Mrs. Latham will just go over your story with you, probably ask you a few questions. No big deal."

"Will Jarrod be there?"

"No. Jarrod's locked up tight. Don't worry about him."

I let out the breath I must have been holding. "I'll be ready when your car comes."

True to my word, I'm watching at the window when the car arrives. It's a plain dark brown sedan. I guess I expected a blue-and-white police cruiser. The driver shows me his credentials, and I follow him to the car. It's probably better this way. Another police car might have worried Mrs. Cooper.

But Mrs. Cooper comes out onto her front porch. She calls across to me, "Stacy, is everything all right?"

"Fine," I call back. She looks at the police driver with such suspicion that I add, "I'm being taken to an appointment with one of the district attorneys who's going to talk to me about Jarrod's case."

"Oh," she says, nodding as though there were a spring in her neck. "Well, just call me if you want anything."

"Thanks." I don't want anyone, especially Mrs. Cooper, to keep an eye on me.

The driver opens the car door for me. I climb in and look back as we pull away from the curb. She stands there, watching, until the car is out of sight.

The driver talks about the weather and a lot of dumb stuff like that. Maybe it's a way of killing time. Maybe he's trying to be friendly. Kids don't waste time talking about things that don't mean anything, but adults do it all the time. I suppose that's one more thing I'll have to learn how to do.

We go through the eastern part of downtown Houston, and again I gawk at more new buildings that seem to have popped up as fast as the red tulips Mom used to plant in the front garden each year.

Markowitz meets the car and walks with me into a building where corridors echo with footsteps and voices. An elderly shoeshine man sits just inside the front entrance. "That's the girl," I hear him tell someone as we pass his stand, and I walk a little faster.

As we finally step off the crowded elevator Markowitz says to me, "I'm sorry you have to go through all this, Stacy. It's just part of the game."

"It's not a game!"

He nods. "Sorry again. Wrong word. It's tough for you and for the rest of your family. I know you'd all rather forget it."

His words slap me into awareness. Of course. This whole thing has been horrible for Dad and for Donna. And now they'll have to relive it all again. Blast you, Jarrod! It's not fair!

Markowitz opens a couple of doors, and we're in a small office. Most of the desk and the top of a bookcase are covered with piles and stacks of papers. Behind a clearing in the center of the desk sits a young woman, large glasses rimmed in a tortoiseshell brown that matches her short hair. She's cool and dignified. She stands and, as Markowitz makes the introductions, appraises me.

"The description the press gave her wasn't far off, was it?" she says, and for some reason sounds almost hostile. "Would either of you like coffee? A Coke?" she adds.

Markowitz accepts the coffee, but I don't want anything. I'm too shaky to hold something that might end up in my lap.

"Sit down please, Stacy," Mrs. Latham says, pointing to one of the two chairs in front of the desk. "Just relax." As Markowitz and I sit down she continues. "Now, Stacy, you claim that four years ago you saw someone run out of the back door of your house."

I have to interrupt. "I *did* see someone. And that was Jarrod Tucker."

"Stacy," she says firmly, raising her voice a little like a kindergarten teacher whose students won't quiet down and get into line, "when this case goes to court—if it does—"

"What do you mean, *if?*"

Markowitz leans over and puts a big hand on my arm. "Take it easy, Stacy. Mrs. Latham is an attorney. She has to make sure that nothing she says can be misconstrued. Right now she's trying to make sure she's got a good case. That's all she means."

"Thank you, Detective Markowitz," she says. "I'm sure that Stacy is old enough to understand the situation."

"I'll try," I answer.

She taps the end of a pencil against the desk and begins again. "All right. Suppose you tell me in your own words what you claim to have seen on the day that your mother was allegedly murdered and you were shot."

"Allegedly shot," I mutter under my breath. Markowitz coughs loudly, and I wait until he settles back in his chair. Then I go through the whole story.

Mrs. Latham interrupts me over and over, snapping questions as fast as Jan used to be able to pop bubble gum. "What exactly did you think you heard? What kind of sound? Do you recognize the sound of a gunshot? Have you ever heard one before? Are you sure you heard anything? Did you know Jarrod Tucker? Had you ever spoken to him? If you hadn't spoken to him, if you hadn't been in his classes at school, how is it you could have been so sure it was Jarrod Tucker on your back porch? It's been four years since that time. For that matter could your, uh, illness, let's say, the time you 'slept,' have affected your judgment or your memory? Maybe both?"

I stand up, slam my hands on the desk, scattering some of her papers to the floor, and explode into tears. "You have to believe me! You're the one who's supposed to make sure Jarrod goes to prison for murder!"

She looks a little frightened by my outburst. "You can't behave like that in court," she stammers.

But Markowitz gently pushes me back into the chair. "She's just a kid," he tells Mrs. Latham.

"She's not many years younger than I am!" Mrs. Latham bristles.

"Don't forget the four years she has to make up for," he answers. He fishes a neatly folded handkerchief out of his pocket and hands it to me. "Stacy, understand that Mrs. Latham is just playing devil's advocate," he says.

"What's that?"

Mrs. Latham looks up at the ceiling as though appealing for help, then back down to me. "It means," she says, "that Jarrod Tucker's defense attorney is going to ask you a great many questions. We're trying to anticipate some of them. We want all the answers *before* we go to court."

I blow my nose and lean toward her, looking her straight in the eyes. "Okay. I want to help in any way I can. But there's a better way to do this. Don't push at me. Don't snap questions at me the way you've been doing it. I came here to work with you, and you're acting like an enemy."

The telephone rings, and she reaches for it so quickly she jostles some papers off her desk. She wasn't the one being rescued. She hands the receiver to Markowitz and says, "It's for you."

His conversation consists of "Good. . . . Clear? . . . Any reaction? . . . I'll check. Thanks." He hands the receiver to Mrs. Latham and nods as though he were in hearty agreement with whoever was on the line. "They did have some clear prints they couldn't make at the time. They check out now. Jarrod Tucker."

"Then you've got physical evidence!" I realize that I'm shouting and jumping up and down in my chair, so I try to calm down. "That means he'll be convicted, right?"

"That means our chances are a whole lot better," Markowitz answers. "A lot of what will happen is up to the judge and the jury and the prosecuting attorney."

We both look at Mrs. Latham.

She sucks in a sharp breath and blinks a couple of times. Finally she says, "Let's start over, Stacy. Maybe I was coming across a little hard and fast. I guess I want to win this case as much as you do."

I sit back in my chair and wait. "Then let's get with it."

"Stacy," she says, and her words are slower, more gentle, "you're very angry at Jarrod Tucker. Are you sure that your emotions are not going to cloud this case?"

"I'm not going to let my anger get in the way."

"How about your resultant feelings of guilt?"

"Guilt? What are you talking about?"

"I mean the common progress in grief. Naturally you'd begin to shift some of the blame from Jarrod Tucker to yourself in cause-and-effect relationships—

for example, your mother's death. If you had been in the house with her, if—"

"No! You're wrong!" I jump to my feet.

She stares at me in bewilderment.

Markowitz stands up. "Mrs. Latham, we've probably covered enough for now, don't you think? I'd like to take Stacy home."

She talks to him as though I were not in the room. "With this emotional instability, I doubt if she'll be a good witness."

"She needs a little time. She'll have it before she has to appear in court."

I take a long breath and force my voice to become steady. "Appear in court as what? I'm only a witness, remember? Or have I suddenly turned into the accused?"

"Stacy—" Markowitz says, but I stand a little taller.

"I'm the victim—on both sides!"

Mrs. Latham slowly rises and says to Markowitz, "Perhaps you can talk to her father. Is she getting any type of therapy?"

"I'll talk to you later," he says, and pulls me out of the office before I can catch my breath and tell her what else is on my mind.

He drives me home in his own car and tries to explain that Mrs. Latham is somewhat new in the department and is trying very hard to prove herself and do things right and that I shouldn't react to everything she said.

"It's going to be a lot tougher than that when Jarrod goes to trial," he tells me. "You'll hear the defense witnesses lie through their teeth, and you'll have to sit there and keep quiet. And Tucker's attorney will blister you with questions, and you'll have to take it."

"Why?"

"Because that's the way the system of justice is set up."

"Justice for whom?"

"Don't be bitter. It's got its flaws, but at least it attempts to give everyone a fair chance."

"Nothing about this seems to be fair. It would have been fair only if somebody had shot Jarrod!"

He doesn't answer. We drive past the Galleria and Neiman-Marcus, and slowly my anger simmers down, like a pot of water with the burners turned off. "Detective Markowitz," I say, "I'm sorry I lost my temper. I acted like a little kid. I won't do it again."

I try to sort out exactly what happened, but one thing puzzles me. "I'll do what Mrs. Latham wants, but she doesn't like me, you know. When I walked in, I could tell that she didn't like me. And I don't know why."

He smiles. "Ummm, could be a little jealousy."

I twist toward him. "Jealousy? About what?"

But he just slowly shakes his head and chuckles. "Stacy, you really are still a little kid."

"You're as bad as she is," I mutter.

"I didn't mean to get you riled," he says. "Let's change the subject."

"Okay. I want to talk about Jarrod's gun."

"I told you. It didn't match the slug and casing we've got on file."

"I know. But when did Jarrod buy this gun? Four years ago he may not have owned one. He might have used someone else's gun—probably one belonging to his father."

He turns to me and smiles. "We're thinking in the same direction. Granted, it's pretty much of a long shot, but we're requesting a search warrant. We can see if Jarrod's father owns any guns, and we can subpoena them for testing. The Houston Police Department has one of the best ballistics experts in the United States. If there is anything to be found out, he'll find it."

"Before the hearing?"

"It doesn't have to be before the hearing."

"I want to be there."

"Have anyone to take you?"

"I'll ask Donna."

He's silent for a minute, and I know he's thinking of what Donna went through in the police station. "Let's leave your sister out of this. I'll send a car for you. The driver will be at your house around two."

"Thanks."

"It's okay. Now, do me a favor and relax."

I lean back against the seat and try to relax. I really do. Especially I try not to think of everything Mrs. Latham said.

But when I'm finally in the quiet, lonely house, it comes back to me. I pick up the picture of Mom that Dad keeps on the dresser in their bedroom. She's squinting against the sunlight and laughing as though someone had just told her a wonderful joke.

"Oh, Mom, it wasn't my fault, was it?" I ask the picture. The picture just smiles back. I sit on the floor, my back against their bed, hugging the picture to my chest. For the first time I wish I could cry. But the tears are locked behind the hard lump of hatred that grows and chokes and burns inside me. I can't get rid of that hatred, and nothing can help me get rid of it. Not until Jarrod is dead!

Chapter Thirteen

Early Tuesday morning Jan calls to invite me to dinner. I promise to come over to her house around five. As soon as Jan is off the phone I call the head counselor at the high school. I find out his name is Mr. Dobbis.

"Oh, we're right up on our toes about your case," he says, and I picture him pirouetting around his office in toe dancer shoes. "Come to the office now if you'd like to," he adds. "We were going to give you a little more time, but I've already met with your seventh-grade teachers, and gone over your records, and have a pretty good handle on a plan for your future studies."

"Will I have to go back to middle school?"

"No. Come on, and we'll talk about what I have in mind."

Dad gives me a lift to the school and shows me a bus stop where I'll be able to catch a bus that comes down Memorial Drive. From there I can walk home.

"Remember, I'll be at Jan's house for dinner tonight," I tell him. "She'll bring me home—probably around ten."

"Then I won't come home for dinner," he says.

"Don't work too hard, Dad."

He just smiles, waves, and drives off.

The high school is a mixture of old brick and modern, with two-story buildings stretching across a large campus. There are lots of trees and a wide grass lawn in front of the school. At the side is a gigantic parking lot. Kids are beginning to arrive for classes, and the street in front of the school is almost blocked with a chain of cars trying to get into the parking lot. I keep swallowing as I go up the steps of what looks like the main building. I have to ask a second time how to find Mr. Dobbis's office, because I'm so nervous I can't remember what the first person told me.

I'm in Mr. Dobbis's office for about an hour, talking about makeup study and exams and the school's tutoring program and summer school, and I leave feeling pretty good. It's going to mean a lot of work, but I can do it. He thinks I can, and I know I can. There's no way I can graduate with my class, but I honestly didn't expect to. With math and science and four years of English and everything I'll have to cram in, I couldn't cover it that fast. But at least it won't take four or five years. I won't be the oldest student in the history of the world ever to graduate from high school.

I smile to myself as I leave his office, hugging the books he gave me, and plunge out into the hall. It's filled with fast-moving bodies, and I find myself pushed aside. I plaster myself as flat as I can against the wall, trying to stay out of the way.

Someone skids to a stop in front of me. "Stacy?" Tony asks. "What are you doing here?"

"Tony! You didn't answer my phone call."

"Yeah. Hey, well, I was busy." He begins to move off. "I'll see you."

"Don't go." I grab his arm.

"Look, I'll call you tonight."

"What I have to ask you won't take very long. You're one of Jarrod's friends. Right?"

The pupils of his eyes flick to each side, and he licks his lips. "Not really friends. He comes to my parties, if you know what I mean."

"No, I don't."

"You're really dense."

It takes just a moment for what he said about Jarrod to sink in. I tighten my grip on Tony's arm as I say, "You're telling me he has a reason for being at your parties. Are you talking about drugs?"

"I gotta get to class, Stacy. Let go."

"Answer my questions, or I'll start yelling and screaming."

Again he seems to check from side to side, then leans close. "So he's a supplier. Most of the kids know it."

"Why hasn't he been arrested?"

"Proving it is something else." He scowls at me. "And don't go telling your cop friends."

Friends. "One more question. Who are Jarrod's friends?"

"A guy like Jarrod doesn't have friends."

"You must have seen him with someone."

He thinks a minute. "Yeah. Sometimes he comes on the grounds here. Sometimes I've seen him at places he hangs out. I've seen Jeff with him. Remember Jeff Clinton? He was at my party. Somebody said he took you home."

I clutch my books to my chest and shiver, but a big guy barges into Tony, knocking him off-balance, so he doesn't notice. "I gotta go, Stacy!" he complains.

A bell rings. The hall is emptying fast. "Go ahead, Tony. Thanks for answering my questions."

"Remember," he says, "keep some of that information to yourself."

I have to lean against the wall for a few minutes. The metal locker is cold, and the handle pokes into my back. But it doesn't seem to matter. Everything seems to be all wrong. Tony must have been lying about Jarrod's friend. It couldn't be Jeff.

I find myself walking down the hallway toward the main doors. I've got to go home.

As I walk into the house, about forty minutes later, the telephone rings. I don't want to answer it, but what if it's Donna? What if it's Dad? So I clutch the receiver and manage to say a weak "Hello?"

It's Detective Markowitz. "Mrs. Latham has some more questions she wants to go over with you," he says. "Do you feel up to it?"

"Now?"

"As soon as we can get you downtown. She wants to get more information from you before the hearing. There are some things you didn't cover in your first meeting."

"Okay."

He pauses. "Uh, Stacy, she's kind of unbending, but

she's a good prosecutor. If you could relax with her—"
The sentence dangles.

"I'll stay calm," I promise him.

"Fine."

"Do I have to testify at this hearing?"

"No. It's just to set a date for Tucker's trial, give his attorneys a chance to ask for a postponement, all that sort of legal stuff. You don't even need to be there."

"But I want to be there."

"Believe me, it won't interest you."

"Yes, it will. Really."

"Get ready," he says. "The car will be at your house in about twenty minutes."

I change from my jeans and blouse to a dress. I want to look just right. If I had a suit, I'd wear that. I can be just as businesslike as Mrs. Latham.

The driver from HPD arrives. I wave to Mrs. Cooper, who comes out on her porch again. How can she be so aware of everything that's going on?

She calls to me as I'm climbing in the police car, "Stacy, it's all right about that car."

The driver shuts the door, so I roll down the window and stick my head out. "What car?"

"Tell you later," she yells.

We soon arrive at the courthouse, and again it's a quick hello to Detective Markowitz, through the lobby with him, into the elevator and up to Mrs. Latham's office.

She's a little less formal with me now, and I don't let her officiousness get to me. If she's a superprosecutor, then that's what I want. For some reason she slows down on the questions, so I don't feel bombarded, and I answer them over and over and go into all the details I can remember.

It doesn't take long. She looks at her watch and says, "Very good. I think I have all the information I'll need for now. I'll go to court and see what I can accomplish."

"I'm going to be at the hearing too."

Mrs. Latham looks at Markowitz, who just shrugs. "Some of the media will be bound to be on hand," she says.

"I thought they had written enough about it," I say. "It hasn't been on TV or in the newspapers lately."

"It will again. They'll cover each new development."

"I don't care. I have to be there." I can't explain to either of them that I need to know what is happening each step of the way, that I need to *see* Jarrod standing before the judge.

We go to another floor, where each door along the hallway opens to a courtroom. Mrs. Latham leaves us, and Markowitz and I enter one of the courtrooms, and slip into seats near the door in the third row. The room is painted a shade of off-white, and the seats are like padded theater seats. A large desk faces us at the far end of the room, and I know that's the judge's bench. Flags of Texas and the United States hang at one side of his bench. There are no windows in the room. I feel closed in, a little panicky, but I won't leave. I huddle against the curved, molded back of the seat and hug my elbows for comfort.

A well-dressed woman enters the room, pauses for just a moment, and glares at me. It's Mrs. Tucker. A man joins her. She murmurs something to him, nodding in my direction. He gives me an angry glance, then ushers her into one of the seats at the opposite side of the room.

A woman bustles back and forth between the judge's bench and her desk. A few other people are in the room, and more straggle in. Four men carrying briefcases push their way through the hinged panel that separates the front section of the courtroom from the seats for visitors. They chat as though they were friends, then separate, going to opposite ends of a long table in front of the judge's bench. Mrs. Latham arrives and begins to talk to a couple of the men. They both look up at me, then go back to their conversation.

"I told you, this will be boring," Markowitz mumbles.

I just shake my head. He doesn't understand how much I need to see this happen.

"Everything going all right for you?" he asks, so I tell him what Tony had said about Jarrod and drugs.

He doesn't seem surprised. He just says, "That won't figure into this case."

"But it shows what kind of person Jarrod is!"

"The trial will be concerned with whether or not Jarrod Tucker was the person who murdered your mother. Whether or not he's supplying drugs now has nothing to do with what happened four years ago."

"You mean, he's going to just get away with the drugs thing?"

"I didn't say that. We have a narcotics department. I can pass along what you told me and let them look into it."

"You should work together."

He stretches out his long legs. "We do work together."

"Well, I think—"

I don't have time to tell him what I think because the woman near the judge's bench suddenly announces the arrival of the judge, and we all stand. A tall gray-haired man strides in, his black robes billowing around him. He sits down, and everyone in the courtroom sits down too.

A door at the far end of the room opens, and two men dressed in tan uniforms come through. A young man in jeans and what looks like a jogging shirt is between them.

"Who are they?"

"Bailiffs," Markowitz whispers, "with one of the prisoners."

"But where's Jarrod?"

"On the other side of that door is a holding pen, where prisoners are kept until it's their turn to see the judge or to be taken back to jail."

One of the prosecuting attorneys quickly goes through charges against the man before the judge. His attorney says something to the judge about the man's lack of a previous record, and the judge sets bail of $5,000. The attorneys go over to talk to the court clerk. Everyone on the judge's side of the railing seems to be talking, but I can't hear what they're saying. In a few minutes the bailiffs go off with the man, and another one comes in with an elderly woman who looks like a bag lady.

"When will they bring in Jarrod?"

"Be patient. I told you this would be boring."

Finally the first two bailiffs return. They enter the courtroom with Jarrod walking between them. He's dressed in a really sharp suit, white shirt, and tie. He looks like a model student here to accept an award. They stop at the right end of the table. The two men who have been sitting there stand and talk to Jarrod. I recognize one of them. He was there at the lineup. Jarrod's attorney. I can't hear what they're saying. They point to a chair between them.

Jarrod's mother makes a little whimpering noise, and Jarrod shifts to look at her. His lower lip curls downward, and he looks like a spoiled little boy ready to throw a tantrum. I think Jarrod hasn't noticed me, but before he sits down, he turns and stares at me. One corner of his mouth twists, and he glares with such fierceness I gasp. I get his message. I couldn't miss it. But I know it as well as he does. Without my testimony there would be little way that Jarrod could be convicted of murder. I know Jarrod would like to kill me if he could only get the chance.

Markowitz seems to know what I'm thinking. He puts a hand on my arm. "Don't worry about him," he says. "He's under guard. There's no way he could get to you."

"I'm not afraid," I whisper. But I am. A little. Even though Jarrod's back is to me, I keep seeing his pale yellow eyes, surprised and horrified as we face each other in our backyard. And I see the gun.

Maybe I'd be more afraid if I didn't hate Jarrod so much. Markowitz and Mrs. Latham might think I want to be here because I'm curious. They couldn't know about the hatred that burns and hurts and makes me want Jarrod to be punished for what he did.

I can't quite follow everything that goes on. I do hear Jarrod's attorney claim that Jarrod has been arrested four times on charges of possession of drugs, he's been given probation in all cases, and he has no record of violence. The attorney asks that Jarrod be released without bail. I want to jump up and yell at the attorney, but Mrs. Latham is talking to the judge, and the judge gives these little nods as if he were keeping time. I hope he's agreeing with her.

But suddenly Jarrod flings himself up, twists, and groans. All the people in the court stare at him like openmouthed statues. He shudders and makes a horrible, retching noise, drops facedown on the floor with a loud plop, twitches, and is still.

Jarrod's mother screams, runs to him, and kneels next to him. "What did you do to him?" she shouts.

The bailiffs have sprung to life. One of them crouches next to Jarrod. The other tries to pull his mother back. The first bailiff calls out to the judge, "He's out cold, but he's breathing. It's not very regular. We'd better get an ambulance."

The judge has stepped down from the dais and is walking toward Jarrod. "It looked like some kind of seizure." He looks at Jarrod's parents. Mr. Tucker has joined his wife and has an arm around her shoulders. "Does he have some kind of medical history we should know about?"

But Mrs. Tucker isn't coherent. She cries and accuses, and a lot of what she's saying is muffled against her husband's chest. Mr. Tucker looks as though he were going to be the next one to pass out.

"He's got a good pulse," the bailiff says.

"Paramedics are on their way," one of the clerks calls to the judge.

The judge gives a final nod at Jarrod, who lies there without moving, and strides back to the bench, his robes billowing behind him like black sails.

After he's seated, he states, "When Mr. Tucker has recovered, we'll set another date for a hearing. For now he'll be taken to the Ben Taub emergency room and kept under guard."

A jabber of noise from the hallway bursts through the door with two paramedics. They run to Jarrod and begin their work. Someone in uniform secures the door.

"Let's go, Stacy. We're in the way here." Markowitz pushes out of his seat, and I follow him.

In the hallway we're met with blinding lights from television cameras. Microphones are shoved in my face. I recognize Brandi Mayer among some other reporters with notepads and tape recorders. They surge at me, asking questions that confuse me.

"Do you still think Jarrod Tucker is the one you saw four years ago?"

"Have you had amnesia?"

"Are you seeing a psychiatrist?"

"How do you feel about those lost four years?"

"How do you feel about Jarrod Tucker?"

I don't know how to answer. I just want to stand still and scream. But Markowitz fields for me, edging through the crowd, tugging me with him, answering some of the questions for me, until an elevator arrives and we can escape inside.

"There will be a lot of this," he says. "Better get used to it."

I lean against the back of the elevator. "In the beginning I thought you'd just arrest Jarrod, and there would be a trial, and it would be over."

The elevator doors open, and he quickly leads me down a back hallway to the parking lot and into his car. When we're out on the street, he finally answers. "There's a lot more to it than that. There will be a trial, but if the verdict goes against Jarrod, his attorney will automatically appeal it, and you'll have to testify again. I've seen his attorney operate before. Unfortunately he really knows how to badger witnesses. Just be prepared for him—and for the press. They'll be interested in you and your family until all this is over."

"My family? But Dad and Donna shouldn't be a part of this!"

"To the media they are."

"Why do they ask so many questions?"

"It's their job."

"But it's not fair!"

"Get used to it, Stacy."

As I climb into the car I glance back at the courthouse. None of this would be happening if Jarrod Tucker were dead. With all my heart I wish he were dead!

Soon after Markowitz has taken me home, Jeff arrives. When I open the door, he says, "Your next-door neighbor just came out on her porch. Shall we sit out on the porch or ignore her?"

Before I can answer, he says, "Let's ignore her. It's hot and I'd like a Coke." He steps in and closes the door. I hear the latch click as the dead bolt turns.

Maybe I look startled, maybe a little scared because Jeff says, "Have to be careful."

He leads the way to the kitchen, and I follow him. It occurs to me, as I put the Cokes on the kitchen table and sit opposite Jeff, that I could run over to Mrs. Cooper's. Or I could tell Jeff what Tony said about him. I don't do anything but watch Jeff and sip at the icy drink.

Jeff raises his head to take a long swallow from the can, and I watch the muscles work in his throat. I'd like to reach out and touch his throat. I'd like to be close to him, to feel his arms around me. I'd love to have him kiss me. I've never felt like this about anyone before. I try to explore my mixed-up feelings, but they don't make any sense.

Jeff puts down the can and tilts his chair back. "You had a rough time at the courthouse."

Suddenly I'm cold. "How did you know what happened at the courthouse?"

"It was on the television newscast," he answers easily.

From where I sit I can see the kitchen clock. "The first newscast won't be on for half an hour."

"Must have been on the radio, then," he says. "I know I heard it someplace."

Jeff is lying. I can tell. Why would he lie to me?

"I heard that you went to the high school this

morning to talk to the head counselor," Jeff says, quickly changing the subject. "Did you get things straightened out?"

Carefully I answer, "For the most part. Making up all that work won't be too bad."

"I hope you still want a tutor."

My voice is so low I wonder if he can hear me. "Yes, I do."

His expression changes. The smile slips, and his eyes become serious. "Tony said you had a lot of questions to ask him."

I can't answer. I don't know what to say.

Jeff leans across the table and takes my left hand. I hope he can't feel it tremble. "Stacy," he says, "don't believe everything Tony might have told you." His eyes look kind of strange, almost sad, as he adds, "Don't believe in anybody but yourself."

Chapter Fourteen

The telephone rings, and I snatch it, grateful for the interruption. It's Brandi. She asks if I'd mind just a couple of questions.

"I'm sorry," I say. "Not now. I—I'm sorry."

As soon as I hang up, the phone rings again. It's another reporter—this one calling long distance from a newsmagazine.

"No," I say. "Not now!"

It rings again, and I just stare at it, shaking my head. "I don't want to talk to reporters," I tell Jeff.

"You don't have to," Jeff says. He puts a hand on my shoulder. He's standing very close to me. "Don't be afraid, Stacy," he murmurs.

How can I tell him that he's the one I'm afraid of?

The doorbell chimes insistently.

Jeff is ahead of me as I hurry to the door. He opens it, but Mrs. Cooper twists around him to thrust a steaming loaf of bread at me.

"Take the potholders too!" she exclaims. "The bread is right out of the oven, and I don't want you to burn your fingers."

I remember my manners. "Would you like to come in?"

Instead of answering, she smiles at Jeff and says, "I thought I'd just stop by for a visit."

"I'm sorry," I tell her. "I'm going to my friend Jan's house for dinner. I'll be leaving here in a few minutes."

"I've got to go too," Jeff says. "Lots of homework. See you later." As he reaches the walk he turns and adds, "Both of you."

Mrs. Cooper seems greatly relieved. "It's just as well. I've got to get home. Dinner to make, you know." She smiles lovingly at the loaf of bread I'm holding. "It's too bad you can't eat that with your dinner, Stacy."

"I'll love it for breakfast," I answer.

She watches Jeff drive off, then says, "Oh, yes— about that car. It's all right."

"I don't understand what you mean."

"The car I told you I saw driving around and around this neighborhood. I've seen it again, but with one thing and another I just didn't mention it to you, but there it was, and—"

I shouldn't interrupt, but I can't stand it. "What about the car, Mrs. Cooper?"

"It's his," she says, and looks pleased with herself.

It takes a moment to register. "It was Jeff's car you saw?"

"Yes," she says. "So it's all right. Enjoy the bread." She's off on a trot to her own house.

I carry the bread to the kitchen. It's yeasty and buttery, and I'm hungry, but I've got something more important to think about than a loaf of bread. Why would Jeff—I can't put the question into words. I'm afraid of the answer.

Our telephone rings again. Automatically I pick up the receiver, and a deep voice begins telling me he's with one of the Houston television stations, and how do I feel about testifying against Jarrod Tucker?

"What do you mean, how do I feel?" I stammer. "I want to testify!"

"You're not afraid of him?"

"Jarrod's in jail."

"For how long?" the reporter asks. "Even if he goes to trial and gets a life sentence, he can be paroled in twenty years—twelve, if he gets time taken off for good behavior."

"That can't be true."

"It's true. Check it out. How does your family feel about your decision to testify?"

"I—I don't know. I don't want to talk to you anymore!"

The moment I put down the receiver the telephone rings again. I won't answer. Those reporters will have to give up sooner or later. I don't want to talk to them. I have to think.

I curl up in Dad's recliner with an apple, taking big, angry bites out of it as I try to sort things out. What's happening is like a nightmare, but it's not something that will go away when I open my eyes. And it's not like the stories I read and the Saturday-morning cartoons I watched when I was a child. The bad guys aren't caught and carried away so that the good guys can live happily ever after. Maybe a jury will give Jarrod the death penalty. Maybe it won't. How long am I going to have to live with fear of this man who has already robbed so much of my life? And it's not just me! What is all this going to do to Dad? And to Donna and Dennis and their baby?

If I had the chance, I would kill Jarrod Tucker.

At first the thought startles me, and I push it away. But it comes back, and I examine it, turning it over in my mind, testing the sharpness of its edges, feeling the hatred that makes it strong.

The phone has stopped ringing, and the silence of the house settles around my shoulders. Late shadows fade the colors of the room like a coating of dust. I should have been at Jan's house an hour ago. I'd better hurry and get ready.

I'm suddenly uncomfortable with the silence because through it pop and creak the settling sounds that houses make. I turn on the television, not listening to words, just wanting noise to blot out the quiet.

The doorbell chimes again, but this time I don't answer it. I peek through the curtains at the front window to see who is on the porch. Mrs. Cooper. She's the last person I want to talk to right now.

She gives up and leaves the porch. She cuts across the lawn to her house. A marked police car cruises around the corner and slows down as it passes our house. Did Detective Markowitz arrange for this? I step back from the window, but not before I see the police car pull to a stop while Mrs. Cooper runs down her walk to talk to the officers. Does she have to know about everything that is going on? The car moves on, and Mrs. Cooper heads back to her house.

Jan is going to wonder why I'm so late. I'm in the

den, on my way from the living room to the bedroom to get my handbag, when I hear a slight rattling noise close at hand. It seems to be coming from the side door that leads to the garage. I stand and listen, waiting for the sound again, but it's the words on the television that I hear.

The announcer is saying, "In an escape while being examined in Ben Taub Hospital a short while ago. A bailiff was shot in the leg when his gun was taken by Tucker. An HPD spokesman told us that an all-points bulletin has been put out for Tucker, who is believed to have stolen a dark blue Pontiac and is thought to be heading out of state, possibly toward Louisiana."

The noise from the hall door that leads to the garage rattles over the announcer's words, and I see the doorknob turn.

I know who's at that door. It has to be Jarrod. He's inside the garage, and soon he'll be inside our house! No one would suspect that he'd come here. He'd have to be crazy. But didn't he warn me he always gets his own way?

For an instant I freeze, unable to move, desperately wondering what I can do. I have to pass the door leading to the garage to get to the front door. Jarrod will have that door open in a minute. I'll run right into him. I can't hide in the house. He'll find me. If I can make the backyard—

As quickly and quietly as possible I move to the back door and open it carefully, wincing at the slight sounds it makes. I shut it and run into the yard. Now what?

I hear one of the Cooper children complaining

about having to come in; then the Cooper back door slams. I take two steps in that direction when I realize I can't endanger their lives. This is between Jarrod and me.

In front of me is the oak tree and the nailed board steps that lead up to the tree house. Jarrod won't look for me there.

I scramble upward, clinging to the trunk and branches. My foot slips as one of the boards tears loose from the tree, and I skin my elbow. I'm so scared it's hard to breathe, and my fingers feel like numb stumps as I pull myself up and drop to the floor of the tree house. Frantically I tuck my legs inside and shove myself against the back wall.

But the tree house rocks unsteadily. I hear a board from it drop to the grass. I inch to the center and sit perfectly still. Miraculously the house steadies itself. My back is against a window, but the window is on the Cooper side and shielded by a large branch. If Jarrod comes outside—and I don't think he will—he won't be able to see me through this window. I wait. There is nothing I can do but wait.

Forever is measured not in minutes but in heartbeats. I can hear the steady thumping pulse in my ears. Shadows are deeper, but time has dissolved into terror.

Then I hear what I've been dreading. The back door to my house opens and shuts. Jarrod is in the yard.

"Stacy?" He mumbles something after that, but again, as on the phone—for now I'm sure it was him—it's as though he were talking to himself.

The voice comes from below me, as soft and shivery as the warm night breeze from the Gulf. I try not to move. Can he hear my trembling?

He chuckles, and the sound is even more fearful than his voice. "You've got to be up there," he says.

Instinctively I shrink back even farther. The boards in the tree house groan loudly, and it rocks.

"I could shoot you from down here," I hear him say. "But I don't want to shoot you. I want you to have an accident." He laughs to himself again.

I hear the sound of his shoes scraping the trunk of the tree as he climbs toward me. "Stacy," he says, "I told you—I always get my own way."

Suddenly a calm sweeps through my mind, and I stop shaking. I am not going to sit here and wait for Jarrod to have his own way. I'm a woman who's able to think rationally, to want *my* own way. And I have a plan.

Slowly, careful to keep the tree house balanced, I slide upward, grasping first the rough edges of the window behind me, then reaching for the branch outside it. I have managed to pull myself out the window, with my feet resting against the lower window frame, by the time Jarrod's arms and grinning face shove into the door to the tree house.

I stare into his yellow eyes. I see the gun.

"If I'm killed, they'll know you did it!" I whisper.

"Not if it's an 'accident.'"

"You're insane!"

He giggles. "Smart girl, Stacy," he says. "I've set it up. That's going to be my defense. Now, let's talk about your 'accident.' My friend and I will take care of it."

"Your friend?"

"This is my friend." For just an instant he takes his eyes from me as he gives a little wave of the gun in his hand.

As hard as I can I kick against the side of the house, swinging into it, throwing all my weight against it.

The house, with a great groan and crash, collapses and falls, taking Jarrod with it.

I scramble down and drop from the tree, into his screams and curses. Jarrod is lying on his back. Some of the boards are under him, and the large part of the tree house covers his hips and legs.

The gun lies near my feet.

I pick it up, hold it carefully in my right hand, and slip my index finger against the trigger.

Jarrod has stopped yelling. He stares at me. I can see the back door of our house fly open. I can see the terror on Jarrod's face, the gleam in his eyes. I can see his gun pointing at me.

"Don't shoot me," Jarrod whimpers, and I realize I am pointing the gun at him.

If I shot Jarrod, wouldn't it be self-defense? And wouldn't it end the trials and the questions and the badgering and the harassment and the nightmares and the worries and the years and years of fear?

Carefully I aim the gun.

Chapter Fifteen

"You can't shoot me!" Jarrod is crying and slobbering. Spittle drools from his mouth and down his chin. Or is it blood? "I didn't mean to kill your mother. I didn't know she was in the house, but she came into the den from the kitchen, and saw me, and said something to me, and I was scared. I didn't mean it, Stacy!"

I try to picture my mother facing Jarrod with his gun. "What did she say to you?"

"She didn't say anything at first. She was smiling. Then she saw the gun, and her eyes got frightened, but she still had a kind of smile on her face. She held her hands toward me and said, 'It's all right. It's all right.' "

"And you shot her!"

He can't talk. He's crying too hard. I aim the gun at his head, just as carefully as he once aimed it at me. My hands have stopped shaking.

But now I can picture my mother. I can see her smile too. I can hear her telling Jarrod, "It's all right." Tears rush to my eyes with such force I'm blinded. I try to rub them away with the back of my left hand.

Choices were so easy when I was a child. Good guy

versus bad guy, and the good guys always won. But I'm no longer a child.

Although I keep the gun pointed at Jarrod, at the top of my lungs I yell, "Help! Mrs. Cooper! Help!"

I hear her scream, "They're coming! I already called the police!"

"I'm all right," I shout to her. "Don't be afraid. I'll keep the gun on him until the police get here."

Someone leaps the hedge and lands beside me, but it isn't Mrs. Cooper.

"Give me the gun, Stacy," Jeff says.

"No!" I don't take my eyes off Jarrod. "Stay away from me. Mrs. Cooper called the police. They're coming."

"I *am* the police. Narcotics squad," he says. "You can give me the gun."

He reaches across and takes it out of my hand.

"My leg's broken!" Jarrod begins to yell again. "She did it. She tried to kill me!"

I look up at Jeff. "How can you be a policeman? You're just a senior in high school."

But, as always, he avoids my questions. He even sounds a little angry. He keeps his eyes on Jarrod. "You could have been killed, Stacy. Apparently you were home and weren't answering the phone. Why not?"

Jarrod groans. "My back. It hurts. I think something's busted. Get an ambulance!"

"It's on its way," Jeff tells him.

"Jeff, I had Jarrod's gun. I could have shot him."

He doesn't look at me. "Could you?"

I shake my head. "No. Not really. I wanted to. I

hated him so much that I really wanted to kill him. I almost did. But then I couldn't do it. Mom wouldn't—"

It's hard to explain. I hope that Jeff understands what I mean. I add, "I really didn't have a choice. Jarrod's life doesn't belong to me." I think of all the problems to come for all of us because of Jarrod, and I give a long sigh.

The yard seems to be filled with people. Mrs. Cooper is talking at a great rate. To me? I hear the high, excited chirps she's making, but the words don't come through. There's a bass note in my ear as an officer with a notebook peers at me, asking me questions. But the only words I want to hear are Jeff's.

He has my arm, propelling me around the rubble and the police officers, through our back door and into the house. The familiar, dusty smells of the room are laced with the pungency of drying apple core and somehow comfort me. I give a huge sigh of relief and lean against the closed door.

"Are you all right? Do you want to sit down? Can I get you some water?" Jeff asks.

I look at him carefully and remember something else. "I know where I saw you before. It was downtown, at the police station. You looked right at me."

He doesn't answer, so I add, "You can tell me the truth. You lied to me."

"I didn't lie," he says. "I've been with the Houston Police Department for two years. I'm twenty-three, but because I look a lot younger than I am, I was put on a special high school assignment with the narcotics squad, and they sent me to the school in your area. Markowitz got worried about you, and I was in a logical position to keep an eye on you, so you became part of my assignment."

"I was just an assignment?"

"Don't look at me like that, Stacy," he says. "I don't want to hurt you."

"Hurt seems to be another part of growing up," I tell him. "One more thing to get used to."

He shakes his head, resting his hands on my shoulders. I like the feel of them. I wish I could tell him so. I wish I knew how.

"There are so many good things about growing up, you can keep your mind on those and climb over the hurts."

"Like falling in love? I think I was beginning to fall in love with you."

"I don't want to be your first love, Stacy."

"You've made that clear. I won't forget. I'm an 'assignment.'"

"Listen to me," he says, and moves nearer. His hands slip from around my shoulders and hold me tightly, pressing my cheek against the base of his throat. "I asked to get taken off the narcotics assignment just so that I could tell you the truth, and I asked because I care about you."

"But you told me—"

"I said I don't want to be your *first* love. I'd like to be the real thing, and I can wait."

My cheek glows from the warmth of his skin through his shirt, and I can hear the steady beat of his heart. I put my arms around him. I'm Stacy McAdams. I'm seventeen. And I'm definitely in the right body!

The Name of the Game
Was Murder

*To Louise Hagen
my sister-in-law and friend
with love*

ONE

clung to the heavy oak door for support, terrified of the old man seated behind the cluttered desk. His gargoyle eyes—magnified by thick, overlarge lenses—were huge, wet shimmers in a pale, shiny-bald head; and he hunched into a tight, stoop-shouldered ball as though at any minute he'd fling out moldy wings and swoop toward me. "What do you think you're doing here?" he snapped.

As long as I could remember, Augustus Trevor had been famous as one of our country's greatest literary novelists, and he was almost as well known for his well-publicized socializing with kings and presidents and a lot of people with tons of money. I had expected to meet the Augustus Trevor with the charming smile and elegant manner—the one I'd seen in so many photographs—but the Augustus Trevor who glared at me from behind his desk was a much older, scowling, mean-tempered person, and I was shocked.

I tried my best to smile but couldn't make it, and I began to sweat. Whether it was from nerves or because of the heat from the smoldering fire in the huge fireplace behind him, I didn't know. "I—I'm Samantha B-Burns," I stammered.

"I didn't ask *who* you are," he snapped. "I asked what you're doing here."

Good question. I was beginning to wonder myself, but I took a deep breath and started over. "I'm here because I'm Aunt Thea's niece. That is, my mother is her niece."

His scowl didn't waver, and I wondered if he understood who I meant. "Thea, your wife," I explained. "I suppose I should have waited for her to introduce us, but I couldn't wait to meet you. You're the reason I'm here. I mean, I've heard a lot about Catalina Island and Avalon, and the great beach and the music, and 'island of romance' and all that, but *you* . . ." His face was crinkling like a dark purple prune, so I quickly added, "but the main reason for my coming is *you*, Mr. Trevor."

His lips parted, and he made a kind of burbling sound, the way babies do before they spit up, so I thought I'd better explain a bit more. "I asked Aunt Thea if I could come for a visit before school begins in September, because I'm pretty sure that I'm going to be a writer, but I don't think I can do it without help, and I've brought some stories . . . I'd be so grateful if you'd read them and tell me if I really have any talent and give me some advice."

It was awful trying to talk to someone whose face was screwed up in agony. "Remember?" I asked quickly, and smiled encouragingly. "Two years ago I mailed you a story I'd written, and I really didn't expect you to answer. I mean I did then, but I don't now because I realize the story wasn't terribly good. I was only thirteen then, but I've been writing something every day—an article in a writers' magazine said to do that if you want to be successful—and, as I said, I've brought these stories. . . ."

Augustus exploded from his chair and scuttled around his desk. "Stop that foolish prattle!" he screeched.

I realized that he was short, too, and that surprised me. It's hard to think of a literary giant as short, but Augustus Trevor was definitely short. I'm five six, and we were facing each other nose to nose.

Still maintaining a tight grip on the edge of the door, I mumbled, "I know I talk too much when I get nervous, and I'm really nervous meeting you, Mr. Trevor."

"Then go home," he said.

"I can't," I told him, although at the moment I wished with all my heart that I could. I hadn't just asked to come. I'd begged Mom and Dad. I'd pleaded. I thought about what Dad had said about how I always jumped into things without thinking, and I had to admit that in this case, at least, he'd been right.

I suddenly realized that Augustus had regained control of his emotions and was speaking to me, so I took a deep breath and tried to pay attention.

"Young lady," he said, "I invited you to leave. The correct response would have been 'I will,' not 'I can't.' What do you mean by saying 'I can't'?"

"I mean that because I was coming here my parents decided to take a trip they've always wanted to the Grand Cayman Islands. That means no one's home, and Mom would really be mad if I went home and lived there alone for two weeks, only I couldn't anyway, because I've got one of those nonrefundable airline tickets and not enough money to get another one, and then there's the matter of food, because all I've got is spending money and . . ."

Augustus grimaced as he reached out and grabbed me, his bony fingertips digging into my arms. "I have better plans than entertaining you," he said. "I am hosting a house party this coming weekend for some very important people, and you'll be in the way."

"Aunt Thea didn't tell me about the party," I answered.

"Thea didn't know about it."

"Maybe you should have told her," I suggested helpfully, and tried a smile. "You can't blame Aunt Thea for telling me I could come and visit, if she didn't know you'd planned something else." Augustus scowled again, and I quickly added, "Look, I'll stay out of the way while your party's going on. I promise. You won't even know I'm here."

And after your guests have left, then maybe you'll be used to having me around, and you'll read some of my stories, I thought, *because if you don't, how will I know if I can really be a writer or not?*

Augustus let go of my arms, and I rubbed them as he stood there silently, looking as if he was thinking over what I'd said. Finally his pupils, swimming like fat fish in goldfish bowls, focused on me. "What room did Thea put you in?"

"It's a big room," I told him. "It's got a huge bed with a dark red spread and canopy and red carpeting and French doors that open onto a balcony."

"I suppose you'll have to remain on the island, but you can't sleep in that room. It's reserved for Buck Thompson."

"Buck Thompson? You mean Buck Thompson the network sportscaster? That guy who does all those shoe commercials with little kids?''

Augustus's only answer was a sneer of disgust in my direction. He strode toward the fireplace and yanked on a long, thin piece of tapestry that hung on the wall next to it. I knew what the tapestry was because I'd seen bellpulls like that in old movies. It was an odd, old-fashioned contrast to the modern computer that sat on his desk.

Suddenly a voice spoke behind me. ''Yes, Mr. Trevor?''

I hadn't heard anyone approach, and I jumped, whirling to face a slightly plump woman who wore no makeup and whose streaked gray hair was pulled back tightly and knotted at the base of her neck. She was dressed in a navy blue cotton dress with a high neck and long sleeves and looked exactly like what she probably was—a housekeeper.

''Mrs. Engstrom, this is the daughter of Mrs. Trevor's niece,'' Augustus said, leaving off my name as though it weren't important. ''Due to Mrs. Trevor's carelessness in not asking my plans, this young woman will be our house guest for a brief period of time. She has been wrongly assigned to the Red Room, so please remove her things and escort her to the tower room at the end of the south wing.''

I smiled at Mrs. Engstrom, but she didn't smile back. She gave me just the briefest of glances and said to Augustus, ''The tower room is quite small and off to itself, Mr. Trevor.''

''The other bedrooms will be occupied. Take her things to the tower room,'' he said with emphasis. ''That will be all, Mrs. Engstrom.''

She nodded and turned, and I quickly followed.

Augustus Trevor was the most disagreeable, obnoxious dork I had ever met; and it made me angry that people read his written words that rippled and tumbled and fell like beautiful waterfalls one on top of the other, and thought that because he wrote super-wonderful stories he must be a super-wonderful person. It wasn't fair.

I had to trot to keep up with Mrs. Engstrom as I followed her across the massive entry hall with its large black and white diamond-shaped tiles, careful not to trip on the edges of the oriental rugs that were scattered over the floor. We went up the sweeping, carved stairway, the sound of our footsteps lost in the heavy carpeting, and turned left, hurrying down the hall to the Red Room. There was no sign of Aunt Thea.

"Which is Aunt Thea and Uncle—uh—Mr. Trevor's room?" I asked Mrs. Engstrom.

"Your aunt's room is the one nearest the head of the stairs," she answered. "Mr. Trevor's is directly across the hall from the room we are in."

"Oh," I said, and felt my face grow warm. I gathered up my suitcase and backpack, glad that I hadn't unpacked them, and again followed the silent Mrs. Engstrom down the hallway, which was dark in spite of the wrought-iron sconces, each of which held clusters of small, low-watt light bulbs.

She stopped outside the last door and threw it open, then stood to one side. Instead of the room I'd expected, I saw a narrow, curving flight of stairs. "It's just a short flight," she told me, "but the stairs are steep, and my knees aren't what they used to be. If you don't mind, I won't follow you."

"I don't mind," I said, and smiled at her again. "By the

way, my name is Samantha Burns. Everybody calls me Sam."

She nodded, but she didn't smile in return. What a household! At least Aunt Thea seemed to be glad I was here.

I shifted my suitcase into my other hand and edged into the stairway.

"I'm sorry," Mrs. Engstrom murmured. I twisted around to tell her not to be, but she was on her way down the hall.

I wondered just what it was she was sorry about. Sorry that I had to clump and squeeze my way up this weird stairway? That I'd had to change rooms? That Augustus Trevor was a mean-minded nerd?

The stairs made only a half circle and ended at an equally narrow door that was arched on top. A large brass key protruded from the keyhole. Feeling something like Alice in Wonderland and hoping I wouldn't shrink, I turned the key, pushed open the door, and entered the tower room.

It was perfectly round, including the part of it that was partitioned off for a tiny bathroom. Inside the room there was only enough space for one twin-size bed, a small chest of drawers, and a chair. I dropped my suitcase and backpack on the bed and walked to the narrow windows that ringed the outer curve of the room. Beyond, in the distance, lay the sea, but the view was marred by the bars set into the stone.

I rested my forehead against the glass and groaned. In spite of gentle Aunt Thea's presence in this house, I was beginning to get scared. "I can't believe this," I said aloud. "I'm in prison!"

TWO

I needed to get out of that room as soon as possible, so I unpacked in a rush, tossing my journal and stories, my shorts and T-shirts and other stuff into the empty drawers. Mom had insisted that I bring two dresses, so I hung them in a tiny makeshift closet I found in the bathroom and threw open the door of my bedroom.

I stopped with my hand on the doorknob, the cold brass key touching my fingertips, and for a moment I stared at it, a peculiar chill shivering around the back of my neck. While I was inside the room, with the door closed, anyone could have turned that key and locked me in.

Stop that! I told myself. *It's not just a key. It's an ornament . . . maybe an interior decorator's attempt to try to carry out a theme in this yucky castle. Big deal. Nobody locks doors inside a house.*

But it didn't matter what I'd told myself. How could I know what people did in Augustus Trevor's house? I grasped the key and turned it in the lock, feeling it grind and grate until there came a deep and final click, then shoved the key into the hip pocket of my jeans and took off down the winding stairs. I had to talk to someone— anyone. I needed to hear a human voice.

Unfortunately, that "someone, anyone" didn't include my parents.

You know how awful it is when you tell your mom and dad you have to do something, and they tell you all the reasons you shouldn't, and you say they're wrong, only they turn out to be right.

"Take it easy, Sam," Dad had told me when I insisted how important it was for me to visit Aunt Thea and meet Augustus Trevor. "You've always been like this—the minute you get an idea you want to rush right into it. Slow down and think this out. If you want to be a writer you can be one. You don't have to depend on Augustus Trevor's help."

"Thea has never invited us to her home," Mom pointed out, and I thought I could detect a slight trace of bitterness as she added, "I wouldn't doubt that her celebrity husband has been responsible for that."

Aunt Thea had visited our family a few times, and we'd enjoyed her visits. She went shopping with me for a really hot jacket, took me to the best beauty shop in town for a terrific new haircut, and taught me how to play cribbage. But Augustus had never come with her, and we'd never been invited to visit them. If it was Augustus Trevor's fault, I honestly didn't blame him. If you could have lunch with the Duke and Duchess of Kent and dinner with Robert Redford, why would you want to hang around with the Burns family of Elko, Nevada?

"Augustus Trevor is one of the world's greatest writers.

He has to place a high priority on his privacy," I said, and winced at how stuffy I'd just sounded.

"Which is all the more reason that it wouldn't be polite to invite yourself," Mom had insisted.

"Don't you see?" I pleaded. "Ever since I decided that someday I'm going to be a writer, I've wanted to meet Augustus Trevor. If I'm in his home for a visit I can get his advice. He'll let me know if I really have writing talent or just think I do. Whatever he tells me can influence my entire career."

"As I remember, you sent Trevor one of your stories a couple of years ago," Dad said, "and he didn't bother to write to you about it or even return it."

"But this time I'd be there in person! Don't you see what a difference that would make?"

Dad gave me one of those looks, and I realized I was overdoing it, but Mom and Dad just didn't understand how much it would mean to me to be guided by Augustus Trevor.

Mom sighed and said, "I suppose you could call Thea and ask if she'd want you to come for a visit. If it wouldn't be convenient, I'm sure she'd be honest enough to say so."

I made the call and started to talk to Aunt Thea about all sort of polite nothing stuff, but I couldn't stand waiting to ask my question and get the answer, so I blurted out, "Aunt Thea, could I come and visit you for two weeks?"

For a few seconds there was only silence. My face grew hot, and my hands began to sweat, but finally Thea said, "Of course you can visit us, Samantha. I'd love to have you as a guest."

"Thank you, thank you, thank you!" I shouted, and

Mom took the phone away from me to chat with Thea and talk about travel arrangements.

Three weeks later Aunt Thea met me at the Los Angeles airport, and we took a taxi to the harbor. We were ushered aboard Augustus Trevor's launch by a couple of crew members and were soon on our way to Catalina Island. His own launch! Wow!

I said something about being eager to see Avalon and the beach, but Thea looked surprised. "Oh, Samantha, I'm sorry," she said. "Our home is on the opposite side of the island, past the Isthmus, and rather remote from the Avalon area, I'm afraid."

"That's all right," I said. "I don't mind hiking it."

She shook her head softly. Everything about Thea was soft, from her pale gray-blond hair, through her light untanned skin, to her eyes that looked like reflections of the washed-out blue of the sky. "We're not connected to the road that runs through the island," she said. "Our only transportation is by boat." Thea gently brushed back a strand of hair that had blown across my eyes and smiled. "Don't look so disappointed, Samantha. We'll see that you get a glimpse of Avalon. We'll take you there in the launch."

Just getting a glimpse of Avalon wasn't quite the same as lying on the beach in my new blue bikini, hoping the lifeguard would notice it was the exact same shade of blue as my eyes. My best friend, Darlene Barkholter, spent two weeks on Santa Catalina Island a year ago, and I heard plenty about the lifeguards at Avalon, who were real hunks. I can't say I hadn't given the lifeguards some thought.

Darlene and I have always been interested in the same

things, from the time we met in third grade. We shared a tree house, wrote countless letters to each other in code all the way through fifth grade, and joined the same clubs in junior high and high school; so I would have shared Darlene's appreciation of the Avalon lifeguards. However, I reminded myself that the reason for my trip wasn't to enjoy watching lifeguards. I had a much more important, literary purpose, so I assured Thea that I didn't mind missing Avalon at all.

She began telling me about something called the Santa Catalina Island Conservancy, which was a foundation formed to preserve the natural resources of the island, and how someday Augustus's 1920s island house would belong to the foundation, but I'm afraid I didn't pay much attention. I relaxed and looked out at the deep blue water and the sky in which clumps of clouds were beginning to gather, their edges darkening like watercolors that had run together. I let the ocean spray sting my face, and I thought about how someday I'd love to have an island home and a boat just like this one. Maybe, someday after I became a famous writer.

Catalina is just twenty miles off the coast of California, so it didn't take us long to arrive. We swung north, went around the far tip of the island, and docked behind a motorboat at a short, covered pier in a small, narrow cove. One of the crew from the launch carried my suitcase and backpack up a steep, winding stairway to the house, while Thea and I followed.

What a house! It was so weird that I wondered for just an instant if I'd wandered onto the set of a Halloween horror movie. Spread out, with corridors rambling in all directions, this ugly stone castle sat alone on a scrubby hill covered with a thick tangle of sage and short golden-brown grasses under wind-twisted oak trees. Beyond were higher hills, blurred purple-blue with mists, and from where we stood we had a picture-postcard view of the sea.

Thea had led me to a large bedroom and said she'd leave me to unpack. I guess I should have stayed there and waited for her, but the moment she had left I went downstairs in search of the man I was so eager to meet, the famous author Augustus Trevor.

That had been a big mistake.

Now, as I walked down the staircase to the landing, my footsteps muffled by the thick carpet, I took my time, listening intently for the sound of another human being; but the house was silent. For the first time I paid attention to my surroundings. From my vantage point on the landing I could look down on the immense entry hall and get a good view of part of the living room as well, and I was amazed to see that the house was cluttered with museum-like stuff. Besides all the heavily framed paintings on the walls, there were wood carvings of animals and people, all kinds of big and little statues (some of them pretty weird), glazed pottery bowls, china plates, and even a crystal bear which sat on a table near a window. Souvenirs from their travels? Gifts from royalty?

As I turned away from the railing my attention was caught by a pedestal which was tucked into the deep angle of the landing. A burnished gold vase with a rounded lid stood on the pedestal, and I stepped closer to examine it. The vase was close to two feet high and about ten inches in diameter, with a wide base. It was graceful and curved and heavily ornamented with designs and markings that looked like scrunched-up little faces.

I reached out my hand to touch the lid, but someone spoke close to my ear, startling me. I jumped and the vase wobbled, but I caught it in time.

"Are you looking for something, miss?"

I turned to see a tall man dressed in dark pants and a white jacket. He was staring down at me with a bland, noncommittal expression, and I'd seen enough British-made television programs on PBS to recognize immediately that he must be a butler.

"I'm Sam," I said. "Samantha Burns. Thea Trevor's niece. I was just looking at this vase."

"That is not a vase, Miss Burns," he said. "It is a burial urn."

"Oops." I took a step away from it. "You mean somebody's in there?"

"Not to my knowledge," he said. "Considering that the urn dates back quite a few centuries and has undoubtedly traveled through many hands, I would assume that by this time it is empty."

That was not a pleasant thought. Somebody thought his ashes would be tucked away in the urn forever, and what happened? Someone carrying the urn tripped? Opened it in a windstorm? Dropped it through an open carriage door? Gross! If my ashes had been lost so carelessly, I'd be angry enough to come back and haunt my urn.

I took another uneasy step away from it. "Mr. uh—uh—"

"My name is Walter," he said.

"Walter, that urn isn't haunted, is it?" I asked.

"I believe there is some sort of legend to that effect,"

Walter answered, "but you will have to ask Mr. Trevor about it. I do not believe in ghosts." He became more businesslike as he added, "Is there anything I can do for you?"

"Yes," I said as I shot another uneasy glance toward the urn. "Can you tell me where my aunt is?"

He gave a slight nod and answered, "I'll take you to Mrs. Trevor. She is in the sun-room."

There was a sun-room in this house? Great! Did that mean a hot tub? An indoor pool? Things were beginning to look up. I trotted down the stairs after the butler and followed him across the entry hall toward the back of the house.

The sun-room was formal and just as overdecorated as the rest of the house, but it did have large windows framed by sheer curtains and heavy drapes. The windows overlooked an uneven landscape of grasses, low shrubbery, and wind-twisted oaks which led steeply down to the sea. Aunt Thea was seated in a heavy wicker chair, her back to the window. Clouds had dimmed the sun, but there was enough brightness left to outline Aunt Thea with an aura of pale green light.

As I came in she looked up and placed a delicate china teacup on the silver tray which rested on the low table in front of her. "Samantha dear," she said, "I'm sorry that you met Augustus so abruptly, without warning. He can be a little frightening, if you aren't used to him."

"It was my fault," I told her. "I couldn't wait. That is, I mean, he's so famous, and he's such a great writer, and I know you would have made the introduction easier." I shrugged and added, "Dad keeps telling me I jump into things without stopping to think."

She smiled. "Impulsive is the word."

I smiled back because I really liked Aunt Thea. As I flopped into a chair I stretched out my legs and sighed. "Impulsiveness says it all. I guess that's something I'm going to have to watch out for in my writing. There's so much to learn."

Aunt Thea reached over and patted my knee. "Be patient with yourself. Becoming a published writer takes years and years of practice and experience. Do you think that Augustus had immediate success?"

Her question caught me by surprise. "Why, yes," I said. "He did, didn't he? His first book won that big literary award and boom!—instant fame."

"His *fourth* book," she said. "The first three were rejected many times over."

"They were?" I mumbled, and tried to absorb what she'd said, but Thea changed the subject.

"I'm sorry, too, that Augustus moved you to the tower room. I know it's small and unhandy, but since he'd assigned the other rooms to his guests—"

"Please don't apologize," I interrupted. "The tower room is a really—uh—interesting room. I—uh—like it."

Thea paused a moment, accepting what we both knew was a polite fib, then picked up a teacup in one hand and a silver teapot in the other and asked, "Would you like a cup of tea, Samantha?"

"Oh . . . yes, thank you," I answered. I'd rather have had a soft drink, but I supposed tea was okay if it had a lot of sugar and lemon in it. Thea handed me a cup and saucer, and even though I was still bemused by what she had said about Augustus's rejections, I noticed there was another cup and saucer on the tray. "Is uh—Mr.—I mean, is your husband going to join us?"

"Why don't you just relax and call him Augustus?" she suggested.

"I—I don't think I could do that."

Aunt Thea took a sip of tea and nodded. "You'll soon begin to feel comfortable with him."

I seriously doubted that, but I didn't have to say so, because Thea went on to explain, "The extra cup is for Laura Reed. She arrived this morning, and she'll be down to join us at any minute."

"Laura Reed!" I nearly dropped my cup. "You don't mean Laura Reed the movie star, do you?"

"The very same," Thea answered. "She's one of Augustus's guests for the weekend party he planned."

"He didn't tell you about the party before I got here," I said, but Thea just shrugged.

"Augustus has always been able to bring home unannounced guests and know they'll be well cared for."

I put down my cup and leaned forward. "Aunt Thea," I said, "I didn't mean to crash his party. I'm sorry if I caused any trouble."

She smiled as she reached out and squeezed my hand. "Don't look so worried, Samantha. You're not the cause of any trouble. Augustus tends to be hotheaded when things aren't going the way he's planned, and during the last few years the painful bouts he's had with arthritis and gout haven't helped his disposition. But I'm sure you'll find that he'll be perfectly charming while you're here. He can be a very gracious host when he wants to be."

Easy for her to say. She hadn't had him throw a temper tantrum right in her face.

Or had she? I got the uncomfortable feeling that she wasn't telling me the truth.

"Hello, Thea."

I rose to my feet as Laura Reed—the famous movie star Laura Reed—glided into the room. Maybe I expected flashing lights and little twinkle stars and a mink coat and a sparkly sequined dress. I didn't expect what I saw: a pretty but quiet woman who wore no makeup. Her blond hair—just a shade lighter than mine—hung straight and heavy around her face, and she was dressed in a simple white blouse and navy blue jeans.

They had to be designer jeans, I told myself as Aunt Thea introduced us. And the blouse—she probably bought it on Rodeo Drive. After all, Laura Reed was a movie star, so she must have a ton of money, in spite of the fact that her last two movies had bombed.

She took both my hands and looked into my eyes as she smiled shyly. Shyly? A movie star? She reminded me more of a mouse. "I'm so very pleased to meet you," she murmured in a voice all sleepily whispery and throaty.

"Thank you," I answered. "I'm pleased to meet you, too."

I was excited at meeting Laura Reed, and one part of my mind was already thinking about what I'd tell Darlene: *Laura? Oh, she was nice. Very friendly. And it's true, her eyes really are a kind of greenish-gold.*

But another part of my mind was registering the fact that there was an odd expression in those eyes. What did they remind me of? She was looking at me, talking to me, and yet she wasn't. I mean, I could see that her mind was somewhere else, and it must not have been a very happy place, because she was nervous. I wondered if Augustus

Trevor's weird house was having an effect on her. Burial urns, tower rooms with bars on the windows—if I opened a closet door and discovered a mummy, I wouldn't be in the least surprised.

Laura had seated herself, so I quickly sat down too, picked up my cup, and tried to sip as nonchalantly as Laura and Thea.

They chatted for a few minutes, mostly about old friends and old parties. I didn't know most of the people they were talking about, and I was a little disappointed that things weren't turning out to be as exciting as I hoped they'd be. My attention began drifting away, but it quickly returned when Laura put down her cup and asked, "Thea, you must tell me. Why am I here?"

Aunt Thea's eyes widened. "Why are you here? I don't understand, Laura. You were invited to Augustus's weekend party, and you came."

Laura shook her head impatiently. "Party? I'd hardly call it a party."

"But Augustus said . . ."

Laura Reed sighed and leaned back against the plumply cushioned sofa. "Obviously, *you* don't know either."

"Know what?" Now it was Thea's turn for impatience. "Laura, please explain what you mean."

"Very well," Laura said. "Augustus wrote, asking me to be here. No. He didn't ask. He *told* me to come. He said there would be a game in which I'd be one of the chief players. His exact words were, 'If you don't take part, you'll soon regret it.' " Laura leaned forward, her golden eyes trained on Thea like piercing spotlights. "I came because I was afraid to ignore his threat."

Thea paled. "You must be mistaken, Laura," she said. "Surely, Augustus would never threaten his friends."

"Friends?" Laura whispered. "I'd hardly say we were friends."

I thought about what Laura had told us, and I had to agree with her and not with Aunt Thea. What Augustus Trevor had written to Laura Reed sounded like a threat to me.

THREE

The tea party was uncomfortable, with Thea trying to be a gracious hostess, in spite of what Laura had told her, and Laura trying to be a charming guest, even though it was obvious she'd rather be anywhere else. To ease the situation they both turned to me.

"You're lucky to lead a normal life," Laura said, and patted my hand. This time her smile was wistful, and her words dragged, plopping themselves down like reluctant feet. "You'll never know what it's like to . . ."

"To be rich and famous?" I offered helpfully.

"To be used," she corrected. "To want to be really loved —not as a star, but as a child, hungry for affection."

I wasn't sure how to answer her, but I needn't have worried because she rambled on about the traumatic people who had affected her adult life, from parents to hairdressers. Thea and I just listened. I stopped being embarrassed by Laura's revelations and began thinking that I'd have a lot of really interesting stuff to tell Darlene.

Even though it was midafternoon, the room gradually became darker, and finally a maid in uniform came in, turned on some lights, and began picking up the empty cups. She had a round, cheerful face, and looked as if she might be only a few years older than me.

Thea went to the window. "It looks as though it's going to pour," she said. "Such odd weather for August."

The maid stopped, tray in hand, and said, "Mrs. Trevor, the radio news said there's going to be a storm. It's part of a hurricane moving north from Mexico."

As she spoke she looked at Aunt Thea with a kind of pity and tenderness. It was obvious that she was fond of Aunt Thea, but I didn't understand why she should pity her.

"Thank you, Lucy," Thea said. "I didn't listen to the radio today. I wasn't aware of a possible storm."

Radio? What about television? It dawned on me that I hadn't seen a single TV set in this house. Two weeks without television? It was hard to imagine.

Thea sat down again and announced, "The launch just pulled up to the dock, which means the other guests have arrived. We'll all be snug and cozy before the storm breaks."

Snug and cozy in this creepy old castle? I didn't believe it.

Laura sat up stiffly and asked in her kind of choking, breathy way, "Who are the other guests?"

"Augustus told me that Buck Thompson is one of them," Thea said.

I eagerly volunteered, "You know who Buck Thompson is, don't you? He used to be a pro quarterback, only now he's a sportscaster on one of the networks." I realized that

I shouldn't have interrupted, so I quickly said, "Sorry, Aunt Thea."

Thea just smiled at me and continued. "And Julia Bryant will be here."

"Julia Bryant!" I blurted out.

Thea raised one eyebrow and said, "I take it that you're familiar with Julia's books, Samantha, although I'm a little surprised that you'd like that type of novel."

"I really don't," I answered, and blushed as hotly as one of Julia's female characters. "I mean, this girl at school was talking about one of them, and she read a couple of scenes to us, and they were kind of wild, but I read some of the rest of the book, and it was boring."

Laura nodded vigorously. "You're right. Julia's novels are sleaze. They're drivel. And the last one on television was badly cast. I was up for the part, but then someone got the idea of casting this twenty-two-year-old with absolutely no talent . . ."

"More tea?" Thea asked, and held the teapot toward Laura as she said, "I'm sure you know that when Julia's novels began making the best-seller list she set up a foundation to help support budding novelists—all in the name of an old friend."

"What a neat idea," I said, and could just see myself doing something like that in Darlene's name. Or maybe I'd put both our names on it. "I bet that made her friend happy."

"Thea should have said *in memory of* her friend," Laura told me. "Julia's friend wanted to be a writer and, as I heard it, wrote dozens of manuscripts, but never had enough courage to send them to a publisher."

"What happened to her friend?"

Laura sighed. "Apparently, she destroyed all her manuscripts, then jumped out of a twelfth-floor window."

"How awful!" I said.

"There's no point in going into any of the arts unless
you have a dedication and determination to achieve,"
Laura began, then suddenly changed direction as a
thought struck her. "Will Julia's husband be here too? You
know Jake, don't you? The poor boy never was able to
make it as an actor, even though he's a *very* attractive
man."

"Augustus didn't invite him," Thea said, and looked
embarrassed as she tried to explain. "He didn't invite Senator Maggio's wife either. That's United States Senator Arthur Maggio of Nevada."

"Has anyone else been invited?" Laura asked.

"One more guest," Thea answered. "Alex Chambers."

I'd heard the senator's name often enough, since we
lived in the same state, but I was a lot more interested in
the dress designer, Alex Chambers. His clothes were high-
class expensive, in tons of magazine ads, and it was a
good chance that if Laura Reed was wearing designer
jeans, *Alex Chambers* was the name on the label.

There was silence for a moment, until Laura murmured,
"I wonder if each of your other guests received the same
kind of threat I did."

"Oh, Laura, now really," Thea began, but Laura turned
the full wattage of her green-gold eyes on Thea and said,
"We're supposed to be players in a game. I just wonder
what the game is going to be."

Aunt Thea informed me that we would dress for dinner,
so I went up to my room and put on a dress and a long

string of Venetian glass beads that Darlene had given me for my birthday. I wondered why anyone who chose to live on an island would want to dress up and live in a castle with maids and butlers, when it made a lot more sense to wear shorts and go barefoot and live in an open, comfortable house where you could clean up by just sweeping the sand out the front door every morning.

I decided that if I became a famous writer, I'd do exactly that. Of course, at the moment I didn't know if I should try to become a writer or not. I was depending upon Augustus to tell me.

We were all supposed to gather downstairs for cocktails at seven, and I wasn't about to go down early all by myself, so I stood by the window and watched a swarm of dark clouds battle the sun, which struck out with shards of red and gold before it was smothered and dragged toward the sea.

The gloom was so intense that I turned on the bedside lamp. I sat on the edge of the bed, where I could keep one eye on the clock, and pulled my journal and a pen from the top drawer of the chest. The writers' magazines I read suggested that writers and would-be writers keep journals and write something in them every day. I had no problem with that because I like to write.

I wrote what I had thought about the sun, but that didn't lead anywhere, so I decided to write a description of the room I was in. Only I went even further and added some cobwebs and dust and the sound of something creeping up the stairs.

At the loud knock on my bedroom door I screeched, threw my journal into the air, and jumped to my feet.

"Are you all right, Miss Burns?" a muffled voice asked.

I staggered to the door, turned the key and opened it. "I'm fine, thank you," I told Walter. There was no way I was going to explain. He'd think I was pretty weird.

Walter looked at me as though he thought I was pretty weird anyway and said, "The guests have gathered in the front parlor, Miss Burns. Your aunt would be pleased to have you join them."

I had been so interested in what I'd been writing that I'd forgotten to watch the clock. "Okay," I said. "Thanks." I watched Walter descend the stairs before I locked the door. I hefted the big brass key in my hand, trying to decide what to do with it. My dress didn't have a handy pocket to hold it.

Inspiration struck, and I opened the clasp on the string of beads, ran the string through the large hole in the middle of the key, and fastened the clasp at the back of my neck. At least I'd have my key with me. I wasn't going to leave it in the door.

The long upstairs hallway was dim and deserted, except for me, and I hurried along, nearly running, because I had the awful feeling that someone—or something—was watching me. I practically galloped down the stairs, pausing only for a few seconds on the landing to glance at the burial urn, which, even in the shadows, seemed to glow.

"Listen, whoever you are," I whispered, "my name is Samantha Burns, and I'm an innocent bystander. I had nothing to do with your urn or your ashes, so if the scary feeling in this house is coming from you, please . . . leave me alone!"

I didn't wait for an answer. I certainly didn't want one! I just ran down the rest of the stairs and joined the lights and noise in the front parlor.

The room was festive with dozens and dozens of glowing candles and bowls of bright summer flowers. I began to relax and enjoy myself, especially after Aunt Thea—comfortably soft and gray in a cashmere knit dress the same shade as her hair—took me by the hand and introduced me to Senator Maggio, Alex Chambers, Buck Thompson, and Julia Bryant. I was in famous company!

Each of the guests smiled brilliantly in my direction and told me they were pleased, quite pleased, very pleased, or terribly pleased to meet me. Julia Bryant did remark on my necklace. "How exciting and unusual! That darling antique key looks so authentic and—hmmm—somehow familiar. Wherever did you find it? Neiman's?"

"No, in my door," I said, "and I don't really think it's an antique, because doesn't something have to be one hundred years old before it's called an antique?" Trying to make polite conversation, I continued. "One of my mother's friends has an antiques store, and she finds some of the most unbelievable things in . . ."

I stopped talking because they hadn't been listening and had gone back to their conversations. I even lost Aunt Thea as Julia put an arm around her shoulders, drew her into the semicircle she'd created with Alex and Laura, and said, "Thea, you must hear about the fantastic charity ball that our dear, generous Alex is underwriting."

I wasn't interested in Alex Chambers's charity ball, so I wandered away from the groups and stood alone, watching them. People-watching is good practice for anyone who wants to be a writer, according to my writers' magazines.

Buck Thompson's face was familiar. It would be to anyone who watched a pro football game on television. He was huge and beefy, his face tinged dark red like a medium rare steak. His hair was brown, thick, and unruly. It was Buck's own hair, not a toupee, so I'd have to tell Dad his guess was wrong. Buck's movements were overlarge and expansive. As he spoke with Senator Maggio, Buck just missed knocking a flower arrangement off a nearby table.

I'd seen Senator Maggio's face in the newspapers. Because he was round and bald I never thought he looked like a senator ought to look—especially one who's being considered as a possible presidential candidate. But he was well groomed. He wore a dark blue suit made out of some silky fabric, and he carried his head high. I wondered if he'd ever had a P.E. teacher like Mrs. Tribble in ninth grade, who kept saying, "For good posture, pretend there's a string at the top of your head, girls, and it's pulling, pulling, pulling you upward."

A laugh tinkled like broken glass, and I turned toward the sound. Laura, in a long, plain gown of deep blue silk, her hair brushed out in a golden glow, looked softer, younger, and prettier in the candlelight. Again she laughed, but the brittle sound told me that she was every bit as wary and nervous as she had been earlier.

Julia had dressed like a twenty-year-old model in kelly green satin, with a skirt hem high above her knees and a low-scooped neckline. Her hair was dyed red, and she wore layers of makeup. If Darlene were here, she'd agree with me that it didn't help Julia Bryant to try to look young. She had to be at least fifty. "No. What you heard was wrong. I'm just an old-fashioned girl," she was saying. "I'm not the least bit mechanical-minded and hate having to use computers."

Alex Chambers smiled from one woman to the other. "You should try computerizing designs," he said. He was tall and slender, with wisps of dark hair and large brown eyes which blinked a lot when he wasn't squinting. I bet he wore glasses when no one was around. He had on tight slacks with a twisted rope holding them up, instead of a belt, and a silk shirt the color of whipped cream. The shirt was buttoned only halfway up, but the opening was filled with a knotted, bright, multicolored scarf.

People-watching was interesting for only so long. I wandered over to a large round table in a nearby corner, which was cluttered with dozens of photographs. In each of them Augustus Trevor—mostly young or middle-aged —was buddy-buddy with someone who looked important and official. I recognized Prince Rainier of Monaco and the Shah of Iran, but the others were unfamiliar.

As I picked up an ornate silver frame, Mrs. Engstrom appeared beside me. She carried a small tray of canapes, but she seemed more interested in the photo in my hand. "That's Mr. Trevor with the late King George the Sixth of England," she said. With her free hand she pointed to one photo after another. "That's King Juan Carlos of Spain, the late king Gustav Adolph of Sweden, King Fahd of Saudi Arabia, the late king Frederick the Ninth of Denmark . . ."

"They're all royalty?" I asked.

"All of them," she said. "In fact, Mr. Trevor calls this 'the Kings' Corner.' " Mrs. Engstrom's mouth had a strange twist to it, as though she thought this was putting things on a little too much.

As Mrs. Engstrom moved on to pass the canapes to the

other guests, Lucy came into the room with a tray of assorted drinks and handed me a glass of ginger ale.

"Thanks," I said. Eager for someone to talk to, I asked, "Where's Mr. Trevor?"

"He'll be along," she said quietly, and glanced back at the open doorway. "He likes to come in after everybody else has been standing around waiting for him."

I wanted to ask more about Augustus Trevor, but Lucy left, delivering drinks to the other guests. Walter was busy too, so I was trying to decide whether to stand by myself, looking stupid, or stand with one of the groups, looking stupid, when Augustus Trevor entered the parlor. Conversations stopped in midsentence as we all turned toward him. In the silence a gust of wind suddenly rattled the windows, and I wasn't the only one who jumped.

Augustus looked like a character in one of the old movies Mom and Dad like to rent. He was casually dressed in a dark red velvet jacket with a belt that tied around his pudgy middle. Augustus also wore dark slacks and loafers without socks, and smiled charmingly at his guests. "How delighted I am that all of you could come," he said, and made a little bow. "Welcome to our humble home."

Laura gave a sigh, as though she'd begun breathing again, and Senator Maggio cleared his throat. Julia was the first to come forward. She clutched Augustus's shoulders and blew smacky kisses near both ears.

"You darling man, I've been so excited. What *is* this wonderful imaginative game you've thought up for us?"

I saw Buck and the senator glance knowingly at each other, so that answered one question. Each of these guests had received the same kind of invitation. *Threat*, Laura had called it.

Augustus chuckled and draped an arm around Julia's shoulders. "All will be explained when the game commences," he said, and went through the room greeting the other guests with the warmth of a gracious host. I could see what Aunt Thea meant when she had said Augustus could be charming when he wanted to be.

Augustus even had a smile for me, which made me instantly hopeful. When the weekend was over and his guests had left, he'd offer to read my stories and critique them. I *knew* he would.

But there was something even more pressing I wanted to ask him. "Tell me about the ghost," I said.

He stepped back, and his eyes bugged out, but he didn't answer, so I said, "You know, the ghost in the haunted burial urn. Isn't there some kind of legend?"

Augustus's eyes narrowed. He hunched forward and grabbed my shoulders as he growled in my right ear, "There's not only a legend, it also has a curse with it. It's as simple as this: Stay away from that urn or there will be nothing left of you."

"That's not a very nice legend," I mumbled, and squirmed out of his grip.

"It's not a very nice ghost," he snapped, and hobbled over to talk to the senator.

What a crab! His charm didn't last long, as far as I was concerned. I felt sorry for the ghost and hoped he'd give Augustus Trevor a bad time.

The dinner was interesting, since I was never quite sure what had been served. There were purple and yellow crunchy things in my salad—things that aren't too common in Elko, Nevada—and the thin slices of meat rested in some kind of creamy sauce with a red design drizzled around the edges. There were rows of forks at the left and one above the plate, but I stopped trying to figure out the silverware and menu so I could listen to the celebrities and what they had to say.

The earlier mood of caution and suspicion had faded, and everyone talked and laughed a lot. Senator Maggio and Buck, who sat across the table from each other, compared notes about bloopers they'd made in high school football, and somehow the senator worked the conversation around to grandchildren and brought out some pictures of two fluffy-dressed little toddlers. He beamed when he talked about the little girls, but since Thea seemed to be the only one interested in them, his grandfatherly bragging didn't have much of a chance.

Julia, who was seated next to the senator, sparkled as she discussed book tours and confessed to sneaking under a fence to get away from a pair of excited fans. Laura, on my right, tried to top Julia's stories by telling us about some of her harrowing experiences on movie sets.

It was fascinating to me to see some of the celebrity glow peel away like banana skins, giving a glimpse of real people inside; and I wondered if these people often hid inside protective skins so no one could guess their thoughts and feelings. I was just a beginner at this people-watching business, but it was obvious to me that Augustus was the only one who was any good at being famous.

Julia, the author, was like an actress playing the role of one of her sophisticated fictional heroines, and yet at times she looked unsure of herself, and I saw her watch the others questioningly, as though she wasn't quite sure they were taking her seriously. Buck, who sat at my left, was just as nervous—maybe even more ill at ease. He grabbed a spoon to finish off the sauce, then dropped it and turned red when he saw me watching him. And now I knew what the expression in Laura's green-gold eyes reminded me of: our neighbor's dog's puppies who wiggled and yipped and looked up with huge, begging eyes at everyone who came in sight, as though they were saying, "Love *me*. Oh, please, love *me*!"

Senator Maggio, no longer a doting grandfather, had become controlled and polished again; and Alex never dropped his smug conceit. Both of them were safe inside their banana skins, and I wondered what it would take to make them come out.

It had begun to rain, not a soft rain or even a steadily tapping rain. It came in bursts with the wind, whipping against the window like small stones, and I was glad none of us had to go outside in that storm.

We had just polished off a tart filled with fresh mixed berries and soft vanilla custard, when Augustus's voice boomed out. "Please give me your attention, my friends. I have an important announcement to make."

FOUR

Buck's water goblet went over, and water sloshed on the table as he grabbed for it. Julia giggled nervously, and Laura sucked in her breath. We all waited quietly as Augustus resettled himself in his chair before he continued.

"As you are all well aware," Augustus continued, "I am a novelist. I have never been interested in writing nonfiction." He paused and smiled. "Until a little over a year ago."

As we waited, none of us knowing what we were supposed to say, Augustus chuckled. "For the past thirty years," he told us, "I have been thoroughly involved in high society's self-centeredness and hypocrisy. It suited my purposes, and occasionally it provided characters and ideas for my stories."

"Oh, my, I knew it. Prince Rainier," Laura murmured. "Was he the basis for—"

Augustus leaned forward with a scowl. "I have not finished speaking," he thundered, and Laura cringed against the back of her chair.

Augustus was silent for a moment, and when he spoke again it was with a smile. "My current manuscript is not another novel. It is a book in which I intend to make public certain shocking behind-the-scenes behavior of a great many very important people."

Julia stiffened, and it was obvious that she couldn't keep silent, no matter how offended Augustus might be. "Are you telling us that we're included?" she asked.

Augustus grinned nastily. "Yes and no," he said.

"What is that supposed to mean?" Buck demanded.

"It means that while doing background research and interviews, in an attempt to supplement my notes and refresh my memory, I stumbled upon a well-hidden secret in the past life of each one of you."

"Ridiculous!" Senator Maggio snapped.

"Oh, is it?" Augustus asked, and his eyes gleamed. "If these secrets are made known, they'll be damaging enough to ruin your reputations, aside from other complications that might result."

"This is absurd," Alex interjected, but Augustus dismissed him with a wave of his hand and went on.

"Each of you committed one very stupid mistake in your past, yet the mistakes were never made public. Was this because you were actually smart enough to cover them, or because you were incredibly lucky?"

"Augustus, I protest!" Aunt Thea said. "You're embarrassing our guests, and—"

"Sit down, Thea," Augustus ordered, and she did.

"You are all highly successful in your careers," he continued, "and normally that takes a certain amount of intelligence. So what is the truth? Are you stupid, or are you not? I'm going to find out. During the weekend we're going to play a game, and you'll be given clues to solve. The clues will lead to a significant treasure—a treasure that in itself will be self-explanatory.

"If you can solve the clues, then you'll prove to me that your stupid mistakes can remain secret, and I'll remove every trace of your stories from my manuscript. For those who can't solve the clues, the world will soon learn the shocking facts from your past."

"This manuscript you're threatening us with—have you written it or are you simply threatening to write it?" Alex demanded.

"Oh, I've completed it," Augustus answered. "It's ready for its final revision before I send it to my agent, who will proceed to read it immediately and send it on to my publisher. In its current form, your mistakes are detailed."

"Where is this manuscript?" Buck asked. He scowled from under his heavy eyebrows, and his anger was so strong that for a moment I was afraid.

But Augustus wasn't. He leaned back and smiled. "Violence won't accomplish what you want, my dear Mr. Thompson. Clear and sharp thinking will."

Buck hunched over in his chair and grumbled, "I don't know what you've got in mind, but you won't get away with it, Augustus."

Suddenly Senator Maggio shoved back his chair and got to his feet. Tiny lines at the corners of his eyes twitched, and his lips were so tightly pressed together, they were pale. "I'm leaving," he said. "Your weekend game is simply an exercise in self-aggrandizement, Augustus, and I want no part of it. Will you please make arrangements for your launch to take me to the mainland?"

"I'm leaving too!" Julia announced, and jumped to her feet.

Everyone got up except Augustus, and even though we were all looking down at him, he still seemed to be the most powerful figure in the room. I think it was because he never stopped smiling that wicked smile, even when he was talking.

"The launch was taken to the mainland and docked there for greater safety during the storm," he said. "I hadn't counted on any of you being foolish enough to refuse to play the game."

"There's a smaller boat," Buck said. "Is that gone too?"

"No," Augustus said, "but you'd have to be quite desperate and somewhat mad to take a boat like that in choppy seas."

The senator must have faced tough opponents before, because he remained calm. "Then I'll remain in my room until the launch is able to return," he said.

He began to turn away from the table, Julia tentatively following him, but Augustus warned, "Just remember, if you leave this room you'll lose your opportunity to have your damaging secret removed from the manuscript. I prefer that you all return to your seats so the game may begin."

"I don't have any damaging secrets," Julia murmured, but she slipped back into her chair.

After a brief moment of hesitation the others followed her lead, even Senator Maggio. Me? I was one of the first to be seated. I didn't want to miss a thing.

Mrs. Engstrom brought in a tray of tiny macaroons and

bonbons and quietly poured demitasse cups of coffee, passing them to the guests, who were all so intent on Augustus, they ignored her.

Aunt Thea, who sat at the far end of the table, seemed paler than usual and close to tears. Most of the guests looked down at their hands or away at the windows, not wanting to meet another pair of eyes, but Alex shrugged, as if he were only going along with the gag as a good sport, and asked Augustus, "You said the clues would lead to some kind of treasure. Exactly what is this treasure we'll be looking for?"

"You'll know it when you find it, and you'll find it through the clues," Augustus said, and his grin became broader.

"Aren't you going to help us?" Laura whispered.

"Of course," he answered. He reached into a deep pocket in his velvet jacket and brought out six sealed envelopes on which names had been printed in bright blue ink. He read out the names, then passed the envelopes down each side of the table to the correct recipient. Even Aunt Thea got one.

"You might call this a warm-up to the game," he said. "Inside each envelope you'll find a personal clue. You can test your skills by seeing what you can learn from what you've been given."

Julia didn't hesitate. She ripped open one end of the envelope and tugged out the contents. "This is a clue?" she asked. "It's nothing but part of an airline schedule, New York to Buffalo."

"And I've been given a train schedule," Senator Maggio complained.

Alex held up an enlarged section of what seemed to be a

detailed map and said with a touch of sarcasm, "Maybe Augustus is suggesting the three of us plan a trip together."

"In Vietnam?" I murmured. I'd been able to read a few of the names on the map.

Alex did a double-take, stared at the map a second, then folded it and dropped it into his shirt pocket. He didn't answer my question. He wouldn't even meet my eyes.

"Study your clues," Augustus said, and hunched over, chuckling to himself like some evil gnome.

Shamelessly, I looked over the shoulders on each side of me. Laura was holding a list of football games and scores, while Buck stared at a list of names and telephone numbers. One was circled: Peeples, Willie.

Laura said. "You made a mistake, Augustus. These football scores must be for Buck. They don't mean anything to me."

But Julia suddenly gasped as she stared at her clue, and the senator, his face darkening, angrily folded his paper into a hard, tight square, and stuffed it into his pocket.

Thea suddenly spoke up. "Augustus, I don't want to be a part of this game."

He nodded toward her, giving a kind of bow, but he said, "Oh, yes you do, Thea."

"How could you?" she whispered. Tears came to her eyes, and her fingers trembled as she folded what looked like a travel brochure—I could read the word *Acapulco*—and tucked it back into the envelope.

"None of this makes sense to me," Laura said.

I reached for her clue. "Would you like me to help you?" I asked. "I'm really good at clues and codes and stuff like that. When we were younger a friend and I spent years making up crazy codes to solve."

I realized that I had the attention of all of them, but Laura didn't seem to notice and said, "Oh, thank you, Sam. If you can figure this out, I'll be eternally grateful."

"Figure it out yourself, Laura!" Augustus snapped. "That's the point of this experiment—to see if you're smart enough to save your own skins!"

"I'm sorry," I mumbled. "I was just trying to help."

"You want a clue?" he went on. "All right, Samantha, I'll give you a clue. In fact, yours may make more sense than all the rest of them." He pulled a scrap of paper out of his pocket and bent over it, hiding it as if he were taking a test, wiggling the fingers on his left hand, while with his right hand he wrote. When he'd finished writing, he folded it over and gave it to Laura, who passed it to me.

When I smoothed the paper out flat I saw a series of numbers and recognized a simple letter–number code that Darlene and I used way back in fourth grade: One stands for *A*, two for *B*, and so on.

7–5–20   12–15–19–20

Insult me with something like that, would he? I crumpled the paper into a wad and glared at Augustus.

The others had been watching, but Laura had been leaning over my shoulder. "Ohhh," she said. "It was written in code, and she figured it out so fast! She *is* good!"

"Perhaps I underestimated you," Augustus said to me.

"Perhaps," I murmured, and tilted my nose in the air until it occurred to me that I probably looked as conceited as Alex.

"Augustus, what did you mean, Sam's clue may make the most sense?" Julia asked.

Still angry, I didn't give him a chance to answer. "It doesn't," I said. "Why would he want to give something special to me? He was just kidding."

The rain increased with such force that when Thea spoke no one could hear her, and she had to repeat, "Augustus, what are we supposed to do now?"

Augustus propped his hands on the edge of the table, elbows protruding like chicken wings, and shouted, "It's late. I'd suggest you all retire to your rooms and meditate on the meanings you've found in your clues."

"What meanings?" Laura asked in a pitiful voice, but Augustus ignored her.

"There'll be another set of clues for you in the morning," he said.

Thunder slammed and rolled around the house, and I wasn't the only one who jumped.

"The storm may interfere with your sleep, but you won't have to worry about any loss of electricity," Augustus said. "We have our own generator."

Everyone began leaving the dining room, and I glanced toward Laura, whose bleak, miserable expression reminded me of the look that our school's halfback, Moose Munchberg, gets whenever he has to take any kind of test. Augustus had told me not to help Laura, and his glance was firmly on me, so I bypassed her, kissed Aunt Thea's cheek, and said good night.

Thea's skin was cold, and she clung to me for just an instant.

"I can help you," I whispered, "no matter what Augustus says."

But Thea shook her head and answered, "Thank you, Samantha. You're a dear girl, but I've already deciphered my clue. Better be off to bed. Breakfast will be served anytime after seven."

I passed Mrs. Engstrom at the dining room door. She stood as quietly and motionless as a mummy—her lips held in a tight, angry line and her eyes glittering in the dim light—so I started when I saw her.

"Good night, Miss Burns," she said.

"Good night, Mrs. Engstrom." I wasn't quite sure what a housekeeper did. Maybe she planned things. Maybe she took care of the cooking. Politely I said, "That was a very good dinner. I liked the . . . uh . . . chicken?"

"Veal," she said. "I'll tell the cook. Good night."

I hurried up to my tower room, eagerly turning on the light and locking the door behind me. The storm was really noisy up here, but in a way I kind of liked the whoosh and slam of the wind and rain. It slapped the walls and rattled the windows in a sort of rhythm, like waves crashing on rocks, while lightning slashed the blackness with blue-white explosions.

I decided to write that description in my journal, but when I sat on the edge of the bed, curiosity got the best of me, and I opened the crumpled wad of paper I was still holding.

I hadn't quickly deciphered it, as Laura had thought. I'd been too angry about the little-kid code. So now I took enough time to work out which letter went with which number and came up with the message: GET LOST.

Funny. Very funny. I didn't see a wastepaper basket, so instead of tossing the paper, I stuffed it into the pocket of my jeans, which were still draped across the bed.

Okay, I thought. *You want me to get lost? Then I will!* The minute the launch came back I'd leave the island, and tomorrow I'd ask Aunt Thea to lend me enough money to get another plane ticket home. I'd stay with Darlene and her family and refuse to let myself worry about what my parents would have to say.

I'd had all I was going to take from this horrible man with his crazy game.

FIVE

I didn't sleep very well that night, and I'm sure none of the others did either. The storm picked up in intensity, and—even with my down pillow wadded on top of my head—the noise of the wind and rain and thunder was incredible.

Was that the creaking sound of a door opening? I sat up in bed, clutching the blanket and sheet to my chin and listened as hard as I could. Footsteps . . . up the little stairs. Footsteps . . . coming closer . . . closer . . . closer. Was the doorknob turning? It was too dark to tell. As the key seemed to rattle in the lock I cried out, "Stop, or I'll shoot!"

A heavy blast of wind slammed against the windows, and I told myself I couldn't have heard soft footsteps under all the noise the storm was making. It had to have been my imagination. My face grew warm with embarrassment when I realized what I had just yelled. How dumb could I get? I must have heard that awful line while my parents were watching their old rental movies, and it stuck in my head. Thank goodness I was off by myself where no one could hear me!

But the key jiggled again just as lightning brightened the room. I saw it. For an instant I think my heart stopped, and my whole body turned cold. Footsteps or no footsteps, what was making the key jump like that?

I climbed out of bed and ran barefoot to the door, just in time to catch the key as it tumbled from the lock.

Someone had poked it out of the door!

As fast and quietly as I could manage, with my hands shaking so violently, they could hardly aim the key, I shoved it back into the keyhole. If someone had wanted my key out so their key could unlock my door, as I suspected, they'd find they couldn't get away with it.

My key hit against something hard, and I thought I heard someone on the other side of the door grunt in surprise.

I waited for the person to try to dislodge my key again, but it didn't happen.

Was someone still there? Had he left when the key trick hadn't worked? Or, with all the noise of the thunder and wind, had I just imagined what I thought I'd heard? Maybe no one had been outside my door at all.

I was scared to death, but still so curious I couldn't stand it. I slid out my key and bent down to peer through the empty keyhole. Lightning lit up the sky, and in that sudden white-bright flash, I saw the gleam of an eye looking back at me.

I screamed. I couldn't help it. And for a moment everything got blurry and fuzzy. My head buzzed, and I thought I was going to faint. Luckily I didn't, because I heard footsteps running away down the stairs and knew whoever had come to my room had gone. What was the person after? I didn't have anything of value. Could it have been my clue? Did someone want to know what message Augustus had given me? I wished Augustus hadn't been so flippant about it. Someone probably had believed him when he said that my clue may have made more sense than all the rest of them.

Clutching the key tightly, I climbed back into bed. I knew I wouldn't sleep. I'd probably never sleep as long as I was in this house!

But at some point I opened my eyes and found that the thunder and lightning were off in the distance and the room had grown lighter. I checked my wristwatch and discovered that it was already eight o'clock in the morning. No wonder I was starving. I bathed and dressed in a hurry, pocketed my key, and hurried downstairs through those dim, gloomy halls, moving even faster as I passed old somebody-or-other's burial urn. I was eager to reach the dining room, which was bright with the light from the huge crystal chandelier. I didn't like being alone. I needed someone to talk to.

Unfortunately, no one else was there.

The table had been reset, and on the sideboard there was an array of covered warming dishes, bowls of strawberries and melon, platters of rolls and muffins, and small boxes of cereal. I was glad to find that this food was familiar, and there weren't any artistic sauces to confuse me, so I helped myself to some of everything except the cereal—I could have cornflakes at home—and sat down to eat.

"Good morning, Miss Burns. Is there anything else you'd like?" As she entered the room Mrs. Engstrom eyed my heaping plate, then walked to the nearest warming dish and peeked inside as though to reassure herself I hadn't taken *all* the eggs. "Please tell me if there's anything you need or if there is anything I can do for you. I want your stay here to be as comfortable as possible."

"Thank you," I said, and then I blurted out, "Mrs. Engstrom, I haven't told Aunt Thea yet, but I will as soon as I see her, and I'm telling you because you probably have to plan for how many there are at meals and all that . . ." I took a deep breath and tried to slow down. "What I mean is, I'm going home as soon as the storm is over and the launch comes back."

I expected her to nod formally, but instead her face softened, and she said, "Your aunt will be disappointed. She told me how much she was looking forward to your visit."

"But not everyone here wants me," I began, and uncomfortably shifted in my chair.

"Your aunt does and she's lonely," Mrs. Engstrom told me.

I nodded. "I'd be lonely too, if I had to live in this castle, away from my friends and the malls and all that. Aunt Thea and—and Aug—and her husband used to travel a lot, and I remember Mom talking about their town house in New York City. I don't understand why they decided to hole up here."

"Mr. Trevor has always come here to write," she said. "He demands complete quiet. When he's working on a book, no one—not even Mrs. Trevor—is allowed in his office."

I didn't mean to pry, but I was curious. "But what does Aunt Thea do to keep busy while they're living here?"

Mrs. Engstrom's lips tightened again, and she said,

"Mr. Trevor has never wanted to hire a secretary, so Mrs. Trevor has always done the job. She answers Mr. Trevor's mail. You wouldn't believe how much mail he gets. There's fan mail, and invitations to speak to various groups, and requests for donations—all sorts of things—and she takes all his phone calls, and watches out that he's not disturbed while he's working or resting."

"But what does she do for fun? I saw a cribbage board in Aug—uh—Mr. Trevor's office. Do they play cribbage? Read? Watch TV?" I sidetracked myself by asking, "There *is* a television set somewhere around, isn't there?"

"I'm sorry," Mrs. Engstrom said. "It's too difficult to get good reception here."

I wanted to ask her more about Aunt Thea, but Mrs. Engstrom's face had closed over, like someone pulling down a shade, and I had to admit to myself that I had no right to get nosy. "All right, I'll stay," I called after Mrs. Engstrom as she turned and moved toward the door.

She stopped and actually smiled at me, and I could see how protective she was of Aunt Thea. I guessed that the staff all detested Augustus and loved Thea, and must be here only because they were paid awfully well.

My mouth was full of hash browns when Laura Reed staggered into the dining room and flopped into a chair. "Coffee," she groaned. "There must be coffee around here."

I got up and brought her a cup of coffee. It was hot and black. She sipped at it for a few minutes, and apparently it did something for her, because she began to wake up. She sat a little straighter, took a deep breath, and looked to each side, twisting to peer behind her.

"Do you want something else?" I asked. "Breakfast is over there." Pointedly, I added, "It's a serve-yourself."

"I'm not hungry," she whispered, and leaned toward me, shoving a folded paper into my hand. "I just wanted to make sure that Augustus wasn't skulking around someplace. Honestly! The nerve of that man! He reminds me of the director on my last picture. Terrible personalities, both of them."

I opened the paper and saw that it was the list of football scores.

"You offered to help me," Laura said. "So help. Okay?"

"Augustus said . . ." Oh, who cared what Augustus had said. I scanned the list. "Have you tried to work it out yourself?"

Laura sighed. "Work out what? I didn't even read it. I don't know anything about football scores or what they mean."

"I don't know all the teams myself," I said. I checked the first of the scores to see if they were in that easy number-code, and they weren't, but maybe there was another kind of clue in one of the numbers. "I'll read the list out loud," I told her. "If anything seems familiar to you, just speak up. One of these numbers might be a locker number, or part of an old address, or something like that."

She nodded, and I began to read: "Final Scores: Rams 14, Buffalo Bills 6; Falcons 13, Oilers 21; Giants 6, Forty-Niners 7; Emerald Bay 1, Stars 0."

There were a lot more listed, but I didn't read them, because Laura let out a tiny, high-pitched shriek, sounding like a mouse being chased by a cat. She clapped her hands to her cheeks, gasped as though she were hyperventilating, and stared at me in terror.

"What happened?" I asked.

"Nothing!" she wheezed, and snatched the paper out of my hand.

"Something I read must have—"

"Never mind! Forget about it!" Laura jumped to her feet and ran out of the room.

She couldn't have worried that much about the scores. Was it the Emerald Bay and Stars teams that upset her? I'd never heard of either team, but then I wasn't that much of a football fan. I buttered a muffin and began to eat it. The people in this house were getting stranger and stranger.

By the time I'd finished breakfast Alex and Julia had come downstairs. Alex had dark bags under his eyes, and Julia looked terrible. The heavy makeup she wore hadn't helped a bit. I tried to make some kind of conversation with them, but Alex made it obvious that he didn't want to talk.

Julia seemed to like to talk about herself, so I said, "I couldn't believe it when Norelle died."

Julia peered at me over the rim of her coffee cup. "Who?"

"Norelle. In your *Sudden Surrender*. I watched it on TV."

"Oh," she mumbled, and then she said, "Oh" again as though she'd suddenly figured out who I was talking about.

"Why did you decide to have her die?"

"I—I guess it just seemed to fit the plot."

"Even though Prince Eric wanted to marry her?"

"Tough luck for him," she mumbled.

"Wait a minute," I said. "I was mixed up. Prince Eric wasn't in *Sudden Surrender*. He was in *Leftover Love*."

Julia seemed flustered, and a couple of drops of coffee

sloshed onto the saucer as she put down her cup. "Oh. That's right," she said.

I chuckled. "I can see how *I* could get mixed up about which of your characters were in which book, but it's funny that you would, too."

She didn't look too happy, so I searched my mind for something else having to do with writing. "When you were first starting out as a writer, did you get many rejections?" I asked.

She had just put her coffee cup to her lips, and she made a kind of funny sputtering sound in it. She managed to wipe off her mouth and chin before she turned and clutched my arm with one hand. Her long fingernails hurt. "What do you mean by that?" she demanded.

Alex had stopped eating to watch us, and that seemed to upset Julia even more. "Tell me," she snapped. "What do you mean?"

Startled, and a little bit scared of her, I tugged my arm away and slid my chair out of her reach. "I—I'm hoping to be a writer too," I said quickly, "and I need to know all sorts of things, and I don't have any writers at home to talk to. Of course, when I was in the ninth grade an author came to visit our school. She's one of my very favorite authors, and I love her books, but she told us that her first book was rejected twelve times, and then the thirteenth publisher—"

"Stop!" Julia cried, and clapped her hands over her ears. "I didn't ask for a history of your life."

"I was just trying to explain," I said. "The visiting author told us her husband encouraged her to keep trying. Did your husband encourage you?"

Julia put both hands on the table to steady herself and frowned at me. "Who put you up to this? Augustus?"

"Put me up to what? I was just trying to be friendly."

She studied me for a moment, then seemed satisfied and went back to staring into the bottom of her coffee cup. "I can't think this early in the morning, so no more quizzes. Haven't you got something better to do?"

"I'm sorry," I mumbled, even more embarrassed because I could feel myself blushing. I pushed back my chair and left the dining room. What a grouch Julia was! I bet she wouldn't tell me about any early rejections of her manuscripts because she'd had a million of them.

In the entry hall Aunt Thea met me with a smile. "I've got fresh orange juice and cinnamon rolls in the sunroom," she said. "You probably didn't feel like eating much breakfast, Samantha. Why don't you settle in with me, and we'll nibble on rolls and enjoy the storm?"

"You enjoy storms too?" I asked.

She put an arm around my shoulders, and I put one of mine around her waist. In spite of my anger at Augustus, I really wouldn't have walked out on Aunt Thea. I was glad that I had told Mrs. Engstrom I'd changed my mind about leaving.

When we'd settled into comfortable chairs in the sunroom, I asked Aunt Thea some of the same questions I'd asked Mrs. Engstrom. Aunt Thea was an intelligent, active woman, and I couldn't imagine that she'd be happy hidden away here, trying to placate her husband. As she talked about some of the famous people they'd visited and who had visited them in New York and here on the island, I tried to figure it out. She was here either because she was still very much in love with Augustus, or because she was afraid of him, or because . . . maybe . . .

I began to wonder if he might have some hold over her. He'd included Thea in the game. Did that mean she had a secret in her past life? One too awful to be made public?

But Thea was Augustus Trevor's wife! What kind of a monster would terrify his own wife?

Laura came into the room and sat on one of the wicker couches. She stretched out and sighed dramatically before she said, "Whatever Augustus plans to do, I wish he'd get it over with. This waiting is horrible. I tried to call my agent, and would you believe, because of the storm your phone is out."

Alex, still carrying his coffee cup, wandered in, stared out the windows for a moment, then perched next to Laura. "I hate rain," he said. "It makes everything look dreary."

"I'm sorry about the storm," Thea said. "I'm sure none of us slept well."

"As a matter of fact I did," Alex said. He drained the cup and put it on a nearby table. "I even slept quite late this morning."

"Probably because you were up so late last night," Laura said.

He shot her a glance from the corners of his eyes. "I wasn't up late. We all went upstairs together, as I remember."

Laura shook her head. "Your room is next to mine. I heard you moving around and your door opening and closing. I looked at my bedside clock, and it was nearly midnight."

I perked up and listened carefully. Had it been Alex at my door?

"I don't know what you heard, but it wasn't me," Alex insisted.

"It couldn't have been anyone else."

"Laura dear," he said, "you're beginning to sound like a busybody."

Laura apparently decided not to continue the argument, but she pressed her lips together in a pout and glared at Alex before she said, "You're such an inspiring person, Alex. It's wonderful how you managed to achieve so much when you had the terrible handicap of a dysfunctional childhood."

"Laura . . ." The word sounded like a warning.

"Even changing your name," she said. "Of course, I suppose that didn't bother you, since you never knew your parents and Alex Chambers has so much more . . . marketing appeal than—what was it? Keriomaglopolous or something like that?"

Thea reached over and patted Alex's arm. "No one's childhood is perfect," she said. "If you had a difficult time, then I'm sure it helped you to be even more sympathetic and understanding of others."

He glanced sharply, questioningly, at Thea, mumbled "Thank you," then stared down at his white ostrich boots as though he hadn't seen them before.

His air of conceit had vanished, and I felt sorry for him for thinking he needed it as a security blanket. Why couldn't he be proud that he'd been able to rise above his early poverty?

Julia wandered into the sun-room, complaining, "So here's where everyone is gathering. No one told me." She dragged a small wooden chair from its place by the wall, in order to sit close to the group. "Arthur's furious," she announced. "He tried to get through to his Washington office, but your phone isn't working."

"I'm sorry," Thea apologized. "We often lose phone service during bad weather."

Laura sighed. "When *is* this dreadful storm going to be over?"

Lucy, who had just arrived with fresh hot coffee, said, "Mrs. Trevor, the weather reporter on the radio said he's not counting on good weather until Monday or Tuesday."

There was a general groan, but Thea said, "Thank you, Lucy. If you see Senator Maggio, will you please ask him to join us?"

"Yes, ma'am," Lucy said, but as she left the room the senator and Buck passed her.

"We heard voices," Buck said, and he pulled up another of the small, straight-backed chairs that stood against the wall. Senator Maggio did the same, squeezing his chair into the circle. It occurred to me that we were like a group of pioneers, drawing our wagons into a ring for protection.

Buck was his unruly, beefy self, but Senator Maggio probably looked worse than anyone else in the room. His face sagged, and his eyes were sunken behind such dark circles, he looked as though someone had punched him.

"I'm afraid you didn't get much sleep last night," Thea said gently. "Didn't the hot milk help?"

"Not a bit," he said, then quickly added, "but you were kind to prepare it for me."

Thea smiled at him. "It's fortunate that we were both restless at the same time."

"So you were downstairs too," Laura said. She smiled and tossed a sharp glance in Alex's direction. "Thea, did you, by any chance, run into Alex? Around midnight?"

Thea shook her head. "It was after two when I decided I'd never get to sleep and I wandered down to the kitchen."

Now it was Alex's turn to stare smugly at Laura.

So . . . Senator Maggio had been wandering around the house last night too. But then, so had Aunt Thea. I still couldn't figure out who had been at my door.

Julia let out a long, aggrieved sigh. "That's neither here nor there," she said. "We're all waiting for Augustus to make his next move. Where is he?"

"He's usually down by this time," Thea said, and looked at her watch. She pressed a little button by her chair, and in less than a minute Walter appeared.

"Will you please see what's keeping Mr. Trevor?" she asked, and with a nod Walter left.

We could hear voices in the entry hall, and we all listened, thinking Walter had met up with Augustus, but one voice was a woman's, and it sounded sharp and agitated. It must have been Lucy's.

"You seem to have a devoted staff," Julia said. "I can't imagine how you'd find anyone willing to live out here away from civilization."

"I suppose we're very fortunate," Thea answered. "Lucy and Tomás, our cook, have been with us just a short while, and Walter only a year or two longer; but Frances Engstrom has been in our employ for over thirty years, and has become a dear and close friend."

"Only you, Thea, would make friends of the household

help," Julia said, and rolled her eyes, but I thought it was nice that Thea and Mrs. Engstrom were good friends.

The senator pointedly looked at his watch and grunted with exasperation, while Buck said, "Take it easy, Arthur. We aren't going anywhere."

"I'd like to get this so-called game over with," Senator Maggio said.

Alex began to answer him, but again we heard voices in the hall, and there was no mistaking that somebody was *very* upset.

We were all staring toward the open doorway when Mrs. Engstrom, Lucy, and Walter appeared. Mrs. Engstrom was pale and she fought to regain her balance as a tearful Lucy clung to her. "Mrs. Trevor," Mrs. Engstrom said, but her voice wobbled and she couldn't continue.

Walter made an effort to collect himself. He stood a little taller, took a deep breath, and said, "Mrs. Trevor, Lucy discovered that Mr. Trevor's bed had not been slept in, so I went to his office to see if he had spent the night there on the couch."

He gulped, and I could see his Adam's apple wobble up and down before he continued. "I'm sorry, Mrs. Trevor. Mr. Trevor is dead."

Thea gasped and half rose to her feet, but Lucy shrieked, "He's not just dead, Mrs. Trevor! There's blood on his head, and there's blood splattered on his desk! Mr. Trevor was murdered!"

SIX

ucy had been right about the blood. There was a
lot of it. We all rushed to the door of Augustus's
office and tried to push and elbow our way inside—but not too far inside. It was as though we really
couldn't believe what had happened to Augustus unless
we actually saw it for ourselves.

Augustus Trevor was seated in his chair, his head on the
desk next to the computer keyboard. One bent arm covered his face.

This was not a TV cop show in which the problem
would be over in half an hour. Augustus Trevor had been
a real person whose life had been taken away. I suddenly
felt sick. For a moment it was hard to breathe, and I found
that I was shaking. I held on to the door frame for support
and took a couple of long, shuddering breaths to steady
myself. The horrible feeling gradually slid away, and I
knew I'd be able to handle the situation.

However, Laura moaned softly and gracefully sank to
the floor, sitting with her back against the wall, her hands

clasped in her lap while silent tears spilled from her closed eyelids. I would have offered to help her—at least bring her a glass of water—except that I'd seen her do exactly the same thing when she was playing the part of a woman whose husband went off to battle in that Revolutionary War movie she starred in a few years ago.

Alex gagged, turned white, and ran from the room, shoving Buck aside with more strength than I'd thought he had.

"Ouch!" Buck muttered as he staggered into the pointed open drawer of a nearby file cabinet.

I suddenly remembered Thea and turned to look for her. She was standing just outside the door, Mrs. Engstrom's arms around her.

"She'll be all right," Mrs. Engstrom said as her glance met mine. "It's a terrible shock, but don't worry. She'll be all right."

I nodded. Thea's face hadn't lost its color, and she seemed to be in good hands.

I went back to the door of the office as Senator Maggio ordered everyone, "Stay away from the crime scene. There's evidence here that should be protected."

"If you're looking for the murder weapon, it's probably that fireplace thing," Julia said, and pointed at the sharp-ended brass poker that lay on the floor.

There were dark stains near the point, so she might have been right; but something else had caught my attention. The mesh screen across the fireplace that would normally have been closed was open, and lying among the ashes were some curled and cracked metal and plastic pieces.

"Look at the fireplace," I told the others. "Someone has burned some computer disks."

In one bound Buck fell to his knees before the fireplace and groped among the ashes, jerking out the disks and making a terrible mess. "There's scraps of paper too," Buck said. "Looks like typing paper."

He got to his feet, one hand holding aloft the disks and a couple of scorched corners from typing paper—one with the page number 395 printed on it—while he tried to wipe the ashes from his other hand on the seat of his jeans.

"Do you think those are the backup disks containing the manuscript Augustus was telling us about?" Julia asked.

"I hope so," Laura answered, and I saw that she was back on her feet.

"Turn on the computer," Julia said. "There must be a file. . . ."

Senator Maggio flipped the Off switch and said, "I've already tried it. There's no file. Everything has been wiped out."

"If someone destroyed the file, the manuscript, and the disks, he's put an end to the threat," Alex said from behind me. Apparently he'd made a quick recovery.

Julia's mouth twisted as she added, "And put an end to Augustus, as well."

"Who did it?" Laura whispered.

A long moment of silence followed as we all realized that one person in this room was a murderer. I could feel tickly drops of sweat skitter down my backbone, and I shivered. "The murderer has to be someone who's familiar with computers," I said, "someone who'd know how to delete the file."

Julia was the first to respond. "I don't use a computer. I write in longhand, and Jake types up the finished manuscript for me."

"I don't use a computer," the senator said.

"Me either," Buck answered.

Alex shook his head.

"Well, don't everybody look at me, for goodness' sakes," Laura complained. "I've never had a reason even to touch one of those things."

I didn't look at her. I glanced from Julia to Alex to Senator Maggio. No matter what they'd just said, a few minutes ago each of them had proved that they knew enough about computers to understand files and disks. Each of them was lying.

"We must notify the police," Senator Maggio said.

"We can't," I told him. "The phone lines are out. Remember?"

This called for another moment of silence. Each of us sneaked appraising looks at the others while trying not to be seen doing it.

Finally, Julia said, "Let's face some plain facts and look at the positive side. Whatever Augustus had in mind for us is over now."

I heard Thea's sharp intake of breath, and I wasn't the only one who was disgusted with Julia for being so insensitive. Senator Maggio scowled at her and asked in a low voice, "Are you forgetting that Trevor's wife is present?"

Julia looked embarrassed, but she said, "All I meant was that the manuscript has been destroyed."

"No, it hasn't," I said.

Everyone turned to look at me. "Everything on the hard disk in the computer was deleted, and the backup disks were burned, along with what looks like a printed copy of the manuscript," I told them, "but Aug-Augustus was a professional writer. He wouldn't print just one copy of his manuscript. He'd have made one to send to his agent— which he said hadn't been sent yet—and one for himself. Even though the manuscript would be on his computer's hard disk and on backup disks, writers always make at least two printed copies of everything they write."

"How do you know all this?" Laura asked me.

"I read the writers' magazines." I turned to Julia for support. "You're a writer. You do the same thing with your manuscripts, don't you?"

Julia's mouth opened and closed and opened again. "Well, sure," she said. "My—um—secretary does."

Mrs. Engstrom asked Aunt Thea, "Is it true what your niece said?"

"Yes," Thea answered. "Augustus always made a second copy of every completed manuscript."

"Where did he keep the copies?" the senator asked.

"He always kept his notes and materials for whatever manuscript he was working on currently in the top drawer of that file cabinet." She pointed, and we all turned to look. It was the drawer that had been standing open. "Since he said the manuscript had been completed, there should have been two copies of the manuscript in that drawer, as well."

Buck peered inside and shook his head. "It's empty."

"Maybe both copies were burned." Laura's voice was high-pitched and excited with hope.

The senator bent to study the contents of the fireplace. "I doubt it," he said. "Considering that we know there were at least three hundred and ninety-five typewritten pages in that manuscript, if not more, there isn't enough ash here to account for two manuscripts."

"If there's another copy, then we should look for it," Alex said.

"Do we really want it found?" Laura asked.

"I think we do," the senator answered. "It will show up sooner or later, and if it got into the wrong hands, it might pose a future threat."

"Are you talking about blackmail?" Buck asked.

No one needed to give the obvious answer, so Julia said, "We'll find the manuscript, then destroy it without reading it. Agreed?"

"Agreed," everyone said.

I was glad that none of them asked *me* to agree, because the real reason for finding the manuscript, as far as I was concerned, would be to read it in order to discover which of the guests had a reason for murdering Augustus.

Buck said, "If Augustus hid it, then it's probably somewhere in this room."

"We could divide the room into sections," Julia suggested. "Two of us could take the bookcase, two the file cabinets, one the desk . . ."

"Ohhh," Laura murmured. "While . . . uh . . . Augustus is still here?"

I couldn't stand it any longer and shouted, "You can't decide to search this room! It isn't your house! It's Aunt Thea's house!"

Thea moved closer and took my hand. Even though I was upset, I noticed that Mrs. Engstrom moved too, positioning herself in such a way that she blocked Augustus's body from Thea's view. She *was* a good friend. I knew that in the same situation, I would have done anything to help Darlene, and she would have done the same for me.

"Samantha dear," Thea said, "what happened to Augustus is horrible beyond belief." Her fingers trembled, and I could feel shivers vibrate throughout her body. "But I've been heartsick at this terrible game—as Augustus called it. I can't believe that he could have threatened and frightened our guests as he did. It was unforgivable of him. I agree with them that the manuscript should be found."

"Before the police get here?"

There was a slight, silent pause, as though everyone in the room had stopped breathing until Aunt Thea said, "I think, under the circumstances, that finding the manuscript *before* the police arrive would be preferable."

That was laying it on the line. I reminded myself that Aunt Thea was one of the game-players, too, and she'd want that manuscript found and all evidence of *her* secret destroyed. I didn't think that finding and destroying the manuscript was such a good idea, but it wasn't my house, my secret past, or my husband who'd been murdered. About the only thing I could do would be to stay out of the way.

"Let's get busy," Julia said.

Senator Maggio took charge by immediately making up a list of rules and assigning everyone places. They went to their particular sections and began removing books, papers, anything in sight—only neatly, putting them back the way they had been, so everything would be in order when the police arrived.

As I watched them work—no one had thought about giving me a job—I had a chance to go over things that had been said, and I began to wonder about Julia. She was a writer. She should know about the importance of manuscript copies. Yet she was the first one to tell us that the manuscript had been destroyed. And at breakfast she hadn't remembered her own stories and characters. I knew, from reading what writers had to say about writing, that after living with her characters for months— maybe even years while she was plotting and writing about them—they'd be like real people. How could she forget them?

Buck had worked gingerly through each side of the desk, opening drawers with a handkerchief, and taking care not to touch Augustus; but he'd finished, finding nothing, and had joined Julia, who was meticulously removing books from the large bookcase and peering behind them.

I had seen something protruding from under the sleeve of Augustus's velvet jacket, near his right elbow. It seemed to be a small stack of envelopes, and they looked very much like those that held the clues Augustus had given to his guests the night before. I quietly walked over and slid out the stack, turned them over, and on the top, printed in bright blue ink, was the name *Alex Chambers, Game Clue #2.*

I thumbed through the envelopes and, just as I thought, there was one for each of the guests and one for Aunt Thea. Augustus had told them he'd have more clues for them to figure out. Obviously, here was the batch he probably had intended to hand out right after breakfast.

Buck leaned against the bookcase, his face more flushed than ever. "That manuscript is not in this room," he said. "Are we going to have to search the entire house?"

"We don't have a choice," the senator told him.

But I held up the envelopes and said, "Yes, you do. These must be the next set of clues."

"Clues for what?" Laura asked. "Weren't they for finding some kind of a treasure?"

I shrugged. "I think the manuscript was supposed to be the treasure."

They all just stared at me, no one saying anything, so I explained. "He said it would be a significant treasure. Okay, what's significant about the treasure hunt? Remember, he said that if you could solve the clues you could get your story removed from his manuscript? It makes sense, then, doesn't it, that the clue solvers would find the manuscript itself?"

"It does make sense," the senator said slowly, "especially since it seems as though the manuscript has been hidden."

"So you might find it through the clues," I said, and again held up the envelopes.

"It's worth a try," Julia said. She stepped up and pulled the envelopes from my hand, riffling through them until she found the one with her name on it.

She shoved the other envelopes back in my hand and started out of the room, but I called out, "Wait a minute. It could take forever if you work alone. Why don't you try to solve the clues together?"

"I don't think so," Senator Maggio said, "not if they're like the first set Augustus gave us."

Thea said, "I'm going to be blunt about it. If your clues were like mine, then they let you know exactly what it was Augustus planned to include about each of you in his book."

"You're right!" Laura said, and groaned. "No one's going to see my clue."

"What if no one understood the clue except you?" I asked. "And what if you put all the clues together and came up with where the manuscript is hidden?"

"I don't know," Buck said, and rubbed so hard at his chin as he thought about it, I was afraid the skin would come off.

"I don't like the idea of sharing information," Julia announced.

"Okay," I said. "It was just an idea. For that matter, you have all weekend to go through every chest and trunk and cupboard and closet in this whole huge house. You might find the manuscript that way."

For a moment they were silent, and I knew they were thinking of all the rooms in this house—each one packed with furniture which could hold a manuscript. The hunt could still be on by the time the storm was over and the police arrived.

"I like Samantha's idea," Alex said, surprising me. "But I want to put a qualifier in there. I suggest we take a short break and read our clues. If they're not as personal as our first set of clues, then it does make sense to share them. We can meet in the dining room in about half an hour."

Laura hesitated. "What should we do about those first clues Augustus gave us?"

"Let's just see what's in this second set before we decide anything," he answered.

Laura glanced at me. "If we're going to try to figure this out together, could Sam help? She showed us how fast she was at figuring out her own clue."

I kept quiet. Now was no time for explanations. Besides, I wanted to be in on the hunt.

"I think Samantha would be an asset to us," Thea answered.

Senator Maggio smoothed down a single strand of hair over his bald head and grimaced. "I suppose we're all in this together. All right. I have no objections."

"Then let's get out of here and get to work," Julia said.

They quickly filed from the room, but I hesitated, picking up a legal-sized, lined note pad and a pen from one side of the desk.

Thea was the last to leave, and I waited for her until she'd quietly closed the office door. She paused only to glance toward the desk. There was no shock in her expression, just an agonizing mix of pain and hurt and sorrow that lasted only a few seconds.

"I deeply regret that you had to see him like this," Mrs. Engstrom said. She took Aunt Thea's arm and ushered her down the hallway and toward the stairs.

I tagged along behind them, walking a lot more slowly than I would have liked. I couldn't wait to see those clues!

SEVEN

One half hour later we seated ourselves around the highly polished table and waited. Julia cleared her throat a few times, Laura sniffled, and Buck made a kind of humming growl that vibrated around his tonsils. We were like members of an orchestra waiting for a conductor to raise his baton as a signal that we should begin.

The senator must have decided to take the lead, because he said, "I assume that we have all read our clues. I, for one, have determined that mine is not personal in nature, as the first clue was."

He removed the sheet of paper inside the envelope in his hand and laid it directly in front of him on the table.

The others—Thea and Laura hesitating more than the rest—finally followed his example.

I had sat next to Laura on purpose, and I brazenly leaned over her shoulder in order to read what was typed on her sheet of paper. Right in the middle of this blank white space were the words ONE WILL BE ABOVE ALL: THE TEN OF SPADES'.

Laura turned so that our noses were almost touching. "Okay, tell," she whispered. "What does it mean?"

"I don't know . . . yet," I said, reluctant to give up my super-sleuth reputation. "We need to see the others."

No one else had spoken. The senator scowled at his paper as though, if he intimidated it enough, it would speak. Buck squinted hard at his clue and rubbed his chin again, while Alex and Julia glanced up from their papers to study the other faces in the room.

"Have any of you figured your clues out yet?" Julia asked. "Mine tells me nothing."

"What does it say?" Laura asked.

Julia held her paper a little closer to her chest and turned toward the senator. "Have we decided if we're going to share them?"

"Oh, for goodness' sakes," Laura said. She slapped her paper out flat on the table where anyone could see it and read it aloud. "Mine is nothing but the name of a dumb playing card. Did we all get the same thing?"

"Not exactly," Alex answered. "Mine begins in the same way: ONE WILL BE ABOVE ALL. But I've got the king of diamonds."

"Jack of clubs," Buck said, and tossed his paper into the center of the table.

"I have the nine of diamonds," Thea said.

"All right," Julia added, and laid her sheet of paper in front of her. "Mine is the queen of hearts."

There was a pause before Senator Maggio intoned, as though he'd just been picked king of the hill, "If this were a card game, I'd beat you all. Mine is the ace of spades, highest in point value."

"Not always," I told him. "In cribbage an ace is at the bottom and only worth one point."

I realized, by the look on his face, that I wasn't exactly his favorite person, so I tried to get back to the subject of the clues. "Does each of your clues begin the same way, with the words ONE WILL BE ABOVE ALL?"

They nodded, and the senator said, "I was trying to make the point that the ace is above all other cards."

"Except . . ." I began, then changed my mind. There was a more important point to make. "Laura's is possessive."

"That's not true," Laura said. "I am not."

"Not you," I said, "your ten of spades. See . . . there's an apostrophe after it. Do the rest of them have an apostrophe?"

"They all do," Julia said. "What does that mean?"

"One more thing for us to figure out," I answered.

Thea interrupted. "Samantha was right in suggesting we work together. Apparently that's what Augustus intended us to do." She sighed and added, "He set us apart with the first clues, then probably intended to see how long it would take us to realize we had to work together on the second."

Julia shrugged and said, "Okay, Sam, since you know so much about it, what are we supposed to do now with these stupid clues?"

"Well," I said, a little nervous because everyone was staring at me as though I had the answer written on my forehead, "we should look for other meanings to the clues and try as many angles as we can."

"Like what?" Laura asked.

"You've got a spade," I said. "What else does a spade mean?"

Her eyes began to glimmer all green and golden as the thought struck her. "Oh!" she said, "a spade! Does that mean we're supposed to dig for something?" She made a face. "In this rainstorm? How could Augustus do that to us?"

"He didn't know it was going to rain," I said, "and we don't know if that's what it means." I looked across the table at Julia. "What about your queen of hearts?"

She tried to look modest and didn't make it. "Perhaps it refers to me as the reigning queen of romantic novels."

Laura's lip curled. "I'd hardly call your stories *romantic*, dear."

Julia had her mouth open to respond, but Thea suddenly began to chant, " 'The Queen of Hearts, she baked some tarts, all on a summer's day.' Could the clue lead to the kitchen? The Queen of Hearts' tarts?"

"Maybe," I answered. I was writing everything down as fast as I could.

"What about a real heart?" Buck asked. "Augustus didn't have one pickled in a bottle or anything like that, did he?"

"Of course not," Thea said, and shuddered.

"I wish he'd had a *change* of heart," Alex muttered.

I ignored them as I looked up at Aunt Thea and said, "You had the nine of diamonds. Does that mean anything special? Like, do you have nine diamonds?"

"More than nine," she answered, "but would the clue have to refer to real diamonds? I've been thinking about the diamond pattern of the tiles in the hallway."

"There's baseball diamonds," Buck added.

"Crystalline carbon," Senator Maggio said.

"What?"

"The chemical composition of a diamond."

I doubted that Augustus had thought in that direction, but I wrote down what the senator had to say, as well.

"Anyone else with a diamond?" I asked.

"I have the king of diamonds," Alex answered.

"King," I said, "monarch, pharaoh, ruler . . ."

"Aha!" said the senator. "Ruler . . . a tool with which we measure. I think we may be on to something here."

Buck shook his head. "I've got the jack of clubs. So what do you make of that? A club is a weapon."

"It may also be something social," the senator answered.

"Oh, yeah," Buck said. "Like a softball club, or the Lions Club, or the Rotary Club." A pleased kind of grin warmed his face. "I just got an award from the Rotary Club in Wickasee, Ohio, for being an outstanding role model to kids."

"That's lovely, Buck," Thea said.

But Julia snapped, "Come on, come on. It's no big deal. We all get awards. What we've got to work on now are these clues."

Laura poked me in the ribs and whispered, "Well? Well?"

"Give me time," I mumbled, and said to the group, "I think we have to keep in mind the words that begin all the clues: ONE WILL BE ABOVE ALL. From what we've learned so far, what do you think this means?"

"If we're talking about the cards themselves," Alex said, "spades are the top suit."

"Suit, maybe," Senator Maggio said, looking firmly at me, "but in card value we're back to the ace."

"Or it could be the king," I insisted.

Alex spoke up. "Has anyone noticed there's a run of ace, king, queen, jack, ten, and nine? Could that mean anything?"

No one answered. In case it did, I quickly wrote down the clues in order along with the initials of the people who held the card clues, hoping this might spell out something. The first part was zilch, and the last three initials spelt out BLT, which made me realize I was awfully hungry and would give anything right now for a bacon, lettuce, and tomato sandwich on white toast. It seemed kind of disrespectful to think of lunch when we were trying to find a missing manuscript and I was trying to discover the identity of a murderer, but I couldn't help it.

Once again I looked at what I had copied under the heading *Game Clues* #2:

ONE WILL BE ABOVE ALL:	THE ACE OF SPADES'	M.
"	THE KING OF DIAMONDS'	A.
"	THE QUEEN OF HEARTS'	J.
"	THE JACK OF CLUBS'	B.
"	THE TEN OF SPADES'	L.
"	THE NINE OF DIAMONDS'	T.

Finally, Julia said, "Let's think in a different direction. If Augustus meant *things*, not *cards*, then in value you can't beat diamonds."

"Good point," I said. I made some more notes.

Mrs. Engstrom appeared at the door. "Are you finished, Mrs. Trevor?" she asked, and her next words warmed my heart. "Lucy would like to set the table for lunch."

"Thank you, Mrs. Engstrom. We haven't finished, but we can take our work to the sun-room," Thea answered.

The senator pushed back his chair. "I don't think we're going to finish, unless we have more to go on than this."

"We could share the first clues," I suggested.

I was surprised when Thea said, "No! I don't think we need to do that. At least not yet."

Buck got up. "What about your clue, Sam? That special clue Augustus gave you. Didn't he say something about it making more sense than the rest of them?"

"He was kidding, because it didn't," I mumbled.

"Didn't it?"

They all stared at me again, but I didn't feel like telling them the rude message Augustus had given me, so I quickly asked them all, "May I keep these clues for a little while? I'd like to study them and see if there isn't something—maybe even in the typing of them—that we're missing."

When no one objected, Buck shrugged and Julia nodded. They left the room with the senator and Alex, allowing me to gather the sheets of paper. Aunt Thea graciously put her clue into my hand and smiled at me, while Laura shoved hers at me and said, "You've got to solve this quickly, Sam. We haven't much time."

She and Thea walked from the room. I hurried to pick up all the sheets of paper and catch up with them, but Mrs. Engstrom put a hand on my arm, detaining me.

"Miss Burns," she said softly, "I hope you'll be able to help your aunt."

"I do too," I said.

"I'm glad that after you find the manuscript, it will be destroyed before anyone has read it."

I liked the confidence she had in me. She didn't say *if* I found it. It was *when* I found it, but she was still looking at me with a pleading, hopeful look in her eyes, so I said, "Mrs. Engstrom, I don't agree. The contents of the manuscript might help us discover who the murderer is."

"If the things he wrote about were made known," she said, twisting the word *he* as though it tasted bitter in her mouth, "they could destroy innocent people."

"Things" had to refer to Thea. I doubted if Mrs. Engstrom cared that much about the others or thought any of them to be innocent. She and I both knew that one of them was a murderer.

Her steady gaze made me so uncomfortable, I quickly said, "Believe me, I wouldn't hurt Aunt Thea for anything," and hurried out of the room.

I didn't join the others in the sun-room. I took my pad and pen and the clues to my room, then walked down the hall to Augustus Trevor's bedroom. I needed more answers, and I hoped I could find them there.

A key, almost exactly like mine, protruded from the keyhole in his bedroom door. The door was locked, so I held my breath while I turned the key and slowly opened the door. The room was so silent and dark, I quickly fumbled for the light switch before I closed the door behind me. It was cold, too, and I felt clammy, as though dampness from the storm had seeped through the walls. I saw that the heating vents had been closed and wondered why anyone would want to sleep in this depressing, cavelike room.

I didn't care for Augustus Trevor's tastes. Over the windows heavy, tapestry-like draperies had been drawn, shutting out most of the light. The massive high-posted, king-size bed was covered with a spread made of the same dull tapestry; and a maroon overstuffed chair, brass lamp, and table were grouped in one corner of the room. The table, chest of drawers, and wardrobe were of dark, carved mahogany, and all sorts of framed photographs of famous people cluttered not only the walls of the room, but also the tops of the chest and the table.

Mixed among the standing photographs were a lot of carvings of animals and fish. I supposed they were very expensive and valuable, but if this had been *my* bedroom, I'd have tossed them out and put up posters instead. Who wants to see, first thing in the morning, a hideous green jade frog with his tongue lolling out. Yuck!

When I cautiously opened the top drawer in the chest of drawers, I could see that the contents had been pawed through. Everything inside the drawer was a mess, and I was positive that wasn't the way Walter kept Augustus's things. Someone had been looking for the missing manuscript and thought, as I had, that Augustus would have kept it close by—if not in his office, then in his bedroom.

Had whoever it was found it?

As I opened the rest of the drawers and looked into them, I was pretty sure that the manuscript had not been found, because the contents of every single one of the drawers had been stirred through.

I found myself standing next to another door, and this one had a key in it as well. I turned the knob, but the door was locked. It had to be the door to a bathroom, but why lock it? I asked myself, and I immediately began to wonder if the person who had searched this room had checked out the bathroom as well. Bathrooms had closets or cabinets. What if Augustus had wrapped his manuscript in towels or sheets, thinking no one would ever think of looking in a bathroom?

Well, I would!

I unlocked the door and opened it to find a large white-and-black-tiled bathroom that was even colder than the bedroom, if possible. Rain beat at the small window, seeping through the crack at the bottom and staining the wall like tear streaks down a dirty face. A white shower curtain closed off the tub, and I ignored it, trying not to think of that scary *Psycho* movie Mom and Dad had rented in which a woman gets stabbed in a shower. I took baths, instead of showers, for months after I saw that movie.

I opened the built-in cabinet that reached from floor to ceiling, and was pleased to see that the sheets and towels and all the other stuff people keep in bathrooms—like extra boxes of tissue and hot-water bottles—hadn't been disturbed.

So I disturbed them. I was neater than the person who'd searched the bedroom had been. I took out stacks of things, looked through, around, and behind them, then put them back the way they'd been. It was hard because I had to work fast, and—unfortunately—it was all for nothing. The manuscript hadn't been hidden in the bathroom.

All that bending and stretching had made me tired. I shoved the shower curtain aside so that I could sit on the edge of the tub, but instead I froze in midair.

I clung to the curtain with fingers as tight and stiff as claws, unable to move. My mouth was open, but not a sound came out, and—as though I were a bird trapped by a snake—I couldn't look away. Augustus Trevor's bloody, twisted face stared up at me from the bottom of the tub!

EIGHT

"**W**hat are you doing in here?" a low voice asked.

That did it. The words broke the spell, terrifying me so much, I nearly fell on top of Augustus. Grabbing the shower curtain for support, I swung around and out and slammed into Walter, who clutched my shoulders and kept me on my feet.

"Downstairs . . . in his office . . . bathtub . . . two of him? No, couldn't be . . . but where . . . why?"

"Be quiet please, Miss Burns," Walter said. "If you'll stop making so much noise, I'll explain." He gave me a gentle push in the direction of the bedroom and pulled the shower curtain closed before he followed me out of the bathroom and locked the door again. This time he pocketed the key.

"Since it will be at least a day or two before the storm will subside and we'll be able to notify the police, I deemed it prudent to—um—store Mr. Trevor's body in a room which could be kept at a cool temperature."

"Oh," I said. "But what about when the police get here? Won't they mind? Doesn't the body have to be just the way it was when we found it? I mean, maybe they'd see clues that would tell who murdered him, although—"

"You didn't answer my question," Walter interrupted, and his tone of voice was less like a butler and more like our suspicious next-door neighbor when she used to ask, "Who threw the ball into my petunia bed? Was it you, Samantha?"

I wanted to be straightforward about everything with Walter, so I told him that I couldn't decipher the second group of clues we'd been given, and I hoped that if I looked around Augustus's bedroom I'd learn something that would help.

"And find the manuscript?" he asked.

"Well, I guess I had that in mind too."

"Did you find it?"

"All I discovered was that someone else searched the room before I did," I answered, and explained about the messy drawers. "Whoever it was must have been looking for the manuscript."

"Do you think they found it?"

"No," I said. "I'm pretty sure they didn't."

Walter rose an inch taller and became a butler again. "Luncheon has been served," he said. "I was sent to find you."

Lunch? I'd forgotten all about it, but my stomach hadn't, because it began to growl.

When I entered the dining room, everyone stopped talking and looked at me. I was getting awfully tired of being the center of attention.

"Well?" Laura asked. "Well?"

"I haven't had enough time!" I happened to glance at myself in the mirror over the sideboard and saw that my face showed my irritation, so I tried to calm down.

No sooner was I seated, with my napkin in my lap and a salad—with more of those strange, crunchy things—in front of me, than Senator Maggio nodded in my direction, peered from under his thick eyebrows, and asked, "Where have you been?"

"In Augustus Trevor's bedroom," I said.

"Why, dear?" Aunt Thea's eyes widened in surprise.

"There are two places most people would hide things in, because they're personal places," I said. "So I figured that Augustus would hide whatever he wanted to hide either in his office or in his bedroom. I thought I'd look."

"Aren't you the one who said we should work on clues instead of wasting time searching for the manuscript?" Julia demanded.

"Well, yes," I said, "but we can't get very far with just one set of clues." I took a large bite of salad. It tasted good, but what *was* that curly purple stuff?

"Wait a minute," she said. "You were looking for *clues*?"

"Both."

The senator put down his fork, his salad untasted. "Augustus spoke of giving us clues throughout the weekend. There must be a series of clues he'd prepared for us. The question is, where are they?"

"What did you find, Samantha?" Thea asked.

"No clues and no manuscript," I said, "but I did find that someone had already searched through all the drawers in the chest and the wardrobe."

No one spoke up. I guess it was dumb to expect someone to say "I did it." Everyone at the table shot questioning glances at the others, though, and everyone except Buck just poked at their salads. Buck ate every bite of his. Oh, well, for that matter, I did too.

Finally, Senator Maggio said, "We have to assume that one of us found the manuscript and is in possession of it."

"No, we don't," I said. There I was, contradicting him again, and it was obvious by the thundercloud expression on his face that he didn't like it.

"What I mean is," I continued, trying to make the situation less tense, "all the drawers were a mess. If the manuscript had been found at some point in the search, then we could even tell where it had been, because some of the drawers wouldn't have been touched. The prowler wouldn't have needed to keep looking."

"Good point," Julia said.

The senator didn't give in graciously. "Perhaps one of us—or all of us—should look carefully through the room to make sure that Samantha was correct in what she found."

"Oh, really," Thea began, but I just shrugged.

"It's fine with me," I answered, "only don't go in the bathroom."

"Why not?" Buck asked.

"Because Augustus Trevor is in the bathtub."

"What?" Julia shouted, and Laura screeched.

"Please, everyone, don't get upset," Aunt Thea quickly said, and she went on to explain why Walter had moved the body—after consulting her, of course.

"I can understand your reasoning," Senator Maggio said, "but the police may not accept it. Evidence leading to the identity of the murderer may have been destroyed."

"Oh, don't be so pompous, Arthur!" Julia snapped. "What's done is done, and for that matter, do any of us care who murdered Augustus? I don't!"

"Me either," Laura said.

I couldn't stand it. Everything that had happened around here was making me crazy. "Please don't talk like that. He was Aunt Thea's husband," I reminded them. "Besides, if you just think about it, whoever murdered him could murder you too."

Laura gasped, but Alex said quietly, "The only one who would need to worry is the person who might accidentally discover the murderer's identity."

"Please!" Aunt Thea held out her hands almost as though she were begging, then dropped them into her lap.

Senator Maggio looked sternly in my direction. "We must respect each other's privacy, Samantha," he said. "I'd like to know why you gave yourself permission to open a locked door."

Walter came in and began removing the salad plates and substituting some kind of soup with chunks of tomatoes and shrimp in it. His expression was unreadable, and he didn't look in my direction.

It didn't matter. I had something to ask the senator. "How did you know that the door was locked?"

For a moment Senator Maggio's eyes widened, and he made a flapping fish mouth while he tried to think of what to say next. But he quickly recovered and answered smoothly, "I passed the door as I was coming downstairs and saw the key in the lock. Just to make sure that the room was secured, I checked the knob and was gratified to discover that the door was locked."

"Did you know that the bathroom door was locked?"

"Of course not," he said. "I'd have no way of knowing that."

I couldn't tell if he was lying or not. I thought he was.

"I can't take much more of this," Alex blurted out. "While we're eating lunch, I don't want to hear another word about the murder! We have to talk about something —anything—else."

There was silence for a moment. Then Buck said, "What d'ya think of the Green Bay Packers' chances this year?"

"Chances for what?" Laura asked.

Buck made kind of a choking sound.

Julia said, "My agent called on Tuesday. *Starved for Love* is going into video."

No one said anything. The only sound in the room was Buck slurping his soup.

"I'm due back in Washington on Friday for those confirmation hearings on Martinez," Senator Maggio told us. "They should be routine. I'm sure she'll get Senate approval."

No one wanted to add to that, so again there was a long, miserable silence. The dining room was an interior room and didn't have windows, but the storm was still loud enough that I could hear bursts of rain and wind slamming against the house.

"After the studio paired me with that overaged bozo on my last film," Laura suddenly said, "I demanded casting approval on the next." She looked at all the uninterested faces and added, her voice gradually fading away, "There isn't exactly a contract yet, but we're working things out, you understand."

Maybe no one understood, because no one answered.

Finally, I laid my soup spoon on my plate, clutched the

edge of the table so hard, my fingers hurt, and said, "One set of clues isn't enough. If you'll share your first set of clues with me, I might be able to help you make some sense of all this."

"Those messages Augustus gave us won't help," Julia answered. "I don't think he meant them as clues. They each contained information that would prove to us that Augustus knew something about us we'd rather no one else knew."

Walter came in to take away the soup plates and bring in chocolate eclairs.

"None for me, thank you," Laura and Julia said together, but Buck reached out and clamped his fingers around Walter's wrist.

"I'll eat theirs," he said. For a moment I felt sorry for him. He was a big guy, and soup and salad probably weren't enough to fill him up.

When we had finished lunch and were waiting for Thea to stand, Alex suddenly said, "Augustus had planned to give us more clues."

"We know that," Julia grumbled.

Alex half stood as he reached into the hip pocket on his very snug jeans. He pulled out a wad of envelopes and laid them on the table. We all stared.

"What are those?" Senator Maggio asked, although we could see the names printed in blue ink and *Game Clue* #3 on them.

"Where did you get these?" Thea asked.

"Where'd these come from? What's this all about?" Buck asked.

"I happened upon them," Alex said.

"Where? When?"

For a moment Alex scowled. "Where and when doesn't matter. The point is, I found them."

In Augustus Trevor's bedroom? I thought. It had to be. He had the second set of clues with him when he was murdered. Maybe he wanted to keep the third set in a private place until he was ready to give them out.

Julia stretched to reach the envelope with her name on it and slid it across the table until she could pick it up. "My envelope's been opened!" she complained.

"What difference does it make?" Alex asked.

"You opened all of them so you could read ours as well as yours!"

"That's right," he said. "I thought it would help me find the manuscript."

Senator Maggio put on his most forceful voice. "I assumed we were working together."

Alex just shrugged.

"Working together seems to be our only chance to succeed," Thea told him.

"You can see, from those playing card clues, that Augustus meant us to share ideas," Julia said.

Alex's voice was sharp as he turned toward her. "Only to a point. Remember, he also said that only those of us smart enough to figure out the clues would win."

Julia pushed back her chair, and her eyes narrowed with anger. "You're saying that Augustus expected some of us to cheat the others? The way you tried to cheat us by finding the clues and hiding them from us?"

"Maybe," Alex said. "In any case, I wasn't able to figure them out. Does that make you happy?"

"Deliriously," Julia snapped.

Laura sniffed self-righteously and said, "At least we know we can't trust Alex any longer."

"No sermons," Alex said. "I've given you the next set of clues. Do you want them, or not?"

Thea rose. "Let's take them to the sun-room."

I ran upstairs to get my pad and pen.

The little door at the head of the winding stairs to my tower room was standing ajar, although I knew I had locked it. I automatically reached for the key I'd shoved into my pocket and pulled it out, along with the folded paper with my GET LOST message on it.

I shoved them both back into my pocket and moved forward cautiously, peering around the edge of the door. The room was empty, but it was obvious that someone had searched it. The drawers of the small chest were open, the few things I'd brought had spilled out, and my jacket was lying on the floor, the pockets turned inside out.

Why would someone do this to *me*? I didn't have anything anyone would want.

Or did I?

Buck had talked about the clue Augustus had given me, repeating what Augustus had said. I'd tried to tell them all that it wasn't true my clue made more sense than theirs, that Augustus had only been joking; but it was plain, from the looks of my room, that at least one of them hadn't believed me. I wished now I hadn't been too embarrassed to tell them that the message had only been GET LOST.

I dumped my things back into the drawers and closed them; picked up the set of clues, pen, and pad, which were scattered across the bed; and left the room, carefully locking the door behind me.

There was something I had to find out. I walked down the long, empty hall, chose a door at random, and tried my key in the lock. It easily opened the door. Rats! As far as protection went, my key was good for nothing. All the bedroom door keys were probably made from the same mold.

I couldn't help glancing into the room. From the tie draped over the back of a chair, I knew it must be Senator Maggio's room. A dresser stood near the door, and I saw on top of it, next to a lap-top computer, the envelope Augustus had given the senator.

Whatever is in that envelope is none of my business, I told myself.

But I answered, *We're dealing with a murder. I need to find out as much as I can about the clues so I can help solve them, don't I?*

Do you want to be as sneaky as Alex?

It's not the same thing, I insisted. *If I solve the clues, it might keep someone else from being murdered.*

I didn't like arguing with myself, so I stepped inside the room, quickly opened the envelope, and found myself looking at a train schedule for a lot of small towns. I had no idea where. One name was circled: Bonino. It sounded familiar, but I had no idea where the town of Bonino was or what it meant as far as being a clue.

I returned the letter to the envelope, put it where it had been, and left the room. I had tucked the key into my pocket and was passing the door of the Red Room when it suddenly opened, and Lucy walked out. She was carrying a dusting cloth and a can of spray stuff in one hand, a small wastepaper basket in the other.

Lucy started when she saw me, but I smiled with relief

that I hadn't been caught in the senator's room. There was a question that had been bothering me, and Lucy could probably answer it.

"The door keys for the upstairs bedrooms are all for show, aren't they?" I asked. "I mean the same key fits every door."

"That's right," Lucy said.

"Isn't that a problem?"

She looked surprised. "Why should it be? The only people who come here are Mr. and Mrs. Trevor's guests. You don't have to lock doors against guests."

Even guests who sneak around in the middle of the night? I didn't want to tell Lucy about my midnight visitor, so I just nodded and said, "So none of the rooms can really be locked."

"Just the wine cellar," she said. "Mr. Trevor kept it locked, and that was a big nuisance for Walter and Tomás, especially when they needed to get wine during the times that Mr. Trevor couldn't be disturbed." She smiled. "Mr. Trevor was silly about that wine cellar. None of us were going to help ourselves to his wine."

A gust of wind rattled around the house, and Lucy shivered. "I wish the storm was over," she said. "I wish the phone company could fix the lines."

"So Aunt Thea could call the police," I added.

Lucy took a step closer to me and said, barely above a whisper, "I'm scared here. Aren't you?"

"Yes," I said.

"It's bad enough Mr. Trevor got himself murdered. I keep thinking that the murderer is here in this house. What if he decides to kill somebody else?"

I shivered and moved closer to Lucy. "Don't let yourself

think like that," I said. "You're perfectly safe. You're not playing the game Mr. Trevor set up. If anyone is in danger, it's bound to be one of the game-players."

"That's not what Walter said," Lucy told me, and her eyes were as round as the curve of her cheeks and face. "We all know that you're the one who's got that special clue that gives you more information than the rest of them put together. If somebody else is going to be killed, it's very likely to be *you!*"

NINE

I had to get out of that dark hallway and away from Lucy, so I ran all the way down the stairs and into the sun-room.

I took the only empty chair. It was one of the hard, straight-backed chairs, but I didn't mind. I tried not to stare as I examined each face. Alex's expression was blank, Julia's was puzzled, and Thea's was concerned; but the other three were steaming. Something had really made them angry. I kept in mind that one of these people was a murderer. One of them had searched my room. And, according to Walter's way of thinking, one of them might be after me!

"Are you feeling well, Samantha?" Aunt Thea asked. "You look a little flushed."

"I'm okay," I told her, and—even though my fingers trembled—I managed to flip some pages over the top of my writing pad until I reached a clean sheet of paper. "What kind of clues have we got this time?"

"Clues?" Laura threw her sheet of paper at me. It

landed at my feet, and I bent to pick it up. "These aren't clues! They're just more of Augustus's nasty comments!"

On her sheet of paper was typed SHE LAID AN EGG, AND IT WAS A DOOZY.

I had to agree with Laura that the statement wasn't very nice. She must have been unhappy enough about the bad reviews of her past two movies. She didn't need an amateur critic's report.

"What Augustus wrote to me isn't flattering either," Senator Maggio said, "and I have no idea why he had to drag my family into this."

"What does your clue say?" I asked.

As a pulse pounded in his neck and his face darkened, the senator read, " 'THE BALD EAGLE HAS MANY KIN.' " He gave me the paper, leaned back, and self-consciously ran the palm of one hand over the top of his smooth, shining head.

"At least he didn't take potshots at your love life," Buck muttered. "It isn't Augustus's business or anyone else's that Eloise and I are . . . well, having a trial separation."

"Is that what your clue says?" I asked. This wasn't making sense.

"Here," Buck said, "read it yourself," and he handed it to me.

In the middle of the paper was typed SHE IS LOST AND GONE FOREVER. DREADFUL SORRY, PAPPY.

"Did your wife call you 'pappy'?" I asked Buck after I'd read his clue aloud.

"No," he said. "No one ever has. We don't have children."

"Maybe this isn't about your wife. Maybe it means something else."

• "Oh, sure. What else *could* it mean?"

I shifted in my chair, which wasn't terribly comfortable, and answered, "I know this sounds crazy, but while I was reading the first part of your clue a tune came into my head. Don't you remember that old song? I think I learned it at Girl Scout summer camp, or maybe it was in kindergarten." I sang, " 'Oh my darling, oh my darling, oh my darling Clementine. She is lost and gone forever, dreadful sorry, Clementine.' "

"Is your wife's name Clementine?" Laura asked Buck.

"No, it isn't," Buck snapped, and his forehead crinkled into a couple of deep creases as he tried to think things out.

Thea suddenly broke in. "If Buck's clue came from a song, then I'm wondering if mine did, as well." She read, " 'DARLING, I AM GROWING OLD,' " then dropped her paper into her lap.

"That's a song, Aunt Thea?"

"Long ago it was a very popular song," she said. "It begins like this: 'Darling, I am growing old. Silver threads among the gold shine upon my brow today; life is fading fast away.' "

Totally depressing, I thought, *and people complain about* our *music!*

"Oooh, what about this?" Laura asked. "What if it's a prophecy of his own death."

"Nonsense," Senator Maggio complained. "It's just more of this stupid foolishness we've been forced into."

Alex gave his paper to me. "Two of the clues may be tied in to songs, but I doubt if mine is. It makes no sense whatsoever."

I read aloud what was typed on Alex's paper: " 'IT WASN'T ENTIRELY JASON'S FAULT.' "

I asked Alex, "Who's Jason?"

Alex shrugged. "I have no idea. I don't know a Jason."

"Jason's a common enough name," Julia told him. "Think about it. The *Jason* Augustus referred to wouldn't have to be a friend. Maybe he's a neighbor or a business associate."

Alex looked at her sharply. "What do you mean by that?"

Julia's eyes widened. "I don't mean anything. I thought we were supposed to try to work out these clues."

"We haven't heard yours," I told her.

"Right," Julia said, and sighed. "Perhaps I'm being oversensitive, but I think my clue also comes under the insult category." She read, " 'TAKE A LITTLE SOMETHING FROM OLIVER, THE POET.' "

"Take what?" Buck asked. "What could you take from a poet?"

"His words," I said.

"I don't get it."

"She means plagiarize," the senator grumbled.

"That's silly," Laura said as Julia's face became blotched with pink. "Julia doesn't write poetry." Laura tilted her head to one side and asked, "Who is this Oliver, anyway?"

"I don't know," Julia said, still embarrassed. "I don't *read* poetry, either."

Buck suddenly got to his feet. "None of this stuff makes sense to me. There's only one thing left to do and that's search this house from top to bottom, and I say we start with Trevor's room."

"Wait a minute," I complained. "This isn't your house!"

"It's all right, Samantha," Thea said. "We must do everything we can in order to try to find the manuscript before . . ."

She didn't finish the sentence, but she didn't have to. The rest of it would have been "before the police arrive."

"I'll go with you," Senator Maggio said, and he tried to match Buck's long strides in an attempt to catch up.

Alex slowly unfolded himself and got to his feet. "I'm going to do a little searching myself," he admitted, and chuckled. "Maybe the butler's pantry. Remember the old saying 'The butler did it'? And a thorough search of the wine cellar might be a good idea."

"What about going through Augustus's desk?" Julia asked him. "Because . . . well, because the body was there, we didn't look very carefully the first time. I'll go with you."

"You don't have to," Alex said. "I prefer to work alone."

"You made that pretty obvious when you kept those clues for yourself, and because of that I don't trust you for a minute!" Julia shouted.

Alex just shrugged. "That makes it mutual," he said, "especially after the sneaky insinuation you made about my business associates."

"What insinuation?" Julia's anger turned to surprise.

Alex didn't answer, so before Julia could continue the argument, I broke in. "You asked me to try to solve these clues, but you're all leaving. I'm going to need help."

Even though all of Augustus's guests—even Aunt Thea —wanted to find the manuscript to destroy it, and I wanted to find it to see if it would give away the identity of the murderer, I needed other thoughts and viewpoints. I wished Darlene were on hand.

Laura shook her head and walked to the doorway. "I wouldn't be any help at all," she said. "The clues are much too confusing. I've got a terrible headache anyway, so I'm going to my room and take a nap."

Julia and Alex, in spite of their differences, left the sunroom together, Laura trailing behind.

Thea motioned me to join her on one of the wicker couches. "I'll do what I can to help you," she said, "but I must be honest with you, Samantha. I believe that the clues may be unsolvable. It would be typical of Augustus to offer false promises just to enjoy watching the discomfort of his guests. I'm afraid that whatever he wrote about us in his manuscript is there to stay."

"Aunt Thea," I asked, "was he always that mean?"

She shook her head. "We had many happy days together when we were young. I made sure his working days were quiet and comfortable, and when we traveled and partied there were always exciting people to meet and interesting things to do."

"I saw the pictures in the Kings' Corner," I told her. "But you weren't in them. Only Augustus."

"Being photographed with royalty was important to Augustus. My presence in the photographs wasn't necessary." For a moment she was silent, then said, "Augustus could be tender and affectionate when he wanted to be, and when he wasn't . . . I accepted it as part of his genius."

"But you fell out of love with him, didn't you?" I asked.

"I suppose so."

"Was he ill? Is that why he became mean?"

"He had bouts of pain, but that was no excuse. There are many people who become gentler through suffering."

"Then why didn't you leave him, Aunt Thea? Why did you stay holed up in this house, away from everything?"

"Marriage is a contract," Thea said, but she looked away from me, and I knew she hadn't given me the right answer. Augustus had been holding something over her head, and it had to be whatever he'd written about in his latest manuscript.

In the silence that followed I listened to the steady drumming of the rain and its gulping gurgles as it rushed through the drain spouts, splashing on the concrete walkways and patios. The storm was no longer violent, but the rain continued to come down as if it would never end.

I stared down at my note pad where I'd copied down *Game Clues* #3:

SHE LAID AN EGG, AND IT WAS A DOOZY	L.
THE BALD EAGLE HAS MANY KIN	M.
SHE IS LOST AND GONE FOREVER. DREADFUL SORRY, PAPPY	B.
DARLING, I AM GROWING OLD	T.
IT WASN'T ENTIRELY JASON'S FAULT	A.
TAKE A LITTLE SOMETHING FROM OLIVER, THE POET	J.

When I was younger, I had thought I was pretty good at making up clues with Darlene and solving them, and I wanted to prove I could still do it, so I refused to give up as easily as the others had. "I'd really like to work on these awhile, Aunt Thea," I said.

"Of course," she answered. "As I told you earlier, I'll help you, but I have no idea how to start."

Could I trust her? I had to. Besides, she was my mother's aunt. "If these are legitimate clues, then each set has to have something in common," I explained. "Nobody wanted to tell me what was in the first set, so I don't know what they were all about. But in the second set we were told that 'one will be above all.' I can only guess that it means the king."

"Arthur insisted it was the ace."

"But you and Augustus played cribbage. There was even a cribbage board in his office. I think he would have thought of the king as top card, and put in the ace just to lead astray all the bridge players."

She smiled. "I'm inclined to agree with you. What else do you get from that set of clues?"

"Nothing," I said. "Just *kings*. Although *king* could mean *ruler* or *general* or *official* or *emperor* or whatever might be in that line."

Wait a minute! I thought. *Kings' Corner.* But there was no place among those photographs to hide a manuscript, and I didn't see how the pictures could give me any kind of help in solving the clue.

Thea said, "Samantha, you saw the first clue that Augustus gave me. It was a travel brochure to Acapulco."

"That's all?"

"That's all."

"But what does it mean? You told me you'd figured it out."

"Wasn't it Julia who told you that these were more messages than clues? That they were Augustus's way of informing us that he had uncovered our secrets. You don't need them to solve the puzzle, Samantha. Please believe me."

While I was thinking about it and deciding that I had to believe Aunt Thea, Mrs. Engstrom came into the room with a teapot and two cups and saucers. "Hot tea tastes good on a rainy day," she said, and gave careful scrutiny to Thea. "Are you feeling well, Mrs. Trevor? I'm sure that this stress is tiring you."

"I'm fine, thank you," Thea said. "There's no need to worry about me."

"I'll be glad when this storm is over," Mrs. Engstrom said as she poured two cups of tea. "Tomás is upset because he's running low on sugar and salad greens and I can't send in my computer order. I wouldn't dare turn on my computer with only the generator to power it."

"How do you shop by computer?" I asked.

"A number of people on the island have a software program with a grocer in Avalon," Thea answered. "We send an order on our household computer, he receives it, and either delivers it or it's ready when we pick it up."

"Well, latest reports on the radio are that the storm should be over by Monday," Mrs. Engstrom said.

I could hear the relief in her voice, but Thea and I glanced at each other with concern. Even though we had different reasons for wanting to find that manuscript, we both realized that we hadn't much time.

Mrs. Engstrom caught the look and asked, "How far have you come on working out the clues, Miss Burns?"

"Not very," I answered.

"Does 'not very' instead of 'no' mean that you've begun to solve it?"

I opened my mouth to say "yes," but thought how weak my guess was on the second set of clues and how I hadn't even begun on the third, so after hesitating just a fraction too long I answered, "No, I haven't."

She stared at me as though she suspected I'd just lied to her, and walked to the other side of the room, where she busied herself straightening magazines and picking up a couple of empty cups that had been left on a side table.

Thea sipped at her tea and said, "Look over your list, Samantha. If you have any questions, just ask, and maybe between us we can come up with the answers."

"Thanks," I said, so grateful for her moral support and so sure she couldn't possibly be the murderer that I confided, "Aunt Thea, I have to find this manuscript before the others do."

"No, Samantha," she said quietly.

"Don't you see, Aunt Thea? If we read the manuscript, we might find out who the murderer is."

"If we read the manuscript, six lives might be ruined."

I squirmed uncomfortably. "But not yours, Aunt Thea."

"Yes, mine too," she answered.

I shouldn't have spilled everything out. I looked around to see if we might have been overheard, but Thea and I were alone. Not knowing what to say next, I got up and went to the desk, opening the lined pad to the page with the number-three clues and spread my notes next to it. I couldn't look at Thea. I didn't want to do anything that might hurt her, but surely she had to understand that someone in this house was a killer and might kill again!

From the corner of my eye I saw her refill her teacup. "I'll wait right here with you, dear," she said, as though our conversation about the manuscript hadn't happened. "If you want my help for anything, just ask."

"Thank you, Aunt Thea," I murmured, and set to work.

I read the clues over twice, and each time I came to a dead stop on Julia's clue. Finally, I looked up at Thea and said, "Do you know any poets named Oliver? The only Oliver I can think of was in that novel *Oliver Twist* by Charles Dickens, and that Oliver was a kid, not a poet."

"We can use the encyclopedia in Augustus's office," she suggested.

"I thought of that," I said, shuddering at the idea of going back into that room, "but it's going to be almost impossible to check out poets by first names."

Thea smiled. "I can give you a start," she said. "What about Oliver Goldsmith, the British poet who lived in the seventeen hundreds? You've studied *The Deserted Village* in school, haven't you?"

"No," I said, "but I like the title. Is it a mystery novel?"

"It's a poem, and I do believe I still remember a few lines from those I once had to memorize about the village schoolmaster." She got a faraway look in her eyes and recited, " 'But past is all his fame. The very spot where many a time he triumphed is forgot.' "

She could have been talking about Augustus. We both felt the impact of the words at the same time and looked away from each other, embarrassed.

I wrote down *Goldsmith* and went on to Buck's clue, writing down the chorus of "My Darling Clementine" and snatches of words from the verses. I could only remember part of them, and I couldn't remember any that had the word *pappy* in them. Aunt Thea had remembered that awful old song about growing old, so I asked, "Do you remember any of the words of 'My Darling Clementine'?"

She put down her teacup and hummed quietly to herself before she answered, "Just snatches."

"Do you remember anything about Clementine's pappy?"

Between her eyebrows a little crease flickered as she thought. "I can't remember him being called *pappy*. Wasn't he a miner?"

"Right," I said. " 'Came a miner, a forty-niner, and his daughter Clementine.' " As I wrote it down I wondered aloud, "So far, this stuff is pretty gloomy. We've got somebody growing old." I checked my notes. "With 'life fading fast away.' Then we've got somebody being forgotten after he dies, and now old Clementine being lost and gone forever. Augustus didn't look on the bright side, did he?"

I got another thought, and this one was too scary to share with Aunt Thea. Was Augustus warning each of his guests that something bad was going to happen to them? And if he was, when was it going to happen? With the weekend half over, we wouldn't have to wait long to find out!

TEN

*D*on't think like that! I cautioned myself. *He's not here to do anything to us, even if he wanted to.* But the memory of his body upstairs in the bathtub was so unnerving that I pushed back my chair and stood up.

"Are you through working on clues already?" Aunt Thea asked.

"Oh, no," I said. "I've made a good start, with your help, Aunt Thea, but I've got some questions to ask two of the others."

"What kind of questions?"

I knew Aunt Thea wasn't prying. She was just being interested. "Well," I said, "I've been thinking that the solution to Laura's clue might be in the name of one of the movies that flopped so badly. I don't remember either of them. Do you?"

"No," she said. "Better ask Laura."

"I have something to ask Senator Maggio, too—the

names of all his relatives. Maybe their initials spell something. I won't know unless I try."

" 'The bald eagle has many kin,' " Thea said.

"You've got a good memory," I told her.

Her smile was sorrowful. "Under the circumstances, the clues would be hard to forget."

I took my pen and pad, with my notes stuffed inside, and headed for the stairway. But I glanced into the parlor and saw Senator Maggio standing alone at the window, staring out at the rain.

As I passed the Kings' Corner I paused to study the framed photographs, but pairs of eyes stared blankly out at me, offering nothing.

The senator didn't acknowledge me as I joined him, and I supposed he was drawn into that swirl of gray sky and grayer sea, its choppy surface shredded by rain and wind.

I waited patiently, then said, "Could I ask you a question, Senator Maggio?"

"If you wish." His voice was as depressed as the view outside the window.

"Okay," I said. "It's about your relatives." But I was sidetracked by my next thought. "Weren't you searching the house for the manuscript?"

"I don't see any hope of finding it before the storm lets up," he answered.

"Then help me solve the clues."

He shook his head. "I don't see how that can be accomplished either."

"Let's try. Why don't you tell me the names of your relatives?"

He turned toward me, startled, but then relaxed. "Oh.

You're referring to the bald eagle's many kin. Frankly, there aren't that many, but I'll go through the list."

He told me the names of his wife, his two brothers, his son and daughter and their spouses, and his two little granddaughters. He reached for his wallet, and I thought for a moment he was going to show me their pictures again, but apparently he decided not to and let his hands drop to his sides, once again staring out the window.

"Everyone makes mistakes," the senator said, so softly that at first I wasn't sure he was talking to me. "Why can't they be forgotten? Why should such a terrible price have to be paid?"

"He didn't know he'd have to pay it."

Again he turned to me, an expression of surprise on his face. "I was talking about past mistakes made by the guests who've been invited here."

"I thought you were talking about Augustus Trevor."

Senator Maggio shook his head. "He's the one responsible for all this trouble."

I nodded. "And he's the one who made the biggest mistake. He invited a murderer to his house."

"You'd better keep in mind," he said quietly, "that the murderer is still present."

I wasn't comfortable about the forbidding look on his face, so I left him in a hurry and trotted upstairs to see if Laura would answer my questions.

On the landing I took time to glance at the names of Senator Maggio's relatives, but they added up to zilch. Except for the first letter of his son's first name (Arthur Maggio, Jr.), the others were just a jumble of consonants: two J's, two K's, two M's, one P, and one H. I not only couldn't make anything out of it, it occurred to me that I'd hardly call this "many kin." I probably expected something like one of those family reunion photos in which relatives are fanned out all over the porch and lawn. Senator Maggio's clue had to mean something else. But what?

The back of my neck prickled, as though someone were watching me, but I looked all around and couldn't see anyone. The burial urn on the stand caught my eye, and I whispered to whatever invisible something that might happen to be hanging around it, "I'm working as hard as I can to get us all out of here in one piece. Be patient, will you? And stop staring!"

I found Laura Reed just where she said she'd be—in her bedroom, but she hadn't been napping. When she opened the door to my knock, her eyes were red, and there were drippy mascara smudges on her cheeks.

"Help me solve the clues," I said.

She shrugged as she stood aside to let me in. "I haven't the foggiest notion how to go about it."

"Well, I do. I mean, it isn't foggy. I want to ask you about your last two films."

Laura perched on the edge of the bed—a high four-poster covered with a dark blue-green quilted spread. There was a heavy swag of the same material over the head of the bed, caught into a kind of gold-colored crown, and at the windows there were draperies to match. Maybe when the sun was out the room didn't look so gloomy. I was beginning to wonder if the person who decorated this house had learned his profession in Dracula's castle.

"I should remember, but I don't," I said as I sat in a narrow gilt chair that stood in front of a dressing table. "What were the names of your last two films?"

"Nobody remembers," Laura said, and she slumped,

hugging her elbows. "Last year was *Daughter of Vengeance.* The year before that was *Lady in Trouble.*" She sighed. "Prophetic, wasn't it? This lady's really in trouble."

I wrote down the titles and looked up. "Maybe not."

She sighed again, a long, dramatic sigh that seemed to come all the way from her toes. "It wasn't murder," she said. "It was a moment of anger, of acting without thinking. It was an accident."

I gulped. "Are you telling me you killed Augustus Trevor?"

Her green-gold eyes glowed like spotlights as she turned them on me. "Of course not, because I didn't. I wasn't even talking about Augustus."

"Then who . . . ?"

"What difference does it make? This is all such a hodgepodge, and my head hurts so much, I don't even remember what we were talking about."

I felt cold all the way to my toes. "You'd said you were in trouble, and then you talked about the murder . . . I mean the way it took place, as though you'd been there . . . and . . . well, it just seemed to fit."

No matter what Laura said or denied saying, she certainly had had the opportunity to kill him.

"Never mind. Forget what I said. I was just thinking out loud." She sat up straighter. "We'll talk about your clues. How do the names of my films fit into them?"

"I don't know yet," I said.

"Augustus makes me absolutely furious," she snapped. "Telling me I laid an egg and it was a doozy! How rude can you get?"

"Maybe he didn't mean you," I told her.

The corners of her mouth turned down, and her voice

was sarcastic. "Oh? Who else but an actor lays an egg? Are you talking about a chicken? A goose? Maybe the goose that laid the golden egg. Wouldn't Augustus think that was a great joke."

A knock at the door made us jump.

Laura opened it to Lucy, who had brought two extra pillows. Laura thanked her, shut the door again, and tossed the pillows onto the bed. "I sleep better with lots and lots of pillows," she told me, but as she sank back onto the bed she became plaintive. "I really don't expect to sleep at all—not until that manuscript is found and destroyed."

Tears glistened again in her eyes as she told me, "I hunted over every inch of this room, even between the mattress and springs. There's a vent into the attic from the closet in my room. I even checked that."

"Maybe we'll solve this puzzle and find the manuscript," I told her.

"How far have you come in solving the clues?"

"Not very."

She drooped again, reminding me of a fading petunia on a wobbly stem. "Wouldn't it be nice," she asked, "if we could live our lives over again and take out all the bad parts?"

"I guess so," I answered, although I'd been lucky enough not to have many bad parts and nothing so terrible that I'd want to live my life over again to miss it.

"If I weren't so miserable, I'd be bored to death here," Laura said, and looked at her watch. "Do you realize it's more than an hour until dinnertime?"

"I've been thinking about it in the opposite way," I answered. "The weekend and the storm will be over soon.

The time we have left to find the manuscript is running out."

Laura groaned. "You came here to cheer me up. Right?"

A loud knock on the door startled us, but we heard Buck call, "It's me, Buck. Wake up, Laura. Open the door."

Laura opened it graciously, holding her head high, as though she were a queen. "I wasn't sleeping," she said. "And you don't need to shout."

"Sorry," he said, and his feet did a kind of fumbling shuffle as he stepped into the room. "This whole thing has got me so riled, it's made me do things I never thought I'd ever do."

"Like what?" I asked, and held my breath, waiting for his answer.

He looked at me with surprise, and I realized he hadn't known I was with Laura. "Like pawing through people's things, searching for that manuscript."

I relaxed. What had I expected? That he'd confess to committing murder?

He nodded toward the legal pad on my lap. "Are you getting anywhere with those clues?"

"Not yet," I admitted, "but I'm trying. That's why I'm here. I was asking Laura some questions about her clue, and I'd like to talk to you about yours, too, if you've got a few minutes."

Buck made a scrunched-up face that answered my question. "I've been going room to room," he said. "I want to search Laura's room too."

"Forget it," she said. "I already searched it."

His eyes narrowed as he studied her. "Did you find anything?"

"Of course not. Don't you think I'd have told every-body if I did?"

Buck didn't answer right away, and Laura's neck and face flushed an angry red. "You don't trust me? You think I'd hold out?"

"I don't know who to trust," he mumbled. "All I know is that somebody here killed Augustus."

Her voice rose to a screech. "You think it was me? How about you? Maybe *you* murdered him!"

"Okay, maybe I did!" he yelled back.

"You did?" I whispered, and clutched the arm of the little dressing table chair.

"No, I didn't. I was just making a point. Any one of us could be the murderer, so who are we going to trust?"

"Please sit down, just for a minute," I begged. "I've got only a couple of questions for you. I need to know how the song 'My Darling Clementine' fits into your life."

"Fits into my life? That's a stupid question. The answer is that it doesn't."

"Maybe I didn't ask my question the right way," I said, and felt myself blush. "I meant, was it a special song for you? Did you hear it at some time under special circum-stances?"

"No," he said. I wished he'd sit down. He was awfully big to glower down on an innocent bystander—me.

"You know the words to the song, don't you?"

He shrugged. "A few words, here and there, that's all."

"Okay, what does 'pappy' mean to you?"

"Beats me. I didn't call my dad 'pappy.' I don't even know anyone called 'pappy.' "

"You're with kids a lot. As you said, you're a role model. Maybe sometime in your past—"

Buck interrupted. "What are you getting at?"

Like a ferocious pit bull, he leaned toward me, eyes glinting in narrow slits, his lower lip curled outward. He scared me so much I jumped out of my chair.

"N-nothing!" I stuttered. "I—I'm just trying to figure out these clues!"

He didn't believe me. Not for a minute. He took a step toward me, and I shrank back against the dressing table, terrified of what he'd say next. But just then we heard muffled footsteps running toward us, and the door was jerked open.

Julia poked her head inside, stared from Laura to Buck to me, and said, "Come on downstairs. Make it quick! I've found the fourth set of clues!"

ELEVEN

"**W**here did you find them?" everyone asked Julia, and as soon as we were all seated in the sun-room, she told us.

"The envelopes were fastened with a rubber band and tucked at the very back in the middle drawer of Augustus's desk under some papers." When no one said anything for a few moments, Julia's voice rose. "Don't look at me as though you think I'm lying. We didn't search that part of the desk this morning. Remember? And we weren't looking for clues. We were looking for the manuscript."

"Julia's right," Buck said. "I went through the drawers on each side, but I couldn't . . . that is, Augustus was . . ."

"Wait a minute," I said. "The first clues he handed out. The second were under his arm, ready to be given out the next morning. But why would Alex have found the third set in Augustus's bedroom, and then this set—"

Alex interrupted. "I didn't find them in his bedroom. I

found them just inside the middle desk drawer in his office." He shrugged. "I suppose if I'd been able to check the back of the drawer I would have found the fourth set of clues."

I felt cold and creepy as the thought hit me. "Were you looking in the desk while Augustus was still . . . ?"

"It's none of your business," Alex said.

"He was *dead*," Laura whispered.

"There's no point wasting time with this discussion," Senator Maggio argued. "Will you please give us our envelopes?"

Julia proceeded to do so, and I saw that on the top of each envelope, next to the players' names, had been printed in that same bright blue ink, *Game Clue* #4.

It was hard to be patient while the suspects—as I thought of them—read their clues to themselves. I wished I had elbowed in on the couch next to Laura, but I was sitting cross-legged on the floor, which was more comfortable than the hard straight-backed chair which had been the only seat left.

Alex was the first to speak. "This clue makes no more sense than the others," he said, and read, " 'MORE SILENT THAN THE TOMBS ARE.' "

I began to write it down but looked up, startled, as Laura burst into tears. "That dreadful, horrible man," she sobbed.

Her clue fluttered from her fingers as she covered her eyes, and I picked it up. On the paper was typed LIKE DAVY JONES'S LOCKER—MINUS THE SEA.

As soon as Aunt Thea calmed Laura down, I asked her if I could read her clue to the others.

Laura lay back against the cushions, one hand pressed

against her forehead, and said, "Oh, go ahead. What difference does it make now?"

I read Laura's clue, then asked Senator Maggio, "What does yours say?"

He shrugged. "I suppose it's a threat: 'DEADER THAN A DOORNAIL, GREEN AS A PEA.' "

Julia's eyes widened. "These are all about death. Listen to mine: 'TEA AND SYMPATHY—DONE TO DEATH.' "

"So that's what this means. I thought—" Buck interrupted himself and read: " 'WHY A SUDDEN DEATH PLAY?' "

"My clue is in line with the others," Thea told us. She handed me her paper, and I read aloud, " 'GIVE UP THE GHOST.' "

With tears in her eyes she said, "Please believe me when I tell you that I have no idea what Augustus had in mind. To bring you here, to force you into playing this horrible game, and then to threaten all of you—all of *us*—with death, is unbelievable to me. I'm sorry. I'm so terribly sorry."

"No one blames you, Thea," Julia told her, and the others murmured in agreement.

Thea was sitting close enough to me so that I could reach out and take her hand. "Aunt Thea," I said, "you're forgetting that these aren't messages Augustus was giving you. They're clues, which means they're supposed to add up to something else."

Everyone stared at me. Since they were all seated on chairs, and I was cross-legged on the floor, I felt like the frog in biology class just before the teacher gets ready to dissect him. I quickly stood up and read aloud the clues I'd written down:

MORE SILENT THAN THE TOMBS ARE	A.
LIKE DAVY JONES'S LOCKER—MINUS THE SEA	L.
DEADER THAN A DOORNAIL, GREEN AS A PEA	M.
TEA AND SYMPATHY—DONE TO DEATH	J.
WHY A SUDDEN DEATH PLAY?	B.
GIVE UP THE GHOST	T.

As I heard them I got a strange feeling. Something about these clues was odd. For an instant I was almost able to grasp the reason, but I looked the list over again and the feeling had gone. I said to the others, "As I already told you, there has to be a common theme in these clues. That's the way it works. Why don't we get busy and try to find it?"

Laura moaned and staggered to her feet. "It's not true it's not true it's not true!" she gurgled as a fresh burst of tears poured down her cheeks. She pushed her way out of the circle of chairs and ran out of the room.

"There's no use in any of this." Buck's voice was deep with despair. He slowly hoisted himself out of his chair and walked away.

Alex stood and stretched before he said to me, "If you can make anything out of 'more silent than the tombs are,' I'll believe it when I see it."

"If I can? How about you? You're the ones who were supposed to figure out the clues and solve them," I told him. "Don't leave it all up to me. I need help."

"Don't we all," Alex said, and left the group.

"Come on," I told the others. "Help me figure out what all this stuff means."

"You said there was a common theme, didn't you?" Senator Maggio asked.

"Yes."

"Well, it's clear. The theme is death."

"No," I insisted. "That's too obvious. There has to be another meaning."

The senator didn't like to be contradicted. The expression on his face was unmistakable.

As he stalked out of the room Julia said, "I'll help you, Sam."

"So will I," Thea added. "What do you want us to do?"

"Help me look for hidden meanings in these clues."

"Let's start with mine," Julia said. "*Tea and Sympathy* is the title of a novel, and it was made into a movie."

"Anything else here that ties in with a book or a movie?" I asked.

We studied the list but came up with zilch.

"There's a clue about football and a clue about sailors," I said. "At least I think Davy Jones was a sailor, wasn't he?"

Julia half rose out of her chair. "Wait a minute! Locker! Davy Jones's locker!"

"Aunt Thea!" I cried out. "Could the manuscript be hidden in a locker?"

Thea looked bewildered and spread out her hands helplessly. "We don't have anything resembling a locker here," she said.

"What about down at the dock? Are there lockers there for gear or equipment?"

"No. There's a large metal chest in the boat shed where equipment for the boats is kept, but the crew members live in the house for employees and keep their gear there."

"Where is this house?" Julia asked.

"Just the other side of the cove."

"All your employees live there?"

"Yes." Thea nodded, then suddenly said, "Except for Mrs. Engstrom, of course. I guess I think of her as more of a friend than an employee. She has a small suite of first-floor rooms here in our home."

Julia thought a moment, then asked, "Is it possible that Augustus hid the other copy of his manuscript in the employees' house?"

"I know he didn't," Thea told her. "During the last few years Augustus became sedentary and rarely went outdoors. I'm positive that Augustus didn't leave the house at any time after he completed his manuscript."

"What if he gave the manuscript to one of the employees to hide? Maybe Walter?" I asked.

Thea shook her head. "Mrs. Engstrom informed me that she immediately questioned Tomás, Lucy, and Walter. They knew nothing about a copy of the manuscript. In fact, they're all frightened about everything that has happened."

"I'd still feel better if we searched the other house," Julia said.

Thea stood, her spine as straight and stiff as the back of the chair she'd been sitting in. "I can't allow anyone to invade my employees' privacy," she said. "However, if you wish, I will ask Walter and one of the others—Buck, perhaps—if they would like to put on raincoats and boots and climb down to the boat shed in order to search the chest." She paused and glanced at the windows, which were blurred with a steady shimmer of rain. As she turned back to Julia, Thea said, "Maybe *you'd* like to visit the boat shed, Julia."

"Well . . ." Julia drew out the word. Her gaze was on the windows. "If no one else volunteers, I'll go."

"I'll ask them," Thea said, and left the room.

Julia slumped against the arm of the couch and pressed her fingertips over her eyes. "It's never worth it," she mumbled. "Nothing is."

"Worth what?" I asked.

She slid her hands down her face and let them fall into her lap as she looked at me. "Peace of mind," she said. "I gave it up too easily."

I didn't want to intrude on her thoughts, but I didn't understand what she was talking about, so I asked, "How did you give it up?"

"With one stroke I traded it for a handful of beans— magic beans." Her laugh was scary because there was no humor in it.

One stroke? Only too clearly I could visualize Augustus Trevor's bloody head. Even though Julia and I were alone in the sun-room, which was growing darker and gloomier by the minute, I blurted out, "Are you talking about Augustus Trevor's murder?"

For a moment Julia looked confused, but as she understood my question she leaned forward, her gaze as penetrating as a laser beam. "Are you asking if I killed Augustus?" she whispered.

"Uh—not exactly. I—I don't know what to think."

"Then I'll tell you what to think." She moved even closer, and her eyes glittered. "Don't try getting inside other people's minds. Don't begin suspecting them, and above all, don't tell other people your suspicions or you might very well find yourself in real trouble."

* * *

Buck and Walter did go down to the boat shed, and they came back to report that, just as Thea had told us, there was nothing but equipment in the metal chest. Buck hadn't been able to fit his overly long feet into any of the work boots on the back porch, and the slicker they crammed him into couldn't fasten across his chest, so he was as grumbly cross as a cold, wet bulldog.

"We haven't much time left in which to find the manuscript," Alex said. "As long as Buck has survived the elements on this first trip, it might be a good idea if he made his way over to the employees' house and took a look around."

"Yeah? What about *you* going out in that mess, instead of me?" Growling as drops trickled from his scalp down his face and neck, Buck grabbed a fistful of Alex's shirt, and for a moment I held my breath, sure that Buck was going to hit Alex.

But Buck suddenly flung Alex backward. Alex sprawled on the sofa, then slid to the floor, while Buck stomped toward the stairs. Alex didn't say a word. He climbed to his feet, methodically rearranged his open collar, tucked his shirt back into his slacks, and walked toward the dining room.

Buck was a very strong man, and he had a temper. Could he have gone to Augustus's office and argued with him? Could he have lost his temper and hit Augustus?

Maybe.

I gathered up my writing pad, the loose papers, and the pen and walked to the parlor. I had a new idea about the photographs in the Kings' Corner. What if a message was tucked inside one of the frames behind the backing? I could hardly wait to find out.

Someone else had been even more impatient. The photos, cardboard, glass, and frames had been separated and were strewn all over the table. What a mess! I was furious at this crude violation of someone else's property, and more than a little angry that whoever had done this had got the idea of searching the photos before I had.

I didn't try to repair the damage. Only Aunt Thea would know which photo went with which frame. I found a seat at a small antique desk in the parlor. I turned on the small green-globed desk lamp and moved a lot of little china and crystal birds, which were arranged in groups on top of the desk, so I'd have room to work. I spread out my sheets of paper and went back to the third set of clues, writing down everything that came to mind. I checked to see if the first letter of each sentence added up to anything, but it didn't, which didn't surprise me. Augustus had planned some tough clues, and he wouldn't waste his time with an easy kid trick. The clues had to have a common theme, and I was determined to find it.

"Samantha."

I hadn't heard anyone come into the room, and I wasn't expecting Alex to speak my name just behind my left ear, so I let out a yelp and jumped up, my papers scattered around me.

"How long have you been looking over my shoulder?" I demanded.

"Not long. I came to see how you were doing."

"You didn't have to sneak up on me!"

"I wasn't sneaking. The carpets are soft. It wasn't my fault that you didn't hear me come in."

I picked up my papers, and tried to look dignified. "Sorry," I muttered. No matter what excuse Alex gave, I still believed he'd been sneaking, but I had to answer his question. "I haven't got any answers yet, if that's what you want to know."

"You've made a lot of notes. May I see them?"

He reached for the papers, and I instinctively drew back.

"What's the matter?" Alex asked. "I thought you said you wanted help. Don't you trust me?"

"No, I don't," I answered. "You opened the third set of clues and tried to solve them yourself." I glanced across the room at the Kings' Corner. "And you're probably the one who took apart all the framed photographs of Augustus with the kings."

Alex shrugged. "So what if I did? There weren't any rules to the game, or instructions to share information. We were simply told to find the treasure and win."

Curiosity took over. "Did you find anything in the photos?"

"No." Alex took the papers out of my hand and I let him. He walked to one of the sofas, sat down, and laid the sheets of paper on the coffee table. I sat next to him and waited while he read every one of my notes.

When he'd finished, he turned and looked right into my eyes. "You made these notes earlier. I watched you. What else have you come up with?"

"Nothing," I said. I wished he wouldn't stare at me like that. I felt as though he were poking around in my brain looking for answers.

"You still don't trust me," Alex murmured.

I inched a little farther away on the sofa as I said, "One person in this house is a murderer, so why should I trust any of you?"

"I didn't kill Augustus," he said, "so it's perfectly safe for you to trust me." His lips stretched into a broad smile, but his eyes were cold.

Alex waited for my answer, but I didn't say a word. I couldn't.

His smile snapped off like a door being slammed, and he got to his feet. "Very well then," he said. "I'll work alone."

As he walked toward the door I jumped up and called, "Wait a minute. Give back my notes."

"No," he said, and that awful smile crept back to his face again. "I figured out what you're doing, Samantha. You want to find the manuscript before the rest of us do because you probably have some odd idea that by reading it you might discover the identity of the murderer, but I'm not going to let you. No matter what I have to do to stop you, I'm going to find that manuscript first!"

TWELVE

I was afraid of Alex, much too afraid to make a scene about my notes being stolen, and I convinced myself that losing the clues didn't make that much difference. I had worked so long on the clues, I had memorized them, so I took three clean sheets of paper and jotted the clues down again under *Game Clues* #2, *Game Clues* #3, and *Game Clues* #4.

The notes, however, didn't come back to mind as easily. I remembered the words of that yucky song Aunt Thea sang about growing old with silver threads among the gold, and I wrote down Oliver's last name, Goldsmith. What else had I jotted down?

Thea called to me from the doorway, and as she briskly came toward me she said, "Samantha, I thought of something that might help with Alex's clue about Jason. Wasn't it something like not blaming Jason because it wasn't his fault?"

I read from the clues: " 'It wasn't entirely Jason's fault.' "

"I have an idea," Thea said, and beamed. "Jason and Medea. Remember the tale? Medea urged Jason to steal her father's golden fleece. What was her father's name . . . ? King . . . oh, dear. Do you remember?"

"Not at the moment," I said, but as I wrote down the sentence I began to get an excited bubbling in my stomach. It was the way I used to feel when I was coming close to working out the answer to some really hard puzzle Darlene had dreamed up for me.

"Do Jason and Medea fit in?" Thea asked.

Did they fit! The pieces of this puzzle began to come together, and in my excitement I gripped the edge of the table. "I don't know yet," I mumbled, and couldn't meet Thea's eyes. "They might. Thanks."

Thea was Mom's aunt, so why couldn't I trust her enough to tell her that she may have given me the answer to solving the third set of clues? What was the matter with me?

I had just opened my mouth to spill the whole thing when Laura appeared in the doorway, looking more like someone who was auditioning for the part of a bag lady than someone who was supposed to be a glamorous movie star. "Thea," she moaned, "do you have any aspirin?"

"Of course," Thea said. "Come upstairs and I'll get it for you."

As they left I sighed with relief. It really wasn't time to tell Thea yet.

I couldn't wait to test my new theory on the rest of the clues in this third group. When I re-read Laura's clue, I smothered a laugh. Laura had said something about a goose that laid a golden egg, and she was right. Augustus hadn't accused *Laura* of laying an egg. He'd been referring to the goose, and there was no doubt about it—a golden egg would certainly be a doozy.

I had the key to the third set of clues, and I was so excited, my fingers trembled.

I stopped making notes. Alex might come back, or someone else who'd feel he could just help himself to everything I'd worked out. In fact, this room was much too public to suit me. I grabbed my things and ran, taking the stairs two at a time and scrambling twice as fast as I passed the burial urn on the landing. Once inside my own room I turned on the light, then slammed and locked the door, collapsing against it and gulping for air.

As soon as I had caught my breath I sat on the bed, my back to the wall so I could keep watch on the door, and went through the third set of clues, one by one. Golden, gold, golden, gold.

"The bald eagle has many kin." Sure. Of course. One of the bald eagle's kin is the *golden* eagle.

That left Buck's clue. "Pappy" was a miner, a forty-niner, and what did the miners in 1849 look for? Gold!

That was it! I had it! I let out a yelp, then slapped a hand over my mouth, hoping no one had heard me. I'd solved two out of the four sets of clues, which proved to me that Aunt Thea had been wrong in suspecting that Augustus had planned to trick his guests. He really *had* worked out legitimate clues for them to solve.

Get busy, I told myself. It was time to tackle the fourth set of clues.

They proved to be a lot harder because I couldn't find anything that linked them together.

It was pitch-dark outside by this time, and my stomach

had begun to rumble up and down the scale with hunger. Sometimes it was difficult for me to understand myself. I was in the house with a dead body, a murderer, and a ghost, and I was hungry?

No matter what the circumstances, I guess some things never change. It had been a long time since lunch, and I hoped that Tomás was working hard on dinner. Maybe, I thought, I should go downstairs before someone had to come all the way to the tower to call me.

I took one last look at the clues and for some reason began to read them aloud: " 'More silent than the tombs are' . . . 'Like Davy Jones's locker—minus the sea' . . . 'Deader than a doornail, green as a pea' . . . 'Tea and sympathy—done to death.' "

The strange feeling came back and began to grow—tingling through my body like a jolt of electricity—until all of a sudden the whole thing made sense!

In reading the clues aloud I heard a letter instead of a word in each sentence. "More silent than the tombs *R*" . . . "Like Davy Jones's locker—minus the *C*" . . .

Aunt Thea's clue was the only one without a letter sound, so I ignored it and wrote the letters next to each of the other sentences. I came up with RCPTY, which didn't make sense in itself, but I suspected it was a word with scrambled letters. No vowel, but a *Y* could substitute. TRYCP . . . PYRCT . . . CRYPT.

Crypt! Oh, my gosh! I was so excited, I bounced up and down, shaking and creaking the bed.

King's Golden Crypt. But where? Where?

A sudden thought stopped me in midbounce. How did Thea's clue work into all this: GIVE UP THE GHOST?

The last part of the clue fell into place as easily as

though someone had whispered the answer in my ear, and I knew! I knew! I knew where the manuscript was hidden!

It should have been obvious from the beginning that only an important official, a ruler, maybe a king, would be buried in a golden crypt! The crypt had to be the golden burial urn with the *ghost* in it!

The knock on my door was so sudden that I lost my balance and rolled off the bed, managing to bang my knee and break a fingernail.

"Dinner is served, Miss Burns," I heard Walter call. There was a pause before he asked, "Are you all right?"

I stuck my head out from under the bed and yelled back, "I'm fine, thank you."

"I thought I heard a . . . a thump."

How could I explain. "You did," I shouted at Walter. "I broke a fingernail. And then I bumped my . . . Oh, well . . . what I mean is . . ." I took a deep breath and calmly said, "I'll be down in a minute."

There was a pause, and I knew he had to be thinking what a dork I was, but he answered, "Very well, Miss Burns," and I could hear his footsteps softly descending the short flight of stairs.

My mind raced as I filed down the rough edge of my fingernail. What was I going to do with my notes? I couldn't leave them in my room. Someone had searched it before and might again. I couldn't even tear the sheets up and put them in a wastepaper basket somewhere, because anyone could come across the pieces and fit them together.

There was only one place I was pretty sure they'd be

safe. I folded the pages up into a tight square and stuffed them into my bra.

It took just a quick glance in the mirror to see that people might wonder why I'd suddenly become lopsided, so I removed the wad, divided it into two wads, and tucked them into both sides of my bra. Good. I protruded a little more than usual, but I didn't think anyone would notice.

But what was I going to do about the expression on my face? I looked as though I'd just discovered America. Or won a lottery. Or got picked for a quiz show.

While I tugged off my jeans and T-shirt and pulled a dress over my head, I practiced making bland, unemotional faces in the mirror. It didn't work.

I could wait until Walter came back to see what happened to me and tell him I was sick, but then I'd miss dinner. At the very thought of going hungry my stomach growled. No. I'd have to go downstairs and tough it out.

As I arrived the group was moving from the parlor toward the dining room, cocktail glasses still in hand. I slipped in between Thea and Laura and tried to look inconspicuous, which was hard to do with my door key and necklace every now and then swinging against the paper in my bra, making a sharp, slapping noise.

Thea and Laura looked at me questioningly, but I just drooped along, trying to keep my eyes on the floor.

"Samantha, are you feeling well?" Thea asked, and I could hear the concern in her voice. I felt guilty at being even the least little bit suspicious of Aunt Thea.

"I guess I'm tired," I answered. Tired. That was a good direction to take. My shoulders slumped, and I dropped into the first chair I came to.

"You've been working too hard trying to solve those horrible clues," Laura said.

The clues! Yes! Bursting with excitement, I almost bounced in my chair, but I was so terrified at giving myself away that I hunched my shoulders and kept my eyes on my plate, which, unfortunately, was still empty.

Thea felt my forehead. "You aren't running a fever," she said. "Maybe a little food will give you an energy boost."

I hoped it would be a lot of food. We started with a Caesar salad, which was a good omen, because at last we were eating something I knew about. I could hardly wait until everyone had been served and Thea raised her fork, but I didn't get a chance to begin eating, because I had to answer questions.

Buck's came first. "Have you got to first base with those clues, Sam?"

"They're tough," I mumbled.

"You made a start, though," Alex said, and again his gaze was penetrating. "As I remember, you wrote down 'Kings' for the solution to the first clues."

"Oh?" Julia asked, and everyone stopped eating to stare at me.

"*Second* clues," I said, wishing they'd leave me alone. "And the king wasn't a solution. It was only my guess." I took a long breath, and calmly added, in a burst of inspiration, "Senator Maggio said I was wrong and the key was the ace."

"That's correct," the senator affirmed. "The ace is always the top card."

"But what does it mean?" Laura asked.

Alex's eyes narrowed. "Ask Samantha," he said. "I think she knows."

I wished he'd stop staring at me like that. Deliberately and slowly I ate a bite of salad. It was delicious, so I took another bite.

"Well?" Alex asked again.

I looked up to see all of them still watching me, and again excitement bubbled up inside me like a soft drink coming out of a can right after you shake it. *I know, but I'm not going to tell you!* I thought, then quickly realized that my facial expression was going to give everything away.

I could see suspicion beginning to cloud Julia's face, and Senator Maggio and Buck glanced at each other. Alex smirked. Had I given away my secret? Suddenly I was frightened.

"What?" Laura asked, holding her hands palms up and staring from face to face. "What's the matter? Julia, why are you looking like that?"

I pulled a Laura trick. It was the only way I could think of to get out of this mess. I closed my eyes, covered my face with my hands, and cried, "You're asking too much of me!"

Immediately Aunt Thea's arms went around my shoulders, and she gently scolded the others. "We are the ones who were supposed to solve the clues and find the treasure. Samantha offered to help, and instead of thanking her, you're browbeating her. Can't you see how tired she is?"

"I'm sorry, Sam," Laura said.

I sat up, patting Thea's hand and nodding to Laura. "Thank you," I murmured. I was glad to get out of that tight spot and extra glad that Walter, who had busied himself at the table, hadn't removed my salad.

We ate in silence for a few minutes, but finally Thea put

down her fork and said, "I think we have to face facts. I felt from the beginning that the game Augustus was playing was that of cat and mouse and not the game he outlined to you. You've seen all the clues. The first set was threats. The rest are impossible. No one could solve them."

"Then why would he go to all that trouble?" Julia asked.

"Just to watch us squirm, to watch us try and fail," Thea said.

"Was he really that cruel?" Senator Maggio asked.

"I'm afraid you know the answer to that question," Thea said.

Her eyes became blurry with tears, and as they spilled over her cheeks I leaned toward her. "Aunt Thea," I begged, "don't cry. I'll tell—"

"Excuse me, Miss Burns," Walter said as I collided with his outstretched arm. I jumped back, and he added, "May I remove your salad plate?"

I nodded and leaned back.

"But what about the manuscript? What about the material Trevor wrote that threatens us?" Senator Maggio was so intent on the situation, he hadn't heard me. I glanced around the table, but no one was looking in my direction. They were as upset about what Augustus had written as the senator was.

I'd been about to tell everything to Aunt Thea—and to the others. *Stay cool*, I reminded myself again. I had to get my hands on that manuscript before the others found it and destroyed it.

I kept my peace during the rest of the meal, which wasn't hard because the suspects had so much they wanted to talk about: Had Augustus actually included their secrets in his manuscript, or had he been bluffing? It was obvious that he had come into possession of some facts, but just how far had he gone in repeating them? Would the manuscript contain only simple hints and allusions or would it spell out the stories in detail?

They complained about hunting for the manuscript copy in every place imaginable. Had this been a complete waste of time? Did a copy of the manuscript even exist? I concentrated on eating a breaded ham and chicken roll, but I listened to every word.

As chocolate fudge cake was served, Senator Maggio said, "I think we can relax and forget the whole thing. I am of the opinion that *if* a copy of the manuscript still exists, it is probably hidden away so carefully that it may never show up."

Laura spoke up hesitantly. "When the police come, they'll search the house. They're better at searching than we are. They'll find the manuscript. I know they will."

Julia groaned and said, "I hate to admit it, but Laura is right."

"What if none of us mentions the manuscript?" Alex suggested. "The police need never know."

"Trevor's computer file was wiped out, and his papers and disks were burned," the senator said, and looked down his nose at Alex with contempt. "They'll have to be told about the manuscript and Trevor's reason for inviting us here. Lying won't help."

Alex didn't flinch. "It wouldn't be lying. It would be avoiding the issue, just as *you* intend to do if we find the manuscript and destroy it."

"That's different."

"How?"

"I suggest," Thea broke in, "that we conduct another detailed search of Augustus's office. There are manuscript boxes in his files, and on the shelves in the office closet are countless boxes with content labels pasted on. No matter what the boxes are labeled, we'll open them and examine everything that's inside."

Finding that Augustus was well organized blew my theory. I had just about convinced Mom that I couldn't keep my room cleaned up because I was going to be a writer, and creative people were not as organized as other people. It just wasn't in their nature to worry about mundane things.

In our search we soon found that if a box was labeled *Correspondence with* The New York Times, that's exactly what it contained. *File folders* was filled with file folders, and *Clippings, Paris, 1962* was filled with newspaper articles from Paris newspapers.

No manuscript.

All that work with no result discouraged the others, but it just made me more impatient. Except for that one slip in which the look on my face might have given me away, I'd managed to cover what I'd learned, and I had actually been able to keep from running off at the mouth. Even more important than that, I'd been able to solve the clues.

I felt kind of proud of myself until I remembered that somehow, during the night so that no one would know, I had to sneak down a dark hallway and remove Augustus Trevor's manuscript from a haunted burial urn!

THIRTEEN

We drifted into the parlor. None of us were comfortable about being together, yet at the same time we didn't want to be apart. I was doing my best to build my courage so that later I could do what I needed to do, and at the moment I didn't have enough nerve to go into that dark upstairs hallway all by myself.

Laura groaned and draped herself across one of the sofas, complaining, "When is this horrible rain going to end!"

Thea answered, "Mrs. Engstrom told me that according to the latest radio weather news the storm has begun drifting north and west and should end tomorrow."

"Which means that your telephone service will resume," Senator Maggio said.

The room was silent as we held our breaths.

"Why, yes," Thea said. "The telephone company will probably be able to make repairs early in the day."

"Then we can put all this behind us!" Julia said.

Alex's lips stretched in that horrible fake smile, and he said, "On the contrary, Julia dear. Remember that a man has been murdered and we're all suspects. The police are going to want to know who committed the crime."

"And they'll search for the manuscript," Laura whispered. "They're going to find it. I know they are."

"There's nowhere left to search," Julia said.

"We have the clues Augustus gave us," Alex said. He turned that smile on me.

"I'm not going to do any more work on the clues," I told him, and met his gaze without backing down. Darlene would have been proud of me.

Mrs. Engstrom came into the room with a tray filled with delicate demitasse cups and a large silver pot of coffee. Silently, she began filling some of the cups and offering them to the guests.

Alex ignored her and kept after me. "Maybe you don't need to work on the clues any longer, Samantha, because you've already figured out the solution. Is that it?"

Senator Maggio slapped his cup on the table so hard that it rattled in its saucer. "I don't want to hear any more about those so-called clues!" he stated. "We have established that they were false and therefore of no value."

"You may have taken it upon yourself to assume that," Alex told him, "but there's no reason why the rest of us have to go along with you."

"Please, please, please don't argue!" Laura begged. "We're in enough trouble. We don't need any more bad things to happen."

At that moment the lights went out.

Laura shrieked, and Buck yelled, "Who did that? What happened?"

With no moonlight or starlight seeping through the heavy cloud cover, the room was completely dark. It was like being swallowed by a large, warm mouth, and I struggled to adjust my eyes, trying to make out shapes or shadows.

Thea spoke from somewhere in the blackness. "The generator's gone out, I'm afraid. We've had trouble with it before when there's been a great deal of wind with the rain. Seepage into the motor, or some problem like that. I don't remember exactly what Augustus said about it."

"Can it be fixed?" Buck asked.

"Oh, yes. Chuck—you met him—he pilots our launch and is our general handyman, and he's very good with the generator. The only problem is that Chuck is on the mainland."

In the distance I saw a pinprick of light. It wavered and shivered and grew in size as it came closer and closer. I tried to yell a warning, but my throat froze and my tongue turned to ice. All that came out was a gargling gulp.

It was just as well I hadn't screamed, because the light turned out to be a candle carried by Mrs. Engstrom. She'd brought a basket of candles and candle holders, and as soon as all the candles had been lit the room looked soft and pretty, as though we'd been having a party instead of scaring ourselves to death.

"With the generator out of service, we won't have heat, so I've sent Walter and Lucy to put extra blankets in all the rooms," Mrs. Engstrom said. "We have a few flashlights in the bottom of the basket for those who want them, and if there is anything at all we can do to make you more comfortable, please don't hesitate to ask."

I liked the idea of a flashlight. It seemed much more

reliable than a candle, so I helped myself to one of the flashlights as well as a candle, kissed Aunt Thea good night, and went upstairs. I had a lot more courage now that I knew Lucy and Walter were upstairs too.

I paused on the landing. The light from my candle touched the carvings on the burial urn, and they winked and flickered like tiny, evil eyes. It would be so easy to grab the manuscript now and run with it to my tower room.

But as I hesitated a voice spoke above me on the stairs. Lucy said, as she came toward me, "I put two extra blankets on your bed, Miss Burns, because that tower room is little with lots of windows and can get awfully cold."

"Thanks," I said.

She stood on the landing with me, so there wasn't anything else to do but climb the stairs and head for my room.

"Good luck," Lucy whispered.

I turned and gave her a quick nod of gratitude. I needed all the good luck I could get.

Once I was in my room I blew out my candle. I wrapped myself in one of the extra blankets and sat halfway down the narrow stairs, leaving the door to the hallway open just a crack. I heard snatches of conversation, a couple of "good nights," and doors closing as the others straggled up to bed. I wished I'd thought of counting the closing of doors. Had everyone gone to bed? Was it safe now to go after the manuscript?

Too scared to do anything else, I waited for a while, then finally got enough nerve to creep down the last few tower stairs and enter the hallway. Although I had the flashlight in hand, I couldn't turn it on. Someone might see the light. So I moved to the left side of the hall, feeling my way along the wall through the blackness. Twice I stopped, listening intently. Had I heard a noise nearby or was my imagination working overtime?

Carefully, one hand sliding against the wall, I moved forward step by step. I had almost reached the top of the stairs when my fingers bumped into something hard and warm, something that jerked away, moving fast.

Before I could do more than gasp, an arm wrapped itself around my shoulders, and a hand pressed against my mouth.

I tried to yell, but Alex said, "Be quiet, Sam." He took the flashlight out of my hand and released me.

I jerked away and brushed myself off, wishing I could see him face-to-face. "What do you think you're doing?" I demanded.

"Keeping guard," he said.

"Guard against what?"

"Against you," he answered. I couldn't see his smile, but I could hear the mockery in his voice.

"Why? What did you expect me to do? Rob you while you slept?" I wished I had bitten his hand while it was against my mouth.

"I think you know where the manuscript is," Alex said.

"Don't be silly." I could hear the quaver in my own voice and regretted not sounding more positive.

"You know where it is and were going to get it."

A door opened, and candlelight flickered into the hallway. "Is something the matter?" Aunt Thea asked.

Smooth as a snake slipping into a hole, Alex answered, "Samantha and I were headed in the same direction—down to the kitchen."

"Oh, dear," Thea said, "you're hungry. The electric

stove won't work, of course, so a hot cup of coffee or tea is out of the question, but there's sure to be cold meat and cheeses, and we can make sandwiches." She tied the belt on the robe she'd been clutching together and stepped into the hallway. "I'll go with you."

"There's no need," Alex said. "We can find everything ourselves."

"Why don't you come, Aunt Thea?" I asked. "You might be hungry too."

She rested a hand on my shoulder. "I can't sleep," she said, "so a visit to the kitchen sounds like a good idea."

Alex turned away, but I had seen the angry frustration on his face. *Too bad for you*, I thought.

Another door opened, and Julia stepped out, carrying a candle. Her robe was neatly tied, and her hair was freshly brushed. "I hope you don't mind my overhearing the last part of your conversation," she said. "I'm going downstairs with you."

"Come along." Thea smiled. "We'll make a nice party out of it."

We walked down to the landing. I kept my eyes away from the burial urn by sticking close to the banister, but that was a mistake, because as I leaned over, looking down into the entry hall, I caught the gleam in eyes that were staring back at me. I started and clutched the banister, but it was only Mrs. Engstrom.

She was still fully dressed, and I wondered why. Had she stationed herself in the entry hall to keep guard, just as Alex had stationed himself in the upstairs hallway? Alex had been waiting to see if I'd make a move, but why was Mrs. Engstrom on watch? Was she protecting Thea?

She met us at the foot of the stairs and led the way

toward the kitchen. "Would you like some wine with your sandwiches?" she asked Thea. "I'll be happy to get it for you. Red? A nice Merlot?"

She opened a door which led to some steep stone stairs, and I said, "I'll get the wine for you, Mrs. Engstrom." I snatched my flashlight out of Alex's hand before he was aware of what I was doing, and began descending the stairs—thirteen of them. I counted.

"The Merlot is on the right, near the door," Mrs. Engstrom called, then added, "It's very nice of you to do this, Miss Burns."

I felt guilty about getting credit for being nice when my real reason for offering to get the wine was to see that wine cellar, which had the only door in the house that could be locked to stay locked. An idea was beginning to grow in my mind. The key was in the door, and it turned easily.

I swept the small room with my beam of light, touching row after row of bottles lying on their sides. I could see footprints smudging other footprints all over the dusty floor. Some of the prints must have been made by Walter when he came for wine, and some were made by Julia and Alex and whoever else might have searched this room for the manuscript. It didn't take long to find a couple of bottles of Merlot. I blew some dust off the bottles and carried them back upstairs.

By this time I was shaking. The house was chilly, but the wine cellar was really cold. As I entered the kitchen I shoved the bottles at Alex, who had to take them or lose them, and said, "I'm freezing! I'm going to run upstairs and get my blanket. I'll be right back."

Alex didn't have time to object, and I was pretty sure

that with Thea there he wouldn't run after me. I scrambled up the main stairs to the landing, swooped the beam of the flashlight in a quick arc to make sure no one was around, and turned it off. Tucking the flashlight under my chin I rested my left hand on the urn to balance it and lifted the lid with my right.

A soft hiss seemed to come from the unsealed urn as warm, stale air swept over my hand like crawly fingers.

I squeezed my eyes tightly shut and tried to keep my teeth from chattering as I whispered, "Listen to me, O Honorable Royal Ghost Person. I'm not your enemy. I'm your friend. I'm sorry if somebody got careless with your ashes along the way. I can't do anything about that, but I can remove the manuscript that's stuffed right down your middle so you can rest undisturbed. Okay?"

I didn't wait for an answer. I really didn't want one. If a voice had come out of that urn, I probably would have dropped dead on the spot. Slowly, carefully, I reached down into the urn until my fingers touched something hard. As I explored the object I knew I'd been right. Hidden inside this urn was Augustus Trevor's manuscript!

I grabbed the tightly rolled sheets of paper, which were fastened with rubber bands, took a firm grip, and pulled. The roll was thick and heavy, but I got it out and tucked it under one arm. As I replaced the lid on the urn, I remembered to whisper "thank you" before I ran down the hallway to my room.

All I wanted to do was read that manuscript, but I couldn't. I had to go back to the kitchen or Alex would know something was wrong. So I stuffed the manuscript inside the pillowcase, straightened the bed, wrapped one of the extra blankets around my shaking self—by this time

I had more than one reason to shake—and hurried downstairs, using the flashlight as a guide.

Alex looked up with surprise as I returned, but Thea and Julia were well into a lively discussion of modern theater as they busied themselves by putting together a half-dozen or so sandwiches, so they paid no attention to me. I huddled into one of the chairs, bent almost double, and continued to shake, tremble, and shiver like a poor pitiful thing beyond hope.

Thea glanced in my direction and broke off in midsentence. "Samantha!" she cried. "Are you ill?"

"I don't know," I said. "I'm cold, right down to my bones."

"You're having chills," she said, and came around the table toward me.

Thea's hand on my forehead was cool and comfortable, so I said what I knew she'd come out with. "I don't have a fever. I'm just cold. That's all."

"Maybe a little food . . ."

"I'm not hungry. I'm cold, and I'm tired. I just want to go to bed."

"That's probably a good idea," Thea said. "I'd suggest that you sleep in your clothes. Wrap up in one of the blankets before you get under the covers. Within a few minutes your body heat should make the bed nice and toasty."

"I'll try it," I said, and stood up, clutching the blanket tightly around my shoulders.

Alex got to his feet and yawned. "I'm tired, too, Thea. I'll see you in the morning."

"What about all these sandwiches?" Julia asked. "I thought you wanted to eat some of them."

"Save them until tomorrow," Alex said.

I left the room with Alex right behind me. Neither of us spoke to the other until we arrived at the door to the stairs that led to my tower room.

I stopped and glared at him. "Where do you think you're going?"

He grinned nastily. "I'm going to close the door at the foot of your stairs and sit with my back against it. You won't be able to leave your room to get the manuscript, because I'll be right here to stop you." He paused, one eyebrow wiggling upward. "Of course, you can always take me with you to get the manuscript."

"I hope you're comfortable sitting out here in the cold," I told him, "because I'm going to bed. I'm not going hunting for a manuscript."

He smiled again. "I'll make sure of that."

I shut the door at the bottom of my curved flight of stairs and heard him settle against it. It was all I could do to keep from laughing as I hurried up the stairs, shut and locked my bedroom door, and pushed the little chair against it, wedging it tightly under the knob.

So far, so good, I thought. I removed Augustus's manuscript from the pillowcase and propped myself against the headboard, the blanket around me, the covers pulled up high. Then—so excited that my breath came in bursts and gulps—I removed the rubber bands that kept the manuscript rolled, spread it out on my lap, and trained the flashlight on the title page.

FOURTEEN

"*Tarnished Gold*, by Augustus Trevor," I whispered aloud to myself, then began to skim through the pages.

There was some fascinating stuff in that manuscript, a lot of it about famous people I'd heard of. I would have loved to read the whole thing, because right away I saw that this was full of secret behind-the-scenes stories I couldn't wait to tell Darlene; but there were four hundred and eighty-two pages in this manuscript, and I didn't have enough time. According to my watch, it was close to one in the morning.

I searched each page for the names of the people Augustus had invited to play his horrible game, but it wasn't until I reached page 105 that I found the first name: Laura Reed. Augustus wrote well, and that was the problem. He drew me right into Laura's story, and I could see this young Hollywood actress who had made a good start and had a promising career to look forward to. But she had a problem that could cause all her dreams to vanish: an equally young husband named Larry, who was jealous of his wife and her new life that excluded him. After an argument in which Larry had insisted she forget Hollywood, Laura had tried to patch things up. The use of a sailboat, offered by a director friend . . . a day on the ocean . . . It should have been idyllic, but late that afternoon a hysterical Laura had brought the boat back alone. According to her story, as they'd turned the boat toward shore Larry had been hit by the swinging boom and knocked overboard. Laura claimed to have searched for him until finally, in desperation, she gave up and returned to the dock. Two days later, Larry's body washed ashore at Emerald Bay.

His death was ruled an accident, but many years later Augustus discovered that the boat had *not* been offered by that director friend. Laura had asked for its use. And it wasn't until later that the owner had noticed that a mallet, which was part of the ship's equipment, was missing. He'd thought nothing of it, deciding it had been misplaced, but Augustus had drawn a different conclusion.

I put down the manuscript, shocked by what I'd read. Augustus had practically called Laura a murderer! Maybe she'd been telling the truth. Then again, maybe she hadn't. If she'd murdered one person who had got in her way, she could have murdered Augustus, as well.

This was heavy stuff to think about, and it scared me, but I thumbed through a few more pages and came to Alex Chambers's name.

I already knew that Alex was a stinker, but I didn't know how truly rotten he was until I read what Augustus had to say about him. Alex Chambers, the famous dress designer, had made investments under a fake corporation name, and these investments consisted of New York sweatshops, staffed by recent immigrants, many of them children, most of them people from Vietnam who couldn't speak English.

I'd seen a television exposé of sweatshops, so I knew exactly what Augustus was writing about: guards and padlocked gates at the doors while people bent over sewing machines ten to twelve hours a day for very low pay. Alex Chambers, who publicly gave generous amounts to charity at balls where the women wore his expensive creations—just how wonderful would they think he was if they knew how much of his income came from badly mistreating workers, many of them children?

Would Alex have killed Augustus to keep his secret from being exposed? It was possible.

Fifty pages on I found Augustus's story about Buck Thompson. In 1979, the last year Buck had played pro ball, he'd fumbled the ball at a crucial time in a big game, and his team had won by a close two points. Buck had claimed a back injury, even spending two weeks in the hospital, but Augustus had come up with an informant, a bookie named Willie Peeples, who'd sworn that Buck had secretly bet on the point spread for this game and other games, and in his manuscript Augustus accused Buck of faking his injury in order to control the score.

I winced, thinking about Buck's commercials and work with kids. What would happen to this well-known role model if Augustus's information was printed? To keep the story from being made public, could Buck have killed Augustus? Buck was strong, and he had quite a temper.

Groaning, hating what I had to do, I kept turning pages until I got to Senator Arthur Maggio. A number of years ago his son had been an attorney for one of the organized crime families—Bonino. So that's where I had heard the name! But the senator's son had gone into corporate law, breaking any ties with the Boninos, and the Maggios claimed to be free from that taint.

But not according to Augustus, who insisted that no one ever leaves the mob. Augustus suggested that the generous funds raised and donated by some of the senator's Political Action Committees had come straight from the Boninos, and wouldn't the crime families love to have a president of the United States in their pocket!

I'd overheard my parents talking about Senator Maggio and how he'd spent most of his life working toward his goal of being elected president. Even though we weren't that close to the presidential primaries, his campaign was already under way. The senator couldn't afford to let Augustus publish that information. So what had he done about it?

My jaw actually dropped open, like in a cartoon, when I read what Augustus had to say about Julia. I'd been told about her good friend who destroyed all her manuscripts and killed herself, but according to what Augustus had discovered, after piecing together information from "reliable sources," that wasn't the way it happened. The manuscripts had been secretly carted off by Julia and her husband, Jake, who had been with her friend at the time she jumped. Jumped or was pushed—who was to say?

It wasn't a simple matter of Julia sending the manuscripts out under her name instead of her friend's name. Julia's husband, as co-conspirator, got into the act first, spicing up the plots with graphic scenes, adding the steamy "Julia Bryant" touches that had made Julia famous. Julia was nothing but a front for the novels!

No wonder Julia didn't remember her own characters. They belonged to her once best friend who'd grown up with her in Buffalo.

Maybe it was staying up so late without sleep, maybe it was the fear that came from being trapped in a house with a killer, or maybe it was the awful feeling of being a spy in other people's lives, but I felt terrible. I hugged the rest of the manuscript to my chest, pulled up my knees and rested my forehead against them.

Augustus must have had enough proof that the stories he wrote about took place, or he would have been sued for writing such things. The people he wrote about weren't likely to be arrested, but they still had something to be afraid of, an urgent reason that the stories shouldn't be published. All of them were dependent on public approval, and without it their careers were down the drain.

If Augustus's information was right, then two of them —Julia and Laura—had already committed murder.

Well, that was that. I hadn't learned a thing except information I really didn't want to know. Any one of the five suspects could have murdered Augustus.

Five? Oh, oh, I'd forgotten Aunt Thea.

I searched the rest of the manuscript, and it wasn't until page 356 that I discovered Thea's story.

In 1962, she and Augustus had rented a private villa in Acapulco, taking with them only Mrs. Engstrom, who—as usual when they traveled—took charge of domestic matters and hired local people to staff the house.

One day Thea went alone to shop in town. Thinking she knew the way, she cut through a back alley to reach a shop on another street. She'd been followed by someone who came up behind her, slashing at the straps of her handbag with a knife. Thea had resisted and in the struggle had fallen, dragging the robber down with her. Thea had managed to stagger to her feet, but the robber lay facedown in the dirt without moving. Thea had grabbed his shoulders, turned him over, and saw the knife protruding from his chest. She also saw he was only a boy.

Terrified, knowing that she could be arrested for murder, Thea ran from the empty alley, caught a taxi, and returned to the villa, where she made the mistake of telling her husband what had happened.

Why had Augustus threatened Thea with this story now—after all this time? Had he really intended to use it in his book? Or was he just trying to make her suffer?

Thea had killed, I told myself, but I quickly answered back, *No! Not Aunt Thea. The death was an accident. She'd never commit murder.*

At that moment the light tap at my door and the whisper of my name were more terrifying than if someone had broken down the door.

"Who's there? Who are you?" I shouted. I threw off my blankets and leaped from the bed. The manuscript pages went flying.

"Samantha dear. It's me—Thea. Will you open the door, please?"

"Yes," I answered. "Right away." I swooped up loose pages and stuffed them together, not caring about the order. Did I have them all? Yes. Thank goodness. But where to put them?

"Samantha?" Thea asked.

I quickly stuffed the manuscript under the mattress at

the head of the bed and stumbled to the door, tugging away the chair and turning the key.

As Thea entered the room she gave me a curious look and again rested a hand on my forehead. "Dear me, it *is* cold up here," she said. "Maybe you'd be more comfortable if you shared my room tonight."

"No, thank you," I said. I took a long, slow breath, gestured toward the chair, and said, "Please sit down, Aunt Thea." I was proud of myself. Just one day ago I would have been so nervous, I'd have given everything away, but through this weekend I'd learned a little game-playing of my own, and at the moment I was calm and cool and in charge of myself. I liked the feeling.

"When I found out what Alex was up to I sent him to his room, and I want to assure you he'll stay there," Thea said. "Such stupidity, sitting in the hallway, practically keeping you prisoner, just because he has the ridiculous idea that you know the location of the manuscript."

I quickly turned away so that she couldn't see my face and fell over the chair. So much for being in charge.

"Are you all right, dear?" Aunt Thea asked.

"I'm fine," I squeaked, although I really wasn't. From my hands-and-knees position I could see a page from Augustus's manuscript lying on the floor, half under the bed, half out. It was too far away for me to reach, and it was in plain view. What if Thea saw it?

Thea bent to lend me a hand and help me to my feet, and my mind raced, trying to come up with a way to cover that page without drawing attention to it.

Zilch. Zero. *Nada.* I was all out of good ideas.

FIFTEEN

Thea didn't sit down, and I didn't either. I kept myself between Thea and that sheet of paper. Surely, if she saw it she'd recognize the print and know immediately where it had come from.

"Have you been able to sleep, Samantha?" Thea asked.

"No," I said honestly, "but I'm tired now."

She smiled and slipped an arm around my shoulders. I kept edging sideways, trying to turn her back to the manuscript page. Thea looked a little puzzled, but she said, "I'm sorry your visit has turned out so badly, dear. I'd looked forward to it with so much pleasure."

"So had I," I mumbled. This was my mother's aunt, and I was treating her like one of the suspects. How could I? She had been married to Augustus and probably had inherited everything he owned. That included his manuscript, so she had a right to know that I'd found it. "Aunt Thea," I began.

But she ignored me, going on with what she had in mind. "Your mother told me that you were bringing some of your stories, hoping that Augustus would critique them for you. I'm sorry that has been a disappointment to you, as well. Unfortunately, Augustus wasn't generous with young writers, and he was not likely to have guided you, either. Your mother said that you felt unable to proceed with a writing career without guidance—"

"Aunt Thea," I interrupted, "there's something I want to tell you."

"Before you do," she said, "I'd like to point out that you must have dropped a page from one of your stories. It's there on the floor, and I know you don't want to lose it."

At that moment we heard a loud thud, a thumping, and a terrible crash.

Aunt Thea and I raced out of the room, down the stairs, and into the hallway, waving our flashlights ahead of us. The beams of light flew from ceiling to wall to floor like flashes of lightning, exposing Julia, Laura, and Senator Maggio, who came flying out of their rooms.

"What is it?"

"What's going on?"

The thumping continued, and we raced toward the source.

On the landing Buck gripped Alex by the shoulders, banging him up and down against the floor. Alex held the open burial urn in his right hand, and he bounced it with all his strength against Buck's broad back.

"Stop it!" Thea commanded. "Stop it this minute!"

There was so much anger and authority in her voice that the two men separated. They sat and stared upward. Alex's self-assuredness had vanished, and Buck pouted like a mad little kid.

"What's this all about?" Thea asked.

"I caught him in my room," Buck growled. "He ran, and I chased him."

Alex smiled as his poise began to return. "I thought Buck was asleep. It seemed like a good opportunity to look at the first clue Augustus had given him."

Buck muttered something, and for a moment I thought he was going to hit Alex, but Alex got to his feet and glanced in my direction. "I realized that Samantha was right. The clues we got weren't enough. If it would help to see the first clues . . . well, I'd just be a step ahead of the rest of you in finding out."

The others were all so angry they began yelling at Alex, but I kept thinking about His Royal Scariness and how furious he must be at the way his urn had been treated. Raising my voice so that it was even louder, I shouted at Alex, "What are you doing with that burial urn?"

Alex looked at the urn, which was still in his hand, shrugged, and placed it back on the pedestal, which wobbled a bit then settled itself. "I needed something to protect myself," he answered.

"You shouldn't have used that burial urn," I told him.

Alex picked up his flashlight and aimed it at me. "Why not? What's so special about this urn?" he asked, and said to the others, "Look at Samantha's face. She knows something."

I knew *everything*, and I couldn't let my face give me away. "I'll tell you what I know," I said. "According to Walter, the urn is haunted."

"I've had as much of this place as I can stand!" Laura wailed, and began to cry.

While they were busy trying to out-shout and out-argue each other, I ran down to the landing, picked up the lid to the burial urn, and replaced it. The urn felt warm to my touch, and I patted it gently. "You must know by this time that the world is full of weirdos," I whispered. "Sorry you had to run into a couple more of them."

In just a few hours it would be daylight and the telltale expression on my face would be easy for everyone to read. I had to distract them. I had to take their minds away from me. The clues . . . Alex had said the clues they had got weren't enough. Okay, I'd give them another set.

"Lend me a hand," I said to the urn, "and you'll soon be left in peace. I've got to get something. If any of them notices that I've gone, will you please distract them?" Oh, well, it couldn't hurt to ask.

I turned off my flashlight and felt my way down the rest of the stairs, across the entry hall, and along the way to Augustus's office. I entered the room and closed the door behind me before I turned on my flashlight.

It took only a few minutes to find envelopes and paper that matched those he'd used for the clues, but I had to scribble with half a dozen pens before I found the one with the bright blue ink. I tucked the pen in my jeans pocket and slipped the paper and envelopes inside the front of my shirt, next to my skin.

It wasn't hard to find my way in the dark going back. The sky had grown lighter, and there were even shadows cast by the moon. Thank goodness the storm was over!

As I neared the stairs I heard Thea ask, "Where's Samantha?"

At that moment there was a crash. Alex let out a yelp, and Buck shouted, "You pushed it! You tried to get me!"

"I did not!"

I took the stairs two at a time and shone my flashlight

beam on the urn, which lay on the floor, the toppled pedestal next to it.

"Yeah? How did that thing fall over if you didn't push it?"

I stooped and gently picked up the urn, straightening its lid and stroking its sides. "You probably knocked it off balance earlier while the two of you were fighting," I told Buck. "If you'll please pick it up, I'll put the urn where it belongs."

The pedestal was heavy, and it took both Buck and Alex to raise it. They tested, to make sure it was secure, before I returned the royal burial urn to its rightful place. "Thanks," I whispered to the urn.

"You're welcome," Alex said.

I stepped past him and said to Thea, "It isn't going to do any good to argue with Alex. I don't care what he does. I'm going to bed."

"Good idea," Julia said, but she glared at Alex. "Don't waste your time searching my room, because I didn't keep my first clue. I tore it into little pieces and flushed them away."

Laura gasped, and I could practically hear her mind begin to work. Her first clue would be the next to go.

"Back to bed, all of us," Thea said. She kissed my cheek, told me to sleep well, and I followed my flashlight beam up to the tower room, again barricading the door with the chair.

I would have loved to sleep, but there was something I had to do first. Just to be on the safe side I put the manuscript pages back in order, rolled them tightly, and fastened them with the rubber bands.

No one was in the hallway. I was pretty sure that none

of them would wander out of their rooms again, so I sneaked down to the landing and replaced the manuscript inside the urn.

"It's terrible to bother you again, Your Excellent Ghost-liness, after all that you did for me, if that really was you," I whispered, "but I can't take any chances. The very minute the police arrive I'll take this thing out of your royal middle, and you'll be left in peace and quiet. Is that all right?"

I thought I detected a faint hum, and it didn't seem antagonistic, so I replaced the lid, ran back to my room, and barricaded the door again.

I was so exhausted, my head hurt and I went into a fit of yawning, but there was one last thing to do before I could sleep. I had to come up with clues that looked and sounded like the ones Augustus had invented so that they'd be accepted. But my clues had to have a single purpose—to lead all the suspects, except one, to the wine cellar.

You can do it, I told myself. *After all, you're a writer.*

If I hadn't been so tired, or if only Darlene had been with me, the job wouldn't have taken so long. On my legal pad I wrote, I crossed out, I wrote some more, and made dozens of changes until I had the clues the way I wanted them. Then neatly, trying to copy Augustus's printing, I wrote the clues, put them into the envelopes, and marked them all: *Game Clue #5*. To follow my plan I added, FINAL CLUE: WITH THIS ONE YOU'RE ON YOUR OWN.

I put the unsealed envelopes on the chest, rolled up in one of my blankets, the covers pulled up to my chin, and closed my eyes. Aunt Thea had been right. Even though the air in the room was freezing, my body heat began working, and soon even my toes were warm. I slept so hard, I didn't move until the sun woke me.

Sunlight! That meant the storm had passed and soon we'd be in touch with the rest of the world. Tag ends of clouds scraggled across an electric-blue sky, propelled by a wind that slapped at the treetops and churned flips of white foam across the top of the rough and choppy water.

I glanced at my watch, amazed to find it was already ten o'clock. I had planned on being downstairs first, and now maybe my plan wouldn't work, because the others were bound to be up. There was nothing else to do but give it my best shot, so I washed my face—there was only cold water—and dressed.

Lucy came from one of the bedrooms and joined me as I walked down the stairs. "Do you need anything?" she asked. "Better tell me now, because Walter, Tomás, and I have cleanup work to do in the other house. One part of the roof leaked badly."

"I don't need anything," I told Lucy. "I'm fine."

But I wasn't fine. I was scared. I had no idea if my plan would work.

I didn't hide the envelopes in my pocket. I carried them in my right hand, and as I entered the dining room, where Laura, Buck, Julia, and Alex were eating cold cereal and bananas, I held the envelopes high, waving them.

"Look what I found," I said. "The fifth set of game clues. They're the final ones too."

Alex leaned forward, studying my face. "What are you hiding?" he asked. "Your face gives you away. What do you know that we don't know?"

"All right!" I slammed the envelopes down on the table. "I read them. I know they have your names on them and they're supposed to be for your private information, but I read them anyway. Okay?"

"It's okay with me," Laura said. "Sam *is* supposed to be helping us."

"She hasn't been any help so far," Alex grumbled, but my embarrassment at being "caught" seemed to satisfy him.

Julia snatched up her envelope and stood, pushing back her chair. "Thea and Arthur are in the sun-room. I'll get them," Julia told us and hurried out of the room.

I'd been waiting for the big question, and as soon as we were all seated around the table, with Mrs. Engstrom bringing in refills of coffee, sugar, and cream, Alex asked it.

"Where did you find this set of clues, Samantha?"

I was prepared. "In one of Julia's books, her main character finds a packet of love letters hidden behind a bedroom mirror. Isn't that right, Julia?"

I paused and looked at Julia, who smiled, then nodded. Of course I'd made all that up, but she didn't know her own books, because they weren't her own books.

"So I looked behind the mirror in Augustus's room, and there was the packet of letters, tied with a rubber band and wedged behind the frame."

"Imagine! Just like in Julia's book!" Laura said.

Alex shrugged, which meant, I suppose, that he bought my story.

Buck scowled at the envelope in his hand. "What does this mean? 'Final Clue: With this one you're on your own'?" he asked.

"I assume that this was Trevor's attempt to separate the sheep from the goats," Senator Maggio said, and he didn't attempt to hide the sarcasm in his voice. "It's fairly obvious that once again we're on our own."

"Samantha read *all* the clues," Alex said. "Maybe we should ask her about them."

I didn't like the disappointed look Thea gave me, but when all of this was over I was sure she'd understand. I had started this, and I had to finish it. "This time it won't help you to share the clues," I said. "All I can tell you is that the clues lead to a place in the house you have to find and go to, and I don't think they'll be hard to figure out."

Laura leaned toward me. "Did you figure it out?"

I nodded.

"Tell us."

"Open your envelope. Look at your clue. You can work it out," I said.

She did, and stared at the words so hard, she squinted. The others read their clues, and I watched their faces intently. Had I made the clues too hard? Too easy?

Five of the clues were the same: ONE ACROSS, THIRTEEN DOWN. WHO FINDS A MESSAGE IN A BOTTLE?

Alex studied his clue intently. All of a sudden his eyes widened and a puzzled expression spread across his face. He quickly glanced at the others, then slid back his chair, picking up the flashlight he'd brought down with him. He casually strolled out of the dining room in the direction of the wine cellar.

Julia murmured "Hmmm" a few times, then said, "Oh! But we . . ." As cautious as Alex had been, she quietly left, going the same way.

I was pretty sure they had guessed the answer I wanted them to come up with.

Thea got to her feet but hesitated. She gave me an odd

look, glanced at those who were left at the table, then walked through the door leading to the entry hall.

Mrs. Engstrom followed her, and that was fine with me.

Senator Maggio looked up from his sheet of paper, then down again, mumbling under his breath. "It must be," he said aloud. He pushed back his chair, snatched up the only flashlight that was left, and strode toward the door to the cellar stairs.

"The first part sounds like a crossword puzzle, but there's no puzzle here. I'll never figure it out!" Laura complained.

She probably wouldn't, and that could ruin everything, so I said, "Then why don't you follow Senator Maggio? He seems to know where he's going."

Laura and Buck scrambled to their feet and ran after the senator.

I followed at a more leisurely pace.

One across . . . the dining room. Thirteen down . . . the stone steps leading to the wine cellar. Five suspects were in the cellar now, probably searching for the manuscript in and among the rows of wine bottles.

They didn't even notice as I walked down the steps. I silently closed the door, locked it, and pocketed the key.

It was time now to join Thea. I'd sent her to the sunroom with the clue ON THE BEST OF DAYS THIS IS WHERE YOU'LL GET YOUR RAYS.

I knew it wasn't worded the way Augustus Trevor would have worded it. Thea had probably guessed that these were my clues and not her husband's, which was why she had given me that strange look. She'd want an explanation, but that was okay. I planned to tell Aunt Thea everything.

SIXTEEN

Just as I flopped into a wicker chair across from Aunt Thea, the phone jangled in my ear, startling me so much that I jumped to my feet and reached for it.

But Mrs. Engstrom was one step ahead of me. She picked up the receiver and listened a moment. "Thank you," she said formally, and hung up, turning to Thea. "The phone service has been restored, Mrs. Trevor."

"Mrs. Engstrom!" I interrupted. "You didn't tell them about the murder!"

"The caller was simply an employee of the telephone company," Mrs. Engstrom answered. "Besides, it is your aunt's prerogative to inform the police, not mine." She walked across the room and began to open the filmy curtains that shaded the windows. The room was bright with sunlight, but the trees outside the windows bent and shimmered in the wind.

"Aunt Thea?"

"Yes, I'll call them," Thea said, but she didn't move. I

could hear the exhaustion in her voice as she added, "I had so hoped that we'd find the manuscript in time."

I sat down and leaned toward her. "We did. I found it."

"You what?"

"I worked out the clues. They gave me the answer."

"Why didn't you tell me, Samantha?"

"Because it didn't seem like the right time until now."

"What does this particular time have to do with it?"

"Aunt Thea," I said, "your husband didn't make up the last set of clues. I did. I think you figured that out, but the others didn't."

"Yes. I wasn't sure what you were doing, Samantha, but I trusted you."

That made me feel awfully guilty, and I hurried to explain, "We don't have to worry about the suspects. They followed my clues to the wine cellar, and I locked them in."

Thea stared at me in amazement. "You didn't!"

"I had to. While they're down there we can talk about what Augustus wrote about them. Maybe together we can discover who committed the murder."

"You read the manuscript?"

"Parts of it. The parts about *them*." My voice dropped to one notch above a whisper. "And about you." Quickly I briefed her on what Augustus had written about each of the suspects.

Tears came to Thea's eyes, and she said, "I don't understand why you weren't open with me right from the beginning." She stood up and reached for my hands, pulling me out of my chair. "Come with me, Samantha. Show me where the manuscript is hidden."

"It's right where Augustus hid it, in that golden burial

urn on the landing." I balked, tugging at her hands. "Aunt Thea, please call the police right away. They'll know how much time went by between the time you found out your phone was working and the time you made the call. If you wait too long it will look suspicious."

Thea thought about this for only an instant. She gave a brisk nod, picked up the phone, and called the police. The conversation was brief, and after she hung up she told me, "They said the sea is still quite rough so they'll have to use one of their cruisers. It will take them close to an hour to get here."

"Then we've got time to talk and try to work this out," I said. "Please, Aunt Thea. I told you where the manuscript is, and you know that no one can get to it except you. Please help me find out who committed the murder."

"Half an hour," Thea said. "That's all." She allowed me to lead her to the nearest sofa and sat down beside me. "Where do we start?"

"Which one of the suspects had the strongest reason for murdering Augustus?"

She shook her head. "According to what you told me they each had a reason. I think it all comes down to personality. Which one would be most inclined to commit murder?"

"I don't think Laura could do it."

"No, and no matter what Augustus claimed about the death of Laura's first husband, there wouldn't be enough substantial proof to make a case. Would scandal hurt her? I don't think so. The publicity might even help her career."

"So Laura's out. What about Julia?"

"If Augustus didn't have solid proof about the death of Julia's friend, it adds up to nothing more than rumor."

"What about leaking the information that Julia doesn't write her own books? That could be damaging, couldn't it?"

Thea sighed. "The people who read the kind of novels Julia writes might be a little shocked at discovering she's simply a figurehead, but I doubt if she'd lose many readers. It's the sensationalism they're interested in, not the author."

"We're making progress. We've already wiped out two suspects," I said, excited by what we were accomplishing. I began to feel like a detective character in a mystery novel. "How about Alex Chambers and the sweatshops he makes a profit from?"

"The city officials have to know about the existence of the sweatshops," Thea told me. "The shops were even the subject of one of the national television news magazines. If the authorities want to make arrests, they can."

"But what about Alex's reputation?"

"If his customers cared more about his treatment of people than about his latest creations . . ." The corners of her mouth turned down and she shook her head. "I'm afraid only a few of them might."

My excitement was giving way to discouragement. "Senator Maggio?" I asked.

Thea sighed. "Don't you think that if Augustus could come up with information about Arthur's ties to organized crime, then some sharp reporters and politicians from the other party could too? Probably they're waiting with the information until Arthur announces his candidacy. Arthur knows this. He's too intelligent to commit murder."

"That leaves Buck," I said.

"I don't know what the statute of limitations is on the crime Buck committed, but he's been out of pro football for years. His reputation would suffer, but would it matter so much to Buck that he'd commit murder?"

"Buck has a bad temper."

"A bad temper isn't necessarily a prerequisite for committing murder. Hate . . . fear . . . there are other factors to take into consideration."

"I can see why Augustus was willing to take out the stories about anyone who was able to solve his clues." I groaned and said, "Aunt Thea, this won't work. With your system we've eliminated all of the suspects."

"What about me, Samantha?" Thea asked quietly. "I'm a suspect too."

"No, you're not," I said. "You're my aunt, and anyway, what happened in Acapulco took place a long time ago. I know there isn't a statute of limitations on murder, but probably no one in Mexico even remembers the case or has any records on it."

"We can't be sure," Mrs. Engstrom said from the doorway.

Aunt Thea looked into my eyes. She seemed even more softly gray than ever, and she kind of folded into herself as she said, "I didn't kill Augustus, Samantha."

I squeezed her hands reassuringly. "I know you didn't. Let's look at this another way. Whoever killed Augustus knew something about computers, because the entire document file was erased."

Thea said, "If you remember, everyone claimed not to

understand computers. It seems as though I'm the only one in the group who knew how to use Augustus's computer."

Computer, I thought. *Computer*. It should mean something. I got a funny, tickling feeling in my mind, but I couldn't grasp it.

"Some of them lied," I said bluntly. "Senator Maggio knew how to turn on Augustus's computer. He even brought a lap-top with him. And Alex understands all about files and disks. Before dinner on Friday he was talking about computerizing his designs. Julia knows computers too, no matter what she claims."

Thea's fingers trembled. "How can we possibly accuse them of lying?"

"Maybe we won't have to. There's something else to go on. The person who killed Augustus didn't know how writers work—that there would be an extra copy of the manuscript. That might be the key."

Key? The moment I said the word, things began to fall into place.

Thea didn't answer. I could tell that she was thinking as hard as I was.

I clutched her hand more tightly now, this time because I was scared and I needed someone to cling to. "Your guests don't know that all the bedroom keys are the same and fit all the upstairs locks, do they?"

"Why, no," Thea said.

"Someone who did know about the keys searched my room, looking for the clue Augustus had given me—the one he lied about when he said it told more than all the others."

"Samantha, believe me. I didn't."

"I know that," I said, "because I know who did."

I twisted around and looked at Mrs. Engstrom, who was standing just inside the doorway, the rolled manuscript in her hands. "*You* knew about the keys, and you use a computer, so you know how they work."

Aunt Thea gripped my fingers so tightly, they hurt. She knew what was coming. "You'd do anything for my aunt, wouldn't you, Mrs. Engstrom?" I asked.

"Yes," she said. "I would." She crossed the room and stood in front of Thea. "When I saw that folder from Acapulco in your hands I knew what that horrible man had done. If his manuscript were published and the contents made known, authorities in Mexico could ask for you to be deported. You could be arrested for murder, Mrs. Trevor." She shook her head. "I couldn't let that happen."

Thea didn't answer. Tears ran down her cheeks, and she didn't even try to brush them away.

"Don't worry. I'm going to destroy the manuscript, so you're safe now," Mrs. Engstrom told her. Her eyes were dulled with a terrible sadness.

I jabbed at the button near Thea's chair. "I'll get Walter!" I shouted.

Mrs. Engstrom shook her head. "Walter won't hear the bell. He's with Tomás and Lucy, working in the other house."

Thea cried, "What are we going to do, Frances? When the police arrive . . ."

"I'm not worried about the police," Mrs. Engstrom interrupted. "I'm going to take the small boat to the mainland. I'll be gone. The manuscript will be gone." She smiled, and it was so chilling, I shivered.

Thea rose to her feet, releasing me, and I rubbed my hands together, trying to bring back the circulation. "You can't take that little boat into rough seas! You'll be swamped! You won't make it as far as the mainland!"

"I'll take my chances," Mrs. Engstrom said. She turned the manuscript roll on end and caught the handle of a long, sharp kitchen knife that she had hidden inside it. "Come, Miss Burns," she said. "You're going with me."

SEVENTEEN

Thea cried out as Mrs. Engstrom grabbed my arm and propelled me out of the room. The point of the knife was aimed at my neck, and I wasn't about to argue.

As we left the house the wind whipped against us. I clutched the railing to keep from falling, and trotted and skidded down the slippery steps leading to the dock. Even inside the shelter the small motorboat bobbed wildly. Out in the bay, waves leaped and crashed and spit foam, and all I could think about was that we were going to drown.

"I'm not a good swimmer," I told Mrs. Engstrom.

She jerked me around and stared at me with eyes dark with despair. "Why didn't you just leave things alone? Why did you have to pry? Only three of us knew what happened in Acapulco. Now you know too."

"I'm not going to tell anyone."

She waggled the knife toward the ropes that fastened the boat to the dock. "Untie them."

I wrestled with alternatives and made an instant choice. "No," I said.

She blinked with surprise. "Do what I told you," she insisted and waved the knife under my nose.

"I can't. We'd both drown in that boat," I said.

Mrs. Engstrom's face crumpled like wadded paper, and she began to cry. She let go of my arm, and the knife clattered to the dock. "I wouldn't have taken you with me," she said. "I just needed you to untie the boat. I can't work those heavy knots."

She rubbed a hand across her eyes and looked into mine. "You're not in any danger. You're Thea Trevor's niece. Do you think I'd do anything that would hurt her?"

Just to play it safe, I kicked the knife with the side of my shoe. It skittered across the dock and plopped into the water. "Come back into the house with me," I told her. "We can wait there for the police."

Her gaze had shifted to a point far over my left shoulder, and I turned to see what had demanded her attention. In the distance, dipping and rising with the waves, came the police cruiser.

"There's just one thing left to do," Mrs. Engstrom said.

Before I knew what she was up to, she opened the supply chest, pulled out a can of gasoline and a tin box of matches and ran toward the open end of the dock.

"It's windy! You'll set everything on fire!" I shouted at her.

She scowled, but didn't take time to look at me. "Don't you think I know what I'm doing?" she demanded.

She tossed the manuscript to the damp ground, saturated it with the gasoline, and lit the match.

I was right behind her with a bucket I'd used to scoop

up water from the bay, but I held it. I waited until Augustus Trevor's damning manuscript was nothing but a squirming, twisting bundle of glowing ash. That's when I let fly with the water.

The pile sizzled and smelled as most of it slid off the dock into the ocean. A few pieces of the wet ash swirled up into the wind and vanished, and I was satisfied that burning embers weren't going anywhere to cause further damage. Neither were the many personal secrets Augustus had so easily blabbed in print.

I rested a hand on Mrs. Engstrom's arm. "Please believe me," I said. "I'll never tell anyone what I read about Thea." Not even Mom. Not even Darlene. That was a promise I intended to keep forever.

Her expression was dubious, so I added, "And I'll never write about it, either."

Her eyes widened in shock. "Write about it?"

"Yes," I said. "I'm planning to become a writer. I thought I couldn't do it without getting help from Augustus, but I was wrong. I don't know why I thought I needed his opinion. I finally figured out that it's my own opinion that counts."

Mrs. Engstrom gripped my shoulders, her fingertips painfully digging in. For an instant I thought she was going to fling me off the dock into the sea, but instead she pressed close to me, our noses almost touching, and said, "You'll never tell what you read in Mr. Trevor's manuscript! And you won't write about it, either! You promised!"

"I'll keep my promise," I insisted.

Her gaze shifted to the police cruiser, and she whispered to herself, "No more games."

With his mind on his manipulations, his mean little digs and complicated clues, it had never occurred to Augustus Trevor that his terrifying game might draw one player too many. He never had a clue that the name of the game was murder.